The Hu

Charly Cox was born in the South, raised in the Midwest, and now resides in the Southwest United States. She enjoys jigsaw and crossword puzzles, hanging out with her husband and her spoiled Siberian husky, visiting her son in Arizona, and traveling.

Also by Charly Cox

Detective Alyssa Wyatt

THE
HUNTING
GROUNDS

CHARLY COX

hera

DK | Penguin Random House

First published in the United States in 2025 by

Hera Books, an imprint of
DK Publishing, a division of Penguin Random House LLC
1745 Broadway, 20th Floor, New York, NY 10019

The authorized representative in the EEA is Dorling Kindersley Verlag GmbH.
Arnulfstr. 124, 80636 Munich, Germany

Print ISBN 979 8 217 25309 8
Ebook ISBN 978 1 83598 332 4

Printed and bound in Great Britain by Clays Ltd, Elcograf S.p.A.

Look for more great books at
www.herabooks.com | www.dk.com

"The past is never dead. It's not even past."

William Faulkner

Prologue

Wiping laughter-fueled tears from her eyes, Brooklyn Knox interrupted her sister, Queenie. "As much as I love hearing about my new niece and nephew, I really do have to go. I've absolutely got to finish grading the rest of my students' Roman Empire research papers before Monday. I'll call you after."

"Fine, but grade fast. I need to practice my adult conversation skills before I permanently start talking like everyone I encounter is six weeks old." In the background, Brooklyn heard the faintest sounds of a baby crying, and Queenie groaned. "Oh no. Not already. I swear I just laid them down two seconds ago. Anyway, go grade. Love you." Like always, Queenie didn't wait for a reply; she simply ended the call.

A familiar twinge rooted deep into Brooklyn's chest, sadness that she and her sister no longer lived a half mile from each other. Two years earlier, when Queenie's husband had received a much better job offer in Missouri, they'd packed up and moved away from their hometown of Slaughterville, Oklahoma.

Depressed that she couldn't just pop in and love on the newborn twins whenever she wanted, Brooklyn snagged the bag of salt and vinegar chips she'd just bought and ripped them open, accidentally knocking her phone to the floor in the process. "Damn it," she muttered, leaning down to pick it up.

As she did, something brushed against her, and then a sudden excruciating pain slashed across her lower back. Gasping, she collapsed to the floor. Seconds later, a pair of dirty sneakers appeared in her line of sight.

With her brain's wiring entirely focused on the searing heat streaking throughout her lower body, she could barely concentrate on the fact that she lived alone with her cat, and no one else should be in her house. Spots danced behind her eyes as she struggled to breathe.

The scraping sound of the shoes crossing her floor finally penetrated the thick fog of agony.

The weight of terror pressed in on her as she tried to twist enough to see who was in her house, but in truth, she already knew. His name wheezed out just as he slammed his foot down onto her back, sending her crashing face-first onto the cold tile floor. Tears and panic blurred her vision.

On instinct, she lifted her hands to protect her head, realizing as she did that they were sticky with her own blood. How had he even gotten in? But of course, she already knew that, too. In Small Town, USA, no one locked their doors – car or home.

As if he were much farther away than mere inches, his voice tunneled down to her, but she struggled to make sense of what he was saying because her organs were being crushed together, leaving no room for her lungs to gather the oxygen she desperately craved.

Just as she managed to suck in enough air so that she no longer felt as if she was suffocating, he flipped her over onto her back, sending an agonizing cascade of sensations sizzling along her nerve-endings. Gripped in his right hand, a bloody, silver-hilted knife shimmered under the light streaming in through the windows. Pinched between two fingers of the other was the miniature, heart-shaped wooden jewelry box engraved with both her initials and his. A gift she'd returned. Along with the note proclaiming his undying love for her.

Had that been just last night? Paralyzing fear fused with her pain, and Brooklyn's eyes drifted upward. "Don't—"

A dark blend of anger and betrayal glared down at her as he jabbed the tip of his knife into the area just beneath her chin, close to her throat. A high-pitched whimper slipped between her chattering teeth.

Another swipe of his knife sliced diagonally from high on her shoulder downward across her right breast, and this time, Brooklyn screamed. Blood soaked through her shirt and spilled onto the floor, the metallic odor tickling her nose. Her brain shouted *run* even though she knew she couldn't.

Just like she knew that her life was likely no longer measured in years but minutes. Unless she could get him to listen. She forced his name up from her clogged throat through trembling lips and then waited for his eyes to meet hers. Her whispered plea crackled in the air between them. "Please."

A fist slammed into the side of her face hard enough that she felt a bone in her cheek crack. A mirage of spots and stars replaced his face.

"Please?" he growled. "Please? You have the nerve to beg after what you did? You made me believe I was *special*." Flames spit from his eyes. "But you know what? You're worse than everyone else. At least *they* never pretended to care." His head dropped, and his voice cracked. "I never wanted to hurt you. I love you."

Brooklyn swallowed back the words that wanted to scream that he was wrong, that he didn't grasp the meaning of the word. Instead, her throat burning like she'd swallowed glass, she croaked out, "Then don't. Don't hurt me." Even as revulsion prickled through her, her fingers lifted to touch his arm. "I care about you." Her voice wobbled. It wasn't a lie; she did care about him, just not in the way he craved. Weak, her hand slipped, sliding down his arm. A shiver slithered along her skin at the unintentional caress. "Please," she whispered again.

In a lightning flash of motion, his head snapped up and his knife slashed one way across her mouth, then the other, silencing her words.

Things like this weren't supposed to happen in little towns, not even in ones named Slaughterville.

Feeling helplessly trapped in her own body, the last thought Brooklyn had as the knife plunged down was that at least it would all be over soon.

Chapter One

Tucked into the darkest corner near the overflowing dumpsters at the poorly lit gas station, the man took several deep breaths and then counted backwards from one hundred in an effort to hold onto his sliver-thin temper. But none of his usual tricks worked to erase the words *she'd* cried out to him as he was leaving. *You don't love me because this is not how you treat someone you* claim *to love.*

Veins straining against his skin, he cracked his neck from side to side, glancing out at the nearly empty parking lot just as a red-haired woman dressed in bright yellow shorts and a pink blouse strolled by. He watched her climb into a two-door, baby blue Jeep, acutely aware of the familiar tingling that started at the base of his spine and zippered its way through the rest of his body. He'd teach *her* to question his love.

The gas pumps, along with the building, blurred into indistinguishable blobs as his hands moved of their own accord down to the gearshift. With his gaze riveted on the Jeep's receding taillights, he shifted into drive and, ignoring the angry honk of another driver whom he cut off, he tore out of the parking lot after the woman. Careful to remain a safe distance back, he welcomed the blend of a dark, winding road and the inky blackness of the cloud-shrouded night that helped conceal the fact he was following her.

Mile after mile, his tires ate up the asphalt until he spotted her brake lights up ahead, illuminating the dark as she slowed and abruptly veered off her current route. His heart rate doubled and then tripled as he passed the unmaintained road she'd escaped down. It was a sign, as clear as the one that put her in his path to begin with.

He counted to five-Mississippi before he pulled off to the side of the road. Already cloaked in dark clothing, he grabbed his ball cap to cover his head. He didn't worry about anyone traveling by seeing a man walking into the thick cover of cottonwoods, lumbering pines, oak, and Rocky Mountain junipers, knowing they'd assume he was "checking for a low tire," as his father used to say whenever he'd stop to use the landscape as his personal restroom.

Using a penlight, the man quickly but quietly ran through the woods, stopping when he spotted the woman's Jeep up ahead. Closing his eyes, he slowed his breathing and then dragged his knife from its sheath.

While she pulled up her shorts, he slipped into place.

–

With her father's dire warnings on the dangers of stopping at a rest area or any other sparsely populated place, especially for a woman traveling alone in the dead of night, ping-ponging around her head, Jennie Killingbeck wriggled in the driver's seat, wishing she'd just used the restroom at the gas station. But after one look at the blackened toilet that she was certain had never been cleaned, she opted to head down the road, even though she knew there were pitifully few places for a woman to use the facilities along her favorite route, the High Road to Taos Scenic Byway.

Since she hadn't really needed to pee so urgently back at the gas station, she hadn't been too concerned. But then she'd finished off her bottled tea, and the pressure dancing in her bladder had her shoving out all thoughts of her father's multitude of safety warnings as she passed miles of road far less traveled than the interstate. However, having made this trip routinely over the past several years, she knew relief was a few more miles ahead on an old, unmaintained service road. And if it came right down to it, she could pull off onto any of the numerous forest roads along the way. Not optimal, perhaps, but far better than the pressing alternative.

She was already reaching into her center console for the hand sanitizer she always carried when she realized her bad luck hadn't yet run its course. A huge and brand spanking new reflective sign reading *Authorized Service Vehicles Only. Do Not Enter* had been erected. She groaned. "Seriously? I just want to pee." In the back of her mind, she could imagine her father's sigh of relief. "Easy for you to say, considering your bladder's not about to rupture," she grumbled aloud, as if her dad were actually sitting in the passenger seat next to her.

Within seconds, she knew there was absolutely no chance of her making it to the next gas station, a rest area, or even a fast-food joint – at least not without having an embarrassing accident first. Without wasting time talking herself out of it, she ignored her rule-following ways, along with the sign, and turned onto the old service path, bouncing along until she could no longer see any hint of the main road, the rough bumps alone threatening to burst her bladder wide open. Just when she thought she'd have to park in the middle of the dirt road, her headlights flashed across a space just big enough to safely squeeze her vehicle into without blocking any possible, although highly unlikely, traffic that may also be on this rugged strip of land.

With one hand on the door handle, her mind whipped through the pros and cons of leaving her car running and the driver's door open. Cons won. She was far too paranoid about leaving her keys in the car and accidentally locking herself out, rendering her stuck and vulnerable. Or the more likely scenario, having some kind of critter deciding to climb aboard to explore the leather interior.

After another slight hesitation, she opted to turn off her lights as well. On the off chance another vehicle did happen along, she didn't want to illuminate herself with her pants literally down. Instead, she turned off the engine and grabbed her phone to use as a flashlight, only to remember the battery had died shortly after she'd hit the road, and she'd forgotten to plug it in. *As usual*, her brother would say. Sighing loudly at her own bad habit, she cursed at herself. "Damn it."

She'd just have to use the moonlight, spotty and meager as it was. Dangerously close to peeing down her leg, she grabbed a few tissues and her hand sanitizer before sliding out of her car and pocketing her keys. She danced the potty shuffle as she waited impatiently for her eyes to adjust before slipping into the even darker shadows of the trees. Seconds later, she moaned embarrassingly loudly at the relief for her bladder, glad no one was around to hear her.

When she finished, she yanked her shorts up and grumbled to the treetops about how much easier guys had it. Then, stepping carefully around the little lake she'd created, Jennie grabbed her keys back out of her front pocket, automatically wrapping her fingers tightly around the pepper spray she carried with her everywhere she went. Overly cautious as she often tended to be, she held the container close to her face and then used her thumb to make sure the business end of the spray pointed away from her. She'd learned that lesson the hard way when she'd accidentally used it on herself once. That crap burned like hell on fire. It wasn't a mistake she cared to repeat.

Just as she was stepping out from the cover of the trees, yet another cloud covered the moon, returning the night to a dark inkwell of blackness. Creeped out by her overactive imagination exacerbated by her love of horror movies, she swiveled her head back and forth as she scurried back to her Jeep.

Even though there was no one else around, vigilance remained ingrained in the very fiber of her being, and so she stopped a few feet away and bent low, checking beneath the car, a carry-over trait she'd inherited from her sometimes neurotically skittish mother. As much as she wished she could break the obsessive-compulsive habit, Jennie simply couldn't climb into any vehicle, day or night, without first ensuring no one was lurking beneath it, just waiting to latch onto her ankles and drag her to her death.

Finally reassured of her safety, she straightened up and pushed the key fob, careful to press only once so just the driver's side door unlocked. No use courting unnecessary danger by unlocking both. Another cautious spillover of a habit, though that one she didn't mind as much since she rarely had passengers to worry about. Off in the distance, an owl screeched.

Darkness mixed with the eerie sounds of nature made Jennie eager to be back in the luxurious confines of her Jeep. But mere steps away, an ominous shape stepped out from the shadows of a thick cluster of trees, blocking her path to the driver's side door.

Jennie screamed.

Chapter Two

A dark cloud of fury hovering over her, Detective Alyssa Wyatt stormed down the front steps of the district attorney's office, her strides long and angry. Directly on her heels but wisely refraining from adding his two cents – for now – was her partner of the past ten years, Cord Roberts.

As she neared her black, government-issued Chevy Tahoe, she ripped her keys from her pocket and jabbed her thumb repeatedly into the button to unlock the doors. She continued taking her displeasure out on the inanimate objects around her as she climbed into the driver's seat and snapped her seatbelt into place, impatiently waiting for Cord to close his door.

He'd barely buckled himself in before she rocketed out of the parking space and pulled into traffic.

"Jesus, Lys, I know you're pissed—"

Alyssa snorted and shot Cord a withering glare. "You think? What was your first clue, I wonder."

As usual, her partner refused to rise to the bait as she spoiled for a fight. Instead, in his usual manner, he chose calm and logic to try to defuse the ticking timebomb she'd transformed into within the last hour. "Somewhere in that convoluted but logical part of your brain," he said, "you have to know that Grace wouldn't have offered that plea deal unless she had no other choice. Plus, the victim's *entire* family agreed to it when she spoke to them beforehand. Heavy emphasis on *entire*."

Grace being Grace Burgess, Bernalillo County's district attorney and a woman Alyssa had the utmost respect for and usually greatly admired. Just not at this moment.

Deep down, she knew Cord was right, and by extension, Grace. But the injustice of it all still churned in her gut. Between gritted teeth, she bit out, "Those *bastards* – heavy emphasis on *bastards*," she snarled, "carjacked, kidnapped, and tortured an eighty-three-year-old grandmother for two days before we were finally able to track them down. Too late to save her life, mind you. And for what? The twenty-year-old vehicle she drove and the sixty-seven dollars she had in her purse?" She shot a heated glare in Cord's direction. "And since the families of both men could clearly afford high-end attorneys, I highly doubt they were motivated by greed so much as taking pleasure in the act itself. For that alone, those bastards deserve to rot and die in prison. Both of them. Not one. Both!" She punctuated each word by slapping her palms down onto her steering wheel. "I guess it's true what they say, it just goes to show what money can buy."

True, only one of the men had committed the actual, physical assault, as evidenced by the recording on his accomplice's phone. That didn't matter to her because it was as clear as red on snow that the accomplice had been more than a willing party as he'd stood by, laughing and recording every tormented moment of Lottie Whitmer's last days. In Alyssa's eyes, though he hadn't technically assaulted or murdered Lottie himself, he was equally culpable as his accomplice.

But none of that mattered because Grace was afraid that without the testimony of that guy against his friend, the well-known and highly successful defense lawyers both families had hired for their sons would poke just enough holes in her case to give jurors a sliver of reasonable doubt in the first-degree murder charge she'd brought against the men. While the plea deal still required a prison sentence, with the lesser charge of second-degree murder, the accomplice who'd recorded Lottie's murder would likely be out in fifteen years or less instead of a life sentence with no possibility of parole, which the first guy was still facing.

Even if she understood that Grace had only offered the plea deal as a last resort to avoid risking the chance of acquittal, Alyssa wasn't yet willing to concede that Grace had most likely made the right call for the situation. Understanding Grace's reasoning behind the difficult decision didn't mean Alyssa had to be happy about it. And God knew, she sure as hell wasn't.

Ahead of her, a long line of cars as far as the eye could see did nothing to help quell or ease Alyssa's edginess and pent-up frustration. When, after enduring a third red light cycle that found her still two car lengths away from being able to make her turn, she growled. "Good for the economy or not, I, for one, will be doing a jig when this movie wraps up. Or at least when they permanently move locations. All these lane closures and traffic jams caused by the film crews and looky-loos — it's worse than Balloon Fiesta traffic. And it sucks." As if the mob of spectators strolling down the streets and on the sidewalks, clogging things even more, were doing it to her on purpose and out of spite, Alyssa glared at them the same way she had Cord a few minutes earlier.

A text notification from Isaac, her eighteen-year-old son, distracted her, and since she was stopped anyway, she grabbed her phone and read the message.

> Hey, M. I'm fine, so don't freak, but kind of want to run something by u. Call me when u can. Seriously tho, I'm fine. I know ur busy, so just when u have 1min. L8r

Cord must've read the worry in her face because he asked, "Everything okay?"

"Don't know. That was Isaac. He says he's fine but wants to talk to me about something."

Stuck in traffic, she figured now was as good a time as any to call. She already knew Isaac wouldn't mind being on speaker while Cord was with her, not only because it happened frequently, but because he'd grown up around Cord. But before she could do anything, the light changed, and her phone rang. A quick peek at her Bluetooth screen showed the caller as Captain Guthrie Hammond.

Alyssa finally made the turn onto a quieter side street and tapped the button to answer. "Captain."

Not one for pointless pleasantries that he found a waste of precious time, Hammond jumped right in, his voice gruff as usual. "Where are you and Cord?"

"We just left the DA's office. We—"

He cut her off. "Good. I need you both here in my office ASAP. It's about your missing person case. Jennie Killingbeck."

Alarm bells shoved out her frustration over the plea deal. "What's going on?"

"Just get here." Without so much as a goodbye, Hammond ended the call.

"What the hell was that about?" she asked. "If he got a bead on Jennie's location, he would've sent us there, not called us in. Right?"

Chapter Three

Back at the station, Alyssa nodded once to Ruby, the surly precinct secretary, who offered nothing more than her usual scowl. Alyssa didn't take it personally. Ruby was that way with everyone. Unless she really harbored a strong dislike for you, in which case her usual surly demeanor looked downright fun and frolicky. For the space of a heartbeat, Alyssa considered asking her if she knew what was up, but just as quickly nixed the idea, knowing the woman would not only refuse to answer but would likely give her a scathing smackdown for even assuming she might.

Steps from the captain's door, Alyssa spotted three more members of her team – Hal Callum, Officers Joe Roe, and Tony White – whose skin remained as colorless as his name, no matter how hard he tried to get a tan. Unless he was sporting a sunburn – or that one horrendous attempt at a spray tan that turned him sickly orange – he could moonlight as a ghost in one of Albuquerque's several supposedly haunted houses or hotels.

Hal Callum rolled in his wheelchair beside her, nodding to the captain's closed door. "There's an important-looking someone in there with him. Been

16

behind closed doors since she arrived. Got any idea what's going on?"

If she hadn't been so preoccupied with knowing what the captain had learned about their missing person case, Alyssa might've laughed at the way Hal, the most upbeat, laid-back man she'd ever met, despite being confined to a wheelchair years ago after being shot in the line of duty, had lowered his voice to a whisper to ask.

She shook her head. "Just that it's regarding the Killingbeck case. He called and said he needed us to report to him immediately. I'll come find you after."

One corner of Hal's mouth quirked up, clearly amused that she'd stated the obvious by saying she'd fill him in. Alyssa rolled her eyes at him, but he, along with Joe and Tony, had already headed back to the incident room the team had eons ago claimed as their own because it was the most spacious and had the most natural light. None of the other detectives even bothered trying to use it anymore.

Alyssa knocked on Hammond's door.

"It's open," came the gruff response.

Inside the captain's office, a woman sat in a chair across from his desk. The way she held herself shouted *official* and *law enforcement*. Something about her triggered a brief but elusive sense of déjà vu for Alyssa. Yet, she was fairly certain she'd never even met the woman.

Hammond, usually abrupt to the point of appearing unfriendly while also earning him the nickname Captain Hothead, drew Alyssa's focus back to him with a clipped, "Close the door."

Still behind her, Cord did as he was told, then leaned his back against it. With Hammond's massive bull chest and Cord's muscular physique and height, the medium-sized room grew infinitesimally smaller. Though one other chair remained unoccupied, Alyssa chose to remain standing.

Once again, Hammond wasted no time. He pointed to the woman with the short pixie haircut. "Special Agent Ryker Newlin with the FBI. Behavioral Analysis Unit."

Even as she wondered what a Fed was doing here, and more importantly what it had to do with her missing person case, Alyssa reached out her hand. "Detective Alyssa Wyatt." She shifted to the side so Cord could make his own introduction.

"Detective Cord Roberts. Pleased to meet you."

What could've passed for a smile briefly crossed the agent's face as she accepted the handshakes and gave a curt nod. "Same." For a moment, Agent Newlin stared at Alyssa the same way Alyssa had stared at her, like she recognized her from somewhere.

The moment passed when Hammond cleared his throat, and Alyssa, Newlin, and Cord all turned their attention to him.

He tapped three fingers on a closed manila folder, a file Alyssa recognized as her current case. "I'm temporarily moving you and your team into Homicide in order to assist Special Agent Newlin."

Alyssa knew her face showed her confusion by the way her forehead gathered all its wrinkles together. "Technically, we cover violent crimes *and* missing persons. But that's beside the point. I thought you said this had something to do with Jennie Killingbeck." She tipped her head toward the file on Hammond's desk, but then didn't bother to wait for an answer before she turned to Newlin, firing out questions like they were bullets. "You know what happened to Jennie? Where she is? And what do either of those things have to do with the Feds?"

Special Agent Newlin leaned down and pulled a thick binder, along with an overflowing accordion folder, from a bag leaning against her chair and then placed both on the edge of the captain's desk. "For the past five years – since early 2018 – we've been hunting a serial killer. Not only is he elusive and extremely careful not to leave behind any incriminating DNA, he also doesn't stay in one place too long. A year, maybe two, at the most. Or at least, we don't *believe* he stays in one place too long. I know that might seem like I'm splitting hairs, but details are details, no matter how minute." She took her finger from the binder and pointed to the now open Killingbeck file sitting in front of Hammond.

Alyssa didn't need a reminder of the details of the case. Early Sunday morning, Jennie's parents had called the Albuquerque Police Department to report her missing when she failed to return home Saturday night after visiting a friend of hers up in Southern Colorado. Since Jennie had been using her father's credit card, they knew she'd refueled at The Last Stop-N-Go gas station near Chimayo between Taos and Santa Fe, New Mexico. While there were no security cameras in the area, the young male store clerk easily recalled seeing her, stating her bright red hair and even brighter yellow shorts made her hard to forget. A familiar but unwanted sense of foreboding slithered down Alyssa's spine as she met Newlin's steady gaze.

"We believe Miss Killingbeck may have fallen prey to our killer. And if we can pool all our resources, APD's and the Bureau's, then we might finally be able to run this sonofabitch to ground."

Always choosing to believe she and her team would find their missing person alive until presented with irrefutable evidence to the contrary, Alyssa tried to temper the flare of annoyance at what she viewed as a premature hint of defeat. "I'm sorry, but we don't know that Jennie Killingbeck is dead – nor would we assume any such thing. And since she was just reported missing yesterday, how did you even hear about our case? More importantly, what makes you think she's somehow fallen victim to your serial killer? Have you tracked him here to New Mexico? And if so, where and when? And why weren't local authorities notified immediately?"

Ryker's mouth tightened into a thin line as she grabbed several enlarged crime scene photos from the accordion folder and silently handed them to Alyssa, who shifted so that Cord could see them, as well. By the second image, Alyssa felt the blood drain from her face. After scanning through the rest, she glanced once at the captain before focusing her attention back on the federal agent.

Ryker tipped her head toward the images. "Clearly, the most obvious similarity is in the women's looks. Each one has that same remarkable, unusual red, shoulder-length hair, and all are in their mid-twenties to early thirties. I believe Miss Killingbeck is twenty-four?"

Alyssa nodded.

A grim expression tightened the muscles in Ryker's face as she continued. "Likewise, all the victims share features that are so strikingly alike, it's as if they were all poured from the same mold. Or at least born into the same family. As you can see for yourself, Miss Killingbeck shares the same characteristics as the other victims. Call it a hunch, if you will, but your missing person's hair color alone is what drew my attention and had me contacting your captain."

When Ryker paused, Cord piped up with a question. "Don't Bureau folks usually work with a partner?"

Ryker's nostrils flared briefly, but still long enough for Alyssa to notice. "Yes," Ryker said, "but I was up in Santa Fe all last week to finish my testimony in the Samuel Ezra human trafficking case."

Both Alyssa and Cord were familiar with the case. Close to six years ago, and after a nationwide manhunt, the FBI had tracked Ezra to Santa Fe. The head of a multistate trafficking ring that included numerous New Mexico counties was finally taken into custody after a tense, eight-hour standoff. After countless delays and antics, the trial was finally underway. In fact, that was probably why Ryker looked so familiar; she'd been part of the takedown.

Ryker continued. "I saw the picture of Jennie Killingbeck on the news this morning as I was packing up and immediately contacted my superior before reaching out to Captain Hammond." She didn't bat an eye as she added, "I believe in listening to my gut. It's rarely proved me wrong.

"I explained my concerns to your captain, emailed copies of our victim photos, and you can see why he agrees we may be after the same guy." She held Alyssa's gaze. "I think I read people fairly well, and I can see in your eyes that, even if you don't want to, you think I'm right, too."

Instead of acknowledging the agent's comment, Alyssa had another question. She nodded to Ryker's files. "You always carry copies of your case files with you when you travel?"

Ryker's stare remained unapologetic. "In this case, yes. These women deserve answers, and their families deserve closure. I've been breathing this case since 2018, and I pore over every bit of information we've accumulated every chance I get in the hopes that I'll finally find that missing piece. In fact, I took them along with me on the one and only vacation I've taken in the last five years – and the guy I was dating ended up breaking things off because of it. So, yes, this case is that important to me."

Ryker's blunt, unabashed answer elevated Alyssa's respect for the federal agent.

"Now," Ryker said, "your captain mentioned you and your team would have no qualms working side by side with me on this. But since I like to do my own research on the people I'm sharing my investigations with, I did some digging myself." Here she paused just long enough for Alyssa to suspect she knew why the agent might recognize her, if only by name. "And I have to admit your team has an impressive track record."

While she may not have appreciated the "digging" aspect, Alyssa had to admit she appreciated Special Agent Newlin's direct, no-nonsense approach. Had the tables been turned, she would've done the exact same thing.

"Getting into a territorial pissing match has never been part of my job description, nor something I've ever understood, to be quite frank," Alyssa said. "So, yes, if the common objective is to stop a serial killer, and in the process locate my missing person, then combining our resources makes the most sense."

Ryker set the photos back down on Hammond's desk, and by the way she stiffened her spine and stared directly into Alyssa's eyes, she already knew she wasn't going to like what the agent had to say next.

"Detective, I believe we'll find Miss Killingbeck, I really do, and while I greatly admire your team's philosophy of believing in the best outcome until you have proof to the contrary, I'm going to tell you right now that if I'm right – and again, I trust my instincts on this – then I want to go on the record by telling you that the likelihood of locating Miss Killingbeck alive is slim to none." Before Alyssa or Cord could argue, she cut them off. "Unlike some of your cases I've read about, the perpetrator we're after doesn't kidnap his targeted victims. He kills them in their homes or wherever he finds them."

Without proof Alyssa refused to accept the Killingbeck case was a homicide already. "I understand, and while I appreciate that information, nothing you've said tells me we should automatically believe the worst. Even if what you say is true, we both know murderers, serial killers included, can change their MO if it suits them."

Instead of being offended by her pushback as Alyssa suspected some federal agents might be, she could see appreciation in Ryker's eyes.

Ryker dipped her head once in acknowledgement. "You're right on all sides. Killers can and do change MOs, for various reasons, some of which we never understand. And I hope Miss Killingbeck *is* still alive. I'd love nothing more than for you to prove me wrong. But in the spirit of being upfront, let me share why I'd like you and your team to be prepared for the opposite outcome."

When Ryker spread the rest of the crime scene photos of the other victims onto Hammond's desk, Cord stiffened beside her even as he moved in closer for a better look.

Ryker tapped each photo once. "Beginning with victim number three, Lauren Grand of Omaha, Nebraska, our unknown subject no longer slipped into his victims' homes and killed them there; he began using remote locations where he'd target a victim and then leave her body.

While the locations are remote, they're often places where it wouldn't take too long for a hiker or backpacker, jogger, or whoever to stumble across the body."

Cord interrupted. "So, it's like he wants them found?"

Ryker glanced up. "That's my belief, yes. And I've wondered, whether he knows it or not, if it's because he wants us to stop him. But that theory will remain an elusive mystery until we nab the guy." She waved her hand over the images. "If you look, you'll notice that each victim had her throat cut and an X slashed across her mouth.

"With Daphne Morrow, victim two, he also severed the tendons behind her knees. Personally, I believe he did this to keep his victim from trying to escape. But I'll get into that more a bit later."

Captain Hammond wiped his beefy hands down the front of his face and leaned heavily into the back of his chair. "Just when I think I can't be shocked by anything anymore, there I go, being proven wrong."

Alyssa tapped on one of the images. "The X across the mouth and the slit throat are part of his signature."

Again, Ryker nodded. "Some serials have more than one. In fact, it's one of the ways we've been able to tie these victims together, aside from their strikingly similar looks."

For the next several minutes, silence settled as Alyssa and Cord studied the women's images. Like Ryker, she tried not to ignore her instincts, and as much as she was loath to admit it, her instincts right then were screaming that Ryker was right, at least in that Jennie Killingbeck could've been targeted by the same serial killer who'd murdered the others. Her gaze flitted from Hammond to Cord and over to Ryker. "I guess it's time you meet the rest of our team so we can get to work stopping this bastard."

Chapter Four

Three heads swiveled in her direction when Alyssa walked into the incident room. She'd barely cleared the doorway before the questions started flying at her simultaneously, with Hal's voice rising above Joe's and Tony's.

"So, who's the important-look—" Hal's mouth clamped shut when he caught sight of both Cord and then Ryker strolling in directly behind Alyssa. His eyes snapped to Alyssa, who jumped right into introductions, pointing to each team member in turn.

"Hal Callum, researcher extraordinaire and our all-around go-to guy for pretty much anything. And I do mean anything." She swung back to look at Ryker. "If you need something unearthed or the internet scoured, Hal's your person." She turned back to Joe and Tony. "Officers Joe Roe and Tony White. Everyone, this is Special Agent Ryker Newlin with the Behavioral Analysis Unit. Agent Ryker has reason to believe the Killingbeck case could be connected to one of the Bureau's ongoing investigations, so we're going to be working with her. I'll let her explain the rest."

But before Ryker could begin, Tony cocked his head to the side, his forehead furrowed in deep concentration as he studied the new, temporary addition to their team. Within seconds, his wrinkles smoothed out. "Ryker Newlin. Aren't—"

The smile of greeting disappeared from Newlin's face, to be replaced with an expression that clearly shouted she'd rather eat dirt than respond to what she seemed to sense Tony was about to ask. But perhaps to continue her streak of being upfront and transparent, she addressed Tony's non-question anyway.

"Yes, I am." She took in the entire team, her clipped explanation one that said she'd welcome exactly zero follow-up questions, though she probably expected them anyway. "My grandfather was the beloved, small-town sheriff now infamous for being the prolific serial killer dubbed The Slicer."

Alyssa mentally snapped her fingers, realizing that it wasn't only from Samuel Ezra's case that she recognized Ryker. True, Ryker had aged a little in the nearly seven years since the story had first broken in Northern Indiana. And not just in the number of birthdays that had passed her by. The emotional burden of learning someone close to you was responsible for a number of ghastly murders... well, that took its toll on the hardened features of Ryker's face.

Back when the truth about Ryker's grandfather had erupted, Alyssa had paid attention not only as a detective, but also because the women's bodies had been discovered a few short hours from her own hometown in North-west Indiana. The case had been sensational because of its small-town draw, but also because their beloved hometown hero had committed the crimes. But what had stunned the nation to its core was that Ryker's grandfather had flown so far under the radar that he'd gone undetected for more than forty years. He'd kidnapped, mutilated, and killed his first victim in 1976. Not all of them in the Midwest. The last Alyssa had heard, they still hadn't closed the case with a final body count.

Alyssa remembered the media coverage surrounding the discovery. It had come after Ryker's grandfather had died of a sudden heart attack, what doctors labeled a widow-maker, and the sheriff's family had been grieving the patriarch who'd been larger than life. And then they'd gone into the storm cellar that ran beneath the house. Found the cages, the chains, the bones. And the one surviving victim knocking at death's door when Ryker had stumbled into the nightmare. The media feeding frenzy had been all-consuming and oh-so-brutal.

At the time, Alyssa's heart had bled for what the woman and her family were going through.

"With my father's encouragement, my brother and I both legally adopted our mother's maiden name as our surname," Ryker was saying. "But people, primarily within law enforcement circles, still recognize mine." Ryker's laughter sounded brittle and forced. "People used to ask me how I got my name, and I always felt like they blamed me for their utter disappointment when they learned it wasn't after Rikers Island. Now, I'd welcome that question over the inquisitive, accusatory stares."

The flush in Tony's cheeks spread across his entire face and down his neck. "It's a pretty unique name. Do you want us to ask you about it now, so we can kind of stumble our way out of this uncomfortable conversation? Or is it too late, and we've already failed the test?"

Alyssa noticed how Tony's gaze drifted over to her when he mentioned "uncomfortable" because he knew that *she* knew exactly which stares Ryker meant – the ones that shouted *How could you not have known!* When the family of the offender worked in law enforcement, it made it even more difficult for civilians to accept they hadn't simply looked the other way.

This time, Ryker's laughter rang out with genuine amusement. "You didn't fail the test because there wasn't one to fail. If you really want to know, my brother named me because, for some reason, my parents thought promising a three-year-old toddler he could name his new sibling was a great idea. Of course, they couldn't have predicted he'd want to name me after a rocking chair, which he pronounced *ryker chair*. In the end, it grew on them, and they decided to stick with it." A smile lifted the corners of her mouth and crinkled the lines around her eyes. "Guess I should be grateful he didn't try to name me after the refrigerator, which he apparently called the *refrāta frāta frāta*."

Everyone laughed, relieved that the blurry elephant in the room had been introduced, acknowledged, and addressed enough that it could slide back into obscurity. Then, Ryker clapped her hands together once and said, "Well, shall we get to it?"

The team followed Ryker's lead as she tipped her head toward the enormous whiteboard covering one wall, which already held several images of Jennie Killingbeck. One was the photograph given to Alyssa by Jennie's family. The others were various pictures taken from Jennie's social media, specifically the most recent ones showcasing her short trip to Alamosa, Colorado.

Ryker made direct eye contact with each member of the team. "Before we begin, I'd like to thank you in advance for your willingness to work with me." As she spoke, she set her binder and bag on the table before pulling out the accordion folder, opening it, and once again removing the photos of the victims Alyssa and Cord had already seen.

"For the past five years, the Bureau has been trying to track the person responsible for these murders. Currently, we've attributed kills to him in three states that we know of – or at least highly suspect. So far as we can determine, he's been active in Oklahoma, Nebraska, and Texas." She pushed the photos toward Hal, who was closest to her. "We have reason to believe he's now operating in your state."

Tony glanced up from the pictures to ask the same thing Cord had already asked. "Don't you Feds work with partners? Will yours be joining us later?"

The question brought on a slight, brief tic at the corner of Ryker's left eye. "No, he won't. But I assure you I've been officially cleared to work with you on this case."

Alyssa had the distinct feeling there was more going on with the partner than Ryker was willing to share with them. As long as it didn't affect their investigation, Alyssa didn't need the details.

Curiosity appeased, Tony tapped his index finger onto the graphic crime scene photos Ryker had set out for them and then pointed toward one of Jennie's images. "Gotta say, it's pretty obvious why you think our missing gal is connected to your serial killer case. So, what can you tell us about this guy, besides the fact that he likes women with hair that reminds me of a Sandia Mountain sunset and that he's clearly sadistic?"

Inwardly, Alyssa smiled at how effortlessly Tony and the others accepted Ryker, as if they'd all been working as part of each other's team for years as opposed to minutes.

Ryker's shoulders relaxed in a way that told Alyssa the agent was in her element. "There's a lot we know, but unfortunately, there's a lot more we don't. I'm not sure how familiar you are with what my job entails, but as a behavioral analyst, part of what I do is analyze evidence and then develop what I've gathered into a psychological profile. From what your captain shared with me about Detective Wyatt—"

Alyssa held up her hand. "Just Alyssa is fine. And I'm going to go ahead and speak for all of us and assure you there's no need to be formal, especially as we're all going to be working together. Just call us by our names." Four heads bobbed in agreement.

Ryker's lips tilted up in a half smile, part appreciation and part amusement. "Noted, and same goes. Just plain old Ryker or even Newlin will do. Back to what I was saying. I know from your captain that this team has extensive experience on serial killer cases, so you may already be aware that many of those individuals begin their killing history by stealing ideas from other well-known or even less infamous offenders, at least at first. For example, the man we all know as BTK admitted in a series of interviews that his inspiration stemmed from the 1959 Clutter family murders in Kansas. It appealed to his inner monster, so to speak, and he initially fashioned his fantasies of murder off that.

"We can use those case studies to begin analyzing patterns in an offender's actions, as well as his victim selection. If we can figure out how a killer thinks, we can begin to predict what his or her next move might be. Basically, we map the mind of the killer, which is harder than it sounds."

"Because serial killers, unfortunately, don't all fit into neat little categories the way people seem to think," Hal said.

"Exactly," Ryker said. "Now as far as this case goes, we've been able to identify the killer's version of a calling card. Or in this case, more than one. He slashes their mouths and cuts their throats."

Ryker grabbed one of the more gruesome crime scene photos off the table and used a magnet to secure it to a blank spot on the whiteboard so everyone could see it more easily. "Of course, studying the victims is as important in creating a profile as the crimes and crime scenes themselves. Understanding a victim's lifestyle can possibly end up being our main lead to tracking a killer. So, here's what we know about our victims so far.

"Twenty-seven-year-old Madison Ortega, physical trainer at a gym in Tulsa, Oklahoma, is believed to be victim one. Her body was discovered after her landlord received complaints of a foul smell coming from the house. According to the police interview, the landlord tried calling multiple times, and after receiving no answer, drove over there. Ortega's vehicle was in the driveway, but she wasn't answering the door, so the landlord let herself in with her key. From what we could gather from the scene, the strangulation marks around the victim's neck – from one of her own silk scarves – and the fact there were no defensive wounds, aside from her own fingernails digging into her palms, we believe the killer took her by surprise in her bedroom. It's my belief that he uses strangulation as a means of getting control over the woman before he slits her throat and carves the X across her mouth."

Joe snorted in disgust. "Jesus."

Ryker attached another photo to the whiteboard. "Twenty-six-year-old Daphne Morrow, victim two, also of Tulsa. According to her family, she moved around a lot and was about to begin work as an administrative assistant via a temp agency. Along with slitting Daphne's throat and the X across her mouth, our unsub also severed the tendons at the back of her knees. Quick sidenote: Madison and Daphne are the only two of his victims that we know of who resided in the same state. Victim three lived in Nebraska, and victim four had recently moved to Texas, approximately four months before her murder.

"Now, while Ortega was found lying face down on her bed, quite the opposite was true with Morrow. Let me back up a second. I want to point out that it's my professional opinion that the killer was unused to this level of violence because after he murdered Ortega, he flipped her back over. As a behavior analyst, what that action says to me is that he needed to stop his victim from looking at him, even though she was already dead."

Hal nodded. "Makes sense in a twisted way. Especially if Ortega was his first kill."

Ryker nodded and continued. "Now, back to Daphne Morrow. She was housesitting for her parents at the time, and the blood trail throughout the home, and specifically at the front door, tell us she may have almost escaped. Since there were no signs of forced entry, and the back door was open with the screen unlocked, we believe that's where he gained entry. You can see from the photos that there was a violent struggle from the kitchen all the way through the living room, where the concentration of blood is heaviest.

"We can also tell from the blood streaks on the door that she made it that far. It's my belief that he severed Morrow's tendons to stop her from getting away. What surprises me about Morrow's case, compared to Ortega's anyway, is that there were no signs of strangulation. My initial thoughts are that he was so enraged with her almost escaping that he wanted to make sure she was conscious and alert for the things he did to her next, the X across the mouth and the slit throat." Ryker paused as she looked around the room at everyone. "Any questions or comments so far?"

Tony's eyes remained glued to the numerous crime scene photos as he spoke. "My initial thoughts are that you're right and that by slicing through the tendons at the back of the knee, he's disabling the victim, stopping her from getting away. That much makes sense, as far as the physical act of killing goes. As for the psychological aspect, I'm thinking there's maybe an abandonment issue or a girlfriend/wife/significant other who left him."

Ryker's eyes brightened at Tony's observation, as if he'd just passed a different test, one he didn't know she'd given him.

"Speaking to the X across the mouth," Tony continued, "I've got to go with a classic case of silencing the victim. It's not to silence them from screaming for help, though, because slitting their throats pretty much accomplishes that goal." He swiped one finger against his own throat, as if they all needed the visual demonstration. "This" – he drew an X in the air across his own lips – "feels more symbolic, as if he doesn't like what they've said, whether the 'they' is the actual victim or someone in his past who he's 'searching' for when he kills these women. The fact that all the victims resemble one another tells me it's probably the latter rather than the former."

Ryker agreed with an animated, "Very good."

"Speaking of screaming," Joe said, "were there any reports of that in either of those cases?"

"Great question, and in both instances, the answer is no. With Ortega, I believe she never had a chance to scream for help, and in Morrow's case, her parents lived in an old farmhouse on a ten-acre plot of land, so even if she screamed, no one would've heard unless they were nearby."

The lines in Cord's forehead deepened. "You said she was housesitting. So, who found her?"

Ryker's eyes filled with something that Alyssa could only describe as empathy. "Her parents."

"Shit," Tony and Joe murmured in unison.

"Yeah, shit," Ryker agreed. "Moving on to victim three. Twenty-five-year-old Lauren Grand, sports trainer. Her body was discovered in 2019 on a jogging trail near Fontenelle Forest in Nebraska almost a year after the Ortega and Morrow murders. Similar to Ortega, Grand's body showed obvious signs of strangulation. From the way the ground was disturbed, we believe she was still alive when she was dragged off the trail and into the trees where he killed her. Also, the blood spatter on the landscape, as well as the defensive wounds on her hands and arms, show she tried to fight off the knife attack. We know she used that jogging trail frequently, and we know that she always did her runs between four and five in the morning when it was quieter."

Ryker paused to take a sip from her water bottle and to give everyone a few seconds.

"Four months before her murder, and nearly two years after Grand's, Jaime Asandro moved from Illinois to Lubbock, Texas. Like Grand, Asandro was found outside near a well-known hiking path where she often went after getting off work as a waitress. Because she knew her friends and family worried about her penchant for going on solo hikes, she always let someone know where she was going and when she expected to be back. When she didn't return, her two roommates waited a couple of hours before deciding to drive to the area themselves where they found her car in the otherwise empty parking lot. Since it was starting to get dark, they called the police and explained the situation. Fifteen minutes after arriving, authorities found Jaime not so hidden in some shrub. From what we could gather, her killer grabbed her from behind and slit her throat immediately before branding her with his signature X across the lips. There was no evidence of a struggle nor any signs of strangulation. Her throat was slit, she was stabbed multiple times, and the X marked across her mouth. Lack of strangulation tells me the killer's rage was already at boiling point, and so the attack, for what it's worth, was quick."

Alyssa's head jumped in a dozen different directions, most of which centered around the horrifying realization that Jennie Killingbeck definitely matched their killer's type with her red hair and athletic build. She really didn't want to believe that her missing person case was a homicide, but she also knew she couldn't deny the implications being presented.

Tony pulled the crime scene photos from the Grand and Asandro cases closer to him. After a few seconds, he looked over to Alyssa. "Just a thought, but we could be looking at a big outdoorsman type of person. Not that it narrows our search much."

Hal lifted his hand, drawing Ryker's attention. "Since none of us here have heard about any of these cases, I'm guessing the Bureau hasn't gone public with this information. Have you considered getting the media involved to help capture him?"

Ryker shook her head. "No, we haven't used the media to draw the unsub in, and this was a conscious decision on our part for a couple of reasons. One, as I said, our offender never stays too long in one place. Except for Oklahoma, where we believe he may have roots. The other, more pressing reason to avoid bringing in the media, is to stop any public mass hysteria."

Tony's eyebrows slammed together. "Wouldn't it be better if the public was made aware so they can be on the lookout? You know, stranger danger awareness and all that?"

Ryker's lips tightened. "It's a debate that we could go round and round on, deciding when to bring in the media. Sometimes we get it right, and sometimes, unfortunately, we don't. But the bottom line is that, for now anyway, I'd like to keep them at arm's length until we have more of a grasp on where this guy's headed. To be blunt, we don't even know if he's still in your state. For all we know, our offender could be traveling frequently for his job or something else entirely and he left immediately after targeting Miss Killingbeck. We just don't know, and getting the public in a panic isn't going to help us."

She moved over to the image of Jennie that Hal had pulled from her Instagram. "I believe when we locate Miss Killingbeck's body, we'll find the same identifying markers as those found on our other victims."

Joe's head snapped audibly in Alyssa's direction, but before Alyssa could respond, Ryker accurately guessed his concern and addressed the entire team. "Look, Det... Alyssa already clued me in that your team considers all your missing persons to be alive until irrefutable proof otherwise." She waved her hand toward the graphic crime scene photos she'd shared with them. "If my instincts are right, and the unsub went after Miss Killingbeck, we can't fool ourselves into believing she survived the attack. As you can see for yourselves, he doesn't just slit their throats; he stabs them repeatedly. The chances of anyone surviving such a violent attack are extremely slim. And while I can see that you might want to hold onto hope, experience warns me that we're not going to find her alive."

Alyssa could see Joe, Tony, and even Hal struggling not to offer a rebuttal, but Ryker didn't give them a chance to launch their counter defense. "Listen, while I admire the way your team has a positive outlook, especially in a field as dark as ours, part of my job is to reconstruct a crime scene based on evidence and then create a profile that connects to behavioral patterns, which will help us track this person down before the body count keeps rising. In Jennie's case, I have to connect those patterns to what we already know or suspect.

"With that being said, why don't you all fill me in on anything you've garnered in the relatively short span of your investigation, considering the case just landed in your laps yesterday."

The team looked to Alyssa. "We don't have much. We were able to interview a few of Jennie's classmates in the nursing program that she hangs out with in their free time."

Cord handed her the file he'd taken back from Hammond when they'd left his office, and Alyssa smiled her thanks as she flipped it open, scanning the notes they had. Summed up, they were pitifully minimal.

"Besides Jennie's parents, the last people to see Jennie before she took off for Colorado were Phillip Waller, Lacey Filmore, and Regina Moore. We were able to speak with them all individually, and they each shared the same story, down to the minute. After their summer classes ended August twelfth, they celebrated with drinks that night and then promised to get together again soon. With everyone on different schedules and with different obligations, they managed to wrangle the four of them together this past Wednesday night before Jennie left for her trip Thursday morning.

"At the last minute, they decided to skip out on the restaurant and instead met up at Waller's apartment. Everyone brought snacks and drinks, Waller ordered pizza, they played some low-stakes poker, and then watched *Fatale* and something called *Painkiller* on Netflix before calling it a night. The girls left at the same time, with Lacey and Regina riding together, and Jennie taking her own car. Nothing that was said during their time together hinted at anything being wrong. Mostly, Jennie was excited to see her friend, Allie, while also being a little sad that they'd practically be across the country from one another."

Alyssa looked to Cord. "Did I miss anything?"

"Nope, that about covers it. Aside from the fact that we were going to reach out today to the friends Jennie had regular contact with that she knew outside of nursing school."

After closing the Killingbeck file, Alyssa slid it over to Ryker. "Everything we have or don't have is right there in your hands now. You can skim through it. Now, you've told us about the victims. Why don't you give us a rundown on the killer's psychological profile you've constructed so far?"

Ryker set the Killingbeck file down next to her. "Well, in addition to the high likelihood of him being light-skinned and highly intelligent, he's arrogant and organized. Specifically in reference to the way he's left his victims in places where they're easily located, we believe he's taunting the authorities, openly daring us to catch him. Like many serials we know of, he believes he'll never be caught and so can afford to be cocky."

Cord interrupted to share something with the others that Ryker had said to him when they'd still been in Hammond's office. "Ryker mentioned earlier that it's crossed her mind to wonder if this guy *wants* to be caught, to be stopped."

Ryker nodded. "That's right."

Joe ran his finger and thumb together over his top lip as he processed that information. "Well, if that's the case, isn't that kind of in direct conflict with his arrogant confidence that he *can't* be caught?"

"Yes, it is," Ryker agreed, "and I'm hoping that'll be the something that trips him into making a crucial mistake." Her eyes landed on the smiling portrait Jennie's family had shared. "As horrible as this may come across, Miss Killingbeck may be that mistake."

Cord turned to Hal. "Earlier, you asked Ryker about involving the media. What were you thinking on that front?"

Like he often did whenever he was trying to put together a theory, Hal rolled his chair back and forth in short, clipped movements. "Well, while I agree with Ryker that it's a crap shoot on when to let the media in, I think, in this case, it could be extremely beneficial" – he twisted so he could see Ryker – "*especially* since this guy doesn't stay in one place too long. If he's like many other serials, he absolutely would *not* appreciate being banded together.

"While they may get their initial ideas from other infamous serials and even idolize them, in the end, they want to stand above the rest, kind of like a game of one-upmanship. So, my thoughts are, if we start right off the bat making comparisons to other killers who might've had similar MOs, this guy won't take it as a compliment but rather a direct slap to his superiority complex, which could cause him to act irrationally and make that one crucial mistake we need to stop him."

Tony's head whipped in Hal's direction. "You want to piss this crazy MOFO off? Have you gone and lost *all* your mind? Why the hell would we want to do that?" His finger jabbed the air in the direction of the victim photos spread out on the table. "You see what he's capable of – and that's just from whatever gets his regular mad on."

Ryker listened but didn't waver from her position. "While I appreciate your reasoning, Hal, I stand by my initial objection. In my opinion, bringing in the media now might be to our detriment, and I'd really like to avoid that mistake, if at all possible. To be clear, I'm not nixing the idea altogether. I'm just asking that we all agree to hold off a little longer. If and when the time is right, I'll be completely on board with using the media to our advantage. Deal?"

Hal nodded, though Alyssa could tell he wasn't completely on board.

Tony shifted in his seat. "Not to sound like an asshole, but there's *got* to be DNA or something this guy has left behind. I mean, besides a trail of bodies. In this day and age, it's damn near impossible not to leave a hair or fingernail or blood or just something. Whatever it is, we're going to find it, and well, then he's gonna have a bunch of us crawling up his ass to bring him down."

Joe's bark of laughter cracked the outer shell of the building tension within the room. Shaking his head, he snorted out, "Sorry, sorry, but damn, that's quite a visual you gave there, buddy. I just got a mental flash of you climbing a ladder into this guy's butt." He snorted again, despite the way Alyssa shook her head and tried to bite back her own laughter. Hal, Cord, and Ryker, on the other hand, did nothing to hide their amusement as they each threw their heads back and laughed long and hard.

When dealing with the darkest side of humanity, they had to take their humor wherever and whenever they could get it. And seeing Special Agent Ryker Newlin's reaction gave Alyssa a good feeling about how well they'd all work together for however long it would take to stop this guy before he moved on. Not that she was already trying to give the agent the boot, but Alyssa hoped that would happen sooner rather than later.

Seconds later, their laughter cut off when a scowling Captain Hammond poked his head in the door. "Dispatch just received a call that someone came across Killingbeck's Jeep. And a body matching her description." He didn't wait for anyone to ask before adding, "Clearly deceased."

Alyssa's stomach plummeted with the grim realization that Jennie Killingbeck was, in fact, part of something much more sinister than a missing person case. Even as the captain was handing her the location information, the team, which now included Ryker, was already mobilizing.

—

The High Road to Taos Scenic Byway, a windy, nearly sixty-mile stretch of road, passed through crinkled badlands boasting scrub bushes, scraggly piñon, and juniper trees. Remote mountain villages, both Spanish and Pueblo Indian, along with generations-old small farms, popped up periodically along the way. Populations ranged from fewer than a hundred to a scattered two thousand, and despite the time of day, very few people were seen out and about. In between the villages and farms, fingers of closed or rarely used forest roads stretched off in every direction. It was one of those closed roads where a ranger had spotted Jennie's vehicle and had gone to investigate why the driver had ignored the "closed" barrier. That was when he'd spotted her body.

If it hadn't been for the flashing lights of a dozen police cruisers, Alyssa might've driven right past the location.

Now, with Joe and Tony opposite them, Alyssa stood between Ryker and Cord as they stared down at the bloodied body of the once vibrant Jennie Killingbeck. Mere feet to the right of her battered face rested a can of pepper spray attached to her keychain. From the moment Alyssa had laid eyes on the images of this killer's four other victims, she'd known down to her core that Ryker's hunch that Jennie had fallen prey to a serial killer was on the money, but still, Alyssa had stubbornly held onto that tiny sliver of hope. Now, with the young woman's body left out on display as if she were a crude Halloween decoration, intense fury filled the space where hope had once rested.

"What the hell was she doing on a closed, abandoned service road anyway?" The heat flushing Alyssa's skin was more a product of her anger and frustration than the hot summer sun. As much as she was loath to admit it, Alyssa suspected they'd already been too late to save the young woman by the time the family had reported her missing.

Silent, she knelt to take a closer look, rage rumbling in her chest at the sight of the slashed throat and signature X crisscrossing Jennie's lips. After a moment, she voiced her thoughts out loud, pointing as she spoke. "The cut throat notwithstanding, the sheer number of stab wounds to her torso and neck point to an incredible degree of hate and bitterness." She glanced over as Ryker lowered herself beside Alyssa. "It doesn't matter that the assailant probably doesn't know the victims; these attacks are very, very personal."

Like Alyssa, anger flashed in Ryker's eyes. "I couldn't agree more."

A shadow fell across Jennie's body as Tony shifted so he could make room for Dr. Lynn Sharp and a team of crime scene technicians. "Yeah, I think we can all agree this SOB is butchering whoever these people represent in his twisted head, not necessarily the victims themselves," Tony said. "Along the lines of what Lys was saying, I suspect the victims just had the grave misfortune of being in the wrong place at the wrong time. No twisted pun intended."

Dr. Sharp greeted Tony, Joe, and Cord by name, then crouched down and said hello to Alyssa before turning to introduce herself to Ryker. "Dr. Lynn Sharp, medical examiner. And you are?"

Though Dr. Sharp was technically one of Bernalillo County's medical examiners, Alyssa had requested her presence at the scene since the body would be transferred back to Albuquerque anyway for the autopsy.

"Special Agent Ryker Newlin. I'll be working with Alyssa and her team on this case." She left out the part where she and the Bureau had been hunting the suspected killer for the past five years already.

"Well, I don't know if 'Welcome to the team' really applies here," Lynn said, "but welcome to the team."

Ryker nodded her thanks and then, almost as if she were speaking to the victim, she said, "If we can figure out 'who' he's trying to kill or even why, then we'll have the answer to who's doing these killings."

Of course, if the actual task was that simple, Ryker wouldn't be in New Mexico now hoping she'd finally get those answers after five long years of trying to end this killer's spree.

Alyssa rose back to her feet and turned to Cord. "We need to get ahold of the Killingbecks before this hits the air waves. I want the news to come from us, not some overzealous reporter."

Chapter Five

Soul-crushing sobs saturated the air around them as Alyssa, Cord, and Ryker sat in Heath and Mallory Killing-beck's living room. Since Jennie's driver's license had been located in her vehicle and because of the violent trauma of her murder, as well as the fact that it would still be hours before Jennie's body could be transported to the morgue for the autopsy, Alyssa had made the judgment call to leave Joe and Tony overlooking the crime scene and the technicians gathering evidence while she returned to Albuquerque to break the news to the family. Like it always did when she had to deliver tragic news, the knot in her stomach tightened to the point of pain the closer they'd drawn to the house.

By the time she'd pulled up in front of the one-story, frame stucco home built somewhere around the seventies, Alyssa's anger had risen to the level of red-hot at having to divulge the worst news any parent could ever receive. Logically, she knew she couldn't save everyone. That knowledge, however, didn't stop the deeply seated *need*, the drive to protect other families from suffering the same fate as her own had so many decades earlier.

Within seconds of exiting the vehicle, she'd shoved her personal demons aside as Mr. Killingbeck threw open his front door and stepped outside, hand cupped to shield his eyes from the late afternoon sun. The somber expressions on all three detectives' faces told him everything he never wanted to hear. His hand dropped, and he stumbled back, crashing into Mrs. Killingbeck, who'd just joined him.

Before Alyssa could utter a single word, both Mr. and Mrs. Killingbeck collapsed into each other under the weight of comprehension, with Mrs. Killingbeck's knees giving out as she crumpled against her husband, whose own grief barely gave him the strength to support her from falling the rest of the way down.

"Good God, I hate this part," Ryker muttered under her breath.

"That makes three of us," Cord said.

It took several more minutes for Alyssa to coax Jennie's parents back inside their home, away from the prying eyes of neighbors. With Cord only a few steps behind, just in case he might need to catch Mrs. Killingbeck, Mr. Killingbeck guided everyone into the living room where Alyssa gently but officially broke the news the family had already guessed.

When she finished, she offered an apology that could, in no way, convey the true depth of anguish she felt for the family. "I'm so sorry."

On the end table, the sudden, upbeat ring tone blasting from Mr. Killingbeck's phone jostled everyone's already ragged emotions. Numbly, Mr. Killingbeck untangled himself from his wife's grasp and answered the phone. It took him less than a minute to relay the tragic news to the caller, ending with a strangled, "Why would she be on that road, son? Haven't I always warned her about stuff like that? Why didn't she listen?"

Through the phone's speaker, Alyssa heard a male voice say, "I'm around the corner. I'll be there in a minute."

Mr. Killingbeck drew the phone away from his ear and stared at it, almost as if he wasn't sure what he was supposed to do with it or perhaps wondering if he stared at it long enough, it would provide all the answers he wanted yet had hoped to never need.

No matter how many times she had to witness it, the sights and sounds of a family torn apart by violence were things Alyssa would never get used to – nor did she want to. Because she never wanted to feel aloof or withdrawn from the personal nature of a case. Which was why she, Cord, and Ryker sat quietly, allowing the Killingbecks a few minutes to begin grasping the fact they'd never hug their daughter or hear her laughter again.

Outside, tires screeching to a stop left behind the distinct and offensive odor of burning rubber. Seconds later, a car door slammed, and a man in his late twenties rocketed through the door and into the living room. Face splotchy and with tears that gave his eyes a murky, rheumy look, he cast one quick glance in Alyssa, Cord, and Ryker's direction before rushing to his mother and squeezing himself into the small space beside her and the arm of the gaudy green couch. Gathering her close to his chest, he held on tight as her gut-wrenching cries grew in volume and severity.

The uncomfortably personal scene made Alyssa feel like an intruder – which, of course, she was. As were Cord and Ryker, who sat as motionless and still as she did. But as much as she hated to disturb them, she and her team had a job to do. Catching Jennie's killer and bringing him to justice being at the very top of that list. And for that, they needed information and cooperation.

So, as much as she hated doing it, Alyssa cleared her throat, reminding the family of their presence – not that they could've forgotten.

Still clutching his mother's quaking frame, Jennie's brother craned his head to look at them. His grief-stricken voice crackled like the sound of loose gravel on asphalt. "Do you have any leads? Who did this to my sister?" Each question tossed out sputtered with so much emotion, it was difficult to understand him.

"We're going to do everything in our power to find that answer for you," Alyssa said.

"How did he k—"

His question dissipated into thin air, lost in the frantic whimpers of Mr. Killingbeck's hoarse cries. "No, no, please no. I c… c… can't hear it. I can't. I won't. Please forgive me." His eyes implored Alyssa to understand.

Not only did she get it, but she would also never blame him for how he felt. Every family was different. Some wanted – needed, even – every grotesque, graphic detail, believing they somehow deserved the mental torture since their loved one had suffered while they themselves had survived. Other families, like the Killingbecks, could barely accept the idea that they'd never hear their loved one's laughter or hug them again, much less be forced to envision the hellish ordeal that had stolen their daughter away to begin with.

Regardless, before it was all said and done, Alyssa knew the family would inevitably end up hearing details they'd rather never know, whether those things were garnered from the investigation, the media, or the courthouse when they eventually caught the killer. Alyssa had once heard a prosecutor refer to this cycle as a psychological tourism of torture for the families.

"I know we've already gone over this," Alyssa began, "but we'd like you to walk us through anything and everything you know about Jennie's trip – who she might've met up with, if she mentioned anyone new, where she went, et cetera. We never know what information will give us that one break we need to apprehend the person who did this to your daughter. And sometimes that information comes in retelling us things we've already gone over."

While keeping one arm wrapped tightly around his mother's shoulders, the Killingbecks' son dropped his gaze to the lanyard around Ryker's neck. His eyes swam with grim and angry understanding. When he spoke again, it was through gritted teeth. "You're with the FBI. Does that mean my sister's death is part of something bigger than my parents and I have been told, that whoever did this to Jennie has killed before?"

Ryker momentarily eluded the question with one of her own. "I'm sorry, but I never caught your name."

"Tommy." He shook his head. "Thomas. Jennie's the only one who still calls—" He choked back tears as he corrected himself. "Who ever *called* me Tommy. Your turn."

Ryker shot both Alyssa and Cord a look that warned she would give just enough to appease Thomas and shut down this line of questioning. "I'm Special Agent Ryker Newlin with the FBI," Ryker said, omitting the Behavioral Analysis Unit aspect of her job. "And yes, I'm here because we have reason to believe your sister may not have been this perpetrator's first victim."

Alyssa suspected the slight tonal change she detected in Ryker's voice had something to do with the fact that she feared that the media could now get hold of this detail and possibly spread panic to the citizens of Albuquerque and New Mexico, not to mention the rest of the country, if or when the national news outlets got wind of it.

A stormy brew of anger and grief spread across Thomas's face. "How many? How long has he been killing?"

Ryker shut down any further questions of that nature with an abrupt, yet not unkind, "stop" signal with her palm in the air. "I'm sorry. I know it's not what you want to hear, but that's information we're not at liberty to share at this time. So, Thomas, why don't we instead focus on what you and your family can do to help us stop this from happening to anyone else?"

Mrs. Killingbeck tightened her grip on her husband's hand before addressing Alyssa's earlier question. "As we shared with the detectives yesterday, Jennie went to Alamosa this past weekend to visit her best friend, Allie Ramirez, before Allie jetted off to Maine."

"How long have Jennie and Allie known each other?" Cord asked. They already knew the answer, of course, but Alyssa understood Cord's purpose for raising the question was to help ease the family into the harder ones they'd soon be forced to juggle.

A faint smile lifted one corner of Mrs. Killingbeck's mouth, softening the features of her face for the fraction of a second that it remained before it slipped away again to her whispered, "forever." Tears splashed onto the back of her hand as she reached her free hand up to clutch at her son's fingers resting on her shoulder in a protective manner.

"They met in kiddie gymnastics when they were around four. Jennie was terrified of the balance beam, though it was only a few inches off the ground, and one day, Allie just walked over and laced her fingers with Jennie's while she walked the beam, the whole while telling her not to be scared and spouting words of encouragement. And when Jennie made it all the way to the end and did a leaping dismount, the two of them bounced around, hugging and squealing like they'd just won the toy lottery. They've been inseparable ever since, sharing their dreams and telling each other all of their secrets."

A tug pulled at Alyssa's heartstrings as she watched each member of the family stare off into the memory laid out in front of them, as if they were all watching it play out on a mental video screen they shared. Mrs. Killingbeck's description of Jennie and Allie's tight friendship reminded her of both Isaac's friendship with his best friend, Trevor, as well as her daughter Holly's long-time friendship with her bestie, Sophie.

Seconds ticked by before Cord grudgingly dragged the family away from their shared remembrance. "Allie sounds like the best kind of friend."

Unable or unwilling to speak, all three Killingbecks nodded in agreement.

In deference to the somber mood, Cord lowered his voice. "You told us that you'd contacted Allie before reporting Jennie missing. Was she able to share anything with you, maybe someone Jennie had been planning to visit on her way home."

Alyssa suspected the reason behind Cord's question stemmed from the fact that Jennie's body had been located south of Truchas, population just over three hundred, and not the most direct route from Alamosa, Colorado, to Albuquerque.

Thomas shook his head. "No. Jennie wouldn't have stopped for a couple of reasons. One, anyone other than

Allie that she might've wanted to 'visit,' so to speak, lives here in Albuquerque or at least in the metropolitan area, and she could've done that any time after she returned. Two, once Jennie was heading back home, she hated stopping. We used to get in rows when we were kids because I'd want to take a break and walk around just to get circulation back in my legs, and she'd throw all kinds of a fit. An explorer, she was not. My sister always preferred to enjoy the scenery from a moving vehicle rather than actually being a part of it." Though the words themselves sounded like a beleaguered older brother, the tone spoke of a cherished closeness between the siblings.

"Anyway," he continued, "Jennie left Colorado on Saturday because she had to work early Sunday, and she wanted to get home as soon as possible so she wouldn't miss out on her sleep. Without a solid six and a half, seven hours, she could put the fear of God into a hungry grizzly. And on that slim chance that she would've had someone she wanted to drop in on, she, one hundred percent, without a doubt, would've let Mom or Dad know. Probably even both."

Still puzzled at the route Jennie had taken, Alyssa said, "You said your sister wanted to get home as soon as possible, yet she chose an indirect route that would take her longer. Do you know why?"

"Less traffic, for one, so that was the way she always went. Plus, that drive was far more scenic, at least when it wasn't too dark. But even at night, Jennie loved driving through all the small villages and pueblos. Her favorite was Chimayo. It bothered Mom and Dad that the cell service along that route was nonexistent more than spotty, but Jennie just claimed that was an added benefit. If she was traveling during the day, she could enjoy the landscape without being interrupted by a call or a text, and if it was night, then she wouldn't be distracted driving around the curves and things."

Thomas's red eyes landed on each of them. "No matter which route my sister chose to take, she was nothing if not highly responsible, as well as undeniably reliable." His frustration at being questioned instead of being given answers the family wanted rang through his words. "I mean, Dad said you spoke with her nursing student friends yesterday. Did any of them tell you anything that would indicate Jennie was anything other than what we've already told you?"

Cord shook his head. "No, they didn't. And I know our questions, and us asking you to repeat things can be extremely trying and maybe even a little disconcerting during this time, but I promise you, like Detective Wyatt mentioned, we're only asking because we want to get those same answers you seek just as badly as you want us to."

Mr. Killingbeck's head dropped, as if it were too heavy for his neck to hold up a second longer. "Thomas is right about Jennie never wanting to stop, so I don't understand why she was even on that road. I've always tried to warn her not to stop in unpopulated places. Not to sound sexist, but she was a young woman traveling alone. And Jennie just wasn't someone who took chances. She wasn't a runner, and in fact, she didn't even go on walks around the neighborhood by herself because she was a self-professed paranoid scaredy cat. Oddly enough, that never stopped her from watching scary movies."

Mrs. Killingbeck's smile was soft but fleeting. "Always with every single light on in the house."

Thomas swiped at the tears spilling down his cheeks. "Actually, her love of horror movies is one of the reasons she was always so scared of anything that went 'bump' in the night. Or day, for that matter. Which is another reason it doesn't make sense for her to have been on that closed road – especially if it really had a *Do Not Enter* sign posted. Which brings us back around to what we've already said: nothing you've told us fits. Jennie wasn't a rule breaker or risk taker by any stretch of the imagination. If she wasn't at work, school, or traveling, she was here at home. I guess what I'm saying is that I can't imagine why she'd have chosen to go down that road willingly. It just doesn't – something's not adding up."

Ryker caught Alyssa's eye before addressing the matter of why Jennie had likely been on that closed service road. "We can tell you this – and I apologize in advance if this sounds graphic – but from the amount of discarded tissue found in the general area, it appeared to be a common enough place for travelers, probably females, to use the bathroom. Be that as it may, we're not ruling anything out. And to be completely honest, what happened to Jennie appears to be a crime of opportunity."

The lines between Thomas's eyes deepened. "What does that mean exactly?"

"There's evidence to support another vehicle may have stopped just past the service road. Whoever killed Jennie watched her drive in there, decided this was his chance to pounce, and so he drove far enough past that she likely wouldn't have noticed, and then he circled back on foot and murdered her."

Thomas, along with his parents, flinched at the harsh reality of Ryker's words. "So, you mean whoever did this was following her?"

"We don't have any of those answers yet," Alyssa said. She had no intention of mentioning that she suspected the killer would've gone after Jennie simply because of the color of her hair even if she hadn't pulled off onto that road. The family didn't need to know that right in this moment. Or ever.

Mrs. Killingbeck collapsed into her husband's side as loud, broken sobs shook her small frame. Only after her sobs finally subsided into less hysterical cries did Cord ask his next question. "You said every time you tried calling your daughter on Saturday that your calls went straight to voicemail. While that could've been a result of the lack of cell service, we did verify that her phone hadn't been charged."

The Killingbecks shared a look amongst themselves before Thomas responded. "Jennie was borderline obsessive about so many things, but keeping her phone charged, unfortunately – not to mention, unusually, for someone so attached to her phone – wasn't one of those things. She was always, always forgetting. Like at least a couple, three times a week. Which was one of the reasons I told Mom and Dad not to panic when they couldn't reach her at first." The knuckles on Thomas's clenched fist turned white. "If only—"

Understanding the internal flogging of guilt threatening Thomas's control, Alyssa offered the only kind of comfort she could. "There's no 'if only.' Even if you'd all begun to worry at that moment, none of you could've known the outcome of this tragedy. And as much as I wish I didn't have to say it, the chances are high that, by the time you'd noticed she was late getting home, it was already too late to help her."

Mrs. Killingbeck suddenly leaned forward and reached over to the coffee table nestled between her family and the detectives. Near the corner was a framed family photograph which she snatched up, caressing the image of her daughter's face before clutching the photo to her chest as her tormented wails once again filled the small room. "Please. This can't be happening. It just can't. Oh God, my baby. My beautiful baby."

The way Thomas and Mr. Killingbeck scooted in impossibly closer to either side of Mrs. Killingbeck and wrapped their arms around her, as well as each other, it was clear Alyssa, Cord, and Ryker would get little else from the family at this time. Still, they waited a few minutes before finally handing over their business cards with directions to call immediately if they could think of anything at all, no matter how random or insignificant it might seem.

While none of them moved to show the detectives and Ryker out, Mr. Killingbeck did lift his grief-filled eyes to meet Alyssa's. "We're happy to turn over all of Jennie's cell phone records, my credit card statements and hers. Whatever you need, we'll provide it. If there's a clue hidden in there anywhere, it's yours."

"Thank you," Alyssa said. "We'll be in touch. And it would be helpful if you could email us any copies you have." She directed his attention to the back of the business card where she'd had Hal's number and email address printed. "Just send them to Mr. Callum's attention."

At the front door, Alyssa glanced back to see the family huddled together on the couch, their arms squeezing each other as their bodies shook with their grief. Clutched between them and pressed against Mrs. Killingbeck's chest was the family photo. As Alyssa followed Cord and Ryker out, she knew she'd do everything she could to stop this twisted killer from causing this kind of pain to other families.

Chapter Six

With a rare morning where he didn't have to rush out the door, the man cracked open one eye to check the time, not surprised to see it was only four twenty-three. Always an early riser, even as a teen, he'd never seen much need to languish in bed for hours. Even during those times when he struggled to fall asleep or didn't make it to bed until after two in the morning, he found he still woke before five.

After a slow stretch, he tossed his sheet to the side and made his way into the bathroom where he brushed his teeth and hair. Then, with a quick glance at his physique in the full-length mirror, he dragged on a pair of gym shorts and headed down the hallway into his spare room that housed his extensive and expensive gym equipment. He grabbed a remote and aimed it at the large monitor mounted in the corner, watching the red light blink several times before finally coming to life. Like most days, *she* lay on her flattened mattress with her back to the camera. A patch of nearly skeletal skin peeked between the bottom of her threadbare shirt and the tops of her dingy gray baggy sweats.

He turned away and headed for his weight bench to begin his rigid workout.

Thirty-five grueling minutes later, his skin shiny from sweat, his breathing rasping in and out in heavy pants, he leaned back against the wall and eyed the pull-up bar before checking the time again. Obsessive about his routine, he calculated how much time he could rest before tackling the least favorite part of his regimen.

When his breath finally began to even out, he mustered the discipline required to finish his workout and pushed himself to his feet. As he did, he noticed she had also risen, her eyes lifting to the hidden camera, even if she couldn't see it. Then again, she didn't need to because he'd made sure she knew it was there, that he was aware of her every move, no matter where he was.

Her motions, unlike his, were slow, cumbersome, and clumsy as her bony fingers curled inside and clutched at the metal collar around her neck before dragging her hands down the length of the chain tethered to the wall, tugging at it once, twice, three times. He had his routine; she had hers.

The collar had been his compromise when he'd moved her here from the tiny cage in the root cellar where he'd originally kept her. To show how much he cared, he'd even had the sink and toilet installed as a special surprise for her. He'd expected her to be at least grateful, if not outright happy, when she'd woken to her new environment. Instead, she'd screamed at him with her wrecked voice.

Like it often did, his mind tumbled down the rabbit hole back to that day.

Anxious for her to wake, he sat on a stool across the room as she finally stirred from the drugs he'd been forced to pump into her for the move. He hadn't wanted to do it, but he couldn't take the risk, couldn't trust her not to try to escape. He watched as she slowly became aware of her new surroundings, as she spotted him. As she became aware of the chain and collar.

Her eyes wide with horror, one hand grappled with the collar while the other yanked on the chain drilled securely to the wall. Wretched sobs crackled from her throat as she screamed at him. "Why are you doing this to me? You say you love me, but rabid dogs are treated better than this!" The fingers of both hands clutched at her collar.

Her words sent him into a rage, and he flew across the room, dragging her up off the mattress by her hair. "You're alive, aren't you? You could just as easily be dead like the others. Is that what you want? Is it?"

What he kept to himself was that it was an empty threat; he loved her too much to kill her. It was why she was even alive at all.

Before the memory could burrow its tentacles so deeply that it threatened his control, he blinked it away and trained his attention on the monitor. He watched as she shuffled across the floor to the metal, prison-style toilet, the crude results of his efforts in saving her life evident in the scarred tapestry of her face and skin. Of course, he saw beyond all that to the beauty beneath. True love like his for her always elected to see deeper than the surface. He should know.

When she finished, she pushed the button on the wall that would take her waste away, and then she moved over to the plastic sink where she ran her hands under the trickling water. Finally, she used her index finger and the tiny tube of toothpaste he provided to scrub at the film on her teeth. He didn't trust her with a toothbrush. In fact, he didn't trust her at all anymore, even if he did love her.

His workout completed, he used a towel to wipe away the sweat glistening on his skin, turned off the monitor, and jumped in the shower. Afterward, he made his way into the basement where her dull but wary gaze met his as he dragged a stool over and made himself comfortable.

Because she'd learned early on, she obediently perched on the edge of her mattress, her eyes wide and glassy as he told her about the woman up near Taos. The woman he'd had to kill because *she* had once again questioned his love for and devotion to her. Sure, he had relationships outside theirs, but that didn't negate what he felt for her.

Like always, as he described what he'd done, he waited for some kind of emotional switch to flip on inside of him. Guilt or excitement – or something. But he felt nothing. For him, they were a means to an end, and that end was to exorcise his rage, so he wouldn't take it out on *her* again. That was how much he loved her, but she stubbornly refused to see it that way.

When he finished with his story, she leaped to her feet and raced to the sink where dry heaves wracked her shivering body. Only then did he leave her alone to stew in this hell of her own making, even if she chose not to accept her responsibility for any of it.

After all, if it hadn't been for her, he never would've had to commit that first murder. Right now, he couldn't think about it; he had his normal routine to attend to. Far too many people relied on him; he couldn't ignore his daily life just to console her.

His jaw clenched at her whispered plea to "Stop if he really loved her." He slammed the basement door closed and slid the deadbolt into place.

Chapter Seven

Monday, August 28

After the dry heaves finally ceased, Brooklyn Knox stumbled back to her filthy mattress where she collapsed in a heap and curled back into a fetal position, as if that could somehow protect her from the insanity of what had become her life.

In her years of captivity, Brooklyn hadn't seen so much as a flicker of sunshine or heard the lyrics to a single song, even in her own head. Except for those times her jailer visited, the only sounds she encountered were those of her own voice and the echoes off the cold, windowless basement walls. Her one light source came from a single dim fluorescent lightbulb screwed into the ceiling high above her head and which remained on at all times, its eerie glow doing nothing to alleviate her fear of what lurked in the far corners or the dark shadows.

Not that those things could be worse than her reality.

She wasn't even allowed to read anymore. Until she'd ruined it, he'd surprised her every few weeks with three or four used paperback novels at a time because he remembered how much she'd loved to read "back then." Some of the books he'd brought her had pages ripped out, but she'd never complained, creating her own story to fill in those places. It was one of the things that had originally helped her maintain her sanity. Regardless, the "privilege" of reading had ended after one of her betrayals, and she'd never "earned" it back.

The shiver rippling across her skin came as much from the cold as her never-ending nightmare. The weight of doubt that she could – or even wanted to – continue holding on pressed down on her, making it difficult to breathe. Five women dead now. Murdered. Because of her. Because she'd been foolish enough to think she could escape him, one way or another. Her mind recalled that first time with such perfect clarity, it could've happened just yesterday.

Every one of Brooklyn's nerve endings throbbed. Finally strong enough to work loose the ropes binding her hands and feet, she tugged at the bobby pin stabbing her in the head. She forced herself to focus, to ignore the painful tingling in her skin. Pushing both hands through the gaps in the dog kennel he kept her in, she fumbled with the lock, crying out when the bobby pin slipped from her grip. She yanked her hand back in and lowered it, blindly groping along the cold ground, a choked sob of relief wrested from deep inside her when her fingers closed around the bobby pin.

What felt like hours later, the unmistakable click of the locking mechanism disengaging was music to her ears, and she wasted no time wrenching the lock away and tucking it inside the pocket of her shorts. She needed a better weapon.

She opened the door, wishing for even a hint of light, and scooted out a pattern that traced from one dirt wall to the next until her hand finally found what she was looking for. A rock. Not a large one – it fit snugly into the palm of her hand – but it would have to do.

Her breathing labored, she crawled around until she found the foot of the stairs. She didn't expend any energy attempting to climb them, knowing by the sounds echoing down to her each time he departed that he always secured the door.

Instead, she eased her way to the right of the stairs and waited, her fingers racing over the puckered patches of skin on her face and chest, bile burning her bruised throat as she did.

She had no idea how long he'd already kept her prisoner in the dark, dank cellar. All she knew was that she'd risen from a fog of delirium brought on by what she could only assume was a massive infection ravaging her body from what should've been fatal wounds. Scratchy woolen blankets had rubbed against the stitches pulling at her skin.

The faint sounds of footsteps and a sliding board above her head sent her heart racing, made her skin clammy. She knew she'd only get one chance to get this right. Weak and trembling, she pushed to her feet and lifted the rock, waiting. She wanted to vomit.

A bright flash of light nearly blinded her, and then he was descending the rickety steps, already chittering away excitedly about a job interview he had in Tulsa. His words and feet froze the second he spotted the open cage door.

She brought the rock down as hard as she could onto his temple just as he turned in her direction.

Brooklyn found herself gasping for air, reliving the way he'd managed to overpower her, the way his fingers tightened around her throat as he slammed her head into the cold ground, screaming out his rage at her ungratefulness that he'd saved her life, that she'd be dead if not for him. Multiple times a day, she couldn't help but wish he *had* let her die because then she wouldn't be enduring this hell.

After her failed escape attempt, he'd made sure she'd never get loose again. And then he'd left. For days. Her only source of water came from the two hanging dog water containers secured to the cage. Her tongue hurt from lapping at the tip to get even the smallest drop of moisture.

When he finally returned, he'd brought back his first tale of murder. Overcome with unfettered rage at her betrayal, he'd stopped at a gym in Tulsa to try to work off his anger. That was when he'd spotted the first woman.

"Her hair caught my attention. She looked just like you that first time I saw you." Anger burned through his eyes as he moved in closer. *"But then she spoke, and all I could hear was your voice telling me that you couldn't love me back, couldn't stop reliving how you tried to get away from me after everything I did to save you! So, I waited for her in the parking lot and followed her home. And then I made sure she'd never be able to betray anyone ever again. Because of you."*

Her surroundings blurred as nausea once again took hold. Gagging, Brooklyn crawled over to the toilet, no longer disgusted when her forehead rested against the cool metal. Daily, the draw to end her torment on her own terms invaded her thoughts. But when it came right down to it, her guilty conscience insisted she couldn't risk another woman's life by trying to end hers. Not after her one and only attempt at killing herself had resulted in the second woman's murder.

Instead, she forced herself to hold onto the belief that one day she'd be rescued. That he'd be stopped.

If she didn't force herself to believe it, she'd lose whatever remained of her sanity. And her sanity was all she had left to bolster the hope. For a while after he'd stopped bringing her books, she'd tried keeping her mind active by pretending she had a roomful of students. The mattress, the wall, even the toilet and sink became her students. She'd even named them. But as more and more time passed, her mind became as beaten down as her body that was slowly wasting away. All she had left now was her natural instinct to survive.

So, until her fantasy rescue became a reality, she simply existed.

Her eyes shifted to the sink that had become her new high bar for luxury. The sink that, when turned on full blast, released slightly better than a dripping trickle. A sink that allowed her to dip her head for a drink of metallic-tasting water whenever she needed it. A sink that allowed her to bathe herself – as much as the dribble would allow – with the tiny slivers of soap he routinely provided.

And at least she had an actual toilet now. As foul and rudimentary as it was, it beat the bucket he'd forced her to use down in the earthy cellar. It was probably why he'd expected her to act as if he'd showered her with the finest jewelry when she'd first woken in this basement.

Against one wall rested a large, flimsy cardboard box filled with a four-roll pack of cheap, scratchy toilet paper and stacked with staples such as crackers, a plastic tub of peanut butter, lunch-size packets of chips, and an eight-pack each of chocolate pudding and sugar-free orange Jello – neither of which needed refrigeration. What never came with these boxes were eating utensils, plastic or otherwise.

The first time one of the boxes had appeared, she hadn't understood what it meant. It had taken her what felt like an entire day to summon up the courage to look inside. When she did, she immediately noticed the handwritten note scrawled in black magic marker that simply read: *Ration wisely.*

During those times, she knew his job, whatever it was, had taken him away for an extended period. She could only guess how long he might be gone based on the contents of the boxes.

And while she knew she'd never be able to escape, it was during these absences that her hope of being rescued soared.

Chapter Eight

By the time Alyssa, Cord, and Ryker returned to the precinct, the media, with their fancy, high-tech police scanner apps, had already gotten wind of Jennie's murder, and so the three of them were forced to maneuver through the crush of bodies shouting questions at them, all of whom received no response, not so much as an acknowledgement of their presence.

All save one – Monty Cannon, the investigative journalist from Channel Twelve, a transport from California who, not that long ago, went on air with news that ended up putting Cord's now adopted children's lives in danger. When Cord heard the man's voice amongst the reporters now, he almost gave himself whiplash as he snapped around to find the man. The death glare from hell may have lasted for only a split second, but Alyssa watched as Cannon slunk a little farther into the safety of the crowd. She didn't bother to evaluate why that filled her with so much satisfaction.

Once inside the building, Cord muttered, "That little weasel might still be an overconfident bag of wind, but I really can't believe he'd actually expect us to answer a single one of his shouted questions. Every time I see the man, I'm just reminded of what he almost cost us."

"I agree," Alyssa said, "but at least we were able to speak to the Killingbecks before the news broke. I guess we can be grateful for that."

Weaving around the desks, Alyssa noticed the curious, over-the-shoulder gawking stares the officers and other detectives shot in Ryker's direction. Like they had with the reporters, they ignored them, closing the incident room door on their inquisitive faces. Though not at all surprised, she was glad to see that Tony was already in the middle of a deep dive into the Killingbecks' financials while Joe scoured through the cell phone records that Mr. Killingbeck had emailed shortly after they'd left the grieving family.

Tony glanced up. "Just heard from Lynn that Jennie's body has been transported to the morgue."

Alyssa thanked him as she settled into a chair near Hal and peeked over his shoulder.

In front of him, a map of Colorado as well as one of New Mexico stretched across his screen. Little red icon pushpins tracked Jennie's journey home before they abruptly dropped off approximately ninety minutes, give or take, before she would've crossed back into Albuquerque's city limits.

Without looking up, he pointed to his laptop. "Since we've got her phone pinging regularly off cell towers along this route – at least where there are towers – I'm guessing her battery died around there." He tapped the screen and then traced a long line down to the service road. "That would make it just a few hours away from where her body was located. That's quite a stretch of time for most people to go without charging their phone. Which, come to think of it, probably wouldn't have even helped since that area's not exactly known for its reliable cell service."

"Yeah, but her phone being dead tracks with what we learned today. According to her family," Alyssa explained, "Jennie didn't have the best track record for making sure to keep her cell charged. Which I find a tad strange since so many people, no matter the age, seem almost surgically attached to the things. And why wouldn't we be, when we rely on them for nearly everything now?"

"Instant information available at our fingertips." Hal snorted. "Remember when we were growing up and math teachers told us we wouldn't always have a calculator available to use? Or when English teachers told us we needed to know how to navigate the library and use the card catalog system for research for some random reason or another? Guess the joke's on them."

Just as quickly as he'd added a little humor, he turned serious again. "I know it doesn't help us too much right now, but if we get a bead on a suspect, there's a good chance we might be able to cross-reference the towers his cell phone bounced off of and see if they match up."

"That'll be the easy part," Ryker said. "But first we need to identify a suspect. Speaking of which, I'm going to make a call here in a bit and see if I can get some help tracking down current locations for the names on the FBI's very short list."

So he wouldn't lose his spot, Tony grabbed a sticky note and placed it on the paper in front of him before facing Ryker. "Guess that answers my next question. None of us got to ask earlier because Cap came in, but I was wondering if the Feds had any suspects in mind, or if we're starting from scratch here."

The lines around Ryker's mouth tightened, transforming her face into a mask of fury or frustration – or both. But it was there and gone so fast that, if Alyssa hadn't been staring directly at her, she could've easily convinced herself she'd imagined the whole thing.

From her bulky bag, Ryker pulled out her own laptop, set it on the table, and powered it up. Her fingers flew across the keyboard in a dizzying blur, almost putting Hal's typing skills to shame. A few seconds later, she angled the laptop so everyone could see better. But before they could crowd around the screen, Hal dragged it over in front of him.

"Sorry. Do you mind?" Though technically, he'd kind of asked Ryker's permission, he didn't wait for her to give it before he performed his own magic, blurting out an excited, "Ta–da" as he cast the contents of her screen onto a blank wall across the room, one they kept clear for this very reason. "Cord, catch the lights, would you?"

While Cord leaned back in his chair to flip the lights off, Hal moved the laptop back over to Ryker. "There you go. Now we don't have to be all up in your personal space just to see the screen. You don't strike me as the kind of gal who appreciates that kind of close contact with folks you barely know, even if you have to tolerate it from time to time. You're welcome."

Ryker's gaze swung from her screen to the wall and back to Hal. "No, I don't. How'd you do that?"

Alyssa swallowed back the laughter bubbling in the back of her throat at the way Hal puffed up in pride.

"I can show you later, if you'd like. It's easy breezy."

Ryker snorted. "Sure it is." She moved over to the wall where the names and images of four men were now displayed in full color. "When the Bureau first got this case, these guys" – she pointed to two of the men – "were the Oklahoma authorities' only suspects. Ernesto Henry had a somewhat short history of violent B and Es in the area, and while he was known to restrain and even pistol-whip some of his victims, none of the assaults were ever life-threatening. Not that I'm downplaying what he did; I'm definitely not. I'm just stating what we know. Plus, none of his victims ever reported Henry flashing a knife. He subdued them, tied them up, stole what he wanted, and left. He only resorted to physical violence such as pistol-whipping if the homeowner resisted being restrained. He was out on bail while awaiting trial when Ortega was killed and was spotted in the area, about a block from the crime scene.

"Leo Brown, on the other hand, had a nasty temper that landed him behind bars more than once, starting when he was in high school. On the day Ortega was murdered, she was one of the witnesses who talked to police after Brown showed up at the gym where she and one of Brown's ex-girlfriends worked. He waited for his ex to get off, and when she tried to call the police because she'd taken out a restraining order against him just a week prior, he smashed her phone and then roughed her up. According to the police report, Ortega witnessed the assault from inside the gym and called the police herself.

"Not even a month after that incident, Brown got picked up for choking his then-current girlfriend and holding her against her will for two days because he 'heard' she was flirting with another guy. Because both assaults took place within such a short amount of time, local police had Brown on their radar. Sidenote: both girlfriends had jet black hair, not red. More than anything, their circumstances landed them on the cops' radar.

"Long story short, not only were both men cleared by the Tulsa detectives, but I also verified their alibis myself. As for Brown specifically, he hadn't yet bonded out of jail for violating the restraining order, so he couldn't have killed Ortega." She looked around the room at the team. "They may be slimy individuals, but neither man is our killer."

She tapped one of the other images. "Dustin Moses of Nebraska. His rap sheet has more charges than the number of years in his life. He's been picked up for everything ranging from minor graffiti as a teen to aggravated assault in his twenties. He did a measly three years for domestic abuse but was released just before the Lauren Grand murder. We looked at him pretty heavily since Grand was the person who reported the domestic assault against her friend."

Cord's spine stiffened. "What do you mean?"

"According to the report I got my hands on, Grand's close friend, Ashlynne Redding, called Lauren one night for help. When Lauren arrived at Redding's house, Moses was already gone, and her friend was reportedly in bad shape. Apparently, Moses had used her as his personal punching bag. Grand, who'd been begging her friend for a month to break things off with Moses because of his temper, called nine-one-one. When the police brought Moses in, the thick ring he had on matched the marks across Redding's body. Not to mention the fact that Redding's skin and blood were found on the ring itself. If I recall correctly, Moses also cracked a couple of her ribs and knocked out a couple of her teeth." The more details she gave, the tighter Ryker's voice became. "All of that just because she had the audacity to turn the asshole down when he demanded sex."

74

"Low life sonofabitch," Tony growled.

Cord clenched his hands into fists.

Ryker noticed, and while she addressed Tony, her gaze did a continuous sweep in Cord's direction. "Maybe," she agreed, "but low life sonofabitch or not, his alibi for Grand's murder was airtight. He was with his parole officer during the time the medical examiner estimated her death to have been. Also worth mentioning is that we can't tie Dustin Moses in any way to Jaime Asandro's murder in Texas."

Ryker, her face and eyes hardening again, tapped on the next man's image, pausing for a fraction of a second, almost as if she needed to get her anger under control before she began. "Marcus Davis works at SCJ Headhunters Incorporated, currently resides in Oklahoma, and was Lauren's boyfriend at the time of her murder. We did some digging to see if Davis and Moses knew each other or had ever run in the same circles, and aside from the Grand connection, they didn't. Omaha authorities cleared him fairly quickly, but I noted several inconsistencies over the course of his interviews. Because of that, and the fact that he'd resided in both states where the three victims lived, I called him back in."

"What kinds of inconsistencies?" Alyssa asked.

"Primarily surrounding their relationship, Lauren's and his, I mean. According to Davis, no trouble brewed between the couple, and they were practically engaged, though, he admitted, not officially." The way she ground the words out, underscoring her clear dislike and skepticism of the man, her use of air quotes was heavily implied. "However, both Lauren's friends and family had a different story to tell. They all said she liked Marcus 'well enough,' but that she'd always told them that Davis was more like 'a friend with benefits' and less like this is 'the one.' I tend to believe her friends, if for no other reason than, although Davis claimed they were a committed couple, he had no idea who Dustin Moses was because Lauren had never confided in him about what one of her closest friends was going through. I don't know about all of you, but that seems odd to me.

"But the biggest reason we liked him as our guy – until we didn't – remained due to the Bureau's background check revealing Davis had lived approximately fifty miles outside Tulsa during the times of Madison Ortega and Daphne Morrow's murders."

Tony, who'd returned to his habit of balancing his chair on its two back legs, slammed down, his spine stiffening as his feet hit the floor. "Say again!"

Ryker's lips pinched together in a way that suggested to Alyssa that clearing this suspect still unsettled the federal agent. Or more accurately, pissed her all the way off. "Trust me, we dug up so much dirt on this guy that all our heads were spinning. However, in the end, while we didn't exactly clear him, there was simply no way to tie him conclusively to any of the murders."

Cord voiced the same question sitting at the tip of Alyssa's tongue. "If I'm reading you right, you haven't really quit liking him for the killer though, have you?"

Alyssa mentally shook her head. Why she was still amazed at how often she and Cord shared the same thoughts at the same time was beyond her. These days, it occurred with an almost creepy frequency. She knew he'd read her mind because he shot her a quick grin and winked before turning his focus back to Ryker, who chewed on the inside of her cheek as she mulled over her answer.

"In light of being completely upfront, I'll admit that yes, I, personally, haven't been able to completely clear him from my list of likable suspects. There's just something about him that rubs me the wrong way, something dark in him that I sense. I can't quite put my finger on what it is, but my gut tells me he's involved in this somehow."

Alyssa nodded her understanding. She'd been there herself, more than once. "For argument's sake, we'll keep Davis on our radar until we can officially rule him in or out ourselves. I'm assuming he's going to be at the top of your list to learn his current whereabouts."

Ryker's smile was anything but friendly. "Damn straight." For the next hour, she continued filling in as many blanks as she could regarding the killer's prior victims. Friends, family members, estranged spouses, ex and current boyfriends, co-workers, gym mates, and everyone in between were cleared. She rounded up her summary by returning to her number one suspect.

"With the exception of Marcus Davis, I can say with a ninety-nine-point-nine percent certainty that the other individuals aren't our guy. If all the stars align, then Dr. Sharp may give us the answers we've been searching for after she finishes Jennie's autopsy."

Alyssa may not have known the federal agent long, but something told her she could trust this woman's instincts, and to her way of thinking, that spoke volumes.

Not for the first time, she had a feeling she would not only like working with Ryker, but found she was actually looking forward to it.

Chapter Nine

After leaving Brooklyn and getting tied up in traffic from an overturned eighteen-wheeler, the man's afternoon had then turned into a taxing day of frustration and overheated tempers. All of which resulted in unraveling the frayed edges of his calm until every little thing that hurtled in his direction came to him through a fuzzy red haze. Unable to exorcise his anger through his normal outlet of lifting weights and strenuous exercise, he took the only option available to him in the moment; he slipped out and went for a long walk. Instead of helping, it allowed his mind to dwell on everything and everyone that had pissed him off. Blood boiling, he flipped the hood of his jacket up and lengthened his strides, fingers clenching and unclenching into fists.

He heard the melodious sounds of quiet happiness flowing from her lips before he spotted her red hair.

Quietly, he moved into the thick cover of trees and watched her.

Seemingly oblivious to her surroundings, she sat nestled in the cozy, nature-made playhouse where little children could host imaginary tea parties or conceal themselves during a thrilling game of hide-and-seek. So secluded, if not quite hidden, it could even work as a place for a brief romantic interlude, should a couple be so inclined to have bugs biting at their asses.

As if she'd intuitively picked up on his lurking presence, she glanced up, head cocked to the side as her eyes drifted left and right, up and down. He hunched further down into the thick cluster of trees. From this vantage point, he could still see her.

Off in the near distance, excited chatter and laughter floated back to him. A rustling sound less than five feet from where he stood cloaked in the landscape revealed two teenagers holding hands and giggling as they passed by, never spotting him in the trees.

He turned his attention back to the woman, gripped by the way she absently twirled her red hair around one finger or brushed bugs off her skin or waved them away from her face. The way she rotated her neck to work out the kinks. The way she swayed from side to side as she hummed along quietly while typing away on her phone. Not the back and forth of texting, and not the active movement of scrolling through social media, but more like she was writing a paper without a notebook.

Her chirpy attitude grated on his nerves. Brooklyn's words, "*If you love me*" buzzed at the back of his mind. *If.* His fingernails dug into his palms.

He watched until the evening shadows lengthened their reach. It had been a while since he'd last seen or heard anyone else on the trail.

Though the light had dimmed, her hair still shimmered under the sparkle of the setting sun as it shifted through the trees. He watched as she glanced up and shook her head, as if she hadn't realized that night had snuck in. With a deep sigh, she stood, her back still to him, and stretched her arms high above her head before bending side to side at the waist.

Without thinking about what he was doing, he shrugged out of his jacket and tucked it beneath one of the bushes before removing one of his shoelaces. Quietly, he pulled his thick leather gloves from the inner pocket of the jacket and slid them onto his hands before stashing the jacket again and rising back to his full height.

Moving slowly, hesitating and listening after each step, he slipped between the cover of trees and the thick foliage protecting her little haven until he'd positioned himself behind her. The faint sound of pop music coming from her earplugs whispered back to him, further masking his approach.

He crept closer. One step. Two steps. Three. When he was close enough to physically feel the heat radiating from her skin, he stopped and wound the shoelace around his hands, snapping it taut.

The woman jerked around, eyes widened in shock and fear when she spotted him. Her mouth opened in a startled scream, but her hesitation in running cost her. He used his height and strength to knock her off balance and then yanked her against him, circling her neck with the shoelace and pulling it tight.

—

Overhead, the rustling sound of the wind through the trees brought the realization that nature had stopped its musical chorus, as if all the birds and bugs and creatures had paused to watch him. After several minutes, he rolled to his knees. Rivulets of sweat dripped down his back, soaking his shirt as his eyes roved over her bloody body, waiting, as always, for just that one tiny sliver of emotion. All he managed to summon was a mild detachment at the damage he could already barely remember inflicting.

He rose to his feet and spotted the armband with the woman's identification. He considered taking it with him and tossing it in a dumpster but decided it was too risky. That didn't mean he couldn't make it a little more difficult for the police to figure out who she was. Though he knew he needed to clear out, he "cleaned" the area as best he could. Convinced he'd left nothing behind but his sweat, he bent at the waist and wiped both sides of his blade across the dirt before sliding it into the disposable cloth he kept inside the sheath.

For several seconds, he simply stood and stared down at the woman's face, the X he'd slashed across her lips quieting the noise of Brooklyn's hurtful words. His earlier rage silenced, he ducked back into the trees to retrieve his jacket, using the inside lining to wipe his blood-spattered face before putting it back on to cover his now ruined shirt. With one last glance around, he casually strolled out of the semi-private hideaway and headed in the opposite direction from which he'd originally entered the wooded area, careful to keep an eye out for any potential witnesses, already spinning a story in his head should he encounter anyone.

Once he was safely locked inside his vehicle, he adjusted the vents so that the cold air conditioning blasted across his face. As his sweat dried, he gulped down a large bottle of water, tossed the empty container onto the floorboard, and grabbed another before draining it just as quickly.

Killing always made him thirsty.

Chapter Ten

Tired of tossing and turning because she couldn't shut off her mind long enough to get more than brief snatches of sleep, Alyssa finally threw off the covers, jumped in the shower, poured herself a travel cup of coffee, and found herself back in the incident room at four forty-five Tuesday morning. By five, the rest of the team had also straggled in, all of them bleary-eyed from lack of sleep but chomping at the bit to end a serial killer's spree.

They were in the middle of rehashing the evidence the FBI had accumulated when her phone chimed with a text. She glanced down to see a message from Allie Ramirez, Jennie Killingbeck's best friend. She opened the message, mildly surprised to see it was only five thirty in the morning.

> I know we said seven, but I couldn't sleep, so I can meet now, if you'd like.

Late last night, Allie had returned Alyssa's call to tell her she was on her way to Albuquerque. Through broken sobs and crackling cell reception, she'd asked if they could meet around seven this morning since she wouldn't arrive at her parents' until after midnight. Her only other request had been that they go to her so she wouldn't have to battle parking near the police station, a difficult task most days, but made even more taxing with filming taking place near the area. The bustling excitement of overzealous swarms of people hoping for a glimpse of two of Hollywood's most bankable stars made navigating the already crowded streets a nightmare.

Alyssa had readily agreed to Allie's request.

She relayed the message to the others now, and less than half an hour later, Allie's father led her, Cord, and Ryker into their living room, where Allie sat on a plush leather loveseat cocooned between a slightly older replica of herself and another older woman who Alyssa assumed was their mother. Both women had an arm wrapped around Allie.

Allie's father spoke softly into the room. "Allie, baby, the police are here to see you."

Allie's hollow gaze drifted up from the light blue carpet. And then, as if their presence drove home the crushing reality of her best friend's brutal murder, she leaned into her sister and sobbed.

Alyssa's heart wrenched at the sight. Every time she had to encounter the friends and family impacted by violence, she felt as if her soul absorbed some of their grief and retained it for later.

After a minute, Allie sniffled, wiped her nose with the tissue clenched in her hand, and stiffened her spine. With eyes red as much from lack of sleep as from tears, she whispered, "Thank you for meeting me here. I don't think I could've—" She let her words trail off as another sob wrenched itself from deep inside her chest. "I'm sorry. I'm sorry." She leaned into her sister's shoulder. "I can't believe this is happening," she whispered. "Just three days ago, we were laughing over silly memories, stupid crushes, and making promises that distance wouldn't keep us from seeing each other several times a year."

"I know this isn't easy, but could you tell us about Jennie's visit?" Alyssa asked.

"She sent me a text around eight Thursday morning to let me know she was on her way. Usually, it takes her about four hours because she drives the High Road to Taos route, but there was a bad accident on I-25 outside of Santa Fe that stopped traffic for a couple of hours, so she didn't get in until almost two." She rolled her eyes lovingly. "I was starting to panic when she hadn't shown up by noon and I couldn't reach her, but as usual, her battery was dead. Luckily, she realized it when she stopped to use the restroom after she got through the traffic jam, and so she sent me a text letting me know why she was running late."

Her tears spilling over, Allie stared down at her clasped hands. Her ragged breaths sounded as if they were being ripped straight from her chest. Several minutes passed before she was finally able to continue.

"We had a late lunch, and then Thursday night, Jennie helped me pack up some more of my things, and later we snacked on some popcorn, shared a bottle of wine, watched a movie, and went to bed around eleven. Friday night we went to the bar and had some hot wings and a couple beers."

"What was the name of the bar?" Cord asked.

"Chicks and Dicks. Kind of like its name implies, it's a western bar, so lots of boots, scoots, and cowboy hats."

Alyssa could practically feel Cord roll his eyes at the bar's name, but he kept his opinion out of his voice as he said, "Tell us about that."

Allie shrugged. "There's not really much to tell. Like I said, we ate some wings, drank some beers, danced a little, and then Ubered home."

Ryker chimed in with a question of her own. "You danced. Alone, together, or with other partners?"

"All of the above." Sensing where Ryker's question was leading, Allie shook her head. "No one bothered us or acted suspicious or anything, if that's what you want to know. I mean, there's the one local regular who's like, a hundred, and likes to ask *everyone* to dance, but for the most part, the bouncers there keep a pretty tight handle on any trouble."

"Do you know if the bar has security cameras?" Alyssa asked.

Allie shook her head again. "No. At least not that I've ever noticed. It's way too small a dive. And like I said, the bouncers keep things in check. I've never even seen a bar fight break out. And I go at least a couple Fridays a month."

"What about any current or past boyfriends? Were you aware of any issues there?"

"Jennie was so wrapped up in her studies that she'd kind of sworn off dating for a bit. She figured she'd have time for that after she got her nursing degree." A broken sob slipped out at her words. "She did go out on a few dates with Derek Clark, the guy she dated our senior year in high school, but they both knew those were what Jennie called 'in-between' hook-ups. They scratched a mutual itch, but they both knew they weren't looking for a future together. I know you probably want to know if it's possible he could've done this, but I saw on Insta that he's in the Bahamas right now with his family."

Alyssa took a second to gather the best way to ask her next question. "Jennie's mom mentioned that you and Jennie have been sharing secrets for a very long time. Did Jennie have anything that she might not have wanted to share with her family? Something or someone that she might not have wanted to worry them about?"

Allie's hands lifted and dropped back down, the frustration on her face as plain as if it were written out in words. "I'm sorry. I know this is going to sound lame, but Jennie's family really is very tight. There's very little she would've shared with me and not them. If anything, she probably overshared." The faintest smile tipped the corners of Allie's lips.

For close to an hour, Allie fielded their questions, but no matter what they asked, she couldn't think of any conflict or person who would've wanted Jennie dead.

Accepting Jennie's best friend had nothing that might point them toward a killer, Alyssa thanked Allie and her family and assured them they were doing everything they could to bring Jennie's killer to justice.

Her voice trembling, Allie looked to Ryker. "When I spoke to Thomas yesterday – Jennie's brother – he told me she might not be this killer's first victim. Is that true?"

Ryker's eyes softened, as did her voice. "Yes, that's our suspicion. But like Detective Wyatt said, we're doing everything we can to make sure your friend's the last."

"Is—"

Ryker held up a palm to halt any further questions. "I know you want answers; so do we. But this is an ongoing investigation, and we simply aren't at a point where we're free to share certain information."

A few minutes later, Alyssa and Ryker climbed into the front of the Tahoe while Cord climbed into the backseat. Ryker laughed at the way his long legs looked in the cramped space.

"I told you I don't mind sitting back there. I'm not even sure what chivalrous code you think you're following, to be honest."

"I'm not being chivalrous. I'm putting cushioning between me and the windshield."

Alyssa rolled her eyes and glanced at Ryker. "That's directed toward my driving." She looked in the rearview mirror at her partner. "Which *isn't* that bad."

"No, it's not," Cord agreed. "Unless you're in a hurry, angry, out of caffeine, or just looking for caffeine. Which, come to think of it, is most of the time." He patted Alyssa's headrest. "I stand by my words."

"I should make you eat them," Alyssa growled, "but I want coffee."

–

Fifteen minutes later, Alyssa pulled into the parking lot of one of her favorite coffee shops. While Cord waited in the long line, she and Ryker grabbed a far corner table, one of the few available.

The two of them sat in comfortable silence until Ryker finally tipped her head in Cord's direction and said, "You and Cord have a natural flow to your relationship, and I've noticed how often you both seem to know exactly what the other is thinking. I like that. In fact, it's refreshing to see how your entire team just seems to gel. Everyone listens to one another, and even when disagreeing, your mutual respect is crystal clear." She glanced over at Alyssa.

"You get how rare that is, right? That you, being a woman in a leadership position, don't find yourself in a constant pissing match with your male counterparts?"

Alyssa leaned back in her chair and studied Ryker. "Oh, I'm well aware. But as my son likes to say, I may only be five-three, but I have a six-foot attitude, so I've got that going for me."

Ryker threw her head back and laughed.

"But since you brought it up," Alyssa said, "I'm just going to point out that I've gotten the general impression that you haven't had that same experience with the men you work around."

Ryker offered a lopsided smile, one that Alyssa had come to think of as her, "Well, no shit" one. "No, definitely not. Not ever in my law enforcement career, if I'm being completely honest, but most recently, not with the Bureau, and certainly not with my current partner. I won't bore you with the details."

More than once, Alyssa had noticed how Ryker's mouth always appeared as if she'd bitten into something bitter the few times anyone mentioned her partner. "Your call, of course. But I doubt it's boring, and I'm all ears if you feel like talking about it. Like I said, your call. No judgment either way."

As if they'd read each other's minds, they both glanced in Cord's direction. He'd moved up a whole two spaces in the slow-moving queue. At this rate, he'd be there another five to ten minutes, at least.

Ryker sighed. "My partner and I never really hit it off. He's one of those over-the-top macho asshats who... well, you know the kind. More than anything, his attitude was more of a buzzing mosquito in my ear. Until this case. Or more specifically, until my refusal to let Marcus Davis go as my lead suspect. I didn't mind that he disagreed with my assessment. I minded that he never spoke to me about it before going to our superior and informing him that he felt 'unsafe' working this case alongside me because my thinking had been clouded with, and I quote, 'a gross refusal to accept the truth.'"

Alyssa reeled back at that.

Ryker's face twisted in anger. "Yeah, he said he couldn't necessarily trust my judgment considering how I couldn't even see that my own grandfather was a monster."

Alyssa barely managed to keep her jaw from dropping open. "Sounds to me like your partner was more threatened by your intelligence than having an actual lack of trust in you. Regardless, hearing that must have stung."

Ryker's eyebrows shot up. "Oh, it didn't sting; it pissed me right the hell off. This happened just before I came to Santa Fe to testify in the Samuel Ezra case. My partner's currently working on another case in South Carolina, which is why I had no trouble getting the okay to work with you and your team. And I assured my boss we wouldn't be needing my partner to join us anytime soon and sent him links to some of your past cases for proof."

Ryker's eyes flickered with guilt as she held Alyssa's gaze. "One of them was the Evan Bishop case. I'm sure you can understand why, but still…"

Alyssa held up her hand. "You don't need to explain." Not only because she did understand but also because she didn't need to tumble down that cesspool of a memory. It was enough for the two of them to accept that they had more in common than just being two women in a male-dominated field.

Ryker jerked her head down once. "Anyway, he didn't need much more convincing after that."

Relieved to have moved on, Alyssa still had to ask. "Look, as insulted as I am on your behalf about your partner questioning your professionalism, I need to know – *was* your head too clouded that you couldn't see other alternatives?"

Just seeing how Ryker didn't become offended at the question itself told Alyssa all she really needed to know. But she waited for Ryker's answer anyway.

"No," Ryker said. "Even when I know down to my core and have evidence to back up my instincts, I always, always keep an open mind. No one is ever completely cleared until we have an arrest and conviction. I get the impression you do the same."

"I do." Both women watched as Cord maneuvered his way through the maze of tables, tray in hand. "Now that we've got that all cleared up," Alyssa said, "I'd just like to go on record as saying that your partner definitely sounds like an asshat of the highest order."

Ryker's grin stretched across her face. "Oh, he is," she said just as Cord found his way over to them and set the tray down.

"You two looked deep in conversation. What'd I miss?" As he spoke, he placed a blueberry muffin and an extra-large take-out cup of coffee in front of Alyssa, a cinnamon roll and a medium-sized frothy coffee in front of Ryker, and a passion fruit tea with a naked everything bagel for himself before taking a seat.

Alyssa took a grateful sip of her coffee and sighed her contentment. "Nothing to do with the case. We were waiting for you." She took a bite of her muffin, washed it down with another sip of coffee, and then said, "Thanks for this. We'll square up later."

Cord waved her words away, along with Ryker's offer of the same. "I think it was nice that Allie Ramirez's new job graciously offered to move her start date so that she could come to Albuquerque to be with her and Jennie's family. But I've got to tell you I'd really hoped to get something more useful. Aside from the Chicks and Dicks dive" – his eyes did an impressive acrobatic roll – "she didn't really give us much to go on. And to be honest, from everything she told us, I have a feeling it's going to be a dead end, which is kind of where we already are."

Cord exhaled his frustration and glanced over at Ryker. "Not implying anything against any of the work you and your partner have done."

Like Cord had with her offer to pay him back, Ryker waved his comment away. "You'd have to try a hell of a lot harder than that to offend me or hurt my feelings. My skin has grown mighty thick over the years. More than that, you're not wrong. It's been five years; we should have much more than we do. That we don't just pisses me off."

Alyssa channeled her inner Hal, choosing to focus on the positive. "You haven't yet made an arrest, but what you have done is cross people off the suspect list, which is part and parcel of any investigation. You know as well as we do that it doesn't matter how good your investigative skills are, finding answers also requires a great deal of luck. And since Hal's doing a little digging of his own into the backgrounds of those same suspects the Bureau has already cleared, if there's something there that the Feds might've missed or overlooked, Hal will unearth it. The man's better than a dog with a bone when it comes to stuff like that."

Cord leaned back in his chair and wrapped both hands around his tea. "Lys speaks the truth. I know the Bureau has its own research experts, but it doesn't have Hal, and I'd place my money on our guy every single day, and twice on Sundays."

Ryker smiled. "I don't. Doubt it, I mean." She tapped on the notebook Cord had brought in with him. "I've got to admit I haven't seen anyone conduct an interview with pen and paper in quite some time. You've heard of this thing called technology, right? Tablets, recorders, et cetera?"

Cord shrugged, but a commotion at the door interrupted whatever he was about to say. Squeals and excited shrieks accompanied the sounds of chairs scooting back and camera phones snapping picture after picture as Hudson Bane and Remington Everwood, two of Hollywood's leading heartthrobs, strolled in, an entourage of paparazzi and fans close on their heels as the actors' security team did its best to keep the crowd from completely mobbing the men.

Ryker kept her gaze riveted on the crowd for a moment before turning back to Cord and Alyssa. "According to the Hollywood rumor circuit, those two have quite the combative relationship, getting along about as well as predator and prey. Do you know what they're filming?"

In recent years, New Mexico had become a hub for the movie industry, but this was one of the only times Alyssa had encountered any of the celebrities often filming in the area. "I think I heard it's a love triangle romance kind of deal, but I didn't pay enough attention to be sure."

Ryker chuckled. "Art mimicking life and vice versa, huh?" At Alyssa and Cord's blank expressions, she laughed harder. "Sorry. I forget not everyone has a secret obsession with celebrity news. About a year back, TMZ reported on a love triangle between Hudson Bane, Remington Everwood, and one of their female costars at the time." She shrugged, a slight hint of pink coloring her cheeks. "Some people give up chocolate for Lent; I give up celebrity news. And now you know something personal about me. Try not to judge too hard."

It was Alyssa's turn to laugh. "No promises there."

Cord joined in the laughter and then cocked his head to the side as he studied the two stars. "They're better looking in person than I would've thought. I guess I figured they'd be, I don't know, just less."

A bemused grin lit up Alyssa's face. "You sound like Isaac." She glanced at Ryker. "Isaac's eighteen and my youngest, as well as the one who says I have a six-foot attitude." She turned back to Cord. "Isaac was really hoping that, in person, both guys would resemble the Hunchback of Notre Dame."

Cord chuckled. "Yeah? Why's that?"

"Apparently, he and Amber" – again, she turned so she could explain to Ryker that Amber was Isaac's current girlfriend – "spotted Remington and Hudson out near UNM one night, and as Isaac put it, she went absolutely 'cray-cray.' The next day, Amber and a group of her friends decided to ditch work and head out to a cattle call for extras in the hopes of getting another peek."

Alyssa's phone vibrated on the table. Hal's name and image popped up, and she snatched it up, jamming a finger into one ear so she could hear. "What've you got for us?"

"What the hell is all that noise? You guys decide to hit up a concert or something? Christ, that's loud."

"Worse. Hudson Bane and Remington Everwood just walked into where we stopped for coffee to go over the case. Anyway, do you have something for us?" Alyssa asked again.

"Another body, unfortunately. A couple out walking their dogs happened across it."

Alyssa felt the air whoosh out of her lungs. "Damn it! Where?" Already she was tossing the remainder of the blueberry muffin she'd barely eaten into the center of the tray so she could throw it out, along with her empty coffee cup.

"Wooded area near Tingley Beach. I'm sending the details now."

Alyssa shoved her chair back, gathered the tray of trash, and with Cord and Ryker on her heels, headed for the nearest garbage bin and exit, pushing none too gently through the congregation of people pressing in on every side of her, almost as if they were trying to block her path.

"Identification?" she asked when they finally stepped outside where she could hear Hal.

"Not that I've heard. I'll send Tony and Joe your way as soon as I hang up."

"Thanks, Hal." Alyssa ended the call, tossed her phone to Cord so he could pull up the directions Hal was texting, and then filled him and Ryker in as she pulled into traffic and hit the gas.

Chapter Eleven

Aside from the thick bevy of flies swarming the area, the first thing Alyssa noticed was the victim's red hair, and her stomach dropped to her feet, even though she'd been expecting it. Two murders in a matter of days – the killer was escalating. They needed to find out why, and they needed to find out yesterday.

She nodded a distracted greeting to one of the officers interviewing the couple who'd stumbled across the body earlier that morning, but her concentration remained on the victim, the way the darkened ground around the body had done its best to absorb all the blood, the way her head rested at an odd sixty-degree angle, and how her lifeless eyes held tenaciously to the fear of her final moments. Clear signs of strangulation showed on the victim's neck, an element of the kill present in all the women except Daphne Morrow and Jaime Asandro, victims number two and four.

Tony, who'd just arrived on scene with Joe, growled low in his throat. "Jesus."

Ryker turned in a slow circle, taking in their surroundings, before pointing at the multiple stab wounds peeking through caked blood and then upward toward the woman's neck and face. "Everything seems to match our killer's MO. He caught her off guard by strangling her. After he had her under his control, he slit her throat and marked her with his signature X."

Joe nodded his agreement. "Makes sense to me, but I'm not Dr. Sharp."

Ryker gave what tried to pass as a smile. "None of us are."

Crouching, Alyssa tuned out the conversations taking place around her and concentrated on what her senses could tell her, not just about the victim, but also where the murder had taken place. While the area was by no means out in the open, it wasn't exactly secluded either. What had brought the woman here? Had she been waiting on the person who'd killed her, the same person Ryker had been hunting for five years, the same person Alyssa now hunted? She immediately dismissed the idea as improbable simply because if the victim had been expecting him, catching her off guard by strangling her seemed unlikely.

A gravelly voice near the yellow tape cordoning off the crime scene yelled for someone to get back or get arrested, disrupting Alyssa's thought process. She rose back to her feet and looked at Ryker. "He's escalating. We need to find out why."

Ryker's tight-lipped expression gave physical proof of her frustration. "So much for making sure Jennie Killing-beck was his last victim."

Tony rubbed one hand down his face. "How does anyone do this to another human being? Christ, it's difficult trying to think like a jacked-up killer on a spree." He stepped back and stood quietly, taking in the entirety of the crime scene, much like Alyssa had done moments earlier. Almost as if he were talking to himself, he said, "This isn't exactly the kind of spot you'd easily notice if you weren't already off the trails and in the thick of the trees and bushes." He pointed to a thick copse of trees that the victim's feet seemed to be pointed at. "See the way those branches are bent and the scuff marks on the ground? It's possible the killer kept himself hidden there." He moved in tight little circles as he continued thinking aloud. "That being said, if someone *was* off the beaten path, or knew about this little slice of semi-privacy, it wouldn't be difficult to hear some kind of scuffle taking place in here."

Ryker took in the surroundings. "Every one of his last four murders are more out in the open than the last. Something's snapped inside him, and he's escalating at a dangerous pace."

"Well, in Jennie's case," Tony said, "that road wasn't a public access, so out in the open, yes, but not as easily accessible, which was probably why her body wasn't discovered for a couple of days." A low rumble sounded in his chest as he ran his hands over his sweat-dampened scalp. "So, not only escalating but also thumbing his nose at the possibility of being caught. Arrogance or something else? Who's to say?"

Cord, who'd just finished speaking with the crime tech videographer, joined them in time to hear Tony's statement. "My vote's on arrogance." He looked over at Ryker. "We know, or think we know, that Ortega and Morrow are the only two of his victims who lived in the same state. Until now, that is. How long between those murders?"

Ryker's answer came immediately with no pause for thought, further proof she'd been living and breathing this case for five long years. "Seventy-three days between Ortega and Morrow's. Almost a full year passed before

Lauren Grand's murder. Nearly two years passed before Jaime Asandro. And approximately eighteen months later, Jennie Killingbeck."

"Damn." Cord's whistle said everything Alyssa – and probably the rest of them – feared. How many more victims would this killer claim if he'd suddenly gone from a minimum two-month cooling off period, if one could call it that, to two murders in a matter of days? And why was he killing these women? More importantly – *who* was he killing when he killed them? His mother? A girlfriend? A wife? A sister? Who? Of course, if they had that answer, they'd probably be a hell of a lot closer to nailing their guy.

In that moment, it crossed her mind to wonder if there were victims in between or even before that they didn't know about or hadn't yet attributed to the same perpetrator. But before she could voice her thoughts aloud, someone yelled for her.

"Detective?" The same crime scene technician who'd greeted Alyssa when she'd arrived waved now to get her attention. "I think we may have found the victim's identification."

Alyssa, along with Ryker and the rest of the team, hurried over to where the technician pointed. Nearly buried beneath leaves and twigs approximately one hundred yards from the victim's head was a shattered cell phone, what appeared to be a pepper spray canister similar to the brand they'd discovered with Jennie Killingbeck's body, and what Alyssa recognized as a runner's armband. In the latter, a driver's license and the top of what appeared to be a credit card peeked through the plastic sleeve.

Sadness gripped Alyssa. Knowing the victim's name always had the heavy impact of making things more personal for her.

She surveyed the ground around the items to evaluate how they'd gotten there, so far from the victim's body. In the dried dirt leading away from the victim, the killer had made what appeared to be a rudimentary attempt to erase his shoeprints. She dragged her gaze from bush to bush, tree to tree until she spotted another broken branch, similar to the one Tony had pointed out, but a cleaner break. She turned back to Tony, an avid hunter and by far the best tracker she knew, and nodded toward the branch. "What do you make of that?"

"Looks like a neater cut. Probably cut it off to use as a makeshift broom to erase his prints. It's what I'd do if I were some psycho nut job trying to cover my tracks."

"Yeah, kind of what I thought. The 'killer cut it' part, not the 'if you were a psycho' part, but yeah, glad you're not. Let's make sure we bag that branch. Maybe we'll get lucky, and he left some DNA on it." Alyssa turned back to the victim's items. "What was the purpose of moving her things?"

Tony's gaze drifted back to where the woman's body lay and then back to the items found, repeating the process multiple times, squinting as he studied smaller squares of space with more intensity before moving onto the next. In a way, it reminded Alyssa of an eagle in search of the tiniest rodent. Finally, he said, "It could be something as simple as just trying to make it a little harder for us to make an identification. He didn't want to risk taking the things with him to toss somewhere else, but he didn't want to leave it out in the open either?" He shrugged.

While Tony did his thing, Alyssa lowered herself once again, pulled a pen from her pocket, and turned the victim's discarded armband just enough that she could read the name peeking through the plastic window. Taylor

Gray, date of birth" – she leaned in closer – "July twenty-fourth, 1996."

As soon as Alyssa voiced the victim's name out loud, Cord placed a call to Hal, relaying the information. When he finished, he said, "By the time we get back to the station, Hal should have at least an initial look into Gray's background. If he hits on something that requires our immediate attention before then, he'll get in touch."

Blood pounding in her ears at the senseless act of violence, Alyssa pushed back to her feet. "Barely twenty-seven years old." Her gaze shifted to Taylor Gray's lifeless form. "She still had an entire life to live in front of her."

"She did," Ryker agreed.

Through the canopy of trees overhead, the sky shone a bright, clear blue, and Alyssa couldn't help but feel like it should be overcast with booming thunderclouds to match the viciousness of Taylor Gray's murder.

Beside her, Joe waited for one of the news choppers flying above their crime scene to pass over before speaking. "So, what's causing this sudden escalation? Because I gotta be real and tell you that I'm more than just a little pissed that this sonofabitch has zeroed in on The Land of Enchantment to go completely off the rails."

"Can't disagree with that," Tony said. "When we catch this bastard, he's gonna wish he'd tempered his tastes to sticking with green chile and New Mexican cuisine. And we better catch him fast because if we don't, it doesn't bode well for our state. Or the red-headed women in it."

Having tracked down more than her share of murderers and serial killers over the years, Alyssa had begun formulating her own tenuous theory – nothing that she'd seen in these last two kills hinted at the killer stalking the women. Even the locations felt random. Still, curiosity had her asking Ryker's opinion. "What's your gut saying? Were our last two victims stalked?"

Ryker's eyes shifted from Taylor's body over to the entrance to this little hidey hole of a space. A group of technicians actively collected, labeled, and measured anything they believed could be evidence. After a lengthy pause, Ryker answered. "I really don't get that impression, no. Like Jennie, this feels more like a crime of opportunity. Unless he'd already been stalking the victims for a long time, or he knew them well enough to know their routines. When we speak to the friends and family, we need to find out if the victim came here often. If she did, maybe that'll give us something more to go on."

Cord, quieter than usual, nodded toward the multiple stab wounds that had turned the skin on the woman's torso into ribbons, and made his own observation. "I've gotta say this attack feels an awful lot like overkill, pardon the phrasing. Which makes me think back to what Tony said yesterday, that this guy's 'killing' someone else in his mind. But what, or who, set him off to make him escalate so quickly?"

Alyssa sighed. "Yeah. I was just asking myself that same question. If we can find an answer to that, we might get somewhere." She turned to Ryker. "Maybe your theory that he wants to be stopped is more accurate than you think, even if the killer doesn't know it himself."

Ryker snorted. "Sure as hell would be easier if he just walked up to us and confessed."

"If only it were ever that simple," Tony said as he stalked away to greet Dr. Sharp, who'd just arrived on scene.

–

With his dark shades and baseball cap, he kept to the outskirts of the crowd and blended in with all the other curious onlookers. Slightly in front of him and to his left, a middle-aged woman with neon orange hair and a nose ring had her phone pressed to her ear. Again. In the last few minutes since he'd arrived, he'd listened to her trying to call someone three different times. With a mumbled curse, she shoved her phone back into her pocket, and he stepped closer, leaned down, and whispered, "Do you know what's going on back there?"

The woman's head jerked up and back, her eyes glazed over with enthusiasm. Craning her neck and using her hand to shield the sun from her face, she tried to cover her excitement with the horrified whisper of her words. "I heard they found a body a few hours ago. A woman. She was naked. Like she was—"

Instead of rolling his eyes at what he knew was complete misinformation, he covered his gasp with one hand and clapped the other over his heart. "Oh, my God," he murmured through his fingers. "I walk these trails all the time, and now… Well, it just seems like no one is ever safe anywhere anymore."

The woman's response was lost in the excitement of two detectives who'd just stepped beyond the yellow crime scene tape, their eyes scanning the crowd as they moved through it.

Searching, he knew, for him.

He watched them, his heart nearly exploding inside his chest when one of the detectives suddenly pointed in his direction. He forced himself to stay put a little longer before slipping away.

Chapter Twelve

While Tony spoke with Dr. Sharp, Joe and Ryker re-interviewed the couple who'd had the misfortune of having their morning walk disrupted by stumbling over a dead body. According to one of the first officers on scene, the husband, afraid his agitated dogs may break their leash and disturb the crime scene or bite someone, had asked if he could take the animals home and had returned to rejoin his wife a few moments earlier, giving Joe and Ryker the chance to interview them separately.

In the meantime, Alyssa and Cord observed the crowd of bystanders lurking outside the crime scene tape, searching for anyone who might stand out or otherwise not quite "fit in." Their primary focus outside the growing pile of looky-loos, however, was the residential neighborhood whose walled backyards looked over the parking lot, the fishing ponds, or the wooded area behind the houses.

Nearby, where a stretch of dirt next to the berm was often used for extra parking, Alyssa debated taking out her phone to record the numerous sets of tire tracks in the dust-dry dirt before ultimately deciding it would be useless. Even she could tell there were no usable tire treads that would help – even assuming their killer had parked a vehicle there. Which, thinking like a criminal, especially one as elusive as their killer, she didn't think he would. It might've been the closest to where he'd left his victim, which made for an easier escape, but it also meant an even higher risk of being spotted by someone. And there was no way someone would've gotten away with no blood on him after that slaughter.

Cord came to an abrupt halt and grabbed Alyssa's arm to yank her to a standstill. Startled, her free hand automatically dropped to the holster of her gun. "What?" Her eyes darted left and right in search of the danger.

Cord's laughter caught her off guard.

"What?" she repeated, this time with a little more irritation coating her question.

"Sorry. Didn't mean to alarm you. I just wanted you to look right over there at the back of that faded blue house. I count three cameras."

She swiveled in the direction that he pointed, narrowing her focus to see beyond the throngs of people. "Sure enough. Even better, the one on the left looks to be facing the woods. Let's see if we can get the owner to let us check it out." With Alyssa leading the way, they moved past the crowd and walked the length of the wall until they could enter the residential area. On the corner, she stopped and counted six houses from the east. "There it is." After checking her watch, she crossed her fingers that someone would be home at this time of day.

"Good thing you counted the houses," Cord said, shortening his longer strides to match hers, even though she'd picked up her pace, "because the fronts all look vastly different than the backs. What color is that anyway?"

Alyssa glanced over to where Cord pointed. She had no clue, but she took a wild stab at it anyway. "Looks to me like someone couldn't settle on one purple color so mixed them together and threw in some smashed blueberries for fun. Puke-purple-gray-blue? Who knows? As Isaac would say, 'Unless there's going to be a quiz, does it really matter?'"

Cord chuckled as they made their way along a crumbling sidewalk and past a yard full of political signs before winding their way up a disintegrating driveway, the cracks in it playing host to a collection of various weeds.

In front of the garage, Cord paused so he could shoot off a group text to Ryker, Joe, and Tony letting them know where they were and what they were doing, and then he leaned in to take a peek inside. "One vehicle. Lincoln Town Car. Maybe circa 2009, give or take a year or two."

Alyssa didn't even question the accuracy of Cord's guesstimate. As the other half of the "any and all things cars" aficionado, with Hal being his partner in crime, she no longer doubted their uncanny ability to pinpoint exact makes, models, or years with little more than a glance at body styles.

At the door, a blazing red color that boldly clashed with the exterior paint job of the rest of the house, Alyssa rang the doorbell. An instant chorus of yappy dogs and skittering claws against an un-carpeted floor greeted her ears. "Good God, it sounds like the owners have an entire pet store in there."

It took nearly a full minute before a tiny, elderly lady engulfed in a pink cardigan two sizes too large for her frame opened the door. She gripped the doorknob with an arthritic hand while using her cane to shoo three equally tiny chihuahuas away, praising them for "saving her dear life" with their viciousness before finally greeting the two strangers on her doorstep. "Yes?"

Alyssa's smile came not only as a way of helping put the woman at ease but because even the woman's voice reminded her of the kind of grandmother she'd always wished she had. She held up her badge and ID and pressed it close to the glassed-in portion of the screen door as she introduced herself and Cord. "Hello. I'm Detective Wyatt with the APD, and this is my partner, Detective Roberts. Do you mind if we come in and talk to you?"

The woman lifted her cloudy eyes from their detective shields. "Are you two part of all that commotion taking place back there in the woods?" Alyssa noticed how the woman held the door a little tighter for balance as she craned her neck to see Cord, whose head just narrowly avoided touching one of the exposed beams threatening to fall from the porch roof.

"We are," Alyssa said. "Detective Roberts and I noticed you're the only home in this neighborhood with security cameras mounted in your backyard, and we were wondering if you'd mind letting us take a look."

The woman lifted her hand from the doorknob and pressed it against her chest, teetering a little as she did, something that had Cord's hand shooting out in reflex as if to catch her, even though he would've had to break through her screen to get to her. Her vision may have been a bit blurry, but she could see well enough to take note of Cord's gesture. She flashed a genuine smile that showed off her dentures. "Well, aren't you just a sweet boy?" She waved his hand away. "But I'm fine. I didn't write 'falling on my face in front of a handsome stranger' in my calendar for today, so you're okay."

With that, she flicked the unlock button on the door and ushered them in. "Quickly now before the girls realize they can escape." Barely inside, two of the girls in question returned to their excited yapping while darting behind a recliner where they could certainly be heard but barely seen. The third one, however, braved the strangers in her house, pouncing excitedly in front of Cord before darting in once to nip at his right ankle.

Despite the reason for their impromptu visit, the scene filled Alyssa with enjoyment even if, sadly, it was too short-lived because the elderly woman called off her attack chihuahua. To Alyssa's surprise, the tiny little dog obeyed instantly, sitting back on her haunches, her entire body trembling like she'd been cast outside in a full-scale blizzard.

With a quick snap of the homeowner's wrist, the other two dogs finally stopped their incessant noise. In the sudden silence, the woman said, "I love them, I do, but sometimes their chatter is enough to drive me to want to drink." Then she introduced herself. "My name is Lois Cutter, but you can just call me Lolo, short for Grandmama Lolo, which is what all my grandkids and now great-grandkids call me."

She waved toward the back of her house where Alyssa could just make out French doors in desperate need of a paint job. "You mentioned having a peek-see at my cameras, and as much as I'd love to help you solve a real-life crime like those shows I watch, I have to be honest. I just don't have any idea how to let you do it.

"You see, my youngest grandson" – she practically doubled her size when she puffed up with pride – "he's just recently turned thirty and still elected to rent a room from me just so I wouldn't be living alone in this old ramshackle house. Anyway, Matty has one of those, whatchacallits on his phone, an applicator or something, and that's how he checks the property whenever he needs to. But he's in Thailand right now, I'm afraid."

Disappointed but not quite discouraged yet, while also noting that Tuesday had already turned into Wednesday over in Thailand, Alyssa asked, "I don't suppose you have any way we can try to get ahold of Matty, do you?"

One bony, crooked finger went to Lolo's lips. "Well, now, if it's almost noon here, then it's already after midnight there, so he could still be up. And he did tell me I can call him anytime if… This could qualify as an emergency, right?"

Alyssa looked to Cord, stumped. In her world, it might qualify as an emergency, but in Lois Cutter's, did it?

Then it didn't matter because, almost as if by divine intervention, a cell phone on a nearby table rang, the ringtone humorously trilling out that "Matty's calling." In her effort to shuffle quickly enough to answer, Lolo tipped off-balance, but this time, she clutched onto Cord's wrist with an almost iron grip when he caught her. Steady once again, she reached up and patted his cheek. "Thank you, dear. Now, could you be a darling and hand that to me? And let's just keep this between us. No need to unnecessarily worry my Matty."

Cord shot Alyssa a look that said he wasn't convinced yet he should release Lolo – or keep it from Matty – and so she grabbed the phone and placed it in Lois's outstretched hand, waiting while the elderly woman fumbled to depress the talk button.

With a fierce look of determination, Lolo finally managed to press the correct button to answer the call.

Apparently, she'd also managed to hit the speaker because a deep, male voice suddenly boomed into the room. "Grandmama, what's going on? Who's there? Are you okay?" Concern leaked through the barrage of questions.

After a quick introduction and explanation, Matty, suspicion still lining the edge of his voice requested that Lolo flip on her video chat so he could check their credentials himself. After a bit of fumbling, Lolo allowed Cord to assist her. Then, finally reassured they weren't nefarious criminals out to take advantage of his grandmother, Matty thanked them and explained his timely call.

"I'd apologize, but you know yourselves how shady this world has gotten. Anyway, my app notifies me of all Grandmama's visitors. If I don't recognize someone, I call. If she doesn't answer, I have one of the neighbors check on her. Grandmama calls it unnecessary, but I call it an extra layer of security for those times I'm traveling or just can't get there right away."

Still on video chat, Alyssa smiled at Matty's thoughtfulness while Cord said, "No apologies necessary. I think it's great and nothing less than what I would do."

"All right. Now that we've got that squared away, let's see if I can get you that look into what's on those cameras. Do you see that rolltop desk against the wall? Inside the bottom right drawer is a laptop and power cord. If you'll just pull that out, I can get you in."

Within minutes, after somehow, someway that Alyssa vowed was a form of black magic, Matty had remotely unlocked and opened the app that gave them access to the cameras.

While they searched, his only request was that he remain on the call — in case they had questions, he said. Which probably held a good deal of truth, Alyssa knew; but she highly suspected it had more to do with concern for his grandmother, especially after learning a murder had taken place practically in their backyard.

—

The cameras only kept recordings for four days before disappearing, and so that's where they began. Cord clicked on Saturday and fast-forwarded through until they finally spotted a woman they recognized as Taylor Gray with her red hair loosely wound into a messy ponytail – a ponytail that had escaped in the fight for her life.

After noting the timestamp as Monday at six forty-six, Alyssa and Cord settled in and watched. Aside from a bottle of water, all Taylor carried was an armband with her phone attached. Though she smiled or nodded at people she passed, her apparent singular focus was to reach the wooded area that would soon become the site of her murder.

For what seemed an eternity, nothing happened. Couples and families moved through and around the same place Taylor had entered the trees. Little by little, as daylight began to fade, the crowds began to disperse and fizzle until very few stragglers remained, at least on camera. Aside from the regular flow of traffic in the area, even the cars disappeared from the parking lot, as well as those parked on or near the berm.

Alyssa, her eyes crossing and on the verge of conceding they would find nothing useful, suddenly spotted the shadow of an individual disappearing into the woods. There was something about him… The hair at the nape of her neck rose.

Her hand flew forward. "Pause, pause!"

At the exact same moment, Cord blurted out, "Did you see that?" He stopped the video and zoomed in, resulting in nothing but the image transforming into a blurry blob of black and gray pixelated dots. He rewound ten seconds and hit play again.

A subtle undercurrent of electricity worked its way up Alyssa's spine. There, under the cover of dusk slowly creeping into night, a tall figure, face obscured by distance, the shade of the surrounding landscape, and by what appeared to be a hooded, multi-colored windbreaker with some type of winged bird on the sleeve, slipped through the cover of trees and bushes and then simply vanished. He was so far into the shadows that if the light hadn't been just so, they likely never would have spotted him to begin with. The timestamp showed seven eighteen. After rewinding and replaying the video half a dozen times without a reappearance, they forwarded through to the current time.

While Cord thanked Matty Cutter and requested he forward Hal a copy of the security camera footage, Alyssa wondered if they'd just gotten their first glimpse of their perpetrator.

A few minutes later, after obtaining Lois and Matty's contact information, Alyssa and Cord made their way back to the crime scene, where they found Ryker now immersed in a deep discussion with Dr. Sharp. The second she spotted them, Ryker offered some parting words to Lynn and then hurried over, meeting them halfway.

"Anything?"

Before they could answer, Joe and Tony joined the huddle.

Between the two of them, Alyssa and Cord managed to fill the three of them in. When they finished, Alyssa felt compelled to play devil's advocate, even though something niggled at the edge of her mind, and she knew that even as the words slipped past her lips that she didn't believe them herself. "We could be getting excited for nothing. This individual could simply be someone out for an evening stroll just like everyone else."

Ryker snorted, calling her out. "You don't believe that any more than I do. Besides, who in their right mind goes out for a stroll wearing a windbreaker at the end of August when the temps are competing with the inner circle of hell?"

Cord crossed his arms and shrugged. "To help protect against bug bites? Or hell, as a man married to a woman who can somehow manage to be freezing in ninety-degree weather – or having a heat stroke in fifty-degree temps – it could be something as simple as this person being easily chilled."

Even though Cord's remark was meant to back up her devil's advocate comments, Alyssa's eyes rolled so far back that it felt like she was trying to get a glimpse of her own brain. "While I won't disagree with the fact that your wife gets cold far more easily than anyone I've ever known, you know as well as I do that her heat stroke days primarily stemmed from her being pregnant, with twins no less."

"Yeah, well, she about froze my—Never mind. We're getting off track here."

Alyssa agreed. "Regardless, we need to find out who this individual is. He – and I'm going with male simply based on stature – may be completely innocent but may also have seen or heard something without even realizing it."

Cord rubbed the back of his neck as he rotated at a slow three-sixty before turning back to Alyssa and the others. "Something in the way that guy moved through the trees – I can't quite put my finger on it, but there was something more deliberate or purposeful than someone out for a casual stroll."

Ryker, her voice vibrating with a quiet excitement, said what Alyssa had thought earlier and what she suspected they were all thinking now. "I think you got your first glimpse of the guy I've been hunting for the last five years. I'm curious if his stature matches that of Marcus Davis."

Chapter Thirteen

By the time they'd finished with the crime scene at Tingley Beach and made it back to the precinct, the clock read four thirty.

Tony, leading the way through the maze of desks, glanced up at the wall clock as he passed beneath it. "Looks like we missed lunch. Again." At the open door to the incident room, he slammed on his brakes without warning, causing Joe to shove him forward when he raised his hands to stop from crashing into him.

"What the hell, man?"

Tony whirled around and stepped right back out, his head on a swivel until he spotted Hal. "Who the hell turned our room into a damn oven? Someone could bake brownies in there."

Hal, an ice pack on his neck and a damp towel draped over one arm, answered Tony's question, the unusual growl in his voice evidence of his own irritation. "AC's on the fritz again. Or didn't you notice when you walked inside the building that it's hotter than Hades and the Earth's core combined? Hell, it damn near melted the whiteboard in the conference room, not to mention my eyeballs. Was afraid my laptop would literally catch fire if I kept using it. But maintenance swears it'll be fixed any minute now. Tempers are starting to fray, so I sure as hell hope they're right."

Even as he said it, the rumbling sound of the air straining to make its way through the vents reached their ears, and within minutes, the feeling of suffocation began to ease, making it more bearable as the team entered the room and got back down to business.

Hal opened his laptop and cast Taylor Gray's Instagram account onto the wall for them all to see. "Taylor Gray. While she's got a Facebook page, she hasn't posted any content on it in over a year. However, she posts pretty regularly on Insta and TikTok. Mostly, those things tend to lean primarily toward physical fitness slash health training videos. Combined, Gray has just over six hundred thousand followers.

"I scrolled through some of her content, and from what I can gather, people either love her non-judgmental approach to fitness while others like to point out her hypocrisy." He looked up. "It seems that from some of the comments, back when she was in high school – which was what, eight, nine years ago? – our victim was more likely to be, and I quote, 'judgy and hateful' end quote."

Hal ran his mouse over one of Taylor's more recent videos. In the background, the musical rendition of "Don't Stop Believin'" played during a rapid succession of stock photos containing individuals of varying ages and sizes as they exercised. He opened the comments and scrolled until he found what he was looking for. "Here, this user says, 'I love how you meet people where they are so they can meet you the rest of the way.' But then another user says, 'All u ppl going on like TG is all that. U wouldn't think so if u'd known her a few years ago. She was hateful then! Hypocrite!'

"Interestingly enough," Hal continued, "is that, so far, I've found zero indications that Gray engages with any of the haters. She doesn't apologize for her alleged past behaviors or acknowledge them in any way.

"But there's still an awful lot of content to dig through. That being said, I did come across one particularly nasty comment posted seven months ago on Gray's video titled, 'How-To For Beginners.' A person who identified herself by the name @allhate went on a rant in the comments, accusing Gray of body shaming and reporting the videos for being harmful and dangerous. A few followers told the poster if she didn't like the videos to just scroll on past, to which @allhate casually suggested they all perform impossible sexual acts upon their own person and then go die."

"Sounds like a lovely person," Tony muttered.

"And Gray didn't respond to any of the comments?" Alyssa asked.

"Not even the ones who jumped to her defense."

"So, why leave the comments visible? Why not delete them? Or hell, delete the entire post?"

Hal cocked one eyebrow. "Hate to say it, but in the world of social media, lots of people thrive on the negative attention because it drives engagement. The more engagement, the better it is for the algorithm, and the more attention they get. In other words, any attention is good attention for some influencers."

Alyssa scanned through the comments herself, and even though she didn't think this was the link that would break the case open, she knew they still needed to explore that thread, just in case. "It's probably a long shot, but let's look into @allhate and see what we can find out."

Hal shook his head. "Already done. @allhate was the handle behind one Annabelle Rogers, divorced and with three estranged children, which doesn't really matter as she is now deceased at the age of forty-seven. After a long bout of an unknown and undiagnosed illness by a host of doctors and specialists, she OD'd on prescription antidepressants and half a bottle of cheap tequila. Apparently, whatever this illness was, it left her bedridden and reliant on whatever help she could get from those people she hadn't already alienated."

"Holy Jesus," Joe breathed out. "No wonder her online presence was so miserable. Sounds like her life had gone to shit."

Ryker, silent up until then, stared at Hal, a baffled look of wonderment on her face. "How'd you manage to find all that out in just a few hours?"

"Well, while I'd like to claim it was my master skills, the truth of the matter is that Annabelle's ex, Jeremiah Rogers, had a lot to spill online after his ex-wife's death. Instead of diarrhea of the mouth, it was diarrhea of the fingers. See for yourselves." Hal clicked over to another open tab where he'd pasted multiple screenshots into a word document. In them, an ugly narrative of a contentious marriage and divorce was on full display for anyone on social media who cared – or didn't care – to see.

Cord scanned the comments, wagging his head the entire time. "Call me behind the times, but I just don't get the need to air everything about your life – or someone else's – for the whole damn world. Whatever happened to privacy?"

Tony lifted his hand for a fist bump. "Preach, brother, but thank God people do post that crap because it sure as hell tends to come in handy for us."

Alyssa redirected the conversation. "Let's get back to discussing Taylor Gray. What about family?"

Hal clicked on Gray's "About" section on social media. "Jacks—"

Almost as if he'd just been waiting for his cue to enter, Captain Hammond threw the door open, waving a yellow piece of paper. "Dispatch just received a missing person call from the Tingley Beach victim's brother, Jackson Gray. Apparently, when the victim failed to meet him for brunch this morning, he tried texting and calling her. When he continued getting no response, he assumed she was busy and forgot, since she's done that before. But when he still hadn't heard from her by late this afternoon, he got worried and drove over to her apartment where he noted her car wasn't in its assigned parking space. He let himself into her place using a key she'd given him and noticed his sister's dog was still in its kennel with a dry water bowl, and he knew then something had to be wrong."

Alyssa snatched the paper from Hammond's outstretched hand and pulled her keys from her pocket. Cord and Ryker went out ahead of her, and she turned back to Hal. "See what else you can dig up on Gray's social life, financials, and even though it's still early, see if you can gather any information from her cell phone, where she might've gone, et cetera. Cross reference all of it with the Killingbeck case first, and then we'll branch out later to include the other victims. But for now, since both victims reside in Albuquerque, let's start there."

She looked to Tony and Joe. "Why don't you fill Hal in on what we learned at Tingley Beach? That way, if there's something there, the three of you can maybe get a jump start on that. We can debrief after we get back."

A few minutes later, Alyssa, Cord, and Ryker battled their way through the clog of congested, slow-moving traffic so they could break the tragic news of his sister's murder to Taylor Gray's brother.

Chapter Fourteen

Tuesday, August 29

Hands trembling, Brooklyn's fingers curled into the single piece of paper she'd discovered next to her on the flattened mattress when she woke. Tears she'd thought herself no longer capable of streamed down her cheeks as she stared at the bold headline highlighted in bright orange, words she'd already read a hundred times.

Beloved Teacher Slain; Body Never Found. Entire Town Still Demands Answers

> *On April 29, 2017, beloved teacher Brooklyn Knox of Slaughterville, Oklahoma, went missing from her home. Tomorrow, August 30, on what would be Knox's forty-third birthday, her older sister, Queenie Knox-Bolton is once again pleading for the public's help, claiming that while she wants justice for whatever happened to her sister, more than anything, she just wants to bring Brooklyn home, to give her the proper burial she deserves.*

Brooklyn tipped her head back and screamed out her rage, her powerless ability to save herself. She continued screaming even as pain rippled along her damaged throat, screamed until her voice went hoarse.

How could Queenie, of all people, not know deep in her gut that she was still alive? How could her own sister give up like that? The reality of it felt like the deepest betrayal. If it had been Queenie missing, Brooklyn would've walked to the ends of the earth and back again, searching. So, what was she supposed to do now?

After all, it was only the knowledge that Queenie was out there looking for her that helped force Brooklyn to keep going, to *not* give up. Even now, if she closed her eyes, she could picture her rescue, could picture Queenie sweeping in, her strong arms and stronger resolve engulfing Brooklyn in her tight embrace, swearing she'd never once given up, swearing she'd always known they'd find her one day, and apologizing that it had taken so long.

Now, with the mocking words of the article he'd left for her while she slept, that fantasy was shattered, ripped away as violently as a tornado tearing through a paper village. If her own sister believed her dead, what purpose did she really have for holding on, especially when it would be so much easier just to give up, to end this insufferable hell.

Brooklyn's blurry eyes dropped to the handwritten note scrawled at the bottom of the page.

> *Even your own sister has given up on you. One day, you'll see and accept that I'm all you have left, that I'll always love you more than anyone else ever will. And I'll be the only one who sees through the scars to your real beauty.*
>
> *Happy birthday a day early. I might not get back in time, so I've left you a little surprise. I know it's always been your favorite.*

The "little surprise" was a chocolate cupcake with lemon yellow frosting and a red heart that he'd placed on the sink. Poked into the center was the nubbin of a used birthday candle. As her gaze shifted toward the sweet treat she used to love, the urge to hurl it at the hidden camera swept through her.

Unable to stop herself, Brooklyn lifted her fingers to her own face and traced the puckered skin, then peered down at the scarred map of her chest and stomach. In her years of captivity, she'd never once seen her own reflection, not even in the scuffed metal of the toilet, but her fingers and mind provided enough of a mental picture for her anyway. That, coupled with his constant reminder that only he could see beyond her imperfections to who she "really was" told her what she really didn't want to know anyway.

A pressure inside her chest felt like someone squeezing a fist around her heart as a voice shouted inside her head: *What does it really matter now? Your own sister has given up, you have no way of escaping, so all that's left is to remain at this monster's mercy.*

The Brooklyn of years ago would've told that voice to shut up. But the Brooklyn she was now simply wondered how long it would be before she completely lost her sanity or the will to survive at all.

Chapter Fifteen

Tuesday, August 29

Not often was Alyssa completely struck by a person's attractiveness, which was saying something, considering the multiple times a day women and men alike risked whiplash snapping their necks around to get a second and sometimes third look at Cord. But she had to admit, Jackson Gray gave her partner a solid run for his money. Unlike his sister, Jackson's hair hinted at a shade that ventured more into a deep chestnut than sunset red. But it was the unusual violet hue of his eyes that struck Alyssa and made it difficult not to gawk. The man could hypnotize people with those irises.

Even bloodshot and puffy, they held her almost mesmerized as the four of them stood on the private porch outside his sister's apartment. Having just sent Alyssa screenshots of his call log and last text message from Taylor date-stamped Monday evening at six thirty-three, two fingers stroked over the final words he'd ever get from his sister.

Heading out to my secret spot in the woods. Feeling inspired to write. See you in the a.m. xoxoxoxo.

Three hug emojis and three hearts followed.

Cord shot her a sideways glance, and Alyssa knew they were thinking the same thing – no notebook or tablet had been found at the crime scene. "Your sister was a writer?" he asked Jackson.

A faint smile did its best to tug Jackson's lips upward, but it fell flat. Raw grief simply overwhelmed the effort. "Poetry. Songs. Nothing she ever planned to publish. And always on the notes app of her phone because she never went anywhere without it, like ever, but also because she tended to be a bit neurotic about the possibility of someone going through her things and reading her work. She never even let me see what she wrote. Her songs and poems were her version of a diary, I guess, so I never pried. For her, it was never about sharing her words; it was always a cathartic exercise for her." His voice grew quieter, and he looked away. "It seemed to help her during those times she'd sometimes fall into a depression."

"Depression over what?" Alyssa asked.

Jackson dabbed a tissue at the corners of his eyes as he stared off into the distance. "Tay was real big into fitness, and she's got over half a million followers on social media." He sucked in a deep breath, glanced down at the ground, and then stared at a spot between Alyssa and Cord. "She's – she was – really good at her job. Really supportive in her videos. But she wasn't always like that. Back when she was a teenager, she could be really cruel about, well, about things." Jackson shook his head. "But she changed. Really changed, not just something she did for show. And some people who knew her back then just didn't want to believe it. As one woman put it, Taylor could change the way she talked, but her true nature would always remain the same." His eyes spit fire when his gaze lifted to meet

Alyssa's, as if challenging her to contradict him. "It wasn't just for show. It really bothered her how hateful she was back then."

Though it wasn't uncommon for age and maturity to change a person from who they were in their teens, Alyssa still needed to ask. "What made her change?"

"She started attending conferences and hearing from the kinds of people she mocked, and it really made her feel like crap. And then not too long ago, she found out some woman who hated on her fitness videos had died. Suicide, from what she could gather, I think. Tay thought she should've done more to reach out to the woman when she read the comments that were being posted. She called me crying one night, convinced the woman's death was her fault, that it was the universe's way of paying her back for 'being such a cruel bitch' back in high school." Both hands scrubbed down the unfiltered anguish on his face before he wrapped his arms around his waist. "I can't believe she's gone, that—"

The squeal of tires braking hard distracted him from the raw emotions erupting from inside him.

A car door slammed followed by thundering footsteps, and Alyssa, along with Cord and Ryker, turned in time to see a tall, lean, and incredibly fit man, probably in his mid to late twenties, racing in their direction, his frantic words carrying in the slight breeze. "Jackson! Oh my God. I got here as fast as I could."

For a second, Alyssa thought the man might bypass the open gate and hop the wall into the porch area. His presence, while not massive, made the tight space feel almost oppressive. Alyssa watched as a myriad of emotions traveled across Jackson Gray's face, as if unwilling or unable to settle on just one.

Treating Alyssa, Cord, and Ryker as if they were invisible to everyone but Jackson, the newcomer pushed past them and grabbed Taylor's brother into what seemed to Alyssa like a suffocating bear hug before pulling back and cradling Jackson's face between his palms.

"Have you heard anything? What can I do to help?" One hand dropped so he could reach behind him to pull his phone from his back pocket. "It'll take one phone call, and I can get a search party started. We can—"

Jackson stepped back against the wall, forcing the guy's hands to drop, the sound ripped from his throat born of crushing torment as he barely choked out what he'd only just learned. "She's dead, Leach. They found her body—"

Leach stumbled backward, nearly bumping into Cord. He didn't even turn. "Dead? What? Where did they find—" With each clipped question, his voice rose an octave.

"Mr.—" Ryker paused as she waited for the man to turn in her direction and introduce himself.

He did so almost reluctantly, as if just realizing he and Jackson weren't the only two on the porch. His head swiveled back and forth several times before his hand shot out for Ryker to shake. As he stumbled through an introduction, Alyssa noted that, while certainly attractive in an unconventional way, Leach paled in comparison to Jackson Gray. "Reggie – Reginald – Leach. I'm, uh… I'm…"

"Leach is my agent." The expression that crossed Leach's face appeared to be one of disappointment or hurt. And whether Jackson noticed or decided to share anyway, he quietly added, "And my boyfriend. I was going to tell Taylor about it when we met up today." A sad smile flitted across his face, there and gone in a second. "She's been telling me it was time to get back in the game. She… she'd have been so excited for me. Especially when I told her I got a part in that new romance movie filming downtown. It's small, but it's a speaking—"

His words tapered off as his body crumbled in on itself. His shoulders sagged under the weight of his grief, and Alyssa's heart fractured at the sight, already sensing the darkness that would invade all Jackson's hours – waking and restless sleep-filled – for the foreseeable future.

She started to redirect Jackson's attention so they could try to begin to understand his sister's final few hours, but before she could, Reggie Leach shifted in a way that revealed a wickedly red, jagged, and clearly fresh scratch stretching just above the collar of his v-neck t-shirt. From the way Cord and Ryker stiffened on either side of her, she knew they'd spotted it, as well.

Cord nodded toward the mark and asked the question burning for an immediate answer. "Looks nasty. Mind if I ask what happened?"

Alyssa, like Ryker, studied Leach's face as it drained to white before a rush of red returned to stain his cheeks. He stuttered, stopped, started again. "My, uh, my ex unexpectedly showed up at my place. He, uh, didn't much appreciate hearing I'd moved on." Leach hung his head and scuffed one shoe against the ground. "He may have gotten a little rough."

Though Jackson seemed nearly immune to hearing this news, Leach turned to him to explain anyway. "It wasn't as bad as it sounds, J. I would've told you if this" – he waved his arms toward the patio door behind Jackson – "hadn't happened to you."

Nodding absently, Jackson's eyes drifted away toward the parking lot. His voice dull, he asked almost absently,

"What about Taylor's car? Yellow Camaro. I don't know the year."

With his attention divided evenly between Jackson and Reginald Leach, Cord answered. "We found it in the parking lot with her insurance and registration inside and had it towed to the yard. We'll need to check it for forensic evidence that might help us track down whoever did this to your sister."

Something in the way Jackson's eyes suddenly widened and shifted from the parking lot to Leach had Alyssa, Ryker, and Cord shooting each other questioning looks. Like Ryker's, Alyssa's hand shifted slightly, just enough that it hovered near her Taser.

"How'd you know where to find me?" Jackson asked. While his words still had to fight their way through the grief, his voice now held a definite note of suspicion, which, in turn, put Alyssa on edge.

Leach's forehead furrowed when his eyebrows shot for his hairline. "You sent a text and told me you were here."

The violet in Jackson's eyes darkened as he drilled a hard, unblinking stare at his boyfriend. "Yeah, but how did you know where *here* was?"

"You told me." Leach swiped his thumb across the phone still gripped in his hand and opened the text messages, turning the screen so Jackson could see it. "You told me over dinner that your sister lived in the Sandia Vista luxury apartments. When you told me you'd gone to her apartment and reported her missing, I came right away. When I got here, I spotted your car and then saw you. What's going on? Why are you acting like I—" His words trailed off as he realized exactly what Jackson had been asking.

Jackson's shoulders slumped.

Alyssa moved her hand to rest on her service weapon. "Mr. Leach, can you tell us where you were yesterday evening between the hours of six thirty and nine?"

Reggie Leach stiffened slightly and turned. His lips thinned out, and his eyes narrowed. "Home. Six thirty, I was waking from a nap. No, no one was with me, and no, I doubt anyone can corroborate that story. But you can always try."

Alyssa noted the way Leach's demeanor shifted from supportive boyfriend to instant attitude. For now, she let it go. With or without his permission, she had every intention of *trying*. She turned her focus back to Taylor's brother. "Mr. Gray, since you have a key, do you mind letting us take a look around inside your sister's apartment?"

The effort it took for Jackson to meet her gaze sent another crushing ache through Alyssa's heart.

"Barkley — Taylor's dog — I let him out of his crate when I came to check on her. He won't bite, but I could put him back, if it'd make you all more comfortable."

An image of Isaac with his dog, Ghost, flashed in Alyssa's mind, the way he'd clung to the comfort and protection of Ghost's neck during those long months when he'd wake from the terror of his own nightmare years earlier. She offered a soft smile. "Why don't you just hold onto Barkley for us while we check things out?"

Jackson nodded weakly, sucked in a deep breath, opened the porch gate, and unlocked the front door. As he pushed it open, Leach blocked Alyssa's path.

"What is it exactly that you're looking for?"

To Alyssa, the question seemed odd and out of place for someone so new to this relationship. "We don't know yet. Is there something you're afraid we'll find?" Then she stepped around him and into the apartment.

–

Almost two hours later, Ryker, Cord, and Alyssa were finally back in the Tahoe. At some point during their search of Taylor's apartment, where they'd found nothing that would help in their investigation, Leach had muttered something about an important appointment and left. He'd returned, however, just as the three of them had finished up and were speaking to Jackson. Leach had stood by Jackson's side, his arms crossed, a scowl on his face.

In the SUV, Ryker, her eyes still glued to Leach, blurted out what they'd all been thinking. "I wonder if he really had an appointment. More importantly, I'd just like to point out that he didn't ask what happened."

From the backseat, Cord said, "I noticed that, too. He asked where the body had been found but never what happened."

Alyssa cast one more glance toward where Jackson and Leach stood talking in the parking lot near Jackson's vehicle. "There's something off about him, that's for sure."

"Or just off-putting," Cord countered.

Alyssa shrugged. "Either way, let's get ahold of Hal and see what he can dig up on the guy."

"Let's also see if Hal can find out how long Leach has been in Albuquerque," Ryker added.

Cord held his phone up like he'd won a trophy. "I sent a text to Hal the second I heard Jackson ask Leach how he knew where to find him."

In the rearview, Alyssa grinned. "Look at you being on the ball and everything." Cord returned her grin, and her smile slipped away. Though it was true there was something about Reginald Leach that didn't sit right with her, she had a feeling their case wouldn't be wrapped up that easily.

Chapter Sixteen

Alyssa, Cord, and Ryker returned to the precinct just in time to hear Joe apologizing to Tony and Hal.

"Sorry, man. I'm really not trying to be a cocky SOB. I'm just tired, hungry, and frankly pissed because it feels like someone started advertising New Mexico as the land of opportunity for serial psychos."

Alyssa shot Cord a look and then stepped inside the incident room. "Someone mention hunger?"

Behind her, Cord and Ryker each balanced drinks and takeout bags from Golden Pride. Immediately, the entire room filled with the mouthwatering aroma of hot food and red and green chile.

Ryker set her bags down on the table beside Cord's and smiled. "Sustenance, New Mexico style. We would've been here sooner with it, but it took longer than usual because, apparently, the film crew couldn't stop raving about Golden Pride, and so the restaurant is currently supplying all the food while the movie's filming in this area."

On cue, stomachs loudly and enthusiastically asserted their appreciation. Like he was afraid it might disappear if he didn't act fast, Tony pounced on a Styrofoam container, announced its *carne adovada* contents, and shoved it toward

Joe before grabbing another and nudging it toward Cord. Within seconds, everyone had their respective favorites and was digging in.

If she hadn't been half-starved herself, Alyssa might've taken a moment to be embarrassed at how the team attacked the food with loud grunts of approval and slurping noises. But considering she hadn't had anything except coffee since the half-eaten blueberry muffin earlier this morning, she couldn't really blame them. And they still had a long night ahead of them.

Around a mouthful of green chile-smothered burrito, Tony managed a thank you. Nodding with enthusiasm, Joe pointed his finger at Tony and spoke around his own mouthful of food. "What he said."

Hal followed up with a "ditto that."

Alyssa nodded toward Ryker. "Don't thank me. It was just my idea to stop. It was Ryker who insisted on footing the bill."

Ryker waved off another round of thanks. "You're welcome. This is just my small way of expressing appreciation for each of you being all in. You have no idea how refreshing it is not to get into a territorial pissing match." She grinned at Alyssa. "I believe those were your words anyway. And now that we have a little fuel inside us, maybe we can start thinking more clearly."

Before it could dribble onto the financial statements he'd been searching through, Tony swiped a napkin across his chin to catch the melted cheese dripping from his fork. "Can't speak for everyone, but you certainly know your way to getting this guy's full cooperation. No pissing matches, territorial or otherwise, coming from my direction."

Ryker's laughter was a full-throated burst of true amusement. Alyssa watched pink crawl up Tony's neck to stain his cheeks, even while he joined in the laughter.

For the next several minutes, they continued to shovel food like they were on a mission to finish it all in an allotted amount of time. When they finally slowed enough to take a breath and sigh in that universal way that proclaimed, "I'm fed and full," Hal wiped his mouth and pulled his laptop over. "Right after you left to interview Jackson Gray, I did a little more digging on Marcus Davis.

"On Thursday, August twenty-third, Davis was in Colorado Springs to meet up with a potential client. He flew into Colorado Springs where he rented a midnight blue Nissan Maxima from Enterprise for an unspecified period of time. I called Enterprise, but they couldn't, or more to the point, wouldn't, give me any other details due to privacy laws and all that. No surprise there."

Hal pushed his wheelchair back from the table and rolled over to a map on the wall where he'd already placed several colored pushpins indicating locations of all the victims known to date, as well as Jennie Killingbeck's travel route. He tapped one of the pins and drew his finger down. "That's only a two-and-a-half-hour drive to Alamosa where Killingbeck was visiting Allie Ramirez."

He returned to the table and dragged his laptop over to him. "What with Davis being your prime suspect, learning he was in the general vicinity, which could make it possible for him to have committed the Killingbeck murder, and then having Gray's death coming so soon on the heels of Jennie's, I thought I'd see if Killingbeck and Gray were connected somehow on social media. Figured it was a long shot, but it's a box that needed to be checked either way. Unfortunately, but not surprisingly, neither victim followed the other, nor have I found any mutual followers. In other words, for all intents and purposes, there seems to be no crossover."

Ryker offered a sarcastic grin. "You mean to tell me that you didn't discover Davis followed both of them?"

"Afraid not. But wouldn't that have been nice? Anyway, I scrolled through both their accounts searching for any similar interests or places they both may have frequented, et cetera. I hit another wall because the two women appear to be polar opposites. Taylor kept her posts about her profession while Jennie's were more of a personal, outgoing nature. For example, I can tell you she enjoyed watching thrillers and that swoon-worthy romances made her want to take long walks on a beach at sunset."

Joe snorted. "If beach walks were her jam, she was living in the wrong state."

"Yeah, well, if she'd been living in another state, maybe she'd still be alive," Tony tossed back.

The weight of that truth settled heavily in the room.

Alyssa turned back to Hal. "What about Reginald Leach? Were you able to uncover anything about him?"

The corners of Hal's mouth tipped down into a frown. "I've got a call in to see if we've got enough to ask for a ping warrant on his phone. But I've gotta be honest; I don't think we do. No judge I know of is going to consider a slew of wonky coincidences a legal leg to stand on. That being said, I did some digging and managed to uncover a few interesting things. First, according to an old Facebook account he no longer uses, it appears Leach moved here in 2018 from Wichita, Kansas."

Ryker's spine snapped straight. "Go on."

"Well, if that excites you, wait until you hear this. Since Kansas is smack dab between the two states with the first three murder victims, I ran a navigation search to determine the distance between Tulsa, Oklahoma, where the Ortega and Morrow murders took place, and then between Wichita and Omaha, where Lauren Grand lived."

Ryker's fingers tried to gouge a hole in the tabletop as she waited while Hal paused to find his notes. When he finally found what he was looking for, he added a disclaimer. "Keep in mind, this could mean nothing, or—"

Ryker cut him off. "Or it could mean everything. So, why don't you just tell us so we can all discuss it."

"Okay, here's what I found; Tulsa is less than one hundred eighty miles from Wichita, which driving, would take about two and a half to three hours, depending on whether or not a person lollygagged. Easy enough to do as a long day trip. Wichita to Omaha is a bit of a longer stretch at just over three hundred miles, making it probably between four to six hours' drive time."

All the air rushed out of Ryker's lungs.

Hal shot Alyssa a look, and she nodded for him to continue. "As coincidences go, I could maybe write off the distance bit. Thing is, when we've got two and three 'coincidences' in a row, it's not so easy to do. But this is also the part where things get a little murkier and a lot more complicated, so bear with me.

"I ran a public records search and found that Leach's father had a criminal record. I reached out to the Kansas Department of Corrections who filled in a few blanks and gave me the name and number of Baxter Leach's public defender.

"In as small a nutshell as I can make it, looks like Reginald Leach was around the age of fourteen when his mother took off, his father fell on some financial hard times, and he moved himself and Reggie to Wichita so his parents could help him out. In 2013, Baxter knocked off a few liquor stores by gunpoint and then took his shot at a bank. He survived a GSW in the aftermath of the holdup and was later convicted for armed robbery. He was beaten to death in his cell a year later, but by that time, the courts had already granted Leach's grandparents full custody."

Hal looked up from his notes. "Before you ask, I'm still trying to get a bead on where the mom is, but from what intel I've unearthed so far, Leach has had no contact with his mother since she left the family. As for Leach's grandparents, his grandmother died in 2015, and his grandfather passed in 2017. Leach sold the family farm, and from what I can tell, moved here shortly after."

Alyssa's pulse quickened. "Okay, that gives us something to follow up on. It might be tenuous, but it's better than what we had." She nodded toward Hal's scattered notes. "What else can you tell us?"

"Between 2017 after the sale of his grandparents' property and 2020, I can't find any online record of Leach's existence. As in, no social media accounts, no credit cards issued in his name, not even tax records. Pretty strange for someone who's an agent to the stars.

"But bringing this back around to Taylor Gray, Reginald — Reggie — Leach, according to his current social media, is a fanatic fitness junkie. Vegan, has his own weight room at home, works out twice a day. So far, I've found nothing else that links them together, including followers. He doesn't have many, so it wasn't difficult to cross-reference his with Gray's. Still, it's something."

Ryker, who'd begun pacing, stopped and looked over at Alyssa and Cord. "*Gym rat* isn't the first word that pops into my mind when I think of Leach. I mean, he wasn't exactly Ichabod Crane thin, but certainly more that vibe than say Chris Hemsworth. Definitely fit and strong enough to be able to overtake any of our victims, though."

Alyssa pulled up a mental image of Reginald Leach, specifically the scratch on his neck. She turned back to Hal. "I don't suppose Leach's socials say when or how he met Jackson Gray?"

Hal shook his head. "Not that I've found. But that's the other thing. And sticking with the theme that this could mean nothing at all, but putting it out there just the same, if Leach is in a relationship with Jackson Gray, it's the only one I've seen since 2020 where he's not linked with a female. And with the exception of one woman in 2021 who had the lightest shade of what I'd describe as strawberry blonde, all the gals Leach was romantically linked to had every shade of hair color *except* red. Not sure if that means anything or not."

"Are the women tagged?" Ryker asked.

"If they were, they're not anymore," Hal said.

Alyssa's head swirled with this new information. "You're right, though. That's just too many coincidences linked together for us to brush off. Let's see if we can find any other connections that might give us more of a leg to stand on." She waved to Joe. "Tell us about the couple who discovered Gray's body."

"Brett and Casey Oxley live in the Huning Castle Apartments right there by Tingley Beach. According to them, they both work the swing shift at The Downs Casino and so they like to walk their dogs early." He checked his notes. "This morning, that would've been around seven. They said they often go through the wooded area, just because it's quieter with less traffic. They didn't notice anyone or anything suspicious, and they didn't see any vehicles in the area that they didn't recognize from their usual daily walks.

"Mrs. Oxley said everything was pretty routine until both the dogs randomly and simultaneously started yanking her and her husband toward a path they don't normally use. At first, she thought they'd spotted a squirrel or something, but when she saw the raised hairs at the back of their necks, like they'd sensed an imminent threat neither she nor her husband had yet noticed, she grew alarmed.

"She tried to warn her husband not to investigate, but he didn't listen. She said the second he slipped out of sight into the place Taylor was found, both dogs went absolutely nuts, barking and growling and straining to break loose from their leashes. Casey Oxley said she got a real creepy vibe, and she yelled over the dogs and told Brett that they needed to leave, but Brett had already spotted Gray's body."

Cord, who'd just finished gathering up the remnants of everyone's dinner and tossing it in the trash, doused his hands with hand sanitizer before flipping open his notebook from their interview with Jackson Gray. "We know the last text Gray received from his sister came around six thirty last night. The Oxleys found Taylor shortly after seven this morning, but she'd clearly been deceased a few hours already. Which means we have, at an estimate, maybe a ten-hour window when her murder took place."

"That's a big window of time," Ryker said, "even if it doesn't seem like it. And I'm going to narrow it down a little more based on what was seen on Lois Cutter's security cameras. If Taylor was spotted entering the woods at quarter to seven, approximately fifteen minutes after she last texted her brother, and then wasn't seen leaving again, I think the likelihood is high that she was killed before it even got dark. We'll need to see what we can find on her phone, but if Jackson Gray was right, and she was typing up poems or whatnot, would she have stayed until nightfall? Maybe, but doesn't seem likely. Or wise. But that's a different debate, I suppose." She paused, brows furrowed in thought. "Something just occurred to me. Doesn't it seem kind of odd to be heading into the woods to write at that time of evening?"

Tony shook his head. "Not here in the Southwest. During the summer months, it's not at all unusual for folks to go picnicking or hiking or whatnot in the evening. The heat's just too damn much sometimes in the daytime."

"That makes sense. Still, if we can find a way to get into Taylor's phone, maybe we can find a timestamp on whatever she was working on, which will help us establish a firmer timeline. Plus, every bone in my body is screaming that the individual wearing the windbreaker who was spotted on Lois Cutter's camera is our killer. Once her grandson gets us that copy, hopefully sooner rather than later, we'll be able to go through it frame by frame and see what might've been missed during the initial look. If it turns out we're right, and this is Davis – or someone else who's the killer – Cutter's footage will just be one more weapon we have to secure a conviction once we arrest him." Ryker turned to Hal. "Despite my intuition, we still need to be thorough. If I ask if you already ran a background check on the Oxleys, are you going to be insulted or just laugh?"

Hal grinned. "Neither. But yes, I did already run it. Aside from a penchant for speeding on Brett Oxley's part and an unpaid parking ticket on Casey's, they're clean from what I can tell. They're just two unlucky people who stumbled into a crime scene."

"Yeah, and if either of their faces was anything to go by," Joe said, "they're not the kind of folks who can stomach committing a violent crime, so definitely not suspects. I think we're good to clear them."

While Joe spoke, Cord flipped through one of Ryker's binders. "I wonder if we take what we learned about Leach and apply it to what the Bureau already has on these other cases, if we'll find the answer we're searching for."

Ryker checked her watch and then pulled out the rest of her files. "It can't hurt for a team of fresh eyes to take a stab at it. And as the saying goes, there's no time like the present."

For the next several hours, everyone pored over files, evidence, and witness statements, sometimes silently, sometimes blurting out something of interest. When her back started protesting, Alyssa paced as she scoured through pages of Ryker's thoughts and speculations scribbled in the margins.

Like she often did when she was trying to work out the missing link, she repeatedly snapped the hair band around her wrist, a habit she knew she had but was rarely aware she was doing until one of the others cast her the kind of look that told her they'd be happy to shove her hairband someplace the sun didn't shine, kind of like Cord was doing now.

Because she knew it would bug him, she grinned at his exasperated expression but stopped the snapping, much to her skin's relief. That was when she noticed the whiteboard. Ryker had used blue painter's tape to stretch different colored string to make it easier to visualize any connections between the victims and the short list of potential suspects. Two names were underlined and circled in red: Marcus Davis and Reginald Leach.

Alyssa studied the board. What were they missing? Her gut told her the answers they needed were already there, hiding; they just had to find them.

—

Close to midnight, Alyssa sat on her couch, her feet propped in her husband's lap. Ghost, Isaac's dog, and Schutz, the dog she'd adopted after the same case that had helped grow Cord's family, perched with their heads on one of Alyssa's legs while she ruffled their fur. She was still trying to get used to the kind of silence that came with having neither of her children living at home.

With Holly moving out a few years ago and then getting married, Alyssa thought it'd be easier when the time came for Isaac to move into the dorms. She'd been wrong. Still, while she missed having them home, even when they bickered, she and Brock had raised them to be independent and to follow their dreams, and so, more than anything, she was proud.

Brock squeezed her foot. "It's weird how different the quiet is without Holly and Isaac, isn't it?"

Alyssa smiled at her husband, who'd waited up for her since he'd already been asleep last night when she'd finally gotten home and was still asleep when she'd left early this morning. "Speaking of our offspring, Isaac sent me a message yesterday that said he's fine but that he wanted to run something by me. I tried calling him back last night on my way home and then again tonight, but he didn't answer, so now we're playing phone tag. Any idea what's going on?"

"Nope. He hasn't mentioned anything to me. But if he says he's fine, don't let yourself go worrying that something's wrong."

Brock knew her so well. "Are you reading my mind again?"

"What kind of husband would I be if I let my skills get rusty, huh?"

Alyssa winked. "Not as good of one, that's for sure, but I'd probably still keep you around just for the foot massages."

Brock laughed and switched his attention to Alyssa's other foot. She moaned and closed her eyes, immediately losing herself in thoughts of the case until she felt herself starting to drift off.

Brock shook her gently. "As much as I'm enjoying this," he said, "you should probably get to bed. If I know you, and I do, you're going to be up and back at 'em in just a few hours. So, sleep—"

Alyssa's phone chimed, and she shot him an apologetic grimace as she yanked it off the table, saw that it was Ryker, and checked the message.

> Call me when you get this. I just learned some new information.

Alyssa swung her feet to the ground, startling the dogs. She leaned over and kissed Brock. "I'm sorry, honey, but this could be important."

Brock pulled her to her feet and hugged her. "I get it. I'm going to bed, but if you're heading back out tonight, come wake me. Love you."

Alyssa returned the sentiment and watched him walk away, then called Ryker, who answered on the first ring.

"Sorry. I really didn't mean you needed to call tonight. I hope I didn't wake you."

"You didn't. What've you got?"

There was no mistaking the excitement sizzling in Ryker's voice. "After we left tonight, I reached out to one of the Bureau's data analysts. Like Hal, she's a bulldog when it comes to research. I didn't expect her to get back to me so quickly, but she did. And you'll never believe what she found." Ryker paused. "Guess who used to live in Wichita, Kansas, in the early 2000s?"

Alyssa's nerves felt tight enough to snap. She didn't want to guess because it was far too late to play guessing games.

Luckily, she didn't have to because Ryker answered her own question. "Spoiler alert: it wasn't just Reginald Leach. Marcus Davis also lived there." Ryker sucked in a breath before blurting out something else that had just occurred to Alyssa. "What if we've been looking at this all wrong? What if Leach and Davis are working together? It's rare for serial killers to team up..."

Alyssa finished Ryker's sentence for her. "But not unheard of."

Chapter Seventeen

His neck burned like the hottest fires of hell where the nails of the woman in the woods had scraped down his skin.

In a way, though, he welcomed the stinging sensation because it helped shift the focus, if only a tiny bit, from what really had him distracted, which was what had happened to him in the wee hours of the morning when he'd woken from a dead sleep, drenched head to toe in sweat.

Feeling sticky and gross, he climbed from bed and headed straight to the shower, all with his heart hammering hard enough that he was finally forced to sit and lean against the wall as the water sluiced over him. Like he had as a child when the inner voices grew too loud, laughing at him, telling him no one would ever love him, that he was worthless and ugly and should just die, he stuck his fingers in his ear, and when that didn't dull the noise in his brain, he pinched his lobes and pulled down hard, waiting for the pain to distract him.

All that managed to do was make his head pound harder. Deep breathing exercises only amped up his anxiety, probably because he kept forgetting to exhale until the shower enclosure began to spin around him and he remembered there was more to breathing than just inhaling.

He picked his conditioner as a focal point and repeated in a near frenzy: "I have complete control over my own mind and body." But no matter how many times he said it, his mind refused to accept it, and his body just didn't care because his stomach threatened a revolt as it shot acid up his throat.

Long after the water ran cold, forcing him to shut it off, he remained where he was, shivering, the towel he'd draped over his front doing nothing to retain his body heat. He had no idea how long he stayed there before he finally managed to get his heart rate back to a normal-ish rhythm, but enough time had passed that the hair plastered to his forehead had gone from dripping to mildly damp. Still wobbly, he forced himself to his feet, using the towel rack to keep himself steady, and made his way to the foggy mirror. He swiped a hand across it and traced the contours of his reflection, reminding himself that he was no longer the weak person he'd once been. He was so much stronger now, physically and mentally.

Within minutes, the entire incident evaporated as if it had never happened. He dropped the towel and posed in front of his mirror, thinking of Brooklyn as he did. In a roundabout way, he had her to thank for getting into the best shape of his life. He'd always known she deserved better than the pathetic creature he'd been once upon a time.

As a child and into his early teens, he'd been prone to bad acne and overeating, which had led to relentless bullying. Daily, he found himself the butt of contemptuous ridicule and the punchline of every joke at all the parties he'd never once been invited to but had heard all about. After one particularly bad day, he'd headed straight to the local gym where his one and only friend helped clean the equipment and locker rooms in exchange for free workouts. While he waited for his buddy to finish up, he decided to take his anger out on the equipment. That day, he'd discovered the benefits of weightlifting.

But it hadn't just been the physical activity that had inspired him. What happened after he left that first day drove his desire to get into shape. While the self-important blowhard asshole on the television droned on in the background, he sank back in time.

Sweat poured down his out-of-shape frame, and he used the hem of his used thrift store shirt to wipe it out of his eyes. As he tugged the garment back into place, he spotted her in the parking lot, laughing at something a beefed-up slab of muscle said. When the guy leaned in to kiss her, something he couldn't quite put a name to bubbled up inside him. Jealousy? He didn't know. All he knew was that it felt wrong and cheap.

But then, she drew back and caught sight of him. Her eyes widened, and he was sure he wasn't imagining the way her gaze darted from him to the gym and back, lighting with pleasure. She wanted him, but not like he was. He knew in that moment that she belonged to him, but first, he needed to change, not only mentally, but physically. In all the movies, that was how the guy always got the girl, right?

So, that's what he had done. Within a year, no one ever dared to call him names or shove him around. Quite the opposite. After his hard-earned transformation, people flocked to him, desperate to either be him or at least be around him.

Everyone except *her*, anyway. The only one who mattered. As his transformation unfolded, something in her had also shifted, changed. With his surge in popularity, instead of desire for him that should be burning in her eyes, the stares she gave him screamed of abject disappointment and judgment.

He hadn't liked it. Not one bit.

When he'd tried to talk to her about it one day, she'd called his behavior *borderline abhorrent*. She'd called his explanations *nothing but excuses*, told him she'd *expected better from him*, and walked away, leaving him standing awkwardly in the nearly empty parking lot, his face burning with humiliation.

Equal parts devastated and furious, he finally realized what he was doing wrong. She wanted to be wooed and charmed. So, he left her flowers on her car. Mostly red roses, daisies, and lilies – he thought he'd remembered hearing somewhere that those were her favorites.

But then his circumstances had changed, and shortly after, he'd been forced to move away. Apart from yearning to be near her, he hadn't minded getting out of that shithole of a town or away from the assholes who inhabited it.

Years later, when he'd finally been free to return, he'd entertained fantasies of her falling into his arms and begging him to never leave her alone again playing out in his head. It wasn't that he hadn't enjoyed other relationships during his time away. He couldn't help himself when people practically threw themselves at him. But no matter how many liaisons or one-night stands he had, he always knew he'd end up going back for his one true soulmate. When that day finally arrived, he devised the best way to approach her, reviewing and revising until the plan was perfect.

Except it wasn't.

When he'd moved, he'd lost touch with his buddy from the gym, but he figured that wouldn't matter, that his friend would give him a place to crash for a couple of days, at least until he could move in with Brooklyn. It had never occurred to him that his friend might've also moved.

Friday night, with the heart-shaped trinket box he'd carved himself now wrapped up nicely, complete with a red bow and a handwritten note, he made his way to her house and left it on her doorstep before sliding into the trees surrounding her property to wait. He wanted to see her face and savor her reaction when she saw it.

Only the happiness he'd expected was not what he got. Instead, she arrived home that evening with a different beefcake than the one he'd seen her with at the gym years earlier. He watched her climb out of the passenger side of his car and walk up the walkway. Saw the way she smiled when she spotted the gift and said something to the guy, who shook his head. Her smile melted away, and her forehead furrowed in confusion.

When Brooklyn and her date went inside, he'd tiptoed to the door and listened, horrified when he heard her mention "he was nothing to worry about" and then labeled him as "confused." Crushed, he'd fought back tears as he knocked. She'd opened the front door, and the second she'd seen him standing there, she'd ordered Beefcake to stay put and closed the door before Beefcake could see him. From inside the house, Beefcake asked if Brooklyn wanted him to call the cops. Probably not an empty threat considering he recognized Beefcake as the sheriff's son.

But the final blow was when she'd returned the gift he'd so painstakingly made for her. Each color, each etching reflected his eternal love for her. Her words, "I'm sorry, but I can't accept this. I just don't love you that way" burned a hole into the very center of his heart. Of course, she loved him. He'd seen the way she looked at him.

He'd tried to make her take the gift back, but she'd refused, touching his cheek and promising one day he'd find his true someone and he'd forget all about her. As if that were even possible. With a sad smile, she'd turned her back on him and gone inside, closing the door in his face and on his dreams. A numbing pain spread through his heart.

Cheeks and eyes burning, he slunk away like a beaten dog. Back in his car, he rested his head on his steering wheel, fat teardrops discoloring his pants as her words replayed on an infinite loop in his mind. When rage began to shove out his hurt and humiliation, he cranked the ignition and drove aimlessly through the streets of Slaughterville, his brain spinning. He just needed to make her listen, to make her see that *he* was the one for her, that no one could love her as much as he did. No one. Not ever.

Later that night, he stashed his car and hiked through the woods behind her house. With a pair of high-powered binoculars, he watched and waited for the beefcake to leave. Even now, he could remember the way his stomach had clenched at the sight of her kissing another man, the way her smile lit up her face, the way she'd thrown her head back and laughed at something the guy had said – all the things she should've been doing with him.

Crushing reality hit him square in the chest, and feeling small and demeaned, he dropped down from the tree and left. With every block he put between himself and Brooklyn, his agony and then his fury grew. For hours he drove aimlessly, alternating between sobbing and screaming. He'd waited so long, and in all that time, his love for her had never wavered. In return, she'd made a fool of him, treated him like he was a nobody, just like everyone else always had. The familiar taunts he'd endured from his own parents, as well as his classmates, snuck back in, trapped inside, forcing him to relive every tormented second of his past. "*You're pathetic – no one could ever love you…*"

In that moment, what he needed to do had hit him with perfect clarity. The following day, he stashed his car in the woods behind her house once again. Only this time, instead of lurking in the trees, he let himself into her unlocked house where he rifled through her lingerie drawer. He pulled out a silky lavender nightie, lifted it to his nose, and inhaled, sliding its softness over his face and running it through his fingers.

For a moment, he fantasized about her wearing it for him, welcoming him into her arms and whispering soft "sorries" as she brushed sweet kisses over his lips. But then Beefcake's face flashed in his mind, and his blood boiled over. He closed his eyes, recalling the way she'd thrown her head back and laughed at the giant slab of muscle. She'd probably been laughing at *him*, making him the butt of her own personal jokes, just like everyone else used to do. And for that, she would pay. He'd show her exactly how un-confused he really was.

So that was what he'd done. Only it hadn't gone down the way he'd planned because, in the end, he just couldn't bring himself to let her die.

Despite how she'd crushed and humiliated him, how she'd made him feel small and insignificant, everyone knew a person never genuinely got over their first and one true love, their soulmate, and so he found that he couldn't kill her, but he could also never let her go.

Someone pounded on his door, dragging his attention fully back to the present. "Jesus, stop banging. I'm coming."

An angry female voice yelled back. "Well, come faster, you're late. Again."

His eyes shot over to the clock, he swore, wrenched the door open, and all but shoved the woman out of his way. Five minutes later, he swung through another set of doors and rushed inside where he found six people sitting around a long table, staring at him with a barely concealed blend of disdain and impatience.

He grabbed a drink off a nearby tray, gulped down what tasted like piss-warm coffee, and barely resisting the urge to spit it back out, asked, "What did I miss?"

Chapter Eighteen

Though it did little to warm the chill across her skin, Brooklyn pulled up the ratty, hospital-style blanket that had more holes than fabric and tucked it tight beneath her chin as she curled into a fetal position with her back against the wall.

According to the article he'd left for her, today would be her forty-third birthday, which meant she'd been a prisoner for the past six years. Six years of being locked up and chained by a man who claimed to love her. Six years of Queenie not knowing what had happened to her and now accepting that Brooklyn was dead, never coming back.

Her anger and disbelief spent, numbness now filled the space once reserved for hope. She swallowed against the painful lump in her throat. Somewhere in the back of her mind, that strong person she'd once strived so hard to be struggled to get her to move, to at least go brush her teeth, but her limbs felt too heavy to move. What was the point anymore?

Six years. She probably shouldn't feel so surprised. In many ways, it felt like decades since she'd been standing in her own kitchen, talking to Queenie on the phone.

As much as she wanted to rail against the unfairness of it all, wanted to scream out her frustration at her own sister giving up on her, in truth, Brooklyn understood that she couldn't really blame her. After all, how long should she expect anyone to hold out hope, when the odds of her being alive after that many years were astronomical?

Brooklyn closed her eyes and tried to picture Queenie and Roy, tried to imagine what Micah and Ronnie would look like, what their personalities would be. Did they laugh fully and freely the way Brooklyn and Queenie used to do when they were at that age? Or were they more reserved, selectively choosing their moments of joy, much like their daddy always had? Did their mom tell them stories about their Aunt Brooklyn, or did everyone find it easier to pretend like she never existed because it hurt too much?

Heat spread outward from Brooklyn's chest as tears full of hatred spilled down her face. Her eyes lifted to the vent near the ceiling where a camera tracked her every movement. The overwhelming urge to mouth the words *I HATE YOU* in case he was watching shook her in its intensity.

She glared at the place where she knew the camera was hidden until the drip-drip-drip of water hitting the plastic basin penetrated her haze of defiance. Her jaw clenched, and she rolled off the mattress. Her movements slow but deliberate, she shuffled to the sink, grabbed the cupcake, and then moved to the toilet. With her eyes locked on the hidden camera, she opened her hand and dropped the "birthday surprise" into the bowl with a satisfying splash before flushing it away and turning her back on the camera — and him, if he was even watching. Her back rigid, she returned to the bed.

She knew in that moment she wouldn't allow herself to give up. She'd survived six years of this hell, and she wouldn't let him steal the last of her hope now. She didn't know how yet, but she *would* get out. One way or another.

This time when she closed her eyes, she willed herself to latch onto hope, to imagine the locked door being opened, but instead of him descending the steps to tell her about another murder, it would be the cavalry come to save her.

The tears pouring from her eyes to stain the flattened mattress beneath her could've been from sadness or hope; she didn't know. She just knew they meant she was still in the fight for her life, that he hadn't completely won. Not yet.

Chapter Nineteen

Wednesday morning, Reginald Leach finally strolled into the police station, twenty-eight minutes past the time he'd agreed to meet Alyssa at the precinct for a formal interview. He paused briefly at Ruby's desk, bestowing her with his charming smile as he cleared his throat to get her attention. His efforts earned him Ruby's irritated scowl at the disruption before he spotted Alyssa headed in his direction.

Like Ruby, Alyssa's face bore no sign of welcome. While she understood that things came up and people ran late, when it came to her investigations, she leaned a little more toward being a stickler for punctuality. It especially rubbed her the wrong way when she needed answers that she suspected the person running late could offer.

One look at Reginald's casual appearance and the laid-back vibe he was trying to present, and it was all Alyssa could do not to greet him with: "Don't be in any kind of hurry; it's not like women are dying at the hands of some psycho killer." She tried to look at him objectively, to determine if he really was the serial killer they sought, or if she and Ryker were onto something when they discussed the possibility that he and Marcus Davis were working together.

Something about Reginald Leach definitely had her BS meter pegging near the top. But was he a cold-blooded murderer? She hoped to have a better sense of that answer by the end of their interview.

Still irritable about his tardiness but trying to mask it so that she didn't immediately start the interview off on the wrong foot, Alyssa greeted Leach. "Thank you for agreeing to come down here to speak with us." Not that they'd actually given him much of a choice as they explained he could either come in, or they could go to his place of employment and conduct the interview there. He'd opted to come in.

Reggie accepted Alyssa's handshake, and then, smiling, he pointed to her auburn-colored hair that came courtesy of a talented hairdresser – or a box when she was in a pinch. "That's a great color on you." He cocked his head to the side and pursed his lips. "Blonde, brunette, or another shade of red naturally?"

Alyssa's mind immediately flashed to the crime scene photos for each of the victims, their throats slit, a giant X slashed across their mouths, their red hair stained with their own blood. Her eyes narrowed, and she abandoned the entire idea of trying not to show her annoyance. "Your boyfriend's sister has been murdered, we have questions for you, and you're late, so if you think flattery will make me forget that, you're sadly mistaken." She turned on her heel with a clipped, "Follow me. Special Agent Newlin will be joining us momentarily."

Reggie's footsteps faltered. "Special Agent? As in the FBI kind of Special Agent?"

Without slowing, Alyssa said, "Yes, and you met her yesterday when we spoke to Jackson." At the second inter-rogation room on the left, she stopped and ushered Leach inside. She reached up and moved the placard on the door over so that it read *Interview in Progress* before following him in. Cord caught the door before it closed completely, and he held it for Ryker, who pulled up the seat next to Alyssa while Cord stood in the corner, arms relaxed at his sides.

Since this interview had the potential to be the lead in the case Ryker had been living and breathing for the past five years, Alyssa let her spearhead the questioning.

From beneath her arm, Ryker produced an unmarked manila folder and laid it down, leaving it closed but making sure Reggie saw it there. It was a tactic Alyssa herself used when questioning a potential suspect or person of interest. If the person was indeed guilty, seeing the folder would make him or her wonder what the police had, which could, in turn, cause some suspects to accidentally give something away without meaning to as they tried to get a feel for what the cops knew.

"Mr. Leach, thank you so much for agreeing to come in this morning. I know your time is as valuable to you and your clients as our time is to us." Alyssa hid her smile at the agent's subtle dig. "We'll try not to keep you too long." Ryker's voice flowed with a misleading syrupy sweetness, and Alyssa mentally settled back, ready to see the special agent side of Ryker come to life.

"Please call me Reggie. That's what my friends and clients call me." His slight fidgeting betrayed the confidence his smile and words tried to convey.

Ryker leaned back, her posture one of relaxed authority, though Alyssa knew better. Damn, she was enjoying this more than she thought she would – or should.

"That's right. You're an agent to the stars. Any big names you care to share with us?" The question was designed to stroke Reggie's ego right out of the gate, and Ryker struck gold with it.

Reggie puffed up like a bearded dragon about to explode. "Got one, but for now, I've signed a confidentiality contract, and so I can't divulge that client's name. But I've also got a few B-listers, which I know doesn't sound all that exciting when we're talking about the glitz and glamour of Hollywood. But not every actor can be Charlize Theron or George Clooney off the bat, now can they? But if or when they *do* hit that mark, I'm right there with them, along for the ride. It's all bank after that."

Only because she could see Ryker's grin in the reflection of the two-way mirror could Alyssa tell that it was full of pretense. It was like watching the crocodile coax the hare to hop onto his head to cross the river.

"I suppose you're right about that. So, we know you represent Jackson Gray. Can you tell us how that came about?"

Reggie hesitated, as if weighing the reason behind the question. When he couldn't find an angle, he leaned back in his chair and answered. "He was auditioning for a role one day, and I happened to walk by and hear him." He flashed a creepy-as-hell grin and winked before adding, "You've seen him; he's hot. And those eyes. Daaay—yum. I offered to help him read. He accepted. On a whim, I waited for him to finish his audition, told him who I was, and asked him if he'd like to go for coffee. He said yes."

"I see. When was this?"

"Couple months back, May or June, I think."

"And did you two start dating immediately then?"

Reggie's head whipped back and forth so many times, it looked like it might snap right off. "No. Jackson played a little hard to get at first. Plus, if I'm being honest, I was still in another relationship."

"The guy who did that to you?" Ryker touched her own neck where the scratches on Reggie's were.

Reggie's face flushed red to the point that the scratches nearly disappeared. "Yeah. We were already on the rocks. It's not like I cheated or left him for J, if that's what you're implying."

Ryker's brows arched. "I wasn't, but thanks for clearing that up, anyway. So, when would you say you two became an item then?"

Another shrug. "I don't know. We flirted pretty heavily for quite a bit, and then about two weeks ago, we kissed."

"And who made that first move?"

For the first time since Ryker began her questioning, Reggie stiffened, his eyes darting over to Cord, sliding over to Alyssa, and then latching onto Ryker. "Why is that important?"

"Oh, it's not. I'm just trying to get a timeline together in my mind. And that means we're" – she waggled her thumb in the air between herself, Alyssa, and Cord – "going to have to get a little personal at times."

Reggie studied her for a moment, his intense gaze trying to read into her words. "Do I have to answer if I feel it's too personal?"

Ryker's alligator smile returned. "Of course not. This is a formal interview, but you're in no way under arrest. Like I said, we're just trying to establish a timeline so we can get to the bottom of what happened to Jackson's sister. You understand. And we know you're eager to help as much as you can."

Reggie looked over to Cord, brows furrowed. "So, I'm free to go whenever?"

It was Cord's turn to shrug. "Far as I know, man."

What Alyssa added in her head was *unless we arrest you*.

Reggie's hesitation lingered as he turned to face Ryker again. "I made the first move. J's nervousness was cute, but I could tell he was into me, just a bit gun shy, so to speak. I guess he'd had a real bad breakup about a year ago, which was what he meant when he told you guys yesterday that Taylor had been encouraging him to get back in the saddle."

"Got it. And so would you say you and Jackson are exclusive then?"

"Yes."

"Yesterday, Jackson mentioned he was going to tell Taylor about you. If you'd known him for a few months already and been exclusive for at least a couple of weeks, did it bother you that he hadn't shared the news with his sister yet, especially considering how close the two of them seemed to be?"

Reggie scrunched his face, confused. "No. Should it have?"

"Just asking."

Reggie, who up until that point had played at the line of ignorance, shocked Alyssa with his next words. He glanced at each of them before focusing his attention on Ryker. "Look, I'm not stupid. I know you all didn't call me in here because you want to talk to me about my love life or my client list. You want to know if I killed Taylor Gray out of what? Some sense of jealousy or anger or something else I can't even figure out? Let me spare you the trouble of doing this dance. I didn't kill her. I don't know who did, and yes, I sure as hell would tell you if I could. And not just because I'm in both a professional and personal relationship with her brother."

Ryker placed both palms on the table and leaned forward. "Okay, then, gloves off. I prefer it that way." She slid one manicured fingernail inside the manila folder and flipped it open. "Tell me about your childhood. Your mom abandoned the family, your dad got sent off to prison where he mouthed off to the wrong guy and got himself killed, and then your grandparents up and died. Did all that make you angry?"

Rage poured out of Reggie's eyes. "Yeah, actually, it did. My whole damn life had been uprooted by the time I was fourteen. Within months, my mom left, my dad lost his job, he yanked me from the only home I'd ever known, shithole that it was, and then he ended up a goddamned criminal. You can bet your ass I was angry."

"Why'd your mom leave?"

Reggie crossed his arms and glared at Ryker. "Hell if I know. You think she had the decency to tell me? I came home from school one day, and she'd cleared out. My dad was at the kitchen table, bawling his damn eyes out, snot running down his face, and all I could think was, *you look pathetic.* He let a woman lead him by the balls and convince him she loved him when she was just waiting for the right opportunity to empty his bank accounts and leave him for greener pastures."

This time, Alyssa's brows went up. "Greener pastures? She left your father for another man?"

Again, Reggie shrugged. "Couldn't tell you one way or another. I never saw hide nor hair of her again after I left that morning for school. And sure, at first, I was hurt, wondered what I might've done, wondered if I just wasn't 'boy enough' for her to be proud of, and then decided if she didn't think I was worth saying bye to, she wasn't worth caring about. You could tell me she's dead, and it wouldn't mean anything more or less than if you told me about some stranger dying."

All three of them, Alyssa, Cord, and Ryker, stiffened at Leach's comment. From the corner of her eye, Alyssa noticed Ryker's finger slide over Marcus Davis's name as she peered up at her.

Alyssa nodded her understanding. "Do you know a Marcus Davis?" she asked.

Reggie blinked once before his mask fell into place, but not before Alyssa noted the panic in his eyes. She shot Cord a look, and his slight nod told her he'd seen it, too.

"Marcus Davis?" Reggie's voice held the slightest wobble that, if Alyssa hadn't already been zeroed in, she might not have detected. "No. Doesn't sound familiar. Why?"

Ryker's alligator grin returned. "You both lived in Wichita, Kansas, at the same time. Attended the same high school for at least a year. You sure you don't know him?"

This time, Reggie's face paled, and his eyes darted to the camera in the corner recording his every response, verbal and physical. His intertwined hands dropped to his lap. "No. Never heard of him." He tipped his chin in a show of defiance. "Hate to be the one to tell you all this, but there were probably close to half a million people who lived in Wichita when I did. Doesn't mean I knew them all, even the ones I supposedly attended school with."

"Hmm." Alyssa let that one expression hang in the air until Reggie started to wriggle in his seat. Still, he refused to budge on his response.

For the next two hours, the interview proceeded in the same back and forth way until finally, Ryker pushed back and stood, indicating she'd gotten everything she needed, at least for the time being.

Alyssa waited until Reggie had reached the door before stopping him with one more question. "Mr. Leach, would you be willing to take a polygraph?"

His posture stiffened like someone had slammed a board against his back. Yet, his face displayed nothing but calm and curiosity when he turned around. "Why?"

"Why would you agree, or why would we ask you to take one?"

"Either. Both."

"Because we're conducting a murder investigation, and the sooner we can clear names, the sooner we can move on and find out who murdered your boyfriend's sister."

Reggie's eyes flickered. "Am I still a suspect?"

Alyssa kept her response deliberately vague. "We're talking to everyone."

A muscle at the corner of Leach's mouth twitched at Alyssa's non-answer.

In a move that Alyssa thought was intentional, Ryker picked up the manila folder and tapped it on the table, her gaze steady on Reggie even as his was drawn to the folder. "*Everyone's* a suspect until we arrest the guilty party."

Reggie dragged his eyes from the folder and dropped every pretense of kindness. He crossed his arms, gripping his elbows with his hands. "Why a polygraph when they're inadmissible in court anyway?"

Ryker countered with, "Why not a polygraph?"

After another intense stare-down, Reggie dropped his arms, shrugged, and turned toward the door Cord now held ajar. "Set it up, and I'll contact my lawyer to be present when it happens."

Her head cocked to the side, her stare practically drilling straight through him, Ryker said, "Sorry. Just one more question before you go. Do you happen to own a multi-colored windbreaker with some type of bird's wing on the sleeve?"

Reggie's eyes widened before he forced his features to relax. "Not that I can think of. Why?"

Ryker studied him for several seconds before answering. "Just covering some bases."

As soon as Cord left to lead Reggie through the maze of desks and cubicles, Ryker turned to Alyssa. "Well, what did you think?"

"Did you see the way he crossed his arms and grabbed onto his elbows? That's a classic sign of nerves. Seems clear to me that Reginald Leach isn't telling us everything. Furthermore, he definitely knows who Marcus Davis is."

Ryker's grin sharpened. "My thoughts exactly. I'm curious what the polygraph will show. Or if he'll really go through with it. Either way, it's going to tell us something, isn't it?"

Chapter Twenty

Wednesday, August 30

On the heels of their interview with Reggie Leach, Dr. Sharp called with an update. As soon as Alyssa saw Lynn's name on her caller ID, she hit the speaker on her phone, propped it against the whiteboard, and answered.

Before Alyssa could finish her greeting, Lynn blurted out her news. "We were able to get DNA off that sliver of fingernail found on Jennie Killingbeck's body."

"Already?" Incredulity rang through that one word of Ryker's. "Even the FBI can't get things done that quickly."

Lynn chuckled. "Favors. It's always nice, not to mention beneficial, when people owe you one, or in my case, multiple. When that person is also family through marriage, well, that makes it that much easier to get things done. And with a case as big as this one appears to be, let's just say I don't lose sleep at night when I call in some chips. Now, as I was saying, we were able to get some DNA, and the lab determined the DNA did *not* belong to the victim."

The team all shared hopeful looks. "Did you get a match?"

Excitement still bubbled through Lynn's voice even as she gave a resounding, "No."

Alyssa's emotions boomeranged from hopeful right back to frustrated, not to mention a bit baffled. "No? Then why the hell are you so damn chipper?"

A giant grin lit up Ryker's face, making her eyes sparkle. Alyssa frowned, wondering what the hell had been said that made the federal agent so freaking happy. Why the hell didn't Ryker, like Alyssa, look like she'd bitten into the sourest of lemons?

She didn't have to wait long for an answer, not that Alyssa understood it when she heard it.

"Phenotyping," Lynn said.

"Phenotyping," Ryker repeated.

Joe's hands shot out, palms up. "Sounds like some kind of torture device used for unruly typists back in the day. Since I'm sure it's not, someone want to decode the scientific mumbo jumbo and tell us what the holy hell phenotyping is?"

Cord and Hal both chuckled at the look Ryker shot Joe's way. Alyssa, however, was in Joe's corner. She didn't like not knowing things, especially when it came to things that could help her solve a case.

"Special Agent Newlin—" That was as far as Lynn got before Ryker interrupted whatever the medical examiner had been about to say.

"Ryker."

"Okay, Ryker," Lynn continued. "I'm actually in the middle of something that I really need to get back to, so I'm going to let you take this, if you don't mind. But one more thing before I go. I haven't started Taylor Gray's autopsy yet, but I can tell you that both Jennie Killingbeck and Gray's bodies have an odd, unique shape surrounding several of their stab wounds, primarily those in the breast-bone area. It suggests to me that the hilt of the knife used in both attacks has a very distinct design. I'm betting that the wounds coinciding with the shape will prove to be the deepest.

"I snapped some photos, and I'll try to remember to shoot you an email before I leave today. If you all can find that weapon, I'm almost certain I'll be able to determine with a high rate of accuracy if it's consistent with the marks on the bodies. Also, just as an initial observation, the bleeding from Gray's nose and mouth, along with the bruising around her neck, are clear signs of strangulation. My prediction is I'll find crushed cartilage in her windpipe. And whatever was used, it wasn't rope. From those markings, I'd guess some kind of twine maybe, or something a little thicker than twine. Anyway, I really do have to run now, but I wanted to make sure I updated you before I let any of it slip my mind or I got too wrapped up in one of my exams. I'll be checking back in again as soon as I get anything else."

Ryker mumbled something that sounded like a thank you while she rummaged through earlier crime scene photos, pulling out four of them and lining them up in a row.

"Thanks, Lynn. As always, we appreciate it." Alyssa ended the call and pointed to the pictures Ryker had on display. "Well, that answers my first question as to whether any of the other victims shared the same type of marking around the stab wounds."

Her gaze shifted to Leach's and Davis's names. "Not that they can't be working together, but it seems unlikely that they'd be working in tandem with the same weapon. Even if they each have their own, only one of them is doing the actual stabbing. So, in that theory, one strangles, one stabs? But that doesn't make sense either because we've seen no evidence of more than one perpetrator being present. I don't know. Something's not adding up for me with that scenario. I'll have to mull it over a bit."

Ryker nodded. "I agree. Even if they're working together, they're not necessarily killing together. As for the strangulation, I've already mentioned that I believe our guy uses it as a means of overpowering the women. In Gray's case, I wonder if it was also a matter of keeping her from screaming out and getting someone else's attention, considering the location of her murder. That spot was hidden, but by no means so well concealed that he wouldn't have been caught if she'd been able to call out for help."

"Sounds as plausible as any other explanation," Cord said. "Now, about that phenotyping. Care to explain why you and Dr. Sharp are so jived about it?"

Ryker perked up at the reminder. "In a nutshell, we can submit a DNA analysis, and the phenotyping will create – or predict – the genetic make-up of the individual whose DNA it is, all based on the markers present."

Eyes bright, Tony dropped his pen and leaned in. "Genetic make-up, as in it'll give us an actual ID?"

Ryker's head tilted back and forth, not a yes, not a no. "Not quite, but close to as good as. Phenotyping can predict skin tone, face shape, eye and natural hair color."

Hal chimed in with what he knew. "I've heard of this. Actually, we all have; we just didn't know the name. It can do all that Ryker said, true, but it can also give us an area or a country of origin of the individual. Genetic ancestry, if you will."

Tony shot out of his seat and interlaced his fingers on top of his head, pacing as he did. "You're right. I *have* heard of it. I think I read an article one night at Lynn's—"

The rest of his face flushed the same color as the top of his head as he stumbled over Dr. Sharp's name. "Uh, yeah, I remember the article said they can even use markers to show age progression, right?"

"Algorithms," Ryker corrected. And if Tony had hoped the federal agent missed or would overlook his stumble, he'd miscalculated. The intensity of the stare she directed at Tony even made Alyssa want to squirm for her teammate. "Is there something I need to know about you and Dr. Sharp, something that could hinder or impact this investigation in any way, shape, or form? More accurately, when we make an arrest, will there be some kind of technicality that a good defense lawyer could spin to get the case thrown out? Because I haven't come this far to have it all bungled on the one-yard line, if you'll excuse my sports analogy."

Where excitement had been mere moments ago, a hint of panic and underlying anger laced Ryker's voice. And for good reason, Alyssa knew, which explained why no one, Tony included, became offended.

Instead, he answered as bluntly as she'd asked. "Lynn – Dr. Sharp – and I had a *very* brief romantic interlude right after Lys's daughter got married a few months ago. We decided pretty quickly that we were better friends than lovers, as cliché as that sounds. The entire thing was so brief that I wouldn't even call our decision a breakup because it never extended past" – again, he cleared his throat – "never extended *into* an actual relationship."

Standing beside him, Alyssa could almost feel the heat coming off Tony's face.

Not quite satisfied, Ryker's laser-like focus didn't waver. "Not that I'm questioning anyone's integrity, at least anyone in this room, but I don't know Dr. Sharp the way you all seem to. However, experience has shown me that sex, no matter how casual both parties believe it to be, can cause strife. And in a criminal investigation, especially one this big, well, you can understand why I need to make absolutely certain nothing jeopardizes it."

As this was her team, Alyssa decided to intervene and save Tony from more squirming. "Ryker, I know it doesn't come naturally for you or any of us, for that matter, but you're just going to have to trust us on this. I guarantee there will be no issues regarding your concerns. No one in this room would risk *any* case, much less one this massive, on a possible bogus technicality."

Ryker's shoulders relaxed just enough that everyone in the room breathed out, almost in unison, the sound whisking away the anxiety that had built up when Ryker feared her case could be in jeopardy. "Moving on then. Aside from the phenotyping angle, the other good news is that with all the advancements in DNA technology, we can also do genetic genealogy tracing."

At Joe's blank stare, Hal filled in the gaps. "If anyone in this guy's family tree has their DNA anywhere in pretty much any system, the phenotyping can help us narrow it down even more. And with millions of people jumping on the DNA where-do-I-hail-from bandwagon, the odds are pretty slim that someone in that familial line isn't in a system somewhere. In fact, this familial DNA is how a lot of cold cases are getting solved now, even the ones invest-igators had long ago given up any real hope of finding answers for. Unfortunately, in some of those cases, the guilty party is dead and so will never have to pay for the crime. But at least some families are getting answers they never thought they'd get."

"Why do I sense a 'but' coming?" Alyssa asked.

Ryker's eyes shifted over to the board displaying the graphic scenes of the murdered women. "Because there is. Phenotyping takes time, and with all signs clearly pointing to our killer escalating quickly, time is a commodity we don't have right now."

Cord pushed off the wall he'd been leaning against. "What if we can cut some of the what-ifs out and speed up that timeline?" He looked over to Alyssa, then Hal, whose wife, Helena, was friends with one of the judges. "What are the chances we can get a warrant to swab Reginald Leach for a comparison match? Then we can just skip the whole phenotyping song and dance and just skip to implicating or clearing the man."

Alyssa answered for Hal. "What we have is pure speculation on our part. Absolutely nothing stands out as significant enough for a judge to issue a warrant. Like Hal mentioned just yesterday, I suspect no judge would even be willing to sign off on a ping warrant for Leach's phone right now. I don't think what this team is viewing as circumstantial evidence that seems to be stacking up is substantial enough yet for us to convince the prosecutor or a judge to go out on a limb that short. And if Leach really does represent a big-name celebrity like he claims to, that limb probably got even shorter. I wish we could circumvent the possibility of looking into this phenotyping thing, but right now, the truth is we may not be able to."

The muffled sound of Hal's phone ringing from his pocket ended the conversation as he pulled it out, took one look, and answered, wheeling himself out of the incident room, his voice growing louder and more animated even as he rolled away.

Curious, Alyssa strained to hear Hal's end of the conversation while listening to Joe and Tony discuss phenotyping, all while the sounds of a breaking news story about Hollywood heartthrobs Hudson Bane and Remington Everwood getting into a knock-down, drag-out brawl on set filtered through all the other noise.

The story completely swept from her mind when Hal reappeared, his eyes glued on Ryker. "Before I tell you, I'm just going to say it's your call, but I think we should really consider getting the media involved now. That way, we control the narrative instead of them getting wind of something and we miss that opportunity. They're going to be in it eventually, so we might as well jump the line and get them to help us as opposed to them hindering and second-guessing every move we make. Think about it while I tell you about this." He waved his phone in the air.

"That was the Torrance County public records department. Let me back up a little. After learning that Marcus Davis was in Colorado Springs around the twenty-third, early this morning, I ran a search through our own state database for recent arrests or tickets just to see if something popped, not really expecting anything to hit, mind you, but hoping, nonetheless. Well, something did. On Monday, the twenty-eighth, around nine-thirty p.m., one Marcus Davis with a Tulsa, Oklahoma, driver's license ran a stop sign near Pilot's Travel Center in Moriarty."

Ryker's blank face told Alyssa that Hal's news meant nothing to her, which made sense since the federal agent wasn't as familiar with the area and therefore couldn't fully appreciate the significance of the time and place.

"Moriarty," she said, "is less than an hour's drive from the Tingley Beach area where Taylor Gray's body was found."

Chapter Twenty-One

Wednesday, August 30

Ryker looked like Hal had just handed her an early Christmas on a silver platter wrapped in a pretty velvet bow. "Did I hear you correctly? We have a police officer who can put Marcus Davis in the area near the time we believe Taylor Gray was murdered?"

"You heard correctly."

Alyssa directed her question to Hal. "Are there any city cameras at Tingley Beach that you can tap into, see if there's a midnight blue, late model Nissan Maxima in the area?"

The way Hal scrunched his face answered her question as much as his words. "I'm good, but I don't know that I'm that good. Most of those cameras over there are directed at the fishing ponds, not the parking areas, but I'll go back and double-check, just to be sure."

Ryker's exuberance tapered off. "How many 'coincidences' is it going to take to prove Marcus Davis is our guy?"

Already standing near the whiteboard, Tony found an unused space and etched out a rough timeline. "We know from Lois Cutter's security cameras that Gray entered the area around quarter to seven. Lys mentioned the timestamp showed seven eighteen when, let's call him, Windbreaker Shadow Guy slipped through the area. That's roughly thirty minutes.

"WSG spots Gray – or maybe he followed her there – we don't know yet. Regardless, sunset is approximately seven fifty, give or take. Let's round up to eight. Depending on how long it takes him to actually finish the deed, it's not too far a leap to get from there to Moriarity in that amount of time. Especially if he was speeding."

Tony glanced over his shoulder at Hal. "We need to find out why he was in Moriarty at all. If he was in Colorado Springs on the twenty-third, did he have another potential client meet-up somewhere around here? In other words, do we know what brought him to this area?"

"Well, that's the thing," Hal said. "While you were interviewing Leach, I grabbed my online shovel and started weeding out the less relevant info. Turns out, that ticket isn't even the most intriguing tidbit. Remember, I'd already been conducting my own research into the FBI's suspect list Ryker provided, and it made the most sense to kick it off with Marcus Davis.

"I started with SCJ Headhunters Inc.'s website since that was the last known employment the Bureau had on him. Turns out, he's one of their most widely in-demand employees, and as such, travels quite extensively for work, which was why he was in Colorado Springs. Just deducing from the bio blurb on the site, it appears Davis has risen quite rapidly through the ranks in the past few years. As a result, his already heavy travel load increased."

While Hal spoke, he pulled up the website on his laptop, navigated to the About section, and cast it to the wall. "You can see here how SCJ boasts personal interaction with the companies that hire them, setting them apart from the quote unquote more impersonal phone calls and Zoom chats their competitors offer. I clicked on Davis's name and here's what I found."

A long list of various businesses, each with an accompanying link, filled the page under Davis's section of the website. Hal scrolled over to a map of the locations and enlarged it. "These may traverse the entirety of the country, but if you look, you can see there's a primary focus in Oklahoma's neighboring states, as well as places within the South and Southwest. For instance, Colorado, New Mexico" – he paused and tapped the screen – "and Texas."

"So, basically every single state where there's a victim, we have Marcus Davis," Joe said.

"Basically, yes. But to be clear, lots of people travel to and through Texas, so just because he was there doesn't mean he's the one who killed Jaime Asandro in Texas. I doubt SCJ will give me the complete rundown of Davis's travels for the past five years, but if we get many more coincidences, the FBI can probably get a warrant issued, if for nothing else, at least his personal property."

If the tables were turned, and this had been Alyssa seeking help from the FBI, she wasn't certain she could be as calmly patient as Ryker appeared to be on the outside. The hard eyes, the tightening of her lips, and the throbbing of her temples, however, suggested an entirely different story taking place inside the agent's mind.

Hal paused to take a swig of his sports drink. "I'll cut to the end. Even though I didn't really think I'd get far, I contacted SCJ on the pretense of following up on a meeting with Davis. When I asked for him, the receptionist informed me he was currently out of town but would be back in the office tomorrow or Friday."

In her first outward show of impatience, Ryker's left foot tapped a quiet but steady rhythm against the floor, and Alyssa crossed her fingers that Hal would get to his point soon.

"I feigned that I'd forgotten that Davis was supposed to be in Colorado Springs, and the receptionist kindly corrected me. Marcus Davis has been at a conference in Angel Fire since Friday, August twenty-fifth, one day *before* Jennie Killingbeck went missing."

Ryker stopped tapping her foot and burst out of her chair, an angry growl erupting from deep in her chest, but Hal still wasn't finished.

"That's less than an hour's drive away from where Jennie's body was found. And that's not all. In her quest to be ever so helpful, the receptionist also told me that the four-day conference was supposed to end Monday, but that when the conferences are being held in Angel Fire, which they have been with increasing frequency over the past few years, Marcus often flies into Albuquerque early and stays a bit longer before and after the conference ends. The only difference this time was that he had that client meet-up in Colorado Springs, so he flew into there, rented a car, and drove to Angel Fire, where his aunt and uncle own a summer house."

Hal grinned in that way of his that said he was quite proud of himself. "I wanted to keep this oh-so-helpful gal talking, and so I told her how much my wife and I loved Angel Fire and asked if she'd ever been to this summer house, and she had. That's when she informed me that Davis always has the place to himself because his aunt and uncle are currently living in Greece and have been for the past seven and a half years."

Alyssa shot to her feet. If Cord hadn't already been standing, she imagined he would have, as well.

"Davis and his uncle have an agreement that as long as Davis pays for the housekeeping and upkeep year-round, they'll continue to let him stay there as often as he likes. Plus, it's good to have someone staying just so the place doesn't appear uninhabited on a regular basis, and with no children of their own, I guess this arrangement benefits everyone. Kind of offhand information but sharing it just the same."

Hal's grin grew bigger because he knew he had scored a gold mine of information, regardless of how circumstantial a prosecutor might find it. "From what I gathered, Davis likes to stay at the hotel instead of the house during the conferences. Perhaps, it's a matter of convenience, or perhaps it's something more. Either way, both before and after these conferences, he hangs his hat at his uncle's place until he heads back to his home base in Tulsa. Maybe it's all innocent and coincidental, or maybe he's building up alibis. But by my calculations, this information moves Davis up my personal list of likable suspects."

Ryker finally stopped scraping a path in the floor. "That's a hell of a lot of information to take in, and damn, that was thorough. Thank you for going deep on this. I also happen to think you're right about controlling the narrative we feed to the media, now more than ever."

She moved over to the whiteboard and scribbled: *Together or Separate?* above *Marcus Davis* and *Reginald Leach*. In red, she added, *Primary Suspects*, and then replacing the cap on the dry erase marker, she tapped it against their names. "I think we can all agree that we now have two very viable suspects in this investigation, not to mention two individuals whom I believe are somehow connected to each other, even if Reggie Leach isn't quite ready to admit that yet. But first" – she glanced from Cord to Alyssa – "I think we need to scoop Hammond in and then bend his ear, not just about the possibility of a press conference, but also because I'm getting on a plane to Tulsa asap, and I'd like you and Cord to accompany me."

"For the record," Alyssa said, "I agree it's time to bring the press on board. The killer has escalated his attacks, and it's our job to make the public aware so they, like Tony mentioned on Monday, can take the necessary precautions for their own safety. But I also want to point out to everyone that involving the media will increase the pressure tenfold on us, especially as the paparazzi will start hammering at the mayor, as well as us, to see if the celebrities in the area are safe with a possible serial killer running around on the loose."

Tony shot his finger gun at Alyssa. "Valid point, Lys. But you know we can handle a little heat from the jackals."

"Okay, then."

"Well, while you guys are doing that" – Joe pulled out his phone – "I'll try to contact Enterprise again. That is if Hal can get me a contact person within their corporate offices—"

Hal scribbled a name on a piece of paper and pushed it to Joe. "Rory McEnroe."

Hal's lips twitched when Joe muttered, "Of course he already has it" under his breath. "So, okay, I'll contact Rory McEnroe to see if we can maybe get the vehicle Davis rented out of circulation when it's returned. I'll assure them that we need it just long enough for us to look at it, you know, just in case Davis is our guy, and he left behind some kind of forensic evidence. Worst the woman can say is no, not without a warrant. But she might just say yes."

An unmistakable sizzle of excitement buzzed throughout the room as the team realized they might finally be closing in on a suspect.

Chapter Twenty-Two

Six years after her sister's disappearance – and if she was being honest, most likely her sister's murder – Charlotte "Queenie" Knox-Bolton still harbored the same burning resentment she had all those years earlier when she'd received the call from the local police in Slaughterville. *Signs of a violent struggle* – those five words still echoed in her head and set off a kaleidoscope of horrifying images she couldn't control or block out.

When Brooklyn had failed to show up for work on Monday, Lindy, the vice-principal and one of Brooklyn's best friends, had gone to her house to check on her. After spotting Brooklyn's car still parked in the garage, and after nearly breaking the doorbell by jamming it repeatedly with her finger, all to no avail, Lindy decided to let herself in.

She hadn't found Brooklyn, but she had stumbled into a vicious scene that resulted in the worst kinds of nightmares for everyone who knew and loved Brooklyn. Though Queenie's husband had strongly advised her not to look at the police photos that one of his friends on the force had provided, she'd ignored him, *needing* to suffer, even if only emotionally, along with her sister. Spatter sprayed on the lower cabinets and on the counters, along with the reddish-brown pools of blood streaking from the kitchen to the back door, told a hellish story Queenie could never erase from her mind.

Two days after that gruesome discovery, when dredging the pond in the woods beyond Brooklyn's property, police discovered what Queenie recognized as her sister's favorite fluorescent pink gym bag emblazoned with her name in bright, flashy purple stitching and a decal of the Roman Colosseum that she'd sewn on herself. A thick yellow tow rope had been wrapped around it multiple times, and two grocery bags of river rocks were tied to the straps in an obvious effort to keep it weighted down. Scavenging prey, most likely catfish, had already begun to tear at the seams of the bag, which had been stuffed with blood-stained kitchen and bath towels, all monogrammed with Brooklyn's initials. BTK, Brooklyn Tammie Knox.

After the serial killer who'd self-labeled himself with those very initials, Brooklyn had considered ripping the monogram off each and every one of her towels. It was only after Queenie had reminded her that she'd inherited the same initials as their father's sister who he'd lost to Sudden Infant Death Syndrome had she relented and re-embraced the gift she'd received when she'd graduated with her dual master's degrees in both English and Roman studies.

Upon the police's discovery, Queenie was seized with a crushing guilt that if she hadn't been so exhausted, she would've realized Brooklyn had never called her back like she'd said she would. Maybe if she had, her sister would still be alive. That, coupled with the relentless pain, nearly squeezed the very life out of Queenie. And for one shameful moment, she'd nurtured the idea of ending her own life, leaving behind her husband to raise their children on his own simply because she couldn't grasp how she was supposed to live with the type of agony that came with imagining what her sister had likely endured.

Or how she was supposed to continue living a life without her sister and best friend to share all the love or heavy loads. Eyes hurting from the tears she held back, Queenie closed her eyes and let herself remember the first time that she and Brooklyn, as young teenagers, had snuck out to attend a bonfire. She couldn't remember why now, but they'd both been grounded for some reason or another – probably breaking curfew – and so they'd waited until they heard the soft sounds of their father's snoring.

Queenie tiptoed into Brooklyn's room, careful to avoid the creaky spots on the floor. Brooklyn's door stood slightly ajar, and she slipped in, closing the door softly behind her. They'd had to sneak out through Brooklyn's window because it was farthest from their parents' bedroom, and it didn't screech the way Queenie's did. After replacing the screen, they slipped through the woods, covering their giggles and masking their fear of being busted.

At the bonfire, they proceeded to drink a little too much cheap beer and even cheaper wine someone in the group had absconded with. The next morning, the two of them had been so hungover that they'd had to take turns holding each other's hair back as the other emptied the contents of her stomach. They'd been absolutely convinced they were literally dying. Later that evening, lying side by side on Brooklyn's bed, dehydrated and utterly depleted of energy, they'd pinky promised that when they grew up, they'd buy houses right next door to each other so they could always be there "in sickness and in health," no matter who they married. Then, when they were too old and gray to do anything else, they'd sit and rock on the porch until one day, they'd just die peacefully together, holding hands.

A childish teenage vow, Queenie knew, but it still tore at her heart that it could never happen now.

For days and weeks and months after Brooklyn went missing, the authorities had pounded the ground and the waterways, combing every inch of the massive acreage of wooded areas and farmland. They'd dredged the pond where Brooklyn's items were discovered and employed two dive teams to search all lakes and bodies of water in Slaughterville, Noble, and the surrounding towns.

Despite their efforts, Brooklyn's body had never been found. And while Queenie knew deep in her soul that her sister had left this earthly plane, until she had hard, physical proof in the form of Brooklyn's bones, she refused to truly accept she'd never see her again.

Usually.

However, during certain milestone moments, Queenie needed to disengage from everyone and everything, including familial duties, and so regardless of the guilt that burrowed deep each time she did it, she escaped to a place where she and Brooklyn had shared some of their best, most cherished memories over the years. Most involved their parents before they'd died, while both girls were still in high school, but many were just the two of them, like the time they decided they were brave enough to have a *Halloween* movie marathon alone in the dark. They'd huddled close together under the same blanket eating popcorn and laughing hysterically at every jump scare.

It was here in that same cabin where Queenie retreated now, alone and away from the furtive, worried glances of her husband, her friends, and even her children. It was here where she always felt Brooklyn's pull and presence the strongest, the one place she could truly allow her grief and bottled rage free rein.

For hours and even days on end, she lost herself in the torturous game of imagining what her sister had endured in what were most likely her final moments. The confusion, the terror, the pain.

And now, on what would've been Brooklyn's forty-third birthday, blood pounded in Queenie's ears while that edgy, twitchy feeling engulfed her so completely that her entire body shook from the effort it took not to shatter every breakable thing within her reach. While she herself continued aging, Brooklyn, who always could've passed for someone a good decade younger than she was, would forever be frozen at thirty-six.

In her usual form of self-torture, Queenie forced herself to picture the way Brooklyn, terrified for her life, must have fought against her attacker. Endless waves of guilt gurgled deep in her gut as she railed against the unfairness of it all. As she had done every August thirtieth since, she opened a drawer and pulled out the card she'd planned on giving Brooklyn for her thirty-seventh birthday.

Her heart aching, she ran her fingers over the embossed lettering of the silver words: *Sister by Birth, Best Friend by Choice.* On the inside flap, Queenie had glued a heart made of red construction paper. On it, she'd written in perfect calligraphy:

> *Surprise! For your birthday, I got you US. That's right. We're moving home!!! Get ready to get sick of us!*

Today's tears dripped down to join the past six years' worth of stains. Like she had with the lettering on the front, Queenie traced her fingertips over the dried spatters, thinking how the pockmarked paper heart mirrored her own. For a fleeting moment, she allowed herself the luxury of fantasizing that Brooklyn was out there somewhere, alive and just waiting to be found. And as the fantasy came to its inevitable end, she asked herself that same burning question – if Brooklyn was alive, then why couldn't she use that odd telepathic link that had connected them from the time they were little girls all the way through adulthood to tell her where Brooklyn was?

Her mind answered for her, even if she didn't want to accept it. Because her sister's death had severed the link that had always connected one to the other, no matter the distance between them.

By now, Queenie recognized the sting of fury racing up her spine, replacing the grief, even if only momentarily.

Six years later, she still had no definitive answers. Not the *who* or the *why*. No one had ever been arrested for anything, something she still had trouble wrapping her head around. Before she returned home to her family, she'd do what she always did – stop in at the police station and demand they get off their asses and bring her sister home.

For now, she thought back to that day that had come, in her opinion, rather quickly on the heels of that first excruciating anniversary. Harold Arnold, Slaughterville's beloved sheriff, had informed the town that all leads had been exhausted or dried up, and the case had gone cold.

That day, Queenie had raged and railed against everyone unfortunate enough to cross her path, including her one-year-old babies, something that still horrified her to this day. It was the primary reason she'd started using the cabin as her escape hatch, never wanting to risk that again. Thank God her husband had been home and whisked the kids outside, pushing them around the block in their stroller until they'd both fallen asleep. After putting them to bed in their cribs, he'd approached her like one might a wounded animal, gathering her in his arms and whispering words of reassurance that neither Micah nor Ronnie would have any recollection of this event. Even though the guilt still ate away at her, Roy appeared to be right.

With the birthday card still clutched in her hands, Queenie let her memories transport her back to the day the sheriff had blindsided her with his announcement.

Seething, she stormed into the police station, ignoring Betsy, the kind matronly lady who tried to tell her the sheriff wasn't available. She knew damn good and well he was. Without knocking, she shoved his door open hard enough that it slammed against the wall, leaving a nice size hole in it from the doorknob. She had the satisfaction of scaring the hell out of him.

She marched up to his desk and slapped both palms down, welcoming the sting of pain that rippled up her arms from the impact. Leaning in as far as she could, she screamed in his face.

"Cold? Brooklyn's case is cold now? All your leads have dried up?" She raised her hands and slapped them down again, rattling his computer, his stapler, and scattering the papers in front of him. One of his pens clattered to the floor, and she saw him glance toward his open doorway and give a slight shake to his head.

"It's goddamn 2018," she yelled, "so why don't you tell me how the hell there can be NO leads. Huh? How? You're going to sit there in your comfy-ass chair and tell me to my face that with all the advancements in DNA and forensic science, your

guys" — she bared her teeth as she sneered the word — "can't find one shred of effing evidence in the bloody scene that was my sister's house! How can you just give up like that? How dare you. How. Goddamned. Dare. You." Each word came out at an ever-increasing screech until, exhausted and crushed, she fell back into one of the chairs across from the sheriff's desk.

She used her fists to swipe the angry torrent of tears blurring her vision. "You knew her, Harold. You knew her. Your boys went to school with us. Mason was Brooklyn's first kiss! And her last date! Hell, we attended barbecues and bonfires in your backyard. Brooklyn wasn't just a faceless name in a crowd to you. How can you say her case is cold? How can you let it be? I thought you cared. Don't you want to know what happened? Am I really the only one not willing to give up so easily?" Her chest tightened until it became increasingly difficult to breathe.

Like it did now, the way it always did when she took herself back to that day.

Perhaps because he'd known her and Brooklyn, as well as their parents when they were alive, Sheriff Arnold had allowed Queenie her meltdown. When he knew she'd finally finished, he spoke gently and calmly, which likely would've pissed her off all over again if it hadn't been for the moisture clouding his own eyes.

"Now, Queenie, you know me better than that. And I never said I was giving up or quitting. I said the leads had dried up. Hell, we've interviewed and reinterviewed this entire damn town and every town in a sixty-mile radius. We've even reached out to all the other police departments to put feelers out, just in case somebody said something, heard a whisper of what might've happened or why. Nobody heard or saw a damn thing. I can't even find one single person who could give me even an inkling of anyone who might've wished her harm. Because nobody did. You know as well as I do that everyone loved your sister. Hell, even her students practically worshipped her. You" – he jabbed his finger in the air at her – "know that." His voice crackled with his own overflowing emotion.

"What about that boy who was leaving her flowers and crap? The one who Mason said had left her another gift that Friday night? What about him?"

Sheriff Arnold leaned back in his chair and sighed. "Queenie, you know better than anyone that Brooklyn never ever gave names because she was so protective of those kids. Hell, she made sure Mason didn't even get a look at the kid through the peephole. And he was too focused on Brooklyn when she came back in to sneak a peek through the window when the kid left."

Without thinking, Queenie said, "What about Mason himself, hmm? He said this mysterious person had left a jewelry box kind of thing for Brooklyn, but no one ever found it." She knew she'd crossed a line, but she couldn't stop. "What if he was lying?"

Sheriff Arnold's eyes narrowed, and his chair creaked with his shifting weight when he leaned forward, palms flat on his desk, and used her given name. "Careful there, Charlotte Marie. I know you're hurting – we all are – but you don't want to end up saying something you can't take back. And you definitely don't want to get tongues wagging." He shot a warning glance to his open door where everyone in the small metal building could overhear every single word, even if Queenie hadn't been shouting.

Defeated and ashamed, Queenie whispered, "I'm sorry. You know I didn't mean that. I know Mason cared about Brooklyn. I remember when he called me up after she went missing and told me about what had happened and asked if I knew who the kid was. I didn't even know she and Mason had gone out. When I talked to her Saturday, she didn't mention anything at all." She choked back a sob. "Because she was trying to cheer me up. I was struggling with the whole new mom-of-twins thing."

"Honey, even if she had told you, you know how secretive Brooklyn was about things like that. Like I said, she insisted Mason stay inside. We questioned every teacher, current students, and any former students we could track down, and no one had ever heard of Brooklyn receiving any gifts at all, much less recent ones. Hell, remember when someone graffitied the football field and broke the school windows? I knew she suspected, if not outright knew, who the vandals were, but she didn't want what she called some stupid prank – thoughtless and criminal as it was – to ruin the kids' lives. That's who your sister was.

"She had a heart of twenty-four-carat gold, but if the gift-giver is the person who did this, well, we'd have better luck finding a ghost than finding someone who could actually give us a name."

Though she knew Harold was right, Queenie couldn't relent. Doing so meant giving up, and she definitely couldn't do that. "This is a small town, Harold. Everyone knows everyone else's business before they know it themselves half the time. How hard can it really be to figure it out?"

The sheriff's mouth turned down at the corners. "Apparently, very." Snatching a tissue off his desk, he removed his glasses and wiped his eyes before replacing them. Then, he stretched his hands out to her – a gesture she stubbornly ignored, feeling only the tiniest twinge of remorse when he accepted her rejection and retracted them.

"I swear to you here and now, Queenie, that I won't stop trying to find out what happened, even on my own time. Someday, something's got to give. But in the meantime, you can't be going off half-cocked like this. It's not healthy for you or your young-uns." He sucked in a deep breath and let it out in a rush. "And as much as I hate to say it, I think we need to accept that we may never locate Brooklyn's body. Whoever did this to her clearly didn't want her found. And I've got to be honest, that doesn't feel like something a kid would be able to pull off."

Five years later, those words still echoed in Queenie's head, and a hollow moan slipped between her lips. True to his word, Sheriff Arnold continued to search for leads when he could. For all the good that did. And true to *her* word, she hounded him faithfully for information, even though she knew she'd be the first call he ever made if something cropped up.

Now, in the bathroom of the cabin, she stared at her raven-haired reflection, barely recognizing the heavily cracked shell of her former self. She wondered what Brooklyn would think of her new appearance. For their entire lives, many people had assumed they were twins. The truth, however, was that Brooklyn had been a preemie and was only ten months younger. The sisters had always loved the shocked faces when people learned they weren't the same age. Until six years ago when Queenie stopped loving how she could so easily see Brooklyn's face every time she passed by a mirror. Just another checkmark in the column of destroyed things that accompanied the tragedy of whatever had happened to her sister.

In one of her suffocating bouts of rage, Queenie had chopped her red, waist-long hair off and colored it the darkest black she could find because it matched the color of her soul and the world around her. The change had been so drastic that, once again, she'd frightened her twins.

Beside her, Queenie's phone chimed with a text notification. She didn't have to look to know that it was from her husband. Despite the way she'd seesawed from clinging to him in the depths of her grief to keeping him at arm's length at the height of her hatred, unable to handle the pity and concern swimming in his eyes, he was always there for her.

She was lucky, and she knew it. And yet, even though she knew he understood, she also knew that, during these times, she took advantage of his goodness. She recalled what Brooklyn had told her once after she called her to cry about a stupid fight she and Roy had gotten into. Brooklyn had listened quietly, and then after the requisite – and clearly unbelievable – "That asshole," she said, "He loves you, Queenie. Lighten up and go easy on him. Before he wises up and runs away with the circus or something. Do you know how much it would suck trying to tell people you were replaced by Bozo the Clown?"

Before the call had ended, Queenie's stomach had hurt from laughing so hard. The following day, she had called Brooklyn back to tell her that, after the dust had settled and tempers had calmed, Roy had repeated something almost identical.

"Well, duh," Brooklyn had said. "I'm always right. And this is where I'll tell you 'I told you so.'"

Shaking the memory away, Queenie wiped the moisture from her palm, unlocked her phone, and opened the message, dread immediately settling like a heavy brick in her stomach, predicting what she knew Roy's message would say. She wasn't wrong.

> I know you need this time, but please come home soon. The kiddos miss you. I miss you. You can't keep shutting us out every year like this. It's not healthy. You're stronger now; you won't lose your temper like you did the first time. Come home soon.

A tear rolled down Queenie's cheek. From the time she'd been a young girl, she'd known she wanted to be a mother. And yet, her sister was always supposed to be right there by her side. And after the twins were born, it appeared she'd get exactly that. Until that dream had been so brutally shattered.

Even so, there were times she'd get up in the middle of the night or whenever she was home alone, when the house was still, and talk to Brooklyn's picture mounted on the mantel at her house. She'd spend time relaying something funny that had happened or sharing the milestones, big or small, as they occurred.

Sometimes, she'd whisper her fears of failing motherhood and wifedom. And often, she'd confide her guilt that, after everything had happened, she and Roy had decided to move back to Oklahoma City, not Slaughterville the way they'd planned. She boasted about the way Micah had tied a string to her wobbly tooth and pulled it out herself; she laughed when she told her how, in T-ball, Ronnie had run the bases backwards, stopping to do a little dance at each before moving on until the boys on the other team were dancing along with him.

More than anything else, though, Queenie begged Brooklyn to please help them find answers, to find *her*.

She swallowed against the self-reproach screaming in her head that if she and Roy had never moved to Missouri in the first place, she would've been there and could've somehow prevented the tragedy altogether. No amount of therapy could convince her otherwise.

She released a shaky breath and then typed out her reply to Roy, deleted it, started again, deleted it. In a fit of frustration, she typed out the only message she knew would silence him, at least for now, and with an almost violent gesture, jabbed the send button before she could change her mind again.

> I'll be home by Friday in time for Micah's soccer game.
> Tell her and Ronnie I miss them.

His reply was immediate, as if he'd already typed it up and was just waiting to hit send.

> I love you, babe. Always.

> I know you do. Luv you, too.

Queenie set her phone down on the counter and slid to the floor, her husband's words the final chink in the dam holding back the rest of her emotions. God, if only she could build a time machine so that she could erase the past and stop all this from happening.

Something soft brushed along her legs, followed by a soft meow. Apollo, the once gnarly-furred, starved, and near-death tiny kitten Brooklyn had rescued shortly before her disappearance, and who now belonged to her, crawled onto Queenie's lap and rubbed his face into her neck, as if telling her he understood, that he missed Brooklyn too. A faint and fleeting smile crossed Queenie's lips as she remembered how Brooklyn had called to tell her that she and Apollo had come to a mutual understanding. Brooklyn fed and housed him and essentially spoiled him rotten, and Apollo allowed her to pet and even cuddle him on occasions. Unless he wasn't in the mood, in which case, a solid scratch along the chin was also perfectly acceptable behavior.

Queenie burrowed her face into the cat's neck. "Oh, Apollo, maybe this'll be the year we find the answers." When Apollo squirmed away so he could make himself comfortable on her lap, an unfamiliar yet not altogether unsettling feeling swept through her, accompanied by a sudden overwhelming feeling that she needed to turn on the television right away. In her heart, she allowed herself to believe Brooklyn was whispering the command into her ear.

Lifting a miffed Apollo from his cozy spot on her legs, she set him aside, pushed herself to her feet, and hurried into the living room of the cabin she and Brooklyn had managed to save after their parents had died. A sense of urgency she didn't try to decipher kept her on edge as she searched high and low for the remote, finally finding it sticking out from the corner of the sofa.

She jabbed the on button, and there on the screen, to the right of the reporter, flashed an image of six women, five of whom could've been Brooklyn and Queenie's sisters or daughters. A jagged, gaping hole ripped open inside her heart, and her throat constricted as all the air in the room seemed to evaporate. A wave of dizziness slammed into her, and she stumbled backward.

Icy coldness replaced the blood in her veins as she crumpled to the ground in a weeping heap. Was this the answer Brooklyn had wanted her to see? Was this the proof that she told herself she needed to accept that her sister was dead, her body discarded, somewhere not even her bones would ever be discovered?

Frightened by Queenie's gut-wrenching wails, Apollo darted to the back bedroom.

By the time Queenie managed to uncoil herself from the cold floor, the sun had gone down, shrouding the cabin in a hazy darkness, broken only by the light left on in the bathroom down the hall.

Unable to bring herself to her feet, she crawled the distance to the couch, and foregoing the energy it would take to crawl onto it, she grabbed the framed photo of her and Brooklyn the summer after she'd turned eighteen and cradled it to her chest, rocking it back and forth as if it were a child.

Over the next two hours, she heard her phone pinging with text notifications and phone calls. She ignored all of them.

So, she wasn't surprised when Roy suddenly appeared. One glance at his face told her all she needed to know. He, too, had seen the news report. Like her, he had come to the same conclusion.

When she hadn't answered his frantic calls, he'd taken the kids to his sister's house and come here, knowing she'd need his strength to get through whatever came next.

Quietly, he slid down beside her and gently gathered her into his arms as he murmured that he loved her, that they'd get through this, that he'd help her, and then fell silent as she shattered into pieces all over again.

Chapter Twenty-Three

Never one to crave or desire the attention of the spotlight, even if it was a necessary evil from time to time, Alyssa had been more than happy to hand Ryker the press conference reins. Not to mention that, after clearing it with her superior in the Bureau, it only made sense for Ryker to take the lead since she'd been the one living this case for the past five years. Besides, much like Alyssa didn't believe in getting into territorial pissing matches, neither did she allow ego to stand in the way of potential results. In the end, they all wanted the same thing.

To stop a killer.

Within minutes of Hammond ending the media's endless shouted questions by directing the viewers' attention to the new task force hotline and walking away, the department's phones had been ringing off the hooks. Since the very first call, not a single one of which could be considered credible, neither Alyssa nor anyone on her team had gotten much more than a twenty-second reprieve between callers. The racket of the jangling phones alone was enough to send her nerves through the stratosphere.

Coupled with the inevitable crackpots claiming psychic abilities or alien abductions, Alyssa was damn near ready to crawl right out of her skin and up the wall out of sheer frustration. To make matters worse, the endless ringing competing with the multitude of voices trying to be heard over one another sent piercing arrows of pain shooting through her temples.

As she listened to the latest dead-end caller drone on about his vision – that "fiery redhead murders" were an apocalyptic sign that Satan had risen from his throne in hell – Alyssa popped two ibuprofen gelcaps in her mouth and swallowed them with the last dregs of cold coffee in her cup. She tossed one longing glance at the empty pot. Would coffee stay hot in hell?

Finding no tactful way to end the current call, she simply scribbled the caller's name and contact information on a notepad, thanked him, and disconnected. From the sounds of everyone fielding calls, the information they were receiving was about as useful as a book of wet matches.

With so many people wasting their time, and worse, possibly making it much more difficult for that one person who may have credible information from getting through, her brain felt ready to explode. She needed coffee and answers, not necessarily in that order. She sincerely hoped that they'd been right in the timing of bringing the media in. Otherwise, this had just become a madhouse of their own making, not to mention it being a colossal waste of everybody's time.

She was about to say as much when Cord, Ryker, Tony, Joe, and Hal all ended their own calls, one right after the other like a set of falling dominoes, and all with the same expression of no luck, when Ruby appeared in the doorway. Something in the grouchy secretary's face as she addressed Alyssa had her intuition antennae perking up.

"Yes?"

Ruby's eyes swept the room, lingering for a moment on Ryker before shifting over to Alyssa. "There's a caller I think you're going to want to speak to. I took line two off so I could transfer her into here. Might I suggest you close the door and let the rest of us out here field the calls for a bit? I think you're all going to want to hear what this woman has to say."

With that, Ruby disappeared again, closing the door behind her, surprising no one except Ryker whose left eyebrow shot up in what could've been amusement or confusion. "Guess closing the door was less of a suggestion and more of a command we were expected to obey, huh?"

Hal snorted. "Stick around long enough, and you'll find that the majority of Ruby's suggestions are not-so-subtle demands." As he spoke, he kept his gaze firmly planted on the door.

Ryker shook her head, but before she could say anything else, the extension rang, and Alyssa snapped up the receiver, automatically placing the caller on speaker as she did.

"Detective Wyatt speaking."

A silence so heavy Alyssa could practically feel the weight of it settled in the room until finally a woman's shaky but determined voice crackled over the line. "Um, hello. My name is Queenie – well, Charlotte Knox-Bolton – but everyone calls me Queenie. The lady who transferred my call said you were the person I should talk to about the Sunset Slayer investigation."

Alyssa and Ryker both rolled their eyes at the ridiculous label the media had already saddled the case with, but she brushed off her irritation at the media's habit of sensationalizing serial killers because something in Queenie's voice had Alyssa's sixth sense roaring to life. Though she couldn't have explained it, she was suddenly overcome with the feeling that this woman was going to turn this investigation on its head... or put it on its feet and give them some traction. Either way.

Alyssa caught the expression on Ryker's face and knew the special agent sensed it, too. "Yes, I am. Is there something you'd like to share that you believe could help us?"

Queenie's response was little more than a whispered cry of anguish. "I don't honestly know if it'll help you or not. But I *do* have information you might find useful."

Alyssa's nerves teetered on pins and needles as she waited for the caller to continue.

"I don't know. Maybe this is a mistake. Maybe—" A breath of defeat accompanied Queenie's words, as if she'd already predicted what the team would tell her and was doubting her decision to reach out at all.

Cord, his deep voice calm and reassuring in that magical, therapeutic way of his, interrupted. "Queenie? This is Detective Roberts. You're on speaker phone with the members of the task force. Ruby, the woman you spoke with, thought your call was urgent enough to patch you through to us. So, why don't you go ahead and take a deep breath and share what you know. Let us determine the validity of what you tell us, as far as being helpful goes. That sound okay to you?"

"Yeah, okay." The quiver in Queenie's voice rendered her words almost indecipherable. Slowly, she began to unpack her story, picking up steam as she went.

"Six years ago this past April, my sister, Brooklyn Knox, disappeared after being attacked in her home." A soft, choked sob slipped out. "There's evidence to support the cops' theory that her killer took her and dumped her body somewhere else. What I mean is that her body was never found. And as much as I hate to say this out loud, I realize I may have to accept that we'll never find her, never get to bring her home. But that doesn't mean I don't want the chance to confront whoever did this to her, to us."

Ryker lifted a finger to indicate she had a question. "Queenie, this is Special Agent Newlin with the FBI. You may have seen me during the press conference."

"I did."

"Did the police ever mention the names of any suspects to you?"

Queenie scoffed. "No. Unfortunately, the police here never had so much as a single solitary lead on any suspects. Not one. How is that even possible in this day and age? Isn't it damn near impossible *not* to leave behind DNA?"

Through Queenie's frustration, Alyssa had homed in on one word. "Queenie, Detective Wyatt again. First, I speak for all of us when I say we're sorry to hear about your sister. Now, you just said, 'The police *here*.' Where exactly is that?"

Queenie released a fractured bark of laughter that bore no hint of actual humor. "Slaughterville, Oklahoma. And no, the irony of the name isn't lost on me. How could it be when my hometown's name held a bigger draw for the news jackals than the actual disappearance of my sister?"

The moment the word "Oklahoma" passed Queenie's lips, Ryker jolted to rigid attention, her eyes straying from curious to hardened and demanding. "Queenie, I don't suppose you can give us an idea how close Tulsa is to Slaughterville."

"About two hours, give or take. I heard you mention in the press conference that two of the victims were from there. Tulsa, I mean. That's one of the reasons I decided to call. But it's not the primary reason." Another determined sigh whispered through the phone line. "I know how this might sound, but every last woman you showed on the news report could arguably pass as my sister or at least be closely related."

A crackle of excited energy swept through the room.

Hal tightened his grip on the wheels of his chair. "Hal Callum, here. Do you happen to have a photo of your sister that you could send to us? Email or text?"

"Yes, of course. I can send either or both."

"Both, but a text might be faster." Alyssa rattled off her number. "Also, would you still happen to have the contact information for the detective in charge of your sister's investigation? If you don't know it off the top of your head, that's fine; we can request those records ourselves."

"I have it in my phone, though to be honest, and I'm not trying to be rude here, but *detective* is kind of a loose term. It's no one's fault, really. It's just that Slaughterville is kind of a small farming community, so until my sister's case, the cops' biggest issues were about stupid antics pulled by bored teens." She chuckled, a downhearted expulsion of air. "Hell, even Brooklyn and I did our share of dumb stuff when we were young. In a town like this, you're either bored or make your own excitement. All that being said, Jimmy Jacobson was the detective officially assigned to my sister's case, but he's got early onset dementia and isn't there anymore. But even if he was, the person you really need to talk to is Sheriff Harold Arnold.

"Even though I've given Harold no small amount of hell for letting Brooklyn's case go unsolved, he's never stopped trying to find out what happened to my sister. In fact, he was the one who called the Oklahoma Bureau of Investigation to request assistance when it happened."

Here, she snorted, the sound brimming with unbridled anger. "They declined, claiming there wasn't enough evidence for them to get involved yet. I didn't even know they could say no. They told the sheriff to call back if he got anything more *substantial*. What does that even mean? All I know is that my sister wasn't rich or famous enough for the OBI to step in. But hey, she was just another missing woman. No biggie, right?"

Completely empathetic to Queenie's rage at a system that had clearly failed her and her sister, Alyssa's stomach folded in on itself. "I know this probably doesn't hold much water with you, but I'm sorry. And we're all listening to you now." Her phone chimed. She snatched it off the table and tapped on her messages.

The blood drained from her face, and she flipped her phone around so the others could see the screen. Ryker took one look and shot out of her seat so fast, she sent her chair crashing to the ground.

Chapter Twenty-Four

Wednesday, August 30

Alyssa's head was still spinning with the implications of what Brooklyn Knox's image meant to their case… and to everything they thought they'd known when Queenie asked, "You just got the text with Brooklyn's picture, didn't you?"

"Yes, we did," Alyssa answered. "And you weren't exaggerating. The resemblance is uncanny." Her eyes swung over to the images of all the other victims, stopping at Madison Ortega's. Her heart sank, and her gaze swept the room, the same expressions of disbelief on the team's faces that Ortega was likely not their killer's first victim after all.

After recovering from his own shock, Hal dragged his laptop closer. Within a matter of seconds, he had pages of search options regarding Brooklyn Knox's disappearance and the presumption of her being dead, including an article written as recently as yesterday.

Alyssa took a deep breath and forced calm into her voice. "Queenie, I know this won't be easy, but I'm going to ask you to back up and start from the beginning." Deep in her gut, she knew Brooklyn Knox was the key to unlocking the full picture, to solving these cases. The key to stopping a killer.

Through a series of throat clearing, sniffles, and muffled sobs, Queenie detailed the events surrounding her sister's disappearance, explained how Brooklyn's best friend had stumbled into the crime scene, and how the authorities had found a gym bag stuffed full of bloody, monogrammed towels belonging to Brooklyn in a nearby pond. Alyssa couldn't help but wonder why someone would go to the trouble of trying to get rid of the bloody towel evidence without cleaning up the crime scene, as well. Something about it didn't quite make sense to her, and she found herself jotting down a note.

When Queenie finished, Ryker said, "Queenie, tell us about your sister." Tension caused the request to sound more like a barked command.

While Queenie spoke, Hal scrolled through online articles, clicked on a website, and then scribbled something resembling a phone number and a name on a piece of paper before sliding it over to Cord who snatched it up and shot to his feet. Halfway to the door, cell phone in hand, he turned and mouthed, "Sheriff Arnold. Catch me up later."

Alyssa nodded and listened as Queenie told them more about her sister.

"Brooklyn taught eleventh grade Honors History, as well as an elective course on the Roman Empire at Noble High, one of the towns neighboring Slaughterville. Teaching was her passion, what she was born to do. She thrived on getting kids to love learning. But it was more than just their education she cared about.

"She would listen to their teenage problems and wear their angst in her own heart, like she herself was going through that very same trauma with them. She cared that much, and because the kids knew it was real, they absolutely loved her. And because they did, she kind of became the safe place for the, let's say, less popular kids."

"What do you mean?" Alyssa asked.

"Well, for one thing, she absolutely did not abide bullying. Period. She had them check that drama at the door minute one. Enemies may not have been friends in her classes, but they sure as hell treated each other with reserved respect when they were in her classroom.

"I'm sure you've heard this from every family member on every case you've ever investigated, but I'm telling you straight up, everybody loved Brooklyn. Everybody. Those in her class and those who weren't, loved her, some of them more than their own parents."

When Queenie paused, Ryker used the opportunity to ask, "Did Brooklyn ever encounter issues with *any* students, parents, co-workers, a boyfriend, a husband? Anyone?" Beneath Ryker's words lurked the unspoken *no one is loved by everyone.*

"Not really. At least not that I know of. Brooklyn was very much married to her job as a teacher and mentor. And while she dated, including an on-and-off-again rela-tionship with the sheriff's eldest son, most of the guys she went out with grew tired of her devotion to her career real quick. But, if she had issues with anyone, she never told me about it, and we spoke practically every day."

After a pregnant pause, Queenie corrected herself. "Actually, I said Brooklyn didn't have any issues with any of the kids, but that's not quite true. About three or four years before she disappeared, there was one student in particular who she was starting to really worry about. I remember she said he was one of the more socially awkward ones − I don't even know if he was one of hers. Anyway, I guess he'd been getting harassed quite relentlessly. If he was her student, then, like I said, it wouldn't have taken place in her classroom.

"I think the main reason Brooklyn even told me about it was more because she was so upset and discouraged that, in her words, these kids simply couldn't foresee the possible ramifications of what they were doing. Or if they did, they chose not to care.

"Regardless, she rounded up who she thought were the biggest offenders, told them if she saw any more evidence of bullying that she'd march them all down to the office. She never really said if it stopped or not, and to be honest, I didn't think to ask. What I do remember is how she just casually mentioned one day that the kid had started working out and getting into shape. And then he moved away. Oh, but before that, around the same time, someone started leaving her flowers on her car, I guess. I'm assuming it was the same kid, but Brooklyn never actually said, so I don't really know."

"I think you may have already answered this, but did Brooklyn give you the names of any of those students?" Alyssa asked.

Queenie's reply was immediate and emphatic. "No. That was something she never did. Like ever. Brooklyn was very much a stickler about maintaining students' privacy, even when it came to talking to other teachers or even to me. Part of that was for their sake, sure, and part of that stemmed from the very real possibility that I might know the family of the kid."

Some of the air in Alyssa's balloon of excitement leaked out.

"Whoever this kid was, I do know that he was in the area before Brooklyn disappeared because he left her a jewelry box or something. She didn't tell me about it.

Mason Arnold, the sheriff's son and the guy she'd been on a date with, told me because he happened to be there when Brooklyn found the gift. He'd just brought her home from their date. Anyway, she seemed concerned when she saw it, so he asked her what was wrong. When he suggested Brooklyn call his dad, she refused, telling Mason the boy was confused not a delinquent, and then I guess the kid showed up at her house."

That got the team's attention. Until Queenie poked another hole in their excitement.

"But Brooklyn being Brooklyn — and fiercely inde-pendent — told Mason to stay put or she'd kick his ass, and trust me, she meant it. She wanted to spare the kid the embarrassment, so she handled it herself.

"Though Sheriff Arnold did his best, he could never figure out who the person was. But I also agree with the sheriff that it seems unlikely that a kid could've committed a crime like this and then hidden Brooklyn's body as well as he did. There's even been speculation it was a drifter passing through."

Despite Queenie's claim, Alyssa heard an undertone of doubt. As for herself, she thought it just as unlikely that a drifter would've bothered to go to the trouble of getting rid of the evidence or Brooklyn's body. She did a quick mental calculation, trying to determine how old Marcus Davis or Reginald Leach would've been six to ten years ago.

Tony shoved a note in front of Alyssa, and she read it, nodding her head. "Queenie, did you happen to recognize any of the women whose pictures were shown during the press conference?"

"No. I think I vaguely recall hearing about the two women from Tulsa back when those murders occurred.

But aside from their names being a blip on my radar, none of them are familiar to me. But just so you understand, I still wasn't in a very good space back then, and while I hope I don't sound callous, I simply didn't possess the bandwidth to read about someone else's tragic story; it just wasn't something I could do. A lot of days, it was all I could do just to drag myself out of bed to take care of my babies." Her voice fell into a whispered cry of anguish. "It never occurred to me that Brooklyn's disappearance could be tied to anyone else or be part of a pattern. Maybe if I had—"

Ryker cut her off. "Putting misplaced blame on yourself won't help us or you. So, let me offer some unsolicited advice – don't go there." Then, with her gaze glued on a picture of Marcus Davis, she said, "Queenie, I know this might not be easy, but I'm going to go through a list of names, and you stop me if you recognize any of them, okay?"

Queenie's answer was hesitant, almost confused. "Okay."

"Dustin Moses?"

"Wait, are these suspects you're asking me about now?" After a weighted silence from Ryker, Queenie answered. "No, the name Dustin Moses means nothing to me." She tried another tactic. "Should it?"

Alyssa admired Queenie's tenacious spirit. After all, it had been six very long, hellish years since her sister's disappearance. Though she herself had been only nine at the time of her own brother's disappearance, Alyssa had still suffered through the torment of waiting and not knowing, so she could fully sympathize.

"Marcus Davis?" Ryker's stare drilled into the phone as if she were trying to breach the solid object to see straight into Queenie's head herself.

"No. Wait. Maybe? I'm not sure. That one sounds kind of familiar, but I don't really know why. It's not someone I or Brooklyn knew well if we knew him at all. It's not really an uncommon name. I just don't know. Maybe a friend of a friend kind of a thing. But like I said, I'm not even sure about that."

A storm began brewing behind Ryker's eyes the moment Queenie had uttered the word, "Maybe." Marcus Davis, her prime suspect, even after her partner had claimed her single-minded focus was making her unhinged, just kept popping up over and over. It was like a bizarre, murderous game of Whack-a-Mole. And it couldn't possibly just be a coincidence. Not anymore.

Using her thumb, Ryker put pressure on the end of a pencil she gripped in her hand. When it snapped, she tossed it into the trash and transferred her energy to a pen she snagged off the table. "Queenie, is there any way you can find out if you or your sister somehow had any type of acquaintance with Marcus Davis, even if fleeting, or maybe find out if he was a former student?"

"I can try."

"I've got one more name for you," Ryker said. "Reginald Leach."

The defeat that whispered beneath Queenie's "No" hit Alyssa's gut like a sucker punch.

They questioned Queenie for a few more minutes, and just before she ended the call, Queenie said, "I can mail you copies of everything I've got, including the initial police report and a transcript of the nine-one-one call that Lindy, Brooklyn's friend, made. Hell, I'll even send you old newspaper clippings and all the internet articles I've printed over the past six years."

Alyssa's heart twisted at the offer. "Thank you, but that won't be necessary. At least not yet. As soon as we hang up, we'll request the official records and get in contact with the sheriff. However, there's more than a strong possibility that we'll be heading to Oklahoma in the next few days, and we'd like to get together with you and maybe have a look at those things then, if you wouldn't mind."

"Of course. I'll do *anything* you need. Oh, I almost forgot – I never took Brooklyn's social media offline. I know her passwords, so I'm happy to send them to you so you can scour her DMs and whatnot." Her voice cracked with raw emotion as the reality of the entire conversation finally caught up to her. "But the truth is I've already gone through all those, and there's absolutely nothing there that I could ever find. I know it probably sounds silly to keep her social media up, but sometimes, it helps me pretend like she's still here."

Even though Queenie couldn't see it, Alyssa shook her head. "No, it's not silly. In fact, if looking through your sister's social media posts is what helps get you through, then you should absolutely keep doing it."

"Thank you," Queenie whispered. "I'm trying really hard to keep my expectations in check because it's been six years with no answers. But for the first time in a very long time, I feel like there's at least a sliver of chance that we'll be able to bring Brooklyn home where she belongs."

"We're going to do our best," Alyssa promised.

After thanking Queenie and ending the call, Alyssa checked the time on her phone, stunned to see that eighty-seven minutes had passed since Ruby had first transferred the call. A few seconds later, Cord rejoined them, and everyone began talking at once.

Chapter Twenty-Five

All the faces of the women he'd killed stared back at him, their piercing eyes drilling him with accusations, confusion, and questions of *why*. All of them together. Connected. Their photographs – three on top, three below – framed against the blue backdrop graphic behind the man speaking at the podium. He blinked. Once. Twice. But their images remained frozen at the center of the media frenzy brought on by the press conference. His breath sawed in and out in uneven hitches as he double-checked to make sure his door was locked before hitting rewind and restarting the video yet again.

He stared at the pictures, as unmoved now as he had been when he'd ended their lives. Their deaths weren't what had him teetering on the edge of panic. That award went to the knowledge that the FBI had somehow linked the women together, and worse yet, had labeled him a serial killer. A serial killer that the media had already dubbed with the ridiculous moniker of the *Sunset Slayer* because the color of the women's hair reminded one of the reporters of a sunset.

The accusation swirled in his head. Serial killers were sociopaths who lacked empathy, who engaged in pred-atory behaviors like stalking and toying with their victims; they *hunted* their prey. Serial killers *enjoyed* the kill.

None of those things applied to him. Plus, an unempathetic person would never have spared Brooklyn's life.

Yes, he'd killed the women. But he'd never gone *looking* for them. Fate had always set them in his path, offering him further proof that saving Brooklyn had been the right thing to do, that they were destined for each other. Serial killers only pretended to love others while his love for Brooklyn was real, even if she refused to believe it.

Plus, he hadn't enjoyed the act. Never once had he done what he'd done for the thrill of it. It was simply something that had to be done to settle his bubbling rage. In that way, it wasn't all that dissimilar to someone climbing into a boxing ring to pound out his aggressions. His weight class, so to speak, happened to come in the form of redheads. If he didn't work out his anger on them, he might end up hurting Brooklyn again instead. And he loved her.

Like an infectious disease that had taken control of his mind and body, a sense of doom burrowed deep. If the authorities had been able to tie those six women together, how much longer before they tied the women to Brooklyn? And from her to him? Or had they already, and this was just the warning shot that they were coming for him?

Was this his first glimpse at staring down the barrel of his downfall? The thought of anyone stealing Brooklyn away from him caused his stomach to spasm.

Paranoia and panic collided.

He brushed his forearm across the sweat dripping from his forehead, accidentally moving the mouse on his keypad in the process. His eyes landed on the folder labeled Nanny Cam. The way the hair on the back of his neck stood up made him feel like he was being watched, and he swept his gaze around his space, floor to ceiling and along the wall, searching for hidden recording devices before he finally clicked on the camera.

Brooklyn sat stiffly on her mattress, the article he'd left for her clenched in her hands, the extra length of chain secured to the collar around her neck and tethered to the wall coiled beside her. He sometimes thought about unchaining her, but he knew he couldn't. Though she'd only tried once, he'd never trusted her not to attempt another escape. He wished things could be different, that he could trust her. But just because he loved her didn't mean he was stupid.

He traced his fingers over the monitor, over the dull hair, sunken eyes, and the protruding ribcage pressing against her nearly translucent skin. Six years ago, Brooklyn Knox had been beautiful and glamorous with a gaze that stole his breath and sank all the way into his soul. He still saw beyond her outward appearance to the stunning woman she'd been before. The woman she'd still be if only she hadn't betrayed him the way she had.

Shame filled him when he thought of how close he'd come to leaving her lying on her kitchen floor, bleeding out, with her back door wide open for the bugs and predators to feast on her like a buffet.

He shook his head. He almost had. But he hadn't. He'd *saved* her. A serial killer would never have done that.

In fact, a serial killer would've killed her after she'd attempted her escape; a serial killer would've killed *her* instead of taking out his anger on someone else when Brooklyn had tried to end her life by dragging a piece of metal down her arm. And a serial killer would've just killed her the one time she'd tried to trick him into believing that she loved him as much as he loved her.

Before he could stop himself, he fell back in time, reliving the painful betrayal as if it were happening all over again, tearing open those scars and making them bleed.

With his arms full, he descended the stairs carefully. He was leaving for Nebraska tonight, and he wasn't sure how long he'd be gone, so he was bringing Brooklyn a box of supplies and three new novels he'd heard some women raving about. He always missed her during these absences, even though, technically, he still saw her every day.

At the bottom step, he paused. Brooklyn perched at the edge of the mattress, head lowered, her fingers combing through her limp hair, as if she wanted to look good for him. When she smiled shyly up at him, he stumbled, nearly dropping the box and spilling its contents. Afraid to hope, his heart thumped painfully inside his chest, and he swallowed, surprised to find his mouth had gone dry.

"What has you so cheerful?" Because she'd betrayed his trust too many times already, accusation laced the edge of his question.

Her lips turned down into a pretty pout as she patted the mattress beside her. "Come sit with me."

His eyes raked the area. "Move over." He wanted to make sure she didn't have some kind of weapon hidden beneath her legs. Not that he knew where she'd get one. But it never hurt to be cautious anyhow.

She smiled in a way that he remembered she used to do when she thought someone was being silly, but she moved, revealing nothing but the depression in the mattress. All the tension in his muscles slipped away, and he sat beside her, his heart seizing when she grasped one of his hands in both of hers. His blood pumped hard and fast as he turned his hand until their palms touched, and he could interlace their fingers.

Then, she leaned into him and whispered the words he'd longed to hear, the words he'd known all along.

"I love you. I'm so sorry I couldn't see before that we're meant to be together. I just wasn't ready to admit it yet, I guess. But you'll forgive me, right? So we can go forward from here." She used her free hand to trace her fingers down his cheek, stopping at the corner of his mouth. "I've been dreaming about——" She stopped, turned away, but not before he saw the way her cheeks were stained red.

With his heart thudding against his ribcage, he cupped her face and turned her back toward him. "Dreaming about what?" Anticipation made it hard for him to breathe.

Warmth spread through his chest as she whispered shyly about her fantasy of the two of them walking hand in hand down the street, going on vacations together, of having him get to know her sister. If he weren't sitting, he might actually float away.

Unable to stop himself, he kissed her, his tongue sweeping along the seam of her lips. When she pulled away, hurt stung his pride.

"I'm sorry. It's just…" – she touched one hand to the chain around her neck – "being with you might be easier if——"

Of course. He should've thought of that himself. His heart feeling almost too big to contain inside his body, his fingers fumbled for the key he kept in his pocket. And then…

Her eyes flickered to the door, a look he recognized. And it wasn't love.

Enraged and humiliated in equal measure, he shoved her away from him and flew off the mattress. His fists clenched at his sides as he stormed across the room, pacing. The urge to take that chain and——

The sound on his computer crackled, dragging him back to the present. He was somewhat surprised to find his fist pressed against his chest, rubbing the ache away. He'd taken back the books he'd brought as a surprise and flown to Nebraska right after that. In the booth behind him at the restaurant where he'd stopped to eat, he'd overheard a woman laughing about how the guy she was sleeping with was a great sex buddy, but it wasn't her fault that he liked her so much more than she liked him.

He dug his fingernails into the palm of his hand and turned to glare at her. His entire body jolted in shock, and he nearly knocked over his glass of wine when he found himself staring at Brooklyn. He blinked once and then again until he remembered this woman couldn't be Brooklyn. He'd moved to the other side of his booth so he could watch her and then followed her home. He remembered his scalding fury when he realized she either had roommates or company. Unable to leave, he'd moved his car a few houses down and then fallen asleep. A crimped neck and fate had woken him early the next morning just as she was backing out of her drive, alone. He followed her to a forest trail. And left her body there for the bugs and scavengers, the way he'd been unable to do with Brooklyn.

The nanny cam crackled again, and he turned the audio up, just loud enough for him to hear over the staticky sounds of bad acoustics. Brooklyn's fingers trembled as she pressed the article he'd given her to her chest and closed her eyes. It was the most she'd moved since he'd last checked in on her earlier in the day. His eyes shifted over to the sink. When he saw that she'd eaten the birthday cupcake he'd left for her, pleasure replaced the ache the memory of her betrayal had brought on. Lips parting in a grin, he dragged the video's scrubber bar back, pushing play when he saw Brooklyn rolling off the bed. Then, he watched as, her defiant eyes locked on the camera, she grabbed the cupcake and dropped it into the toilet, flushing it away, before returning to the mattress and turning her back on him.

Red hot fury swallowed the excitement he'd felt just moments ago, and he slammed his fists down on the table, rattling the computer. He'd given her that article to prove that *no one* could ever love her like he did, even after everything she'd done to him. And this was how she repaid him for his thoughtfulness.

Barely aware of doing it, he dragged his knife from its sheath. It was her fault, not his, that he couldn't trust her, that the two of them couldn't make beautiful memories together like millions of other couples.

Each second he stood watching her stoked the fires of his rage until it felt ready to boil over. If it hadn't been for her, the FBI wouldn't be calling him a serial killer and hunting him down like a rabid dog that needed to be put down. If it weren't for her, he never would've killed those women in the first place, would never have found himself in this position. Maybe it was time to teach her a lesson. *Spare the rod, spoil the child.* The old Bible quote his grandfather used as justification for beating him with a stick popped into his head.

"Or" – he glared at the screen – "spare the rod, spoil the woman you love." His phone vibrated on the table beside him, but he ignored it. His mind filled with ways to make Brooklyn see that he was doing this for her own good. Less than a minute later, his phone vibrated again and then again.

Before he could check to see what was so urgent, someone knocked. Halfway to the door, he remembered the nanny cam and reversed his steps. He logged out of the app and slammed his computer shut. With one hand on the doorknob, he returned the knife still clutched in his hand to its sheath, caressing the hilt as he did and covering it with his shirt.

The smile of greeting on his lips died as soon as he swung open the door.

A tall woman with an athletic frame that reminded him of the person Brooklyn used to be the first time he'd ever seen her stood before him. Her brilliant green eyes expressed a nervous blend of young energy and confidence. But it was her red hair that struck him and kept his gaze riveted.

Her fingers fidgeted with the buttons on her blouse. "Hi. I was told to—"

He cut her off. He already knew why she was here. What he didn't know was who she was. "What's your name? I don't think I've seen you around here before."

The corners of her mouth tilted up in a shy smile. "Macey Travers. I just recently started."

She had a voice like bubbly champagne. He returned her smile. "Well, Macey Travers, nice to meet you. Why don't you come in a minute while I grab my phone and a few things?"

As he snatched his phone off the table, he glanced down and saw eight missed calls and six unread texts. With the press conference still fresh in his mind, he knew who they were from without even looking, and he didn't want to hear it. His hands curled into fists. *That* was another problem he'd have to take care of. And quickly.

He wasn't a monster, but he still wouldn't suffer from a guilty conscience for ending what he should've ended long ago. The guy had become too much of a liability.

Chapter Twenty-Six

Because of the vast circle of people Hal knew all over the country and in damn near every industry, along with his absurdly efficient talent of narrowing his search abilities to get exactly what he wanted, Alyssa had electronic copies of the Brooklyn Knox investigation in a fraction of the time it would've taken her or anyone else on the team to get them.

Tony had immediately gotten to work updating the victim map on the wall. A red pin, along with a miniature photograph of Brooklyn, joined the others. Each colored pushpin allocated a victim's home, as well as the location of her murder. Another pin had been added to include the pond in which police divers had discovered Brooklyn's gym bag filled with bloody towels. Blue and green pins indicated places where Leach and/or Davis, their two prime suspects, were known to have resided. Colored string stretched across the map to tie, even remotely, any links between the men and the victims. The visual was only the beginning of an incomplete story taking shape.

In addition to all of that, Hal had printed off no fewer than a dozen articles surrounding the mystery of Brooklyn's disappearance.

Spread across the table were crime scene pics for each woman. Alyssa and Cord studied those while Ryker cross-referenced the initial police reports of the other victims with Brooklyn's case, and Joe and Tony scanned through the hours of crime scene videos, each of them hoping to find that one crucial connection that would break the case wide open. In the meantime, Hal ran a search through the National Crime Information database to see if there were any other cases that matched their victim profile. Though Ryker said she and the Bureau had done this years earlier, they now had new information that would widen the search for possible victims.

Alyssa's stomach twisted into a knot of anxiety at the mere possibility.

More than two hours in, and Hal had compiled a plethora of missing or murdered redheaded women, but the cases he'd found had either been solved or didn't fit the main parameters of their search, including how the victim was killed. Though she told herself she knew better, Alyssa allowed herself to hope.

With images of the Knox crime scene in her hand, she got up and walked over to the map, tilting her head from side to side, as if by viewing things at a different angle, an answer might reveal itself. Something about Brooklyn's case scratched at the back of her mind like a physical sensation.

She returned to the table and compared the images in her hand with each of the other victims' crime scene photos. Why would he move Brooklyn's body somewhere else when he hadn't done the same with the others? There was no evidence that he'd even tried. It didn't make sense. Unless…

"He didn't kill her." Everyone stopped what they were doing to stare at her.

"He didn't kill her," she repeated. "The first two women were killed in their homes *and left there*. Every other victim was located where she was murdered. Not once did our guy go out of his way to hide her body. Six women, six locations. *Except* for Brooklyn Knox. And sure, it's possible he decided it was too much trouble disposing of a body where it wouldn't be found, but I don't think that's it because he left four of his victims out in the open. He doesn't care enough about them to dispose of them, to hide them. Simply put, he *doesn't care* if they're found. Something happened after he attacked Brooklyn that made him change his mind about killing her."

Skepticism showed in the lines of Cord's face as he tipped his head toward the gruesome and graphic images of Brooklyn's blood-smeared kitchen. "Even if he was overcome with remorse or regret and changed his mind, you know as well as I do that the chances are less than slim for someone to survive that kind of attack. So, what did he end up doing with her body?"

While Cord's point was valid, Alyssa didn't answer because she was studying the aerial photos Hal had just pulled up on Google Maps. Nestled behind Brooklyn's house was a heavily wooded area that had been thoroughly searched. Her body couldn't have been left there.

She talked through the scene playing out in her head. "Even if it wasn't under the cover of dark, it wouldn't be difficult to slip through those woods without being noticed. Even carrying a dead-weight body."

"But that doesn't answer the question of where she is." Cord turned to Hal. "Can you pull up a map from 2017 so we can compare it to this one?"

With a few clicks, Hal had two maps cast side by side onto the only available space on the wall. Ryker leaned back and flicked off the lights.

For several seconds, no one spoke. Not surprisingly, it was Tony who spotted an old ATV path barely visible in the woods. He drew a path from that spot to Brooklyn's house. "We know whoever killed these women must be strong enough to overpower and then kill them. A fit person could park his car up here and tuck it out of the way so no one spots it and then hike in the rest of the way. For whatever reason he decides to move the body, and pumped up on adrenaline, he hauls her body back to his car. Tosses her in the trunk, and…"

He let his words trail off because that was where his supposition ended.

Her lips pursed as various theories flitted in and out, yet always returning to the same primary thought, Alyssa shifted her focus to Ryker.

Ryker's eyebrows shot up. "Wait a minute. You're not—You're not actually suggesting Brooklyn Knox is still *alive*, are you? After six years? Like Cord just pointed out, that's one hell of a bloody crime scene for anyone to survive." Her hand waved over the photos as evidence.

Threaded through the incredulous doubt, Alyssa detected the faintest hint of possibility in Ryker's voice.

Trying to temper her own spark of hope, Alyssa shook her head. "If I'm being completely honest, no, not really. I mean, it hardly seems likely after all this time. But then again, I repeat: why hasn't her body ever been found?"

Alyssa's personal history with a kidnapped sibling played around the edges of her thoughts. How could it not? She only had to spare a fleeting look in Cord's direction to know her partner had guessed exactly where her mind had tripped back to.

"I know it's rare," she said, mentally shaking herself out of it, "but it's not unheard of for a kidnapper to hold his victim hostage for years. Decades in some cases. Just in the past few years, think about how many women presumed to be dead have been located. It's mind-boggling, for sure. But I'm going to go back to that one sticking point for me. Every single one of this guy's presumed victims has been discovered. I find it more than a bit peculiar that Brooklyn's body is still missing.

"And even though the sheriff in her case doesn't think someone so young could get away with this kind of extensive crime, we can't dismiss out of hand the idea that one of Brooklyn's former students did this. If he left her a gift like Queenie and the sheriff's son claimed..." She looked at Hal. "Did you ever find out if Marcus Davis or Reginald Leach lived anywhere in that area, or if it's possible either was ever a student at Noble High?"

Hal frowned. "Not yet. I contacted the school district and left two messages already, along with one email. Told them it was of the utmost urgency that they get back to me asap, but crickets so far. You know you're going to know the second I get word. However, I did call a cop buddy who retired up to Angel Fire a few years back. I gave him a brief rundown, and I didn't even have to ask; he offered to swing by and take a quick look at the house Davis's uncle owns. According to him, the house is dark and quiet, and the hotel said the conference ended before noon on Monday. So, what I'm trying to tell you is that Davis is currently in the wind."

"And according to Rory McEnroe at Enterprise, the car still hasn't been returned," Joe chimed in, "and she couldn't guarantee she'd be able to get that vehicle pulled from being cleaned and re-rented anyway, especially without a warrant. But at least she didn't shut us down completely. Well, except for sharing the vehicle's current location, that is."

Alyssa rubbed the back of her neck. "I understand why they won't give us his location without a warrant to back up our request, but at the same time, would it really hurt to bend a few rules now and then?"

Joe snorted. "Now, Lys, what would you say if you found out some stalker had called up and given the same song and dance to some soft-hearted person who just wanted to help, and as a result, someone ended up hurt or dead because of it?"

Alyssa narrowed her eyes. "Don't preach logic to me when I'm feeling frustrated waiting to get a bead on a suspect's whereabouts. Especially when the coincidences are starting to pile up just a little too high for Marcus Davis to be completely innocent. Not that I'm excluding Leach right now. There's something there, too; we just don't know what it is yet."

Just then, Ryker's phone rang. After a quick glance, she announced it was her superior checking in and asked Alyssa if she could borrow her and Cord's closet of an office for some privacy, excusing herself as she answered. Before she walked out, she hit the mute button on her screen and said to the team, "We don't have all the answers yet, but we're getting closer. I can feel it."

Chapter Twenty-Seven

Wednesday night, Alyssa locked her Tahoe and headed inside the restaurant, almost immediately spotting her family tucked away in a back corner. Relief spread across Brock's strained smile when he glanced up and saw her. One arm shot in the air, waving, as if she hadn't clearly already seen him.

The smiling hostess behind the podium greeted Alyssa. "Good evening. How many in your party?"

"They're already here." Alyssa snuffed out the guilt she felt anytime she took time to do something normal, even if it was with her family, when she had a case to solve. But it had been days since she'd done more than exchange texts with her children.

Her daughter Holly and Holly's husband Nick shifted around when they saw Brock waving. While Holly's face looked about as pained as her father's, Nick's was his usual mask of patience. Alyssa watched as her son-in-law wound one hand beneath Holly's blonde hair and massaged the nape of her neck. He smiled his greeting as Alyssa wove her way through the crowded dining area until she reached their table where Amber, Isaac's girlfriend, carried on a hearty conversation all on her own. She didn't so much as take a breath when Alyssa settled into the chair beside Brock.

If over-animation had a name, Amber would be it. It wasn't at all difficult to see how the girl had been captain of her cheerleading squad in high school. Though a bit on the obnoxious side, no one could deny the contagiousness of her excited chatter. "And OMG! Like seriously, he totally, totally kissed me on the cheek after he signed my poster. Eeek! Can you even believe it?" She shoved her arm in front of Isaac, nearly knocking his soda out of his hand. "Pinch me, baby, so I know I'm not dreaming."

With a scowl that could rival an annoyed librarian chastising unruly children running around the bookshelves, Isaac scooted his chair back and crossed his arms across his chest. One eyebrow shot up. "You might oughta consider soaking in some hand sanitizer instead of wondering if you're dreaming. Do you know how many other girls he kissed *before* you? And that's just in the few minutes leading up to your little meet and greet."

Alyssa coughed to cover up her startled laughter. No wonder her husband perched on the edge of his seat like he was contemplating an escape to let her deal with the drama.

Amber's face scrunched up, clearly displeased with Isaac's response. It didn't, however, stop her from carrying on for another full ten minutes, not even halting her play by play when the waiter came over to see if they were ready to place their orders.

Holly offered an apologetic smile before mouthing, "A couple more minutes, please." The waiter's eyes dropped to the top of Amber's head before offering a lopsided grin, nodding, and walking off to help another table.

Either because he was starving, finally fed up, or both, Isaac interrupted his girlfriend's animated monologue. "Amber, can we please take a beat to look at our menus and order? Also, we haven't actually seen my mom for, like, ever, and it'd be nice to, I don't know, get to at least tell her hello."

Everyone at the table sat back, stunned. Isaac rarely exhibited anything except laidback humor. He reserved his other moods strictly for his family and his best friend, Trevor. Amber's mouth dropped open, and then she huffed out a loud, "Rude." If eyes really were windows into the soul, then Amber's soul was really pissed off at the moment.

She shoved her chair away from the table so far that it forced a waitress carrying a load of drinks to sidestep rather quickly. For a heart-stopping second, Alyssa and the surrounding diners watched as the heavy tray teetered in the waitress's palm. A collective sigh of relief rushed out when she managed to get the tray re-balanced. Though she shot Amber a wilting look, Amber was too preoccupied with being offended by Isaac to notice.

Spinning on her heel, Isaac's girlfriend tossed a parting remark over her shoulder as she stomped away. "You know you don't have to be so mean to me."

The thought that popped into Alyssa's head was that Amber's exit would make for great television. A little uncomfortable with the entire scene, she cut her focus over to her son.

Isaac's hands were on the table, clenched, and he muttered something under his breath that sounded a lot like "nightmare" before he offered a blanket apology and stood to go after his girlfriend. But first, he melted Alyssa's heart when he came around the table, wrapped his arm around her shoulder for a quick hug, and dropped a quick kiss on the top of her head. "Hey, M. Hi. And don't worry; your hair is safe. My mouth has been nowhere near the '*oh so dreamy Mr. Romance.*'" He fanned his hands in front of his face and pretended to swoon.

Alyssa couldn't help it. She threw her head back and laughed until tears leaked from the corners of her eyes. Two steps away from the table, Isaac turned back again. "Um, would one of you mind ordering me the nachos, extra jalapenos. I'm sure if I can talk her into coming back in, she'll…" – he cocked his thumb toward the window where Amber could be seen pacing outside – "want a soft chicken taco a la carte."

Brock's smile said he felt for his son. So did Nick's. "You got it."

Isaac's shoulders dropped like a man preparing himself for a possible execution. Only after he slipped from view did Holly turn back to the table. "PhD in drama much? I have so many questions. The first one would be, why does he stay with her? I'm not even convinced he still *likes* her."

Nick's grin spread across his face, and even though Alyssa could tell Brock didn't want to be amused, his eyes gave him away. It took Holly all of a nanosecond to catch on to Nick's meaning, and she elbowed him in the side. "Eww. Gross. That's my brother you're talking about."

Nick's grin only grew wider as he shrugged. "You asked. And for the record, I didn't answer. I can't help it if your mind decided what you think my smile implied."

Before they got off on a separate tangent, Brock interrupted. "Hey, why don't we focus on what we want to order first?"

Since perusing the menu was little more than an exercise in reading since they rarely alternated what they ate at Sadie's, they made their decisions and then set the menus to the side. Holly immediately turned to Alyssa, burning curiosity shining in her eyes. "So, I saw Captain Hammond and that FBI agent on the press conference today. Serial killer, huh? Did you guys get a ton of cray-cray calls after that?"

After Isaac had been kidnapped a few years earlier, Holly had chosen to forego her Ivy League scholarship at Cornell University in favor of remaining closer to home to study criminology. While Brock had initially struggled with her decision, there was no denying the way Holly came to life when she discussed the cases she'd studied, and he knew she'd found the right career path for her. And though Holly knew Alyssa couldn't share details of her ongoing investigations, she never stopped trying. It always made Alyssa's already proud heart swell a little more.

"Yes, we did. And—" Alyssa stopped midsentence when she spotted Cord, Sara, and their four kids enter the restaurant. "Hey, there's Cord and Sara."

Shelley and Shane, their twins, saw Alyssa – or rather Nick – before Cord or Sara did, and the whole restaurant knew because Shelley squealed with toddler delight and ran through the maze of tables and over to Nick, where she excitedly leaped into his waiting arms and hugged his neck tight enough to cut off his circulation.

Shane, in turn, climbed into Holly's lap. Abigail and Carter, the two siblings Cord and Sara had adopted after their mother had been slaughtered, stuck with their parents as they approached the table. Alyssa's heart lique-fied once again when Abigail, slightly older than the twins, turned to Cord, arms raised for him to hold her. Crowds still tended to send her cowering back inside her shell.

Carter, the bravest little boy Alyssa thought she might ever have met, and always the staunch protector of not only his birth sister, but also of his adopted siblings, sucked in a breath and walked over to tuck himself into Alyssa's side. Despite her love and devotion to her job, Alyssa had always been a wife and mother first, and she couldn't deny that special oomph of pleasure at getting to add godmother to the list.

She squeezed Carter back and risked a light kiss on the top of his head, much like Isaac had done to her. "You've grown another foot, I swear."

Abigail's head popped up from Cord's shoulder, and she plopped her thumb from her mouth. Her face scrunched as she stared at Alyssa like she maybe wasn't the brightest bulb in the house. "No, he didn't. See?" She pointed to Carter's two sneaker-clad feet.

It took everything Alyssa had to keep a straight face as she peeked down and then back up. "Yes, yes. You're right. I can see that now. Thank you."

Shane twisted in Holly's lap and squeezed her cheeks between his palms, making sure she was paying attention to him. "Want to hear the joke I made up?"

Holly smiled. "Of course!"

Shane's grin turned him into Cord's mini-me. "What do owls say?"

Her eyes sparkling with amusement, Holly did her best impression of Winnie-the-Pooh thinking before she shook her head and said, "I don't know. What?"

Shane giggled. "Owlbuquerque. Get it? Owl-bu-querque!" His little body doubled over as he howled in laughter. Everyone at the table – and a few of the surrounding ones – joined in.

They were still chuckling when Sara excused herself to let the hostess know they would still be needing their own table. For the next several minutes, Alyssa divided her time listening to all four of her godchildren rambling at once as they told everyone about everything since they'd last seen them.

When Isaac returned to the table with a slightly mollified and much quieter Amber in tow, Abigail promptly released Cord's neck and threw herself into Isaac's waiting arms. A glance around showed some diners were equally as smitten as Alyssa, while others sneered in that way that said they preferred children never be allowed in a restaurant setting.

Finally, Sara sent a text that their table was ready, and Cord finagled the kids away, heading across the large expanse of the dining area. Over the next hour, everyone chattered and laughed together. Everyone except Amber, who scrolled on her phone and spoke only when someone aimed conversation directly at her.

Brock had just finished paying the bill when Alyssa's phone chimed with a text. She flipped her phone over and read the words that sent her heart sinking to her toes.

"We've got another one."

Chapter Twenty-Eight

Close to ten Wednesday night, Alyssa rolled down her window as she pulled up to one of the patrol cars blocking the entrance to Macey Travers's neighborhood. Beside her, Cord, who'd left his car at the restaurant with Sara, was on the phone with Hal. The officer waved to his partner, who backed up enough to let her through. Neighbors huddled in small groupings as they watched the action taking place at the very last house at the end of the block. To the north, bulldozers and other construction vehicles lined the otherwise empty mesa, ready to begin yet another residential build.

The flashing strobe lights nearly blinded Alyssa as she parked five houses away, the closest she could get. Off in the distance but growing closer, she heard the urgent cry of an ambulance's sirens.

Cord ended his call with Hal and the two of them headed up the walkway, where Alyssa spotted Ryker waiting for them in the doorway.

"We need to get a bead on where both Marcus Davis and Reginald Leach were tonight," was how the agent greeted them, her voice vibrating with barely restrained fury. Alyssa was right there with her.

"I agree." She motioned behind her. "Paramedics are almost here. I'd like to see what we've got before they take her away."

"This way." Ryker led the way into the kitchen where a young woman lay sprawled across her kitchen floor between the center island and refrigerator. It was like looking at a more updated version of the Brooklyn Knox crime scene.

In the living room, a movie was paused. On a champagne leather sofa, a man in his mid to late forties sat pale-faced and shaking, both arms wrapped tightly around his middle as he rocked back and forth.

"The victim's father," Ryker said by way of explanation. She shook her head. "Thank God for overprotective dads, that's all I can say. From what we can gather so far, the dad sent our victim a text asking her to call him. Said he just had this 'intuition' that something was wrong. And even though he told himself everything was probably fine, and that his daughter would give him hell, he got in his car and raced over when she didn't call or text back. I guess he lives about ten minutes away. Anyhow, when he got here, she didn't answer. The front door was locked, but Macey's car was parked out front, and so he let himself in with his key." Ryker waved his hand. "This is what he found."

"If the door was locked, how did Macey's attacker get in?" Cord asked.

Ryker pointed to a back patio door. "When the police arrived, they said that door was slightly ajar. So, best guess right now is that the unsub slipped in that way."

One of the crime scene analysts shifted, and Alyssa watched as two officers applied pressure to some of the victim's wounds. One of them glanced over her shoulder, her face red and panicked. "Where the hell are the para-medics?"

When the officer moved, Alyssa got her first real glimpse of the victim. The first thing she noticed was the striking red hair splayed out as if a photographer had posed her for a sick photoshoot. The silk pajama shirt she wore was little more than tattered cloth adhering to the multiple stab wounds on her chest. At first glance, Alyssa thought the attack couldn't have taken place too long ago because blood still bubbled from the X slashed across the victim's mouth. Angry red lines marred Macey's neck, but her throat hadn't been cut. Alyssa took in the father's countenance as he continued speaking to one of the officers, and then her gaze darted to the open back door. Had his arrival interrupted Macey's attacker?

Regardless of the reason, Alyssa was grateful that he hadn't stuck around to make sure he'd finished the job. "How in the hell does anyone survive that many stabbings?" Though the question had been rhetorical, muttered under her breath, Ryker answered anyway.

"Grit. Pure and simple."

"Whatever it is," Cord said, "it's nothing short of a miracle."

The same officer who'd demanded to know where the paramedics were growled. "Well, grit or not, we might still lose her if—"

The officer's words were interrupted by a deep, gravelly voice shouting, "Paramedics coming through."

Joe and Tony rushed in just behind the paramedics.

As they frantically worked to stabilize Macey Travers enough to transfer her to the stretcher, the atmosphere shifted from somber and angry to urgent and critical.

Alyssa, Cord, and Ryker stood back and watched the flurry of activity as one of the high-level EMT paramedics got an IV started while the others did what they could to slow the flow of blood. Someone snapped, "She's crashing."

Alyssa's heart sank. "Come on, fight," she whispered. It took her a second to realize the voice she heard wasn't her own echo.

Ryker, her attention riveted on the men and women fighting to save the woman's life, whispered her own words that matched Alyssa's. "Come on, fight."

A loud exhalation of relief rushed out when someone shouted, "We've got her back."

Cord and Tony cleared the way for the paramedics to get through while the young woman's father walked so close behind, one of the EMTs appeared to have two heads and three arms.

Within minutes, Macey Travers was loaded into the back of the ambulance, and they were on their way to Presbyterian Hospital.

Alyssa's phone vibrated in her pocket, and she pulled it out, noticing she had two texts, one from Brock, one from Isaac. She ignored them and answered the incoming call. "What did you find out, Hal?"

"I just got an email from Marcus Davis's receptionist. Davis has a flight out of Colorado Springs tomorrow night. Of course, she didn't divulge his current location, but you know as well as I do that Colorado Springs is less than a six-hour drive from here."

"Hal, I love you," Alyssa said.

"Yeah, I know. I'm a loveable kind of guy."

"What about Reginald Leach?"

"Still working on it. But I got the judge to issue a warrant, and the moment it was cleared, we were able to ping his phone. And Lys? It last bounced off the towers about a mile from where you are now. Also, the same judge signed a warrant to pull the Maxima from Enterprise's circulation when Davis returns it."

Alyssa swung around to tell Ryker, but the agent was standing close enough that she'd already overheard enough to get the general idea.

Her face was a hardened mask of determination.

The team was closing in. Just not fast enough for her. Or the women being attacked.

Chapter Twenty-Nine

A chaotic upheaval of muddled thoughts hammered at him from all sides, as if a host of people had taken up residence in his head and were fighting to talk over each other. He raked his fingers through his hair and paced the small confines of his kitchenette area, the grating sound of his boot heel scratching the gritty, un-swept floor, scraping at his calm. What had he just done?

This afternoon when he'd opened his door to Macey Travers, her hair rivaling the most vivid sunset, it was like fate had given him a second chance with Brooklyn. She didn't just look like her, she *sounded* like her. And the way she'd *gazed* at him, as if he were her entire world. If Brooklyn refused to love him after all he'd done to protect her, Macey would.

Throughout the day, he'd found himself making excuses to be near her, to ask her questions, to learn everything he could about her life, her favorite songs, her favorite movies. Later, when she'd shyly admitted that she'd considered following in her mother's footsteps and becoming a teacher, he'd known their destinies really were intertwined.

He thought of the way her cheeks had flushed so prettily when, unable to stop himself, he found himself whispering a line from a poem he'd once read: *Compared to your beauty, every rose pales.*

He tucked the strand of hair he'd twirled around his finger behind her ear, enjoying the little sting of electricity that the heated flush of her skin against his brought.

Getting her address had taken just a few simple clicks on the computer; learning she lived alone had been a wink from Fate. He played it back in his mind, trying to pinpoint where it had all gone wrong.

Unfamiliar with the area, he used his phone to navigate to her neighborhood, pleasantly surprised to see it backed up to the undeveloped mesa behind her house. Out of caution, he parked a few blocks over and jogged back. For a long time, he peeked over her wall and watched her carry a glass of wine into her living room, watched her turn her television on. Only when he was absolutely positive that she was alone did he make his way around to her front door where he paused to make sure she didn't have a doorbell camera. That she didn't convinced him it was yet another sign that they belonged together. Anticipation tightened his stomach as he knocked. When he stepped back so she could see him through her peephole, he nearly toppled a dead plant that she probably should've tossed ages ago. He made a note to do that for her. It would just be one of many things to come.

He heard the faint metallic sound of something being moved behind the door, and he waved, knowing she was being safe and checking to see who'd be at her door at this hour.

The door opened, a flush of pleasure staining her cheeks and sending a tingle of pleasure from the top of his head to the soles of his feet.

"Oh, um, hi." She slapped her hand over the cute way her voice squeaked and glanced down at her silk pajamas, her blush deepening even more. She leaned out, peered left and then right,

her perfect eyebrows arched in confusion. "Did I—did I forget something at work?"

He chuckled at the way her blush stained her cheeks the prettiest pink. "No. I know it's late, and I should've called or sent a text before just dropping in, but well, I didn't have your number, and so" – he held his arms out to his sides and smiled his most charming smile – "here I am. Can I come in?"

Confusion mixed with something else crossed her face before she shook her head just a bit and stepped back, waving him inside, closing and locking the door behind them.

His eyes dropped to the way her fingers wound together then lifted, to the way she flipped her hair out of her face with a simple twist of her neck. She giggled, a soft, nervous sound. "I'm sorry. I'm not… I'm not really sure… would you like a drink?"

He shook his head. He hadn't realized it then, but that was where things had started to go wrong. The simplicity of it all should've warned him that something was off. He'd followed her to the kitchen, and when she turned to grab a glass, he'd slipped in behind her, nuzzling her neck, kissing the soft flesh of her skin.

His heart raced as he waited for her to fall back into his embrace, to turn in his arms and wrap herself around him. Only that wasn't what she'd done. Instead, she'd recoiled from his touch and whirled around, shoving him back as she did.

"What are you doing?"

Her outrage had sparked his.

He closed his eyes, pictured Macey Travers lying on her kitchen floor, blood soaking through the tattered remains of her silk pajama shirt, tears leaking from the corners of her eyes, the accusation in them telling him that she didn't want him, that he wasn't enough, that she'd never love him. Just like Brooklyn never had. The whisper of sound slipping past her mutilated lips: "I don't understand."

A noise had penetrated his red-hot haze of fury before he could finish the job. He'd shoved to his feet, careful not to step in blood. Quickly, he'd slipped through her back door and over her wall.

Panic ate a hole in his stomach now. For the first time in six years, he didn't know what to do. From the second Macey Travers had stepped into his view, he'd known her fate was sealed, that they'd forever be tied together. He just hadn't thought it would be like this.

He opened his eyes. Maybe he was looking at this all wrong. Maybe the universe had put Macey Travers in his line of sight to show him it was finally time for him to let go of Brooklyn, no matter how much he loved her. No matter how hard he tried, no matter what he did for her, it was time to accept she'd never love him back, not in the same way he loved her.

Like someone had pulled the plug on his panic, his anxiety drained away. While his heart settled back into its normal rhythm, he grabbed an apple out of his fruit bowl and tossed it high before snatching it out of the air. Feeling lighter and freer, he whistled a happy tune and stepped outside.

He was, without a doubt, exactly where he was supposed to be.

And as much as he realized now what he needed to do, he also knew he couldn't watch Brooklyn die, couldn't risk changing his mind again. He'd have to think of a different way.

He waited for that familiar pang that told him he wouldn't be able to go through with it, surprised and a little sad when it didn't come. Complete freedom and a fresh start sat within his reach.

Patience was the key. The timing had to be perfect.

His eyes fell to the counter where his phone taunted him with two voicemails sitting unheard, a dozen unread text messages, and a slew of missed calls.

He snatched the phone up and scrolled to the number he needed. But as his finger hovered over the call button, he noticed the red scratches Macey's fingernails had inflicted crisscrossing the back of his hands, and the phone clattered back to the counter. He may have come home and washed the blood away in the shower, but he couldn't so easily wash this away.

Chapter Thirty

At nine forty-five Thursday morning, Alyssa, feeling every second of the lack of sleep she'd gotten since receiving the call about Macey Travers, strolled out of the hospital. On the downside, Travers was still in a touch-and-go fight for her life. Which meant the team still had none of the answers they were searching for. On the upside, the young woman's condition had been upgraded from critical to critical but stable. According to the doctor, they were far from out of the woods, but he remained cautiously optimistic that, at the very least, Macey Travers would survive her attack.

At just after one this morning, Macey's trauma doctor had joined them in the intensive care waiting area to give them and Macey's father an update. Afterward, Alyssa and Ryker both had insisted Cord call an Uber and go home. There was nothing he could do there at the hospital, and Carter, unable to sleep, had sent him no fewer than six texts needing to know where his dad was and that he was safe. With each message, Alyssa's heart broke a little more. As strong and brave as Carter had always proven to be, he was still just an eight-year-old little boy whose mother had been brutally slain while he hid in another room with Abigail. Knowing that his new dad went after the bad guys who did stuff like that gave him serious separation anxiety, along with a host of other fears.

Only after a promise that he'd be the first call she made if something in Macey's prognosis changed did Cord relent. Ryker made it another hour before conceding that she either needed to find an empty hospital bed or go back to the Albuquerque hotel she'd moved into late Tuesday night.

Before she left, however, she made Alyssa practically vow a blood oath that she'd also go home and attempt to get some sleep if nothing changed within the hour. Grudgingly, Alyssa had agreed. Which, to be honest, had probably been the main reason she'd finally dragged herself through her front door shortly before four this morning.

By six forty, with barely two hours' sleep, guilt won out. She needed to stop this killer, and she couldn't do that if she was lying in her own bed. She hadn't even waited for the water to heat up before standing under the cold spray and taking the fastest shower known to humankind. Dressed and hair brushed using fingers and a hairband, she gratefully snagged the travel mug of coffee Brock held out to her as she rushed out the door with a mumbled apology.

At seven fifteen, she and Mr. Travers were still impatiently waiting for word, and Cord called to let her know that first, Carter, who'd been unable to sleep until Cord got home and crashed next to him in his tiny bed, was doing much better. The main reason for his call, however, was to let her know Reginald Leach's attorney had reached out. The polygraph exam he'd agreed to was scheduled for eight thirty. Captain Hammond wanted to get it done before Leach or his attorney had a change of heart, so Cord and Ryker handled that while Alyssa waited for a full update on Macey's condition.

At a little after nine, she'd gotten permission from the medical staff and Mr. Travers to slip in and see Macey. With the belief that Macey could somehow hear her, Alyssa had stepped to the bed and promised the young woman that they'd find the person responsible for doing this to her, to bring that person to justice. For several minutes, Alyssa took in the tubes and machines keeping Macey's heart beating, stared at the jagged X slashed across her lips and the defensive wounds on her hands.

Through it all, Alyssa couldn't shake the parallels between Brooklyn and Macey, and not just their attacks. Even though each of the killer's past victims fit the same general description, the uncanny resemblance between Brooklyn and Macey was unmistakable. While she'd still been at Macey's house, Alyssa had spotted a framed photo of Macey with her father. It was like stumbling through a time jump as she stared at an image of a woman who could've been a much younger version of Brooklyn.

Which led Alyssa to the same question she'd had last night – had Macey's attacker had a sudden change of heart, much like she suspected had happened with Brooklyn, or had he been interrupted and slipped out the back door?

With an endless collection of questions churning in her mind, Alyssa stepped through the hospital's automatic doors and blinked, a little startled to be greeted by such a bright, sparkling, cloudless day. After the events of the past week, she half expected the world to be gray with a cold, drizzly rain to match her mood.

On her way to the car, Alyssa debated the wisdom of her plans to fly to Oklahoma with Cord and Ryker. Though Joe and Tony would still be around, she wondered if either she or Cord should also be available in case Macey woke. Her phone buzzed in her pocket, pulling her from her internal debate. Cord's name flashed on the screen. They must've finished the polygraph. Her stomach suddenly felt like a small pin cushion in a giant needle factory.

"How'd it go?"

"You first," Cord said. "How's Macey?"

"About like you'd expect. She's still deep in the woods with a helluva long path to go before she's out, but the doctor seems, in his words, cautiously optimistic. So, nothing we haven't heard before. Unfortunately, we won't be able to get any answers out of her for a while yet. Now you."

"Overall, the examiner called the results inconclusive – except for one very spectacular lie. Want to hazard a guess that won't really be a guess?"

More pins joined the pin cushion. "Reginald Leach lied about knowing Marcus Davis or about who killed Taylor Gray."

"You got it. But that's not all, Lys. We asked about the other women, too, including Brooklyn Knox, and there's definitely something there he doesn't want to share. Whether he killed all of them himself, or if Davis did, or they're in on it together, Reggie Leach knows a hell of a lot more than he's letting on. A lot more. But his attorney is a bulldog."

The name Cord dropped made Alyssa's heart plummet to her toes. Kurt Guerra. For Cord to call Leach's lawyer a bulldog didn't even hit the same ballpark. A poisonous viper would be a far more accurate description.

The headache brewing just behind Alyssa's temples throbbed in time with her heartbeat. "If Leach retained someone as powerful and expensive as Guerra already, that signals Leach knows his lies are starting to unravel. It's only a matter of time before his house of cards comes crashing down."

Whatever Cord said in response was drowned out by Hal's shouting. "Is that Lys you got there on the phone? Don't let her hang up. She's gonna want to hear this. You all are." Even muffled, Alyssa could hear that Hal sounded out of breath. Cord hit his speaker button.

"You'd think I'd just run a sprint instead of rolling in my chair." Hal's humor when it came to being in a wheelchair often sprouted its head at the oddest times.

Alyssa shook her head and laughed anyway. "What do you have for us?"

"You're never going to believe it. The 'shithole' Reginald Leach claimed to have been glad to ditch when his father moved him to Wichita was none other than Noble, Oklahoma. The town right next to Slaughterville where Brooklyn Knox taught high school. I'm still waiting to hear word about whether he was one of her students, but the second I find out, you'll know it."

All at once, the pieces of the puzzle shifted just enough for some to start falling into place. They weren't there yet, but the answers were closer. And Alyssa knew, unless something major changed in Macey Travers's condition, she needed to be on that flight out this afternoon to Oklahoma. She knew all the way to her bones that the answers they needed were there in Slaughterville. "What about Leach's connection to Marcus Davis?" she asked.

"All I can say for sure is what we already know. Davis and Leach attended the same school at the same time when they lived in Wichita. I did learn that Davis has a half-brother he doesn't really keep in close touch with, but I decided I'd try and reach out to him anyway. Was easy enough to get his contact info, so I called and left a message. Was honestly a bit surprised he called me right back.

"Turns out Davis doesn't really keep in touch with his brother because their father, who now needs round-the-clock care for a brain disease, lives with him, and well, let's just call a spade a spade. Or in this case, we'll call the dad a narrow-minded, bigoted child abuser, who thought Davis and, according to the half-brother, 'some other kid who may or may not have been Leach' were romantically involved and demanded the two end their friendship. Shortly after that, the family moved to the Nebraska area."

"Where Lauren Grand lived." Ryker's voice startled Alyssa because she'd forgotten she was even there.

Cord asked the same question Alyssa had. "I wonder if Davis could be the ex-boyfriend who roughed Leach up the other night."

Alyssa's head wobbled back and forth. "I swear you had something implanted in my brain to read my mind. I was just about to ask the same thing. I think Davis being the ex is more than just a strong possibility. If Davis's father really was abusive, it could be a learned pattern of behavior, and the whole apple slash tree thing. Maybe Davis knew Leach had moved to Albuquerque and came all the way down from Angel Fire, expecting a hook-up, and then lost it when he learned Leach had moved on with Jackson."

Hal threw in a new theory. "Maybe Davis wanted his uncle to hold onto that summer house in Angel Fire because it was their place to meet up in secret."

Something about all this didn't quite fit. "If Davis and Leach were romantically involved, that doesn't really explain why either man would be killing women who resemble Brooklyn Knox. We're still missing a huge piece of the puzzle here."

"Yes, we are," Ryker agreed. "But I'm betting that piece is waiting for us in Slaughterville."

Alyssa glanced at the clock. It was already inching toward ten thirty. She'd been so involved in absorbing all the new information that she'd barely registered the fact that traffic had come to a near standstill. She did a quick mental calculation and made the decision to take the next exit and head back toward home. "Listen, I'm stuck in traffic, and my navigation shows it's going to be at least half an hour before I get through this mess, which means by the time I get to the precinct, I'll just have to turn around and leave to go pack. So, I'm going to skip that step, and just meet up with you and Cord at the airport. Call me if anything comes up in the meantime."

Alyssa disconnected the call and grabbed her cup before she remembered she'd emptied the contents before she'd ever made it back to the hospital to check on Macey Travers.

"Damn it," she muttered. She needed caffeine, food, and sleep, and she'd take them in that order.

Chapter Thirty-One

Thursday, August 31

After several delays, one exhausting layover in Denver, and a raucously loud flight full of energetic athletes who'd just won some major competition, Alyssa, Cord, and Ryker finally landed at Will Rogers Airport in Oklahoma City.

Only to discover their reserved SUV had been accidentally rented to someone else. Thus beginning a new waiting game, which had Alyssa barely managing to hang onto her last shred of patience. While they waited, she scrolled through her text messages. One from Brock asking her to let him know when she landed. Two from Holly wishing her good luck on the case and another to ask when she'd be returning. One from Isaac in which he apologized *again* for the debacle at dinner with Amber. But the ones from Hal and Tony were the ones she wanted.

Tony:
No change in MT's condition. Will keep u posted. Obvs

Alyssa checked the time. Eight thirty-seven. Tulsa was a
ninety-minute drive away, and they had an early morning
meeting with the sheriff in Slaughterville. But at least their
hotel in Moore, Oklahoma, was a short twenty-minute
drive, which made tomorrow's drive only a half hour.

Alyssa shot off a quick thanks, shared the update with
Ryker while Cord tucked himself into a corner so he
could talk to Sara and the kids, and then she did her best
not to pace impatiently in front of the customer service
desk while they waited for a different rental. Hunger,
nerves, and her general dislike of being in crowded
airports all conspired against her, testing every ounce of
her self-control. Ten minutes later, whether the rental
gods were with them, or the manager could see the thin
sliver of patience Alyssa was clinging to, they were being
led out to their upgraded SUV.

Fifteen minutes after that, Alyssa hit the interstate.
"First place I see that isn't fast food, we're stopping. I'm
so damn hungry right now, I could eat roadkill."

Ryker pretended to gag. "Thanks for the visual. That
ought to help me keep my dinner down, whatever that
might be."

"I aim to please." Just as they came over a hill,
Alyssa spotted a digital billboard of a local family-owned
restaurant that proclaimed to have the "Best Barbecue

West of Kentucky." For as hangry as Alyssa was, the sign could've decreed they offered the second worst in the entire nation, and she still would've risked it. At this point, she felt like Isaac often swore he did – her stomach was gnawing on her spine.

Luckily, when she took the exit and spotted the restaurant, the overflowing parking lot, despite the hour, indicated the restaurant's claim might just be accurate.

Seventy-five minutes later, their bellies full and their patience restored, the three of them headed outside, where Alyssa glanced up, soaking in the night sky so dark and cloudless that the canopy of stars above their heads looked almost make-believe. On the drive to the hotel, the brightness of the moon helped light up the wooded landscape. A short drive later, they arrived at their hotel and said their goodnights. Less than forty minutes later, Alyssa's head hit the pillow, but instead of sleeping, she couldn't stop trying to fit all the random pieces of the puzzle together.

Maybe it was because she was in Oklahoma, but she just couldn't shake the feeling that Leach, Davis, and Brooklyn were all connected. She just didn't know how. Yet.

But more than that, her head swam with the same question that had been tickling the back of her mind since she'd learned about Brooklyn's case: where was she? She knew Cord was right, that the likelihood of Brooklyn being alive was slim.

Still, she couldn't help but ask herself: if – and it was a mighty big "if" – Brooklyn really was alive somewhere, that meant she'd been a prisoner to a serial killer for six years. And if that was true, what kind of mental state would they find her in?

Once again, she pushed out thoughts of her own family. This was about finding Brooklyn. Dead or alive, she deserved to be brought home.

Chapter Thirty-Two

He'd known that Macey Travers's appearance in his life had been fated, and now he knew he was right, just not in the way he'd thought. She wasn't replacing Brooklyn; no one could. He'd been out of his mind thinking otherwise, even for a second. No, Macey was put in his path so she could show him that it was time to move on.

To finish what he should've done six years ago. What he'd done with all the other women he'd killed because he couldn't kill her. He accepted that now.

And when a golden opportunity presented itself, it was just further proof that he was doing the right thing. A scene from a movie popped in his head. *Prove you really love her; let her go.* Of course, that had been a broken love story about a toxic relationship. Still, the same sentiment could be applied here.

He rushed around the house, locking windows, bolting doors, and packing. He checked the time on his watch and swore. He was running out of time. He needed to leave fifteen minutes ago.

In the workout room, he took a minute to look around. Out of everything here, he'd miss his equipment the most. More out of habit than anything else, he grabbed the remote and switched on the monitor mounted in the corner. Brooklyn appeared on the screen, her head tilted back as she stared up at the ceiling, as if she could somehow sense this was the last time they'd be together.

For a moment, he faltered. Could he really do what he needed to do? What if he gave her one more chance?

When she turned her face toward the camera, her physical appearance, for the first time, hit him. Who was he kidding? Even if she confessed her feelings, he could never allow her out in the public eye, not now after all these years, not looking like that.

There would always be speculation and accusations.

No, he could see it now. It was better for them both if he just killed her. It would be a clean break, like ripping off a band-aid. He'd find another love, and his heart would heal.

Besides, it wasn't a true love story if it didn't have a tragic ending because everyone knew that in every love story, someone had to die. He was sure he'd read that somewhere.

This time, when he looked at Brooklyn's broken form, all he saw was freedom to start over.

He checked the time on his watch again, relieved to see he really couldn't take the time for one final goodbye. It was probably for the best anyway if she didn't know what was coming.

With one last longing glance toward the basement, he whispered, "Bye, Brooklyn." Then, ignoring the stabbing pain inside his chest where his heart should be, he rushed around the house, setting the wheels in motion.

Chapter Thirty-Three

Early the next morning, after a quick stop in the dining room for a continental breakfast that consisted of coffee and a Danish, Alyssa, Cord, and Ryker were on the road heading to Slaughterville. Despite the reason for their visit, Alyssa couldn't help but be in awe of the landscape around her. Even though she'd grown up in the Midwest, it had been a long time since she'd enjoyed this kind of countryside. Close to seven thirty, they pulled into the gravel parking lot of the Slaughterville Police Station.

Inside, a woman in her late fifties greeted them with a welcoming smile and a natural charm that couldn't be more opposite to Ruby's usual scowl. Alyssa wasn't used to such chipperness so early in the morning.

"Good morning. I'm Betsy. Y'all must be the detectives from Albuquerque. I keep thinking I'll get there one day for the Balloon Fiesta. I hear it's spectacular."

Cord flashed his megawatt smile. "Nice to meet you, Betsy." He accepted her handshake as he introduced everyone. "I'm Detective Cord Roberts." He shifted to the side. "Detective Alyssa Wyatt and Special Agent Ryker Newlin. And you should definitely make sure you visit one day. I promise the Balloon Fiesta is an experience you'll not soon forget."

"Well, now, I'll do that. But y'all aren't here to jabber about my travel dreams, so let me just lead you on back to Har—" – she waved a hand in front of her pinkening cheeks – "I'm sorry. Sheriff Arnold's office."

Alyssa and Ryker exchanged grins when they saw that "leading them back" was a whole six steps away.

After firm handshakes all around, Sheriff Harold Arnold swung his arm in a wide arc toward a nearly full coffee carafe. "Betsy's coffee on her worst day is still better than any of those fancy shops. Can I offer you a cup?"

Alyssa pretended not to see Cord's knowing smirk. "I'd love a cup, thank you."

Like Cord, Ryker declined. After one sip, Alyssa nearly moaned out loud. Sheriff Arnold hadn't lied about Betsy's skills.

Behind his desk, Arnold's chair groaned its protest as he settled his hefty weight into it. He traded his smile for a scowl as he bypassed further chitchat and got right down to business. "I'm glad you're here." He shot a pointed stare in Ryker's direction. "Brooklyn's case has needled me for every single one of these past six years. Queenie told me that she mentioned how Brooklyn and my oldest boy, Mason, dated off and on through high school and every now and again as adults, whenever both were without a significant other." He folded his hands together and steepled them under his chin. "I'm also aware that Queenie informed you that Mason was the last person to see Brooklyn outside of the person who attacked and took her."

His head tilted slightly to the side, the sheriff paused. "I don't expect you to take my word for it, but I'm telling you now that my boy didn't have a thing to do with this. Fact is, whatever happened to Brooklyn messed him up pretty bad. To the point that he moved away about three years back. Not far, mind you. Just over the border to Arkansas City, Kansas."

Only because she'd studied a map of where all the victims had been found in relationship to where they could track Davis and Leach's steps did Alyssa recognize the town's name.

Sheriff Arnold leaned forward and snatched a tissue from the box near his computer and wiped the hint of moisture that had suddenly clouded over his eyes. "As I'm sure you could tell driving in, Slaughterville's a pretty small town. So, it wasn't just my boys who knew the Knox family. Back in the day, I attended school with Brooklyn and Queenie's mama and daddy. Good folks, those two. For six years, I've had to live with the weight and disappointment of knowing I failed them. If they were still alive, Brody and Candace – Brooklyn and Queenie's parents – they probably wouldn't be able to look me in the eye. Can't say as I'd blame them, seeing as how, a lot of days, I can barely look at my own reflection."

His attention returned to Ryker, his hardened eyes full of accusation. "Apologies, ma'am. Can't help but put a little of that blame at the steps of the Oklahoma Bureau of Investigations. Maybe if they'd stepped in when I asked, we wouldn't be meeting here today. And six more women would still be alive."

Ryker brushed the comment away. "No apologies necessary. I don't work for the OBI, and even if I did, you still wouldn't owe me an apology. Frankly, I'd be pissed, too. Correction: I *am* pissed."

Cord pulled the sheriff's attention back to him. "You mentioned that if Brody and Candace were still alive... When did they die?"

"When the girls were still in high school. Drunk driver spun his car straight into the path of an eighteen-wheeler hauling logs. Awful scene, that."

"What happened to the girls?" Ryker asked.

"Well, now, their mama's brother, as next of kin tried to take them in, but those girls were having none of that. They put up a squall the likes I'd never seen from them."

"Why's that?" Cord asked.

"How I recall is that Buster, er, Austin Frank, Candace's brother – had been estranged from the family for, lordy, some time. Brody, Candace, and I were still in high school ourselves when he got on the outs with his folks. Anyway, Buster got himself in with a rotten group and ended up involved in an armed robbery over in Moore. Just so happened, if you can believe it, a rival gang was trying to knock off the store at the same time, and the two groups found themselves in a shoot-out. The clerk called the cops, and when all was said and done, two individuals and one officer had been killed.

"Now, Buster, he sang like a canary, cut himself a pretty sweet deal since he didn't have a firearm in his possession when the police hit the scene. Did only about eight years before getting sprung early for good behavior. Lots of irate folks when he got out, I can tell you that much. Candace and her family had visited him a few times in prison, but he never showed an ounce of remorse. In fact, he saw himself as one of the victims. Anyhow, Candace went to her own grave believing her brother's choices broke her parents' hearts and killed them before their time."

Alyssa felt the weight of that story clear to her bones. "Do you happen to know Buster's current location and contact information?"

"Sure don't. After the courts ruled that Brooklyn and Queenie could be placed under the care of Brody and Candace's best friend, Buster learned he wasn't getting a lick of inheritance, not so much as two nickels to rub together, and he got real hurt-like. He tried to appeal to the girls, but they held their ground, and so he tore outta town. But not before he left behind a path of destruction the likes of an F-3 twister."

Harold Arnold wiped one hand over his thinning hair and down his face, a mix of what could've been shame and embarrassment tinging his sun-leathered cheeks with color. "Guess I shouldn't have said that last bit, seeing as I'm the law and the whole innocent until proven guilty thing. You see, everyone knew who'd broken all the windows and kicked in all the doors at Brody and Candace's house before setting fire to the barn. But nobody could ever prove it was him. And then he just up and disappeared."

A dozen follow-up questions swirled in Alyssa's head, but she went with, "And that was it? No one ever heard from or spoke to Buster again?"

"Well, now, I wouldn't rightfully say that. I believe he came back shortly before Brooklyn went missing. He didn't stick around long, though. Maybe a couple days, three at most. From what I hear tell, he was looking for some money."

Alyssa imagined her face wore an identical expression as that emblazoned on Cord's and Ryker's.

Sheriff Arnold noticed. "Let me be clear here, so you three don't go getting your hopes up and pinning the tail on the wrong donkey. Buster couldn't have done it. He'd gotten into some bar brawl and landed his ass in the county jail over in Tulsa at the time of Brooklyn's attack."

Though she believed the sheriff, Alyssa figured it wouldn't hurt for Hal to do a little digging. If nothing else, it could offer a little more insight into the family dynamics. And at this point, the more information they could gather, the better.

Sheriff Arnold pushed himself to his feet. "Let me show you the files we've got on Brooklyn's case." As he led the way to a closed door down the short hallway, he said, "I understand you're meeting up with Queenie over at Brooklyn's old house. I thought I'd tag along, if you don't mind."

"Not at all," Alyssa said. "On the contrary. We'd appreciate your input."

Inside the room, the box of evidence that hit Alyssa the hardest was the sports bag with the Roman Colosseum decal and the mounds of bloody towels, discolored as they were. She hadn't realized until that moment exactly how much hope she'd pinned on finding Brooklyn alive somewhere. Her heart heavy, she studied the evidence in front of her. No one could survive that much blood loss. There was just no way.

Chapter Thirty-Four

Just before eleven Friday morning, Alyssa and Cord stood with Sheriff Arnold in front of Brooklyn's home. Ryker remained in the rental, updating her superior while assuring him that there was no need for him to pull her partner from the case he was working on, nor any need to send another agent in his place because she had Alyssa and her team.

Alyssa admitted to feeling more than just a hint of pride hearing Ryker tell her superior that Alyssa, Cord, Hal, Joe, and Tony were "just as good, if not better" than any federal agents she'd ever worked alongside. They'd arrived at the Knox home shortly after, and so she had no idea what Ryker was saying now.

The soft purr of an engine pulled Alyssa's attention from Ryker's conversation, and she turned around as a silver minivan bumped along the long gravel drive, a cloud of fine dust trailing behind her, coating the car when it came to a stop. Inside the vehicle, a woman with sleek black, chin-length hair kept a tight grip on the steering wheel. Even from where she stood, Alyssa could see the woman's knuckles turning white. Despite Queenie's dark hair, the resemblance to Brooklyn was clear.

Sheriff Arnold strode over to greet her. Brooklyn's sister had barely uncurled her tall, willowy form from the minivan before the sheriff was reaching out to bring her in for a somewhat stiff, one-armed hug. After what appeared to be an awkward exchange between the two, Arnold led Queenie over to Alyssa and Cord.

Queenie wiped her palms down the front of her summer dress before shaking their hands. "I'm so sorry I'm late." She shifted her body slightly away from the house and sucked in a deep breath. "All of this has been so much harder on me than I realized. It's just — and please don't take this the wrong way — I'm afraid to let myself hope we'll finally be able to bring my sister home after six years."

Cord offered a warm, understanding smile. "I don't know many people who wouldn't feel the same if they were in your shoes."

A few seconds later, the car door closed, and Ryker joined them. She shook Queenie's hand, introduced herself, and then pointed toward the house. "Thank you for setting this up. We know it's not easy asking you to walk through the place where your sister was attacked."

Queenie brushed away a single tear and pulled a house key from the pocket of her dress as she led the way to the front door. "Eileen Crosby, the lady who bought the house, only lived here for six months after moving in. Not to get all *woowoo* on you or anything, but she swore Brooklyn haunted the place." Queenie's voice cracked. "Anyway, it freaked her out enough that she moved and rented the house out. The same couple who've been renting it since just moved back to Oregon so they could live closer to their grandchildren. So, aside from the furnishings the family left behind, the place is completely empty."

At the front door, painted a sunny yellow to match the railing around the porch, Queenie closed her eyes and sucked in a deep breath before inserting the key into the lock. "I guess it's not going to get any easier."

Inside, the brightness of the open floor plan felt at odds with the brutal tragedy that had taken place six years earlier. Silently, the five of them made their way into the kitchen, which, both Queenie and the sheriff agreed, looked much the same as it had when Brooklyn lived there, with the exception of new tile and a new granite-topped island in the center. At the entrance to the kitchen, Queenie stopped and wrapped her arms around her middle, swaying. Her head tipped toward the opposite side of the counter. "That's where Lindy found her." Her voice crackled with barely repressed emotion.

Cord looked over to Sheriff Arnold. "Does Lindy still live in the area?"

"She does, and being as how this is a small town, everyone already knows you're here, and she's as eager to speak with you as you are her. She's still the vice-principal of the high school, so we can either meet her there, though she'd rather avoid that if possible, or we can head over to her house. She's just a skip yonder on the other side of those trees."

Alyssa's eye followed the sheriff's finger to a wide window that looked out into what had once been Brooklyn's backyard.

Using the knowledge she already had and the photos she'd seen, Alyssa formed a mental picture of Brooklyn's attack as the sheriff walked them through the crime scene.

Cord alternated between scribbling down notes and using his phone to record what the sheriff was showing them.

The violent energy emanating off the walls of the house sent chills skittering up and down Alyssa's spine. Only after they'd inspected each room and stepped outside into the fresh air of the backyard did she finally feel able to take a complete breath.

Queenie stopped her with a hand on her arm. "Do you mind if I ask what you were hoping to find? I mean, it's not like there's still a crime scene here that you can get forensic evidence or anything. Can you? I think the video I took before I had the house professionally cleaned would be more helpful."

Ryker swung around. "You recorded your own video? Why?"

Queenie's eyes shifted to the left. "I don't really know. Punishment? Knowledge? Hope that I'd find something in it that the police overlooked? All of the above?"

"Do you still have it?" Ryker asked.

"Yes. It's saved in my cloud."

Sheriff Arnold squeezed Queenie's shoulder. "Ah, honey, I've told you a hundred times, punishing yourself won't do you or anyone else any good. Nothing you did or didn't do caused this." He hunched down until he was eye level with her. "You living here instead of Missouri wouldn't have prevented this."

Queenie's eyes darkened. "You don't know that, though, do you?"

A haunted expression on his face, the sheriff shook his head. "I should never have let you talk me out of hiring someone to clean the place, shouldn't have listened when you said you needed to do it yourself. If I'd known—"

Ryker broke the tension between the sheriff and Queenie by asking, "Do you mind sending us a copy of your video? It never hurts to have more information."

"Sure. I'll shoot you an email as soon as I get home. But I've studied that thing like a straight A student cramming for a major exam. If there's something there, I haven't found it."

Out in the yard, overgrown trees lined the edges of the property on either side in both the front and back, making a natural fence, not that there were any neighbors threatening to infringe upon the property line.

Queenie turned in a slow circle. "I guess I expected things to look different somehow." She nodded toward a weathered gazebo with midnight blue chairs nestled around a glass table. Her eyes took on that glazed look of someone seeing a memory only their mind could see. "I remember when Brooklyn bought that. Roy, my husband, helped her assemble it while I painted the chairs. We used to sit out here for hours and trip down memory lane."

After a few seconds, Sheriff Arnold led the group to a point just inside the tree line. As soon as Alyssa slipped into the trees, she felt like she was stepping into a new world where the forest simply swallowed them up. The sheriff retrieved one of the crime scene photos he'd brought along. He glanced at it once before handing it off to Cord.

Dragging one finger through the air, he drew an imaginary line along the ground starting from the trees and heading toward the house and then back again. "You can't see it now, of course, but if you look at that picture, you can see those deep impressions that look like shoe prints. We took a cast of them, but they turned out to be pretty common in brand and size. Anyway..." – he tapped the photo Cord held between his fingers – "first thing I noted when we found those was that they go back and forth several times. But the ones leaving the house are deeper than the ones entering the residence." Something sparked in the sheriff's eyes. "That tells me he was weighted down on the way out."

Queenie shuddered.

Cord snapped a few more comparison pictures on his phone, and Sheriff Arnold guided them deeper into the trees until they emerged into an abandoned cornfield. Across the way, maybe a quarter mile, they could see the back of three more farm-style houses. Beyond that, to the left, approximately what Alyssa would estimate as two city blocks, was a park, a sparkling pond at its center.

"That's where they found the sports bag and the towels," Queenie whispered as she angrily wiped her tears away with her fingers.

The way Sheriff Arnold stared at the pond gave Alyssa the impression that the sheriff thought if only he stared long and hard enough, the answers they'd always wanted would magically appear. He sniffled once and turned slightly to the side as he swiped at a tear. Then, clearing his throat, he said, "We had the towels tested, of course, but we were told the water destroyed any chance of obtaining usable DNA." A flash of anger and frustration registered on his face before he shook it away. "Back then, that field there was full of old farming equipment, logs, and a rock quarry. I can't remember the name of the company that purchased the land, but the farmers in the area fought whatever the guy's business was, and so, if I remember correctly, he moved his enterprise to Oklahoma City."

What Alyssa heard was that it wouldn't have been difficult for Brooklyn's murderer to go undetected as he trudged through the field and over to the pond to discard the bag. More importantly, he could've easily gone undetected as he carted Brooklyn Knox's body away.

"You mentioned not being able to find usable DNA from the towels or bag," Alyssa said, "but what about the house itself? I haven't looked through all the evidence records, but from what I've seen so far, there's been no mention of DNA. Am I to take it that none was found?" Disbelief coated her question.

"Actually, forensics identified DNA from my boy, Mason, as well as Lindy, the friend who came looking for Brooklyn. And one very partial DNA profile that we've found no matches for."

Alyssa's eyes shot over to Ryker. If they could get the phenotyping done, they had something to compare it to.

The five of them spent another half an hour walking the length of the pond and inspecting the area before seeing everything they'd come to see. While Queenie locked the house up, the rest of them discussed what they knew of Brooklyn's case and updated the sheriff on their list of possible suspects.

He recognized Leach's name, but not Davis's. "Didn't know that family well, since they only lived in Slaughterville a short time, maybe a couple of months before they moved to Noble, but I heard his name a few times with some of our locals."

By the time Queenie rejoined them, her hands were curled into fists, and her face had hardened. "Find who did this to my sister, to all those other women. I want answers, but more than that, I want him dead, and I'm not going to apologize for saying or feeling it. I don't care if you put an arrow through his damn brain. Just stop him. Ever since I saw that press conference, my nightmares have gotten worse, and this time, each one of those women become Brooklyn, and he kills her over and over again."

In her pocket, Alyssa's phone rang, but she let it go to voicemail and said the only thing she could say. "We won't stop until we find him."

Queenie squeezed Alyssa's hand with a vise-like grip. "Thank you." Her eyes swept from Alyssa to the others. "All of you. For the first time in six years, I'm allowing myself to hope. You have no idea how that feels."

Queenie couldn't have been more wrong, but Alyssa didn't correct her.

Chapter Thirty-Five

Back at the sheriff's office, Alyssa parked her rental and watched as Sheriff Arnold climbed out of his SUV and greeted a young man who'd been leaning up against a plum-colored Dodge Charger. By the way Arnold grabbed the guy and pulled him in for a back-slapping hug, as well as the resemblance to the sheriff, Alyssa guessed the mid-fortyish man must be one of Sheriff Arnold's sons.

Seconds later, her guess was confirmed.

"Mason, these are the detectives and special agent I told you about on the phone. Detectives, this is my boy, Mason, the one who was on a date with Brooklyn the night before she went missing."

Mason reached out to shake each of their hands. "Sorry that I didn't tell anyone I was coming. I wasn't sure I'd be able to get away. I'm sure you have questions for me, and I thought it might be better if you asked those in person, so here I am." He turned to his father. "We'll just use your conference room, if that's okay."

Sheriff Arnold clapped his son on the back and then wiped the sweat beading on his forehead. "What do y'all say we get out of this heatwave and into the air conditioning?"

Inside, Mason greeted the squeal-happy Betsy with a giant bear hug that lifted her two inches off the ground and apologized once again for not letting anyone know he was coming.

The sheriff interrupted his son's mini homecoming party by turning to Alyssa. "I'll get those boxes of evidence ready for transport, and Betsy here will have the paperwork ready for you to sign by the time you finish talking with my boy."

With that, he nodded once and walked off. Mason leaned low to kiss Betsy's offered cheek, exacted a promise of a slice of her apparently famous apple pie, and then led everyone to a conference room half the size of the incident room back at their own precinct. Mason moved around the table and sat down, immediately rocking his chair onto the back legs exactly like Tony always did.

Alyssa, Cord, and Ryker had barely settled themselves into their own seats before Mason opened the conversation himself. "Look, I just want to mention that there's not much I'm going to tell you that you can't read in the police reports from six years ago."

Alyssa appreciated Mason's directness as it saved them time. "We understand, and instead of asking you a bunch of questions, why don't you just run us through that night first, and we'll go from there?"

Mason set his chair back down on all fours. "Okay. Well, BK – Brooklyn – and I ran into each other at the supermarket in Noble Thursday evening and started shooting the breeze, and then I asked what she was up to Friday night, and we made plans to go out. Just a couple of friends." The smile he flashed didn't quite reach his eyes. "Not to be disrespectful to Brooklyn, but I guess I should admit I knew we wouldn't just be heading out strictly as friends. Chances were strong we'd end up in bed; we often did. That night, however, we didn't."

The sheriff's son sucked in a deep breath, closed his eyes, and exhaled slowly before opening them again. His gaze slipped away, unfocused, as if he were seeing the memory of that night in his head as he told them about it.

"I'd just brought her home from dinner, and when we were walking to her door, she noticed a gift propped up against a potted plant near her front door. It was wrapped in silver paper with a fancy red bow around it. She picked it up, looked at me, and shook her head, and that's when I realized she thought it was from me. The look on her face when I told her it wasn't – her smile just kind of faded away, and I could tell she was really bothered.

"As soon as we got inside, she opened it. It was a jewelry box with a little note inside. I don't know what the note said, and she wouldn't tell me. I could see something carved into the jewelry box, but Brooklyn put it away before I could see. Then she told me about a student who'd kind of developed a crush on her a few years back, told me that he'd left flowers on her car a few times."

"One of her students?" Cord asked.

Mason shook his head, a haunted look of regret causing him to avert his eyes. "I honestly don't know. All I can tell you is that it was a student who used to attend the high school."

Mason's breath shuddered out as he lifted his gaze to meet Alyssa's. "I asked her if she ever reported those incidents to the principal or anyone else, and of course, she said no." This time anger hardened the planes of his face. "She never wanted to embarrass any of the kids, whether they were her students or not. She always claimed they were young, and she didn't want some silly thing they did because they had a childhood infatuation to affect them. You see, this kid wasn't the first boy – or girl – to crush out on her. She genuinely cared so much, and yeah, she was hot to boot, so it didn't take much for some of the kids to confuse that for love.

"When I told her she needed to tell my dad, it wasn't because I actually expected her to file a complaint; I just thought he might have some helpful advice or something. She shot the idea down, told me this kid had moved away a few years before. She assured me he was just confused. And then the kid showed up."

"And you didn't get a single glimpse of this kid?" Ryker failed to disguise the doubt in her voice.

Mason shook his head. "Nope. Not so much as a peek. Brooklyn ordered me to stay inside, or she'd kick my ass – and she meant it – then she told me she'd handle it. She stepped outside and closed the door behind her. As much as it hurts my masculine pride, I listened. Partly out of respect for her wishes and partly because I knew she could probably handle herself. That being said, while I didn't look, I stayed close to the door just in case she changed her mind and needed me. She didn't, and when she came back inside, she no longer had the gift. All she'd say was that she returned it and told the kid she couldn't accept it. She got mad when I kept asking who it was, said it wasn't important."

Mason's eyes clouded over, and he jerked his head to the side as he wiped the tears away with his sleeve. "I wish I'd tried harder to find out. Hell, I wish I hadn't pissed her off and had stayed the night. But you know the saying about wishes, right?"

"And you don't have *any* idea who this kid could've been?" Ryker asked, her skepticism still evident.

"None."

Ryker glanced at Alyssa, then Cord, before turning back to Mason. "Do you recognize the names Reginald Leach or Marcus Davis?"

Mason tilted his head back, thinking. Finally, his lips pursed in disappointment, he shook his head. "Sorry, no." Then his gaze bounced from Ryker over to Alyssa and Cord. "Should I? If they were students at Noble High, Lindy would be able to tell you. Or might be able to. She didn't start working there until the year prior to all this. So, she wouldn't have known all the students. Or at least that's what she told me and the police back then."

Alyssa had already read that in the police interviews she'd skimmed, but she still planned on asking when they met with Lindy later that afternoon. They spent nearly thirty more minutes going over that night, but aside from Mason leaving near midnight when it was clear Brooklyn wasn't "in the mood," there was nothing more he could add that the team didn't already know.

By the time they finished speaking with Mason and gathered the boxes of evidence, it was time to meet with Lindy at the high school. There, Lindy offered no new information. She reiterated what they'd already read: that Brooklyn hadn't shown up for school, hadn't answered her phone, and when Lindy went to make sure she was okay, she'd let herself in, and immediately known something was wrong. She'd called Brooklyn's name as she went toward the kitchen, and that was when she stumbled into the nightmare. She'd immediately backed out and called nine-one-one.

Before they'd left her office, Lindy had handed over a decade's worth of Noble High's yearbooks. They'd thanked her and gone on to interview several other teachers, as well. To the last one, they all claimed not to have heard so much as a whisper of a kid leaving her gifts, either at the time of her disappearance or before. And just like Queenie had claimed, Brooklyn Knox was probably one of the most well-respected teachers or individuals Alyssa had ever heard of.

Alyssa thanked everyone for their time, and she, Ryker, and Cord climbed back into the rental. A quick peek at the radio showed the time inching close to one forty-five. Inwardly, she groaned. They still had a nearly two-hour drive to Tulsa ahead of them, and her stomach had decided to launch its highly vocal protest that it needed more than coffee and a Danish to survive.

She turned the ignition and cranked the air. "Fast food okay with everyone? We can eat on the road."

"Fine with me," Ryker said while Cord mumbled something from the backseat that Alyssa decided to take as assent.

She glanced at Ryker. "Any thoughts on which one?"

"Huh?" Ryker's brows threaded together. "Oh, you mean any thoughts on food." The furrows in her forehead evened out. "No preference." She twisted slightly in her seat to ask Cord and then shook her head. "Whatever's fast and on the way."

Alyssa grinned. "You know, I like you more and more all the time."

Ryker chuckled. "Good to know."

Twenty minutes later, they sat in the drive-thru lane of Wendy's waiting for the late lunch crowd to inch forward. In the meantime, Cord busied himself scouring through the dozens of police interviews he'd pulled from one of the evidence boxes.

Finally at the window, Alyssa handed over her credit card, grabbed the drinks and food, instructed her navigation system to resume the quickest route to Tulsa, and then headed for the interstate.

While Cord's focus remained glued on what he was reading, she and Ryker went over what they knew about all the cases, hoping if they bounced thoughts off each other, someone would drop that elusive piece of information they needed to find and stop a killer.

Alyssa slammed on her brakes when she suddenly came upon a wall of red lights. Traffic had come to a standstill caused by construction closing two of the three lanes for the next twenty miles, according to the sign. Resigned to the inevitable, she used the rearview mirror to peek at the top of her partner's head.

"Have you heard anything we've said at all, or are you completely absorbed in those police reports?"

Still not looking up, Cord said, "In a nutshell, your gut tells you that Brooklyn Knox was most likely our killer's first victim, despite her body never being found, which Ryker believes could hold the key to the entire case. If Brooklyn was victim one, then that would also most likely explain the *who* the killer is seeing when he murders these women. Which would make sense if it's a former student who became obsessed with her."

His hands shot out to stop the file from sliding onto the floor when Alyssa suddenly swerved to avoid a battered old truck that cut her off.

"Jesus. How I haven't had a heart attack being in a car with you, I'll never know."

Alyssa scowled. "Hey! That wasn't even my fault. And I'm a good driver!"

Cord offered a lopsided grin with his apology. "Sorry. You're right. Anyway, how'd I do on the listening front?"

All Alyssa could do was shake her head in amazement. She should never have doubted him. "How you stay so absorbed in whatever task you're working on and still store everything we said into some compartment in your brain is beyond me."

"You've clearly forgotten that I've got four kids at home, all still in the single digit age bracket. More often than not, they like to descend on me all at once as soon as I walk through the door. Instead of jockeying for position on who goes first, they tend to tell me all about their days all at the same time. Not that I'm complaining." The smile that broke out didn't just light up Cord's eyes; it lit up his entire face. "As such, I've learned to pick out the key points, so they all know I heard them."

Ryker twisted in her seat and nodded toward the file in Cord's hand. "Anything new catch your eye?" The way she asked made it clear she didn't really expect a yes. And she didn't get one.

"Nope. To be honest, I'm mostly scanning to see if anything jumps out at me that could possibly prove to be even a tiny link between Brooklyn and the Tulsa murders. If there's anything there at all, I'm not finding it yet."

"Well, maybe we'll get lucky when we reinterview Marcus Davis," Ryker said. "Providing he really did get back to Tulsa."

Alyssa's phone rang yet again, and she took her eyes off the traffic to see Hal's name.

"What've you got for us, Hal?"

Hal chuckled. "You know you should really practice your phone etiquette. Try saying hello before I develop a complex that you're only using me for my mad research skills."

"Hi, Hal. How've you been? We really need to get together for coffee one of these days. What've you got for us?"

Laughter filled the cab of the car. "See. Was that so tough? Never mind. Don't answer that." Like a light switch, Hal flipped off the humor and got down to the reason for his call. "I just got off the phone with the Last Stop-N-Go clerk, the one who remembered Jennie. Anyway, he mentioned remembering a dark-colored sedan pulling to the side of the building. But the person never came in, and he didn't give it much thought because he figured they were just using the dumpster. He called because he hadn't seen anything on the news about anyone being arrested for her murder and wanted to tell us, quote 'just in case.' And before you ask or get your hopes up, that's literally all the information he could provide. He didn't have a make or model, no license plate, and he didn't even notice when the car left exactly, other than it might've been around the time he recalled Jennie leaving. And the only reason he noticed at all was because he remembered someone laying on their horn right after Jennie pulled out of the parking lot."

"And Marcus Davis's rental was a dark-colored vehicle." It was a statement, not a question.

"Correct," Hal said. "Along those lines, Enterprise contacted us about an hour ago to let us know they've pulled the Maxima from circulation. I coordinated with Colorado Springs PD to get it towed to their impound lot for their techs to go over. They'll give us a shout before they begin so that someone on our team can be there for that."

Ryker's mouth dropped open. "Alyssa wasn't lying, was she? You really are the best, Hal."

Alyssa grinned. "Don't let a federal agent saying that go to your head."

"You already know it did. Now, how are things going there?"

"Unfortunately, we don't have much more than what we already knew. We hit one brick wall after another with the bullied kid angle. According to Lindy – Brooklyn's friend and the vice-principal who'd gone to check on her – as well as the principal and a few other teachers we were able to interview, they made it clear that bullying, like everywhere else, is unfortunately common, and many instances go unreported, either because of fear of retaliation or whatever. In other words, they could think of no one who stood out during Brooklyn's time there. Moreover, Queenie nailed it when she claimed her sister was tight-lipped when it came to dropping names because no one, Lindy included, knew anything about any gifts being left for Brooklyn. So, another bust."

Hal swore softly. "I was hoping for a name or two to use as a springboard, but I'll keep digging. Are the three of you finished in Slaughterville now?"

"We are. We're on the road to Tulsa. We wanted to speak to Dustin Moses—"

Hal interrupted. "He's the one who did time for domestic assault after Lauren Grand reported him for the assault against her friend, right?"

"Right. But if we're going on the assumption that all these murders link back to the same killer, then Dustin Moses is the wrong tree to bark up. Ryker spoke with the Omaha PD, and Moses can't be Jennie or Taylor's murderer because, after serving his entirely too brief sentence for his attack on Redding, in which he clearly didn't learn his lesson, he happened to assault another woman. That woman's brother happened to be a cop. Moses has been incarcerated for the past six months. We can cross him off our list, too. We're currently heading back into Tulsa to see if we can speak to Marcus Davis. Before you go, have there been any changes in Macey Travers's condition?"

"Not that I've heard. You'll be the first to know."

Alyssa tried to tell herself that no news was good news, but it didn't stop her stomach from hurting or thinking no news could also mean worse news. She thanked Hal and hung up, picking up speed after the construction ended. The closer she got to Tulsa, the harder she prayed they'd finally get somewhere with Marcus Davis.

Chapter Thirty-Six

Friday, September 1

Tipping the scales at two-eighty and hovering at a solid muscular six-foot three, Marcus Davis stood slightly taller than Cord. A ragged red scratch ran down the length of the right side of his face. To say he didn't look happy to see them standing on his front steps was a massive understatement.

He leaned in his doorway, his glare bouncing off Alyssa and Cord before staying glued on Ryker. "You again? Really? How much longer are you going to ride my ass? Just because you can't solve your case, you're damned determined to pin those murders on me. And now you're back with your buddies, to what, strong-arm me into a false confession? Screw you. Screw all of you. I've already told you, *you're barking up the wrong damn tree!*" He spit each word out through gritted teeth.

Alyssa slapped her hand against his door before he could close it on them. "Now that you've expressed how you really feel, we'd still like to ask you a few questions. If you want to make this more official, we can have you go downtown to the Tulsa police station. They've kindly offered their interrogation rooms to us."

Davis snarled, his entire face transforming from pissed to downright frightening. Alyssa could see why Ryker felt strongly that he could be their man. She intended to find out one way or another. If he was, he'd know they were back on his trail, and if he wasn't, they could clear him for good and move on.

"So, would you like to invite us in, or would you like to take a ride downtown?" Cord prodded. "Your call."

Marcus shot a look over his shoulder before turning back to them and holding the door open for them to enter. "Sonofabitch. But I'm going to tell you this one time only; the first hint I get that this is going wrong, that you're taking my words out of context, I'm cutting it off and calling in my lawyer. I'm probably a damn idiot for not doing it first anyway."

Inside his cluttered house, he swore again. "This is just bullshit. I've got nothing to hide – still – so let's get it over with." He shoved an orange cat to the floor and sat in a grossly stained blue recliner. He neither bothered to clear a spot on the sofa overflowing with all sorts of clothing, nor did he offer them a seat anywhere else.

From the looks of the place, Alyssa would've been too grossed out to sit anywhere anyway. If a person's environment was indicative of their mindset, "organized" was not at all an attribute she'd assign to Davis. "Chaotic" was much more like it. But then, if he really was their killer, could this be a sign of his escalation?

Primarily because she suspected it might take them longer if Ryker was the one asking the questions, Alyssa decided to take the lead. "Why don't we go back six years, and you tell us where you were living."

"Why? You already know I was living outside Tulsa. Isn't that why you guys want to pin this shit on me? I lived in the relative proximity of the murders? Because I'm the only man who did, I guess."

"Look, man," Cord said, his diplomatic mannerism almost instantly cutting the tension in the room in half. "I know you're pissed over the whole thing, but this'll be a lot easier if you cut the attitude and help us out here. If you're as innocent as you claim, I'd think you'd want to clear things up and get us out of your hair sooner rather than later. Frankly, if you're as innocent as you claim, I'd like to mark you off our radar myself so we can get on with finding the real culprit. What say we help each other out with that?"

As if Cord had sprinkled cheery fairy dust in the room, Marcus Davis turned into a different person, making it obvious why the company he worked for had crowned him their shining star as a marketing rep. The charming smile alone made it simple for Alyssa to picture the man standing on a street corner selling snow in the middle of a blizzard. Which didn't mean he wasn't guilty. In fact, all it showed her was that he could schmooze his way through anything.

Davis settled deeper into his chair. "Look, I can appreciate how you want to nab this bastard. Trust me, I want you to, too." He raked his fingers through his hair, and blew his breath back out, a nauseating odor of onions accompanying the exhalation and making Alyssa fight not to wince.

Cord touched his own face. "Why don't you start with telling us how you got those scratches."

Marcus pointed to his cat. "Minx. When I got home last night – or rather early this morning – she didn't exactly welcome my apology when I scooped her up. She's mean like that."

True or not, Cord accepted Davis's answer and moved on. "Why'd you end up moving so quickly after Lauren, a woman you claimed to be practically engaged to, was murdered?"

Marcus shifted in his seat and stared out a window partially covered with a ghastly red curtain. "I'd just recently gotten the job at SCJ Headhunters, and that's why I left Nebraska and moved back here. After Lauren… after she died and then hearing that she didn't reciprocate the same feelings for me as I'd had for her, like I thought, I jumped right into a relationship with a woman I met online. She lived in Muskogee, and so when I moved back, she let me stay with her for a while until I found a place of my own. I stayed there about a month. And shortly after I moved out, she broke it off with me."

He narrowed his eyes at Ryker. "And no, her breaking it off didn't piss me off so bad that I went on a murder spree. Just in case you were going to ask. Like you did last time."

Aside from Ryker lifting one brow, she gave no reaction to or comment on Davis's statement.

"Do you mind if we get her name?" Cord asked.

"Cora Brighton. She still lives in the same place."

Cord scribbled the information into his notebook. "You two stay in touch at all?"

"Hell, no. You stay in touch with any of your exes?"

Cord shrugged. "I did at one time. Lost touch with most of them. You said she broke it off after you moved out. What happened?"

Marcus shrugged. "Damned if I know, man. Maybe she was just on the rag that week or feeling extra hormonal. Got me."

In her head, Alyssa offered another opinion. *Perhaps because you're a bit of a slob, not to mention your heavy leaning on the side of misogyny?*

Where Alyssa had kept her thoughts quiet, Ryker did no such thing. She snorted. Loudly. And exactly in the way Alyssa's mother-in-law, Mabel, would label highly unladylike. "Of course. A woman's menstrual cycle or hormones could be the *only* possible reasons for breaking it off with someone as charming as yourself. Give me a break."

Marcus remained unfazed by Ryker's comment. "Look, I don't know why she broke it off. Maybe she found someone else. We stopped having sex about two weeks after I moved in with her."

"And she never said why?" Alyssa tried and failed to hide her skepticism that Marcus had no idea what had caused a rift in the relationship.

"I never said that. She just said she 'wasn't feeling it,' you know?" Marcus again looked to Cord.

"Feeling what?" Cord asked.

"She didn't think we were going to go the distance, I guess. And yeah, she wasn't wrong. She was fun while it lasted, and after everything that went down with Lauren, no way was I ready to settle down with a wife, a white picket fence, and two-point-four kids, a golden retriever, and a dying goldfish from the state fair."

"Did you know Madison Ortega, Daphne Morrow, or Jaime Asandro?"

Both hands shot up in the air. "No. Well, I mean I know of them because I read about their murders. But I had nothing to do with it. Hand to God. I've already sworn to this a dozen times."

Ryker cocked her head to the side. "Daphne Morrow worked temporarily as a receptionist at the SCJ branch here in Tulsa. Only she went by Daphne Gilbert then. You sure you want to stick with that story?"

Alyssa's head snapped in Ryker's direction. When had she learned that information? Ryker refused to look at either Alyssa or Cord.

All the color drained from Marcus's face, and he shook his head, vehement in his denial. "Jesus, lady, you really want me to be guilty of this instead of finding the real guy? You know tossing me in prison for it just means the real murderer is free to keep killing, right? Like, you get that?"

His head continued moving back and forth as he turned his pleading gaze to Cord. "Look, if whatever you said her name was worked there, then I didn't know it. The Tulsa branch has close to a thousand employees, and more often than not, I work remotely. Other than meetings, I rarely set foot in the building. Anyone there will confirm that." A mottled blend of red burst color back into his face as he divided his glare between Ryker and Alyssa. "I swear on a stack of Bibles a mile high that *I didn't do this*. I'm innocent."

Hoping to take advantage of his distraction upon hearing the news of Daphne Morrow slash Gilbert, Alyssa asked about his most recent trip. "Speaking of working remotely, we understand you've spent some time in Colorado and New Mexico over the last week."

Davis glared at her. "Yeah, so? Is there a question there somewhere?"

"Were your travels work or pleasure related?"

"Both. I flew to Colorado Springs to meet with a client, then I drove down to Angel Fire for a conference, then I came home."

"On Monday, August twenty-eighth, you were pulled over for running a stop sign in Moriarty," Alyssa said.

If them having knowledge of that bothered Davis, it didn't show anywhere on his face or in his body language. "I repeat: yeah, so?"

"What were you doing in Moriarty if your business was in Angel Fire? That's a nearly three-hour drive."

Marcus Davis rolled his eyes. "Jesus. My 'business' wasn't in Angel Fire. I had a conference there. My uncle owns a house there. I didn't realize I wasn't allowed to explore the state in my free time. What the actual—Never mind. I wasn't in Moriarty for anything particular. I'd heard the Manzano Mountains had some good hiking, so I did a little exploring. Afterward, I stopped at the McDonald's in Moriarty to grab a salad and something to drink." Davis swore under his breath. "What with the ticket and now this, I can promise you I'll never go back, that's for damn sure."

So far, his story seemed believable if not one hundred percent verifiable yet. So, Alyssa asked one of the questions she most wanted to see his reaction to. "Tell us about your relationship with Reginald Leach. When's the last time you saw or spoke to him?"

If Davis hadn't been sitting down, she was certain he would've toppled over. "Reg—Reggie? Why?"

Alyssa didn't answer.

Marcus raked his fingers through his hair, tugged once, then dragged his hands down his face before dropping them to knead his thighs. "I saw Leach a few days ago up in Angel Fire when he came by to visit. Sometimes he crashes there; sometimes he doesn't."

"Were you the one who roughed him up for moving into a new relationship?"

Marcus recoiled as if Alyssa had reached out and slapped him. "What? No. Did he say I did? Jesus. No.

288

No! We weren't… I mean, we never… Look, it wasn't like that for us. We were friends. That's all. But back in the day, my dad thought Leach was my boyfriend because he overheard Reggie telling me he wasn't, like, purely straight or whatever. I didn't care then, and I don't care now. But my dad said Leach and I couldn't be friends anymore. I hadn't lived here long, and Leach was about the only friend I had at the time, so we kept in touch anyway. And yeah, for a short time, Reggie thought he liked me, but he moved on when I told him I'm strictly straight."

"You said you and Leach kept in touch anyway. Even after Leach moved away from Wichita?" Cord asked.

For a second, Davis fell silent, and then suddenly, his head snapped up, his eyes widened, and his mouth dropped open. "Oh shit! You don't think *Reggie* did this, do you? No way, man. No way. I would've known."

"Would you?" Alyssa asked because she was genuinely curious if he believed what he was saying.

"Hell, yes. We might not have seen each other all the time, but I was as close to a best friend to Reggie as a person could get."

Ryker frowned. "Reginald Leach doesn't seem like a shy guy. I'm betting he has a few friends."

"Sure, fake friends, maybe. People who want to use him as a stepping stone, but I'm telling you Leach couldn't have done this, either."

"Did you know Jackson Gray, Reggie's current boyfriend?"

Marcus looked away again, but not before Alyssa caught the flicker of doubt in his eyes. "I knew of him but never met him. Reggie told me he'd met him at an audition in Texas." Slowly, almost as if it physically pained him, he turned his gaze back to Alyssa and then settled back on Ryker. "And yes, I heard about Jackson's sister on the news. It was playing in the hotel. No, Reggie and I didn't discuss it when he dropped in to see me. I didn't even think to ask him about it, and he never brought it up, so, make of that whatever you want. But I'm telling you yet again, lady, I didn't do this. And for what it's worth, I don't think Reggie did, either." His laugh held no humor. "But I'd rather you tether your hook to him than me."

Ryker ignored that. "You said you explored the state a little. Did those explorations take you to Taos, by any chance?"

Marcus frowned. "Well, not technically. But it's only, what, a forty-minute drive from Angel Fire? Taos has never been my jam. Too artsy for my tastes. I guess their skiing areas are great, but so are Angel Fire's, so I tend not to venture over to Taos." His sigh hinted that he was nearing the end of his patience. "Why? Did someone get their feelings hurt in Taos, and you need to pin that on someone, too?"

Ryker's eyebrows shot up. "In a manner of speaking, you could say that. If by hurt feelings, you mean, did another woman get murdered, then yeah, someone's feelings got real hurt up in Taos. While you were in the area, I might add."

This time, all the color drained from Marcus's face. "Holy shit. I didn't… I mean, I didn't know. Okay?" His gaze shot over to Cord. "Christ, I didn't know. Shit. Shit. Maybe it's time I end this interrogation and call my lawyer." Marcus's voice shook in a way that sounded real to Alyssa.

"It's your call." Cord jerked his head toward Marcus's phone. "You can ring him now and have him meet us at the police station, if that's what you're comfortable with."

The expression on Marcus's face reminded Alyssa of the proverbial deer caught in the headlights. He didn't know which direction to go. Finally, pressing the heels of his hands into his eyes, he muttered, "Damn it!" He glanced up again, a hint of fear in his voice. "I hope I don't regret this, but I'll keep answering your questions. I've got nothing to hide. I'm innocent."

Because she was beginning to think Ryker might not be right about this guy, Alyssa breathed a sigh of relief at not having to navigate through an attorney blocking every question with advice not to answer.

"I have another name for you then." Ryker moved in a few inches closer to Davis. "Brooklyn Knox."

The blank expression on Marcus's face could've been faked, but Alyssa didn't think so.

After giving it a few seconds, he finally answered with a definite "No."

Ryker didn't relent. "Ever been to Noble or Slaughterville, Oklahoma?"

Davis scooted back in his chair, subconsciously trying to get farther away from Ryker's advancements. "Probably. I really can't say one hundred percent one way or the other. If I was, it was probably just driving through."

For the next hour, they grilled Marcus before Alyssa finally felt like they'd gotten enough. At the door, Marcus Davis took her by surprise when he offered his hand, beginning with Ryker.

"Look, I know I'm an asshole, okay, but I swear on my late grandma's grave, I didn't kill anyone. Not now. Not ever. I hope you find who *did* do it, and soon. And I pray to God it's not Reggie. And I don't want you to find the guy just because I'm sick of being under the FBI and now New Mexico police's cloud of suspicion. From what I heard on the news, those women didn't deserve to die like that."

Ryker studied him. "You know how bad it'll look to us if you call up your old buddy Leach as soon as we leave and warn him about our conversation, right?"

Davis scoffed. "Like I said, I don't think he's your guy any more than I know I'm not, but I'd still rather you hang your hat on his head than mine, so—"

Despite the growing gut feeling that Davis wasn't their man, after all, Alyssa tried to keep in mind his remarkable salesmanship. "We appreciate your cooperation. We'll contact you if we have any more questions."

"Sounds fair, but I sure as hell hope you don't." With that, Marcus closed the door behind them.

Back in their SUV, Alyssa started the ignition and drove away before sharing her initial thoughts, unpopular though they may be. "Ryker, I know you liked him for these murders, but I have to say my gut isn't in alignment with yours. I believe him. I don't think he did it. I don't even know if I think he was smart enough to pull it off. But going just off his personal environment, Marcus Davis is *far* from being an organized individual, which is in complete odds to the psychological profile you built yourself."

Ryker sighed and leaned her head back against the headrest. "I know. And frankly, I think you're right. There was something completely different in Davis's mannerisms this time. In all his other interviews, he was far removed from being forthcoming. If you think his arrogance at the beginning was bad today, you should've seen him a few years ago. He was unbelievably and obnoxiously full of himself. But beyond that, I don't think he has the wits or patience to go about a murder spree the likes of what we're dealing with."

Cord piped up from the backseat. "I agree with both of you, but let's not entirely cross him off our list just yet. I want to see what Cora Brighton has to say, as well as talk to some people at SCJ Headhunters. But if Davis isn't our guy, and Leach is, we're now at risk of Davis letting Leach know, despite the warning."

"Nothing we can legally do about that," Alyssa said. "It's not like we can ban him from talking to the guy. But I believe him when he said he'd rather the focus be on his old friend than himself, so I doubt he'll say anything. Besides, Leach already has a pretty good idea he's on our radar. So, I say let's go talk to Cora Brighton and see what she has to say."

With everyone in agreement, Alyssa put the SUV in gear and waited for Ryker to enter Brighton's address into the vehicle's navigation system.

–

They didn't get back to their hotel in Moore until after midnight. Cora Brighton offered nothing new, aside from validating what Davis already told them, as far as their relationship had gone. Before they'd left, Ryker had asked her if she'd ever met Reginald Leach, but Cora claimed she'd never heard of him. The employees at SCJ, while kind and accommodating – most likely due to the shocking revelation that Davis had called to request that they answer any questions the "cops" had – revealed nothing new. Which, in a way, was kind of a step forward, when Alyssa really thought about it. It helped them put Davis another step in the way of being cleared.

Not much closer to any answers, they'd head back to Albuquerque in the morning and debrief the team. Despite everything, Alyssa couldn't shake the feeling that a break in the case was near.

Ignoring the time, she sent Hal, Joe, and Tony a text, including Hammond at the last minute, even though she knew it would drive him nuts.

> We need to keep tabs on Reginald Leach.
> I think we might be getting close enough to request a search warrant for both his residence and vehicle.

She wasn't even slightly surprised to see Hal's immediate response.

> I'll get on it first thing.

Chapter Thirty-Seven

After yet another long flight and tedious layover, Alyssa, Cord, and Ryker landed back in Albuquerque forty-five minutes later than the two-fifteen arrival time they'd expected. The second the plane's wheels hit the tarmac, Alyssa took her phone off airplane mode, and the screen immediately filled with a list of missed calls and texts.

Almost all of them were from Hammond and the team. She opened the top one from Tony.

> MT awake. Still high on pain meds but we can get in there to talk to her. Let me know when you land.

Alyssa showed her phone to Cord then Ryker. And realized their plane had stopped its taxi to the terminal. The captain's voice explained they were waiting for another plane to clear the gate but that they'd be disembarking soon and thanked everyone for their patience, especially during the more turbulent moments of the flight.

After scanning through the rest of her messages, she shot Brock a quick text.

> Just landed. Rough flight. Not sure when I'll be home; heading to hospital to speak with Macey Travers. Will try to txt later. Love you.

Brock's reply came less than a minute later.

> Good luck. BTW, Mom's here, and Isaac mentioned something about stopping by later today. So did Holly. Love you.

The usual pang of guilt settled onto Alyssa's shoulders. She hoped she'd make it home in time to see everyone, but it didn't do any good to make promises the family knew she might not be able to keep. So instead, she shot off a *thanks* and a heart emoji. Her personal business taken care of, she tucked her phone back into her pocket and settled in to wait.

The delay only lasted about five minutes, but with Macey Travers awake, as well as the antsy attitudes of all the passengers, herself included, it felt more like five hours. After finally disembarking, Alyssa seriously considered leaving her luggage in baggage claim and returning for it later. But since it rarely took long, she figured she could stand to be what passed for patience a little longer.

Only after she made it through the long line of vehicles paying for parking did her tense muscles start to relax as she shot down the interstate, lights flashing but siren silent.

Because it was Labor Day weekend, and many people had left town Friday, traffic was lighter and smoother flowing than Alyssa had anticipated.

They weren't quite as lucky with parking downtown at the hospital, and it took nearly fifteen minutes of cruising the enormous parking lot to find a space. Inside, she tried to temper her expectations, knowing that Macey, if she were alert enough to talk to them, may still be unable to answer their questions.

Outside Macey's semi-private room, a positive sign in itself that she no longer needed to be in the intensive care unit, Alyssa took a deep breath and then, along with Cord and Ryker, stepped inside the tiny cubicle space of a room. Thankfully, the other bed remained empty, allowing them the privacy their questioning would require.

Both of Macey's parents sat in the hard plastic chairs that Alyssa knew acted more like torture devices than anything offering a modicum of comfort. Having already met Mr. Travers, Alyssa introduced herself and the others to Macey's mom.

"I'm Detective Wyatt. We met your husband the other night."

Mrs. Travers spared only a brief glance as she took Alyssa's offered hand, and in a way that was clearly not intended to be a snub, returned to squeezing her daughter's fingers instead of also shaking Cord's or Ryker's hands.

Alyssa stepped to the bed, her heart sinking at the nearly vacant stare that appeared in Macey's eyes. It didn't bode well, but as she often did in situations like this, Alyssa let her instincts guide her.

"Macey, I'm Detective Wyatt" – she pointed to Cord, then Ryker – "and these are Detective Roberts and

Special Agent Newlin with the FBI. I know you might not feel up to it quite yet, but we need to ask you a few questions about what happened at your house Wednesday night."

Tension immediately traveled down the young woman's entire body as evidenced by the way she stiffened beneath the covers. Mr. Travers, hovering like a hawk, noticed and shouldered his way in to grip his daughter's other hand.

Mr. Travers brushed the hair out of his daughter's eyes, kissed her forehead, and whispered something only Macey could hear before righting himself and nodding his head for Alyssa to continue. In complete odds with the turmoil churning inside, Alyssa forced calm into her voice. Witnessing any victim's emotional trauma, not to mention the outward physical damage, never failed to impact her on a personal level.

"I know you might be afraid to talk to us, to tell us what happened," she began. "But we really need you to tell us what you can." She hesitated, conscious of the damage done to Macey's mouth, the stitches pulling the skin tight. "It might be easier for you if you write it down."

Macey briefly turned her unblinking stare in Alyssa's direction before directing her vacant gaze toward the room's only window. Macey's mother repeated Alyssa's question. Macey removed her hands from her parents' grips and tugged the hospital blanket higher over her throat, hiding the dark bruises of strangulation, but aside from that one movement, her lips remained closed.

Alyssa understood how difficult it was for any victim to talk about an assault, but she also needed answers in order to stop this from happening to someone else. "We're sorry for everything you've endured, and we *need* you to know and understand that we're on your side and are working tirelessly and diligently to run down every single lead to capture the person responsible for doing this to you. We want to bring you – and his other victims, including the ones who were unable to escape with their lives – the justice you all deserve."

A haunted look replaced her vacant stare even as a flicker of hope flashed across Macey's face. The tears pooling in the corners of her eyes spilled over. Several silently tense seconds passed before Macey's gaze drifted to the hospital tray nearby.

Mr. Travers followed the direction of Macey's stare. Understanding dawned, and he pointed. "Honey," he said to his wife, "the notebook."

After flipping the spiral open to a clean page, Macey's mother handed her daughter the notebook and pen sitting atop it. With trembling hands, Macey wrote, each letter seeming to take a heavy toll. Three words later, she turned the notebook around.

Alyssa read the choppy, scribbled words out loud. "How many others?"

Macey blinked twice.

Ryker caught Alyssa's eye to let her know she would take this one. "Seven others. You would've been number eight if your father hadn't shown up at your house."

Mr. Travers's head snapped up. "Seven? The press said six."

Macey squeezed her eyes closed and clutched tightly at the hospital covers before grasping at her father's hand as he took hers in his much larger one, offering the only protective comfort he could. The beeping machines provided a nerve-wracking concert as they all waited for Macey to continue. When she did, it was difficult to miss how the physical and emotional struggle drained her strength as she scratched out her next words.

Again, Alyssa read them aloud. "Don't know." She raised her eyebrows. "You don't know? Are you saying you don't know who did this to you or that you can't describe him?"

From the way Macey's eyes suddenly shifted away, Alyssa knew the young woman wasn't being honest.

Macey pressed the tip of the pen hard into the paper and scribbled dark, heavy lines beneath the same words, taking her anger and fear out on the page.

Alyssa and Cord exchanged knowing looks. "Did you know the person who did this to you?" Understanding and compassion softened her question.

Macey's eyes darted around the room, almost as if she were searching for a means of escape.

Which gave Alyssa the answer Macey couldn't. She knew her attacker and was too frightened to admit it. It wasn't the first time Alyssa had seen this. "Macey, do you recognize the name Reggie Leach?"

Macey's lower lip trembled, but she shook her head *no*. Again, Alyssa didn't believe her.

Neither did Ryker. "Macey, I know it's not easy after what he did to you, but you have to trust us. We're on your side, and we want to make sure the person responsible is brought to justice. You can help us make sure that happens. You just need to be honest and talk to us."

In response, Macey closed her eyes and refused to open them again. It didn't take long before her breathing evened back out, and her chest began to rise and fall in a steady rhythm that indicated she'd slipped into the welcome abyss of the drugs in her system.

Frustration, even if they understood why, settled in as Alyssa and the others had no choice but to accept they'd get no answers from Macey, at least not today.

Out in the corridor, Mr. Travers apologized. "I'm sorry. Give her some time. She's terrified right now. Rightfully so." Eyes filled with accusation found Ryker. "All those women on the news that could be Macey's sister… well, I'm trying real hard to tell myself this is no one's fault but the sonofabitch who did this, but I've gotta tell you, it's really difficult not to ask why you haven't caught the guy before now. Aren't you the goddamned FBI?"

Though Alyssa was certain Mr. Travers's words must have felt like arrows piercing the skin, Ryker kept her emotions and voice in check. "There's absolutely nothing I can say that will make any of this better, I know that. But trust me when I tell you that, from the deepest depths of my being, I'm sorry. I know that doesn't change anything, but I really am."

Mr. Travers may not know it, but Alyssa did. Ryker's words weren't empty. She really was sorry. It was why she'd been breathing this case for the past five years, and as such, felt Macey's attack on a personal level.

Mr. Travers swallowed, then nodded once. "Thank you for that. My Macey's always been such a trusting little girl, but—" He wiped one hand down his face. "God, do you have any idea what it's like to see your own child lying in a hospital bed, terrified out of her mind? Do you have any idea what it's like knowing you weren't there to protect your own child?"

Mr. Travers's questions were all rhetorical, and had he not been so preoccupied with worry for Macey, he probably would've seen that yes, both Cord and Alyssa were acutely aware of what that was like.

"Look, maybe Macey will talk to us when she wakes up. I promise I'll tell you anything she shares with us." His voice cracked with raw emotion. "You asked Macey about someone named Leach. Is he the person you think did this to my girl?"

Alyssa didn't know how to answer that question, so all she said was, "We're working every angle we have right now."

Macey willed her breathing to remain steady as she listened to the detectives leave her room. The hand her father had been holding felt cold to the touch.

Before this job that she'd fallen into, Macey had volunteered every other weekend as a victim advocate for those who'd suffered violent crimes, usually in the form of domestic abuse or sexual assault. And while she believed the three individuals in her room meant well, she knew down to her core that they'd never believe her. Because she didn't believe it herself.

And if she couldn't even trust herself, how could she expect anyone else to?

The man who'd done this to her was so much more powerful than she was, and with just a few words of spin, could destroy her reputation, her entire livelihood, not to mention what he and his attorneys could probably do to her family.

Silence was better. Safer.

It's not. You know it's not. Macey's heart constricted at the battle waging war inside her head.

Traitorous tears strolled down her cheeks, and when her mother softly brushed them away, Macey suspected her mom had known all along that she'd been faking sleep.

Her tears fell harder, and she wondered for the umpteenth time since waking if she wouldn't have been better off if her father hadn't shown up, if she'd died there on her kitchen floor. No pain. No pressure. No *knowledge*.

The voices in her head prodded at her again. *If you keep this a secret, anyone else he attacks is on you. If someone dies because you kept quiet, you were a willing party to that. You have to tell someone. You don't have a choice.*

Beneath her blanket Macey clenched her fingers into tight fists. She didn't want to think or feel anymore.

But when unconscious relief eluded her, Macey imagined being brave enough to grab the notebook and admit the truth. *Tall, wavy brown hair; scar over his right eyebrow.* The attack flashed in her mind so vividly that she could feel the rope tighten across her throat, could taste the fear, the horror. The agonizing memory of the knife piercing her skin over and over ripped Macey from the security of the hospital bed and sent her tumbling back to Wednesday night, returning her to that terrifying moment when she realized he meant to kill her.

Her voice crackling, she forced out an anguished whisper. "I don't understand."

Tears blinded her as her mother gathered her into her arms, crying with her and murmuring, "It's okay, baby, I'm here. You're safe now. It's okay."

Chapter Thirty-Eight

Saturday, September 2

Relieved to finally get a chance to be at home with her family, Alyssa walked into her kitchen and, for a surprising moment, considered turning back around and returning to the station. From the number of vehicles parked out front, she'd known she'd be stepping into a full house. What she hadn't expected was the brewing battleground of noise and what sounded like a burgeoning argument between Brock, Holly, and Isaac.

Inhaling deeply, she pulled on the remaining strings of her patience, and since she was asking for miracles, she added a little prayer for wisdom to weather whatever new storm was brewing because she wasn't sure she had the bandwidth to deal with a family drama. Storing her weapon, she sucked in a deep breath and headed into the fray. While the loud discussion continued, Brock leaned down to kiss her cheek. Except for her own children, who simply spared the briefest of looks in her direction, everyone else, which included Alyssa's mother-in-law, Mabel, Nick, Nick's twin, Rachel, and Holly's best friends, Sophie and Jersey, all waved or offered cheerful greetings. Ghost, Isaac's dog, pressed against his side as Schutz abandoned Holly and trotted over to Alyssa, nudging her hand for a pat.

The only person who appeared either oblivious or indifferent to her entrance was Amber. Isaac's girlfriend sat in a corner at the bar, leaning back against the wall while she scrolled through her phone. If Alyssa had to hazard a guess, she'd swear she'd seen more of the top of Amber's head than she had the girl's face since the moment Isaac had first brought her around to introduce her to the family.

When the chaotic argument in the kitchen threatened to break the sound barrier, Alyssa whistled, the trilling vibration purposely shrill. At once, everyone stopped mid-quarrel and stared at her. "What in God's name are you all carrying on about?"

Just as quickly as the argument had ended, everyone plowed in with their own explanation at the same time. This time, she yelled. "Hey!" Then she pointed to Isaac, who seemed to be the most animated and around whom the entire argument seemed to be centered. "You. Talk."

Alyssa couldn't help but notice that Amber still didn't stop scrolling on her phone.

Isaac scowled. "All I said was that I wondered if college was for me."

Alyssa's eyebrows felt like they should've flown off her face for as fast as they shot upward. "Excuse me?"

"I said—"

"I heard you the first time. What I meant was, why?"

The glare Isaac bestowed on her was a rare thing, which told Alyssa this was more than just her eighteen-year-old youngest child considering giving up a degree. A light bulb went on when she realized this was the "something" he'd mentioned running by her a few days earlier. Not wanting to risk putting words in his mouth, she waited.

Brock and Holly, however, had no such qualms as they both took the brief seconds of silence to launch back into their rebuttals. Before Alyssa could do more than open her mouth to demand calm once again, Isaac slapped his hand down hard on the granite countertop.

"What the f—"

His voice trailed off into a mumble as Alyssa audibly snapped her neck in his direction, her narrow-eyed glare daring him to finish his curse. As she'd explained to him more than once, just because he *could* say something didn't mean he *should*. Especially in front of his grandmother.

"What the *hell*, okay?" Under his breath, he added, "It's not like I'm legally an adult or anything. I can swear if I want to."

While he didn't roll his eyes, Alyssa could see the effort it took her son not to. "You can," she agreed. "But I think there's a much bigger issue at play here, don't you?"

Running his hands through his overly long, wavy hair, Isaac's shoulders dropped as he turned to his mom, palms up, pleading with her to understand. "I don't know why everyone's freaking the f—freak out. All I said is that I'm thinking of taking a gap year. Not everyone is destined for some grandiose college degree they'll probably do nothing with anyway."

Isaac's gaze swept over to his girlfriend for the briefest moment before passing over his father to land on Holly, then back to Alyssa.

"I'm not Holly, you know."

Until that moment, Alyssa had been listening with her head, not her heart. But something about how he made that last comment hit her. Hard.

As it did Brock and Holly both.

Tight-knit and banding together every time the going got rough, the four of them turned to each other and tuned everyone else out. Something besides an unwanted college degree was at the root of Isaac's pending decision, and Alyssa suspected she knew what that might be. Her eyes still on her son, she started to ask for the room, but Nick and Mabel were already shooing everyone else out of the kitchen. Even Amber, focus still firmly glued to her screen, followed the retreating group.

In the family room, the television went on, blasting news about a house fire in Taos before someone muted the sound and a lively debate over what to watch ensued. Alyssa, crossing her fingers that she'd say the right thing, addressed her son's real, hidden issue. "I know Trevor took this year off, so the two of you aren't sharing a dorm the way you'd always talked about. You haven't really said much about your dormmate, so I guess I assumed things were going well. Regardless, no one said you have to live on campus, either."

"Your room here is still your room, son," Brock added. "You know that. Just like Holly's is still Holly's."

Holly shoved back from the table and walked over to her brother, who now towered over her at an imposing six-foot-two. She touched his arm and laid her head just below his shoulder. "And I'm married now, so that should tell you something. But also…" – she shot a warning look at both Alyssa and Brock – "Nick and I have a spare room, so you can always stay with us. That way you're not living at home."

Isaac closed his eyes and dropped his head to rest on top of his sister's, and Alyssa knew in that moment they'd all nailed it. Though extremely rare now, Isaac still had the occasional nightmare that had his terrified screams waking him. The thought of his dormmate – or anyone outside his family or best friend, Trevor – hearing those screams terrified him almost beyond reason.

Brock set his coffee mug down and reached out his long arm to squeeze Isaac's shoulder. "In case you haven't noticed, son, we have some smart women living in our midst. What I'm saying is: you have options." His hesitation, though slight, was still notable as he added, "If continuing college is what you decide you want to do."

Relief spilled from Isaac's eyes in the form of tears. "I guess I knew that. I just…" – he swallowed – "stupid fu—damn nightmares." As if shaking off the images in his memory, he did a whole-body shake.

One hand lowered to bring Ghost even closer to him. "Why do people have to figure out who they want to be as soon as they turn eighteen, anyway?" Isaac moaned. "I mean, who made that stupid rule? I don't know what I want to do for the weekend half the time, but now suddenly everyone wants me to have my entire future mapped out?"

"Well, I don't know about everybody," Alyssa said, "but I can tell you that neither Dad nor I expect you to have that answer any more than we would've expected Holly to if she hadn't already known. Do we want you to continue your education? Yes, of course. Is it our choice to make for you? No. Because regardless of how important *we* think it is, ultimately, you'll be the one living the life you choose. With that in mind, make your decisions count."

She pulled her son down into a hug and whispered into his ear. "You'll figure it out. Maybe not today, but you will. And the nightmares are few and far between now. Don't be so hard on yourself." Then, she stepped away and grinned up at Isaac. "And as for this weekend, I believe I recall you promised Grandma you'd help her organize her garage."

Isaac's cheery disposition returned with a comical groan. "What was I thinking when I agreed to that?"

Holly grinned. "That you could borrow her sporty little Camaro when you and Amber head to wherever you're going for Spring Break in March."

As if she'd been standing in the shadows waiting to be summoned, Amber shuffled into the kitchen, her eyes on Isaac. "I thought you were going with me this weekend for the auditions."

Ghost, his eyes on Amber, shifted his body in front of Isaac. While he didn't quite growl, he did bare his teeth.

And if Alyssa hadn't been staring directly at her son, she would've missed the way his eyes narrowed for that split second before he flashed the most insincere, fake smile she'd ever seen him sport. "Sorry, babe. Grandma can't really move things in her garage herself, and I did promise. Maybe Jill can go with you instead?"

The mention of her best friend didn't appease Amber's clear displeasure. "We'll talk about it later." The way she said it sounded a lot like a warning. Alyssa and Brock stared at each other, but then Amber practically bounced herself between Holly and Alyssa and squealed at ear-splitting decibels as if she weren't clearly irritated with Isaac. "Ohmygod, do you want to see something?"

Without waiting for an answer, Amber thrust her phone at them so she could show them the pictures she'd snapped of Remington Everwood and Hudson Bane. The second snapshot was a selfie, in which Amber, lovestruck superfan written all over her face, gazed over her shoulder at the two Hollywood heartthrobs.

While Holly did a much better job at faking enthusiasm, probably more for her brother's sake than anything else, Amber's oohs and aahs and, frankly grating giggles, flew right over Alyssa's head because she had zeroed in on one thing. She was staring at a multi-colored windbreaker with a bird's wing on the sleeve exactly like the one they'd seen when they viewed Lois Cutter's security footage. Her mind raced as she tried to determine if the man wearing it now matched the height of the man they'd seen lurking in the trees near Tingley Beach where Taylor Gray's body had been discovered.

"Amber, would you mind texting me copies of those pictures?" Only years of experience dealing with criminals and skittish witnesses allowed Alyssa to keep control of her voice as she made the request.

That didn't stop Isaac's mouth from dropping open or Holly's attention shifting from Amber's phone to her mom's face. Alyssa knew by the way her daughter leaned forward and her eyes lit up that she sensed Alyssa had seen something crucial in the photographs. Practically bouncing on the balls of her feet now, she peeked back over Amber's shoulder to see if she could see what her mother had seen.

Brock, too, held Alyssa's gaze with his own. The only person in the room who remained oblivious to the sudden mood shift was Amber, who rambled some incoherent thing about how legit it was that Alyssa recognized Bane's and Everwood's "eternal hotness."

Alyssa fought to keep her impatience in check as Amber finally navigated to the share button on her phone. Seconds later, Alyssa's phone buzzed with the notification, and she cut Amber off mid-squeal as she excused herself to call Cord and Ryker.

Chapter Thirty-Nine

Saturday, September 2

Something in the air shifted, and Brooklyn jolted upright. Her eyes darted around the room, up to the door at the top of the steps, and then back down to the floor, her gaze sweeping every square inch of the space before lifting to the air vent near the ceiling. Within a matter of minutes, her eyelids felt too heavy to hold open, and the need to lie down and sleep pressed in on her. Her body listed to the side, the sensation of falling causing her to jerk upright before her head hit the cement floor.

In the back of her mind, she heard a voice – Queenie's? Her mom's? Mason's? – demanding that she not obey her body's instincts, that if she did, she'd never wake.

Feeling as if her limbs were moving in slow motion, she sank back onto the thin mattress, barely registering the pain that rocked her bones or the way her head bounced off the wall hard.

Warmth flooded her from the inside out. At first welcoming the sensation, it soon became uncomfortably hot and suffocating. Through sheer grit and determination, she pried her eyes open. A thick, heavy smoke flowed through the vent, filling the basement.

Her lungs spasmed just before she was wracked with a violent coughing spell that burned her insides with every painful inhalation.

This was wrong. She needed to move, scream for help. But she also just wanted to close her eyes and dream that when she woke, she would be anywhere but here.

Chapter Forty

Back at the precinct, Captain Hammond strolled into the incident room and started emptying what felt like every single thought that had worked its way through his mind from the moment Alyssa had called and dumped her suspicions on him. When he spotted the side-by-side images of the man they'd seen in the woods near Taylor's body and the selfie Amber had snapped, he stopped. Enlarged, the windbreaker certainly appeared to be the same.

"It's possible," Hammond said, "that he was wearing that windbreaker in an effort to remain as incognito as possible. I've read stories that celebrities do that sort of thing. Just because he was in the area doesn't mean he killed her. Jesus, what a damned mess!"

The team had already considered this, and while Alyssa knew the captain was right, her gut told her that they weren't watching a famous person trying to hide his face from fans so much as to conceal his identity because he had just murdered a woman.

Ryker was on the same page as Alyssa. "With all due respect, Captain Hammond, I think that's a fine spin if we were in front of the cameras going public with this right now, but every bone in my body is screaming *that man* is the person I've been trying to run to ground for the past five years. In fact, I know it is."

Cord, who'd been on the phone for the past several minutes, ended his call. "That was Mr. Travers. As soon as Lys told me what she'd seen on Amber's phone, I got to thinking back to our interview at the hospital with Macey, how we got the impression she wasn't telling the truth when she said she didn't know who did this to her, so I contacted Macey's father to find out if there could be any possible link. Turns out Macey was just hired a few weeks ago as a runner on the film set."

Hammond released a string of curses.

"It makes sense why she might be too afraid to admit the truth. In this whacked out world we live in, I'm sure she was terrified that if she accused an A-lister of being her attacker, her career would be derailed, and his rabid fans would do the modern version of stoning her alive on social media and in the news. They'd pry into every corner of her life and kick over every pebble to prove she was a liar or unreliable or hell, just being opportunistic. She'd be blackballed everywhere she went, and not just in the Hollywood scene. Everyone would know her name, and I don't mean that in a good way. She knows it, and that's why she didn't want to tell us."

"Holy—" Hal's palm smacked down on the table, effectively cutting off everyone's chatter. He swung his head around, his eyes wide as they landed on Alyssa. "Come check this out. While you guys were arguing, I've been running through the footage from Lois Cutter's security cameras. I slowed it way, way down, which is probably the only reason I spotted this. Look."

The entire team crowded around Hal and his laptop, waiting. They all noticed it at the exact same moment.

Almost as if they'd practiced it, everyone in the room exhaled in a loud whoosh of air.

For a hairbreadth of a second, the man on the camera shifted as he brushed something off his sleeve. In doing so, the edge of his windbreaker lifted, catching on something before he could yank it back into place. Upon closer inspection, Alyssa could just make out what appeared to be a sheath. Though the image was a bit grainy, they could still see the hilt of a knife. And while she couldn't make out the design to see if it might match the marks made on the victims' bodies, all of it combined to seal Alyssa's conviction that they had their killer. She turned to Hammond. "Seen enough yet?"

Hammond wiped a hand down his face before he leveled a stare at Alyssa, the one that announced he was probably going to say something to set her teeth on edge. She steeled herself.

"Before you go accusing me of it, what I'm about to say has absolutely nothing to do with giving the rich and famous more leeway than the average Joe."

"Why's it always gotta be the 'average Joe?'" Joe mumbled.

No one laughed.

Already, Alyssa didn't like where Hammond's comment was headed. Not that long ago, she'd lit him up when he'd balked at her suspicions regarding a slew of extremely wealthy individuals whose names she and her team had tied to a heinous, massive, multi-state sex-trafficking ring. He hadn't forgotten her reaction – or the fact that she'd been right – and she hadn't ever fully forgiven him for disregarding her educated opinion backed by evidence.

Hammond's attention shifted to Ryker. "Special Agent Newlin, you aren't officially under my command, but I'm going to need you to listen up, too."

If the captain wanted the entire team on pins and needles, he succeeded spectacularly. "I think it might be prudent to cut down on the national media nightmare by letting Mr. Hollywood come to us instead of the APD flooding the studio and causing a stir the likes of which I don't want to deal with. Let's give the man a chance to explain before we go all *Die Hard* on him."

Alyssa sputtered. "Give him a chance to *explain*?" To call her gobsmacked and beyond pissed would be an understatement. "You mean give him a chance to get his acting skills turned on and get his story straight? Because that's what's going to happen if we let ourselves lose the element of surprise here."

"Actually..." Ryker moved to stand next to Hammond. "The captain may be onto something." She cut Alyssa off when Alyssa turned her furious glare in her direction. "Hear me out. I don't like it any more than you do. Trust me. When word gets out – and it definitely will – that the APD hauled one of Hollywood's two leading sweethearts in for questioning, regardless of the reason, our entire case and everything I've been working toward for the past five years could be put in serious jeopardy. Like Cord mentioned a few minutes ago, his fans will do everything they can to discredit us."

While she explained, she stared at the map on the wall, the one where all the victims' faces, eight of them now, had been pinned. "I'm not taking that risk. Especially now that we're this close to closing in. Call it intuition or voodoo for all I care, but I won't gamble on everything slipping out of my grip because of a media gaffe."

Tony, who'd been silently tapping his fingers on the table, now placed them over his mouth as he pinched his lips together before sharing his thoughts. "Is there any way to cross reference where his movies were being shot to see if they coincided with any of the murders? Or all of them, for that matter?" Though he'd addressed the room, everyone knew Tony's comment was really directed at Hal.

Hal beamed from his royal purple wheelchair. "Already on it. And of course, we already know that filming is taking place here. The timing also fits for the Grand and Asandro murders in Nebraska and Texas. The only three where I don't see a connection with the movie industry are: Ortega, Morrow, and Knox. Which might make sense since he only had bit parts in movies and didn't really hit major celebrity status until after that romantic thriller *Soulmate Symphony* came out in 2019."

Joe put forth another option. "Look, I think we can all agree that, despite what we're seeing, Reginald Leach is somehow tied up in all this. His polygraph was inconclusive, except when asked if he knew who killed his boyfriend's sister. When he said no, the polygraph clearly showed he was lying. So, what if we bring *him* in for questioning?" He looked at Alyssa. "Didn't you say he mentioned that he was some hot shot celebrity's agent? Who could be more hotshot than that right now?" He tipped his head toward the man spotted on Lois Cutter's camera footage.

Joe had a point. But bringing in Leach instead of the man responsible held too many elements of cinematic drama for Alyssa's tastes. Her fingers itched to snatch her keys from her pocket and head straight to the studios and let the team figure their way out of this theatrical labyrinth.

What she did instead was ask, "What are you thinking that will accomplish?"

"Show Leach the picture, tell him we think he's involved in these murders. He already knows he's on our radar. Let's just see if he gives something up. Even if it's just to save his own ass."

"Leach's attorney isn't going to let him cooperate," Alyssa countered. "Plus, bringing him in – or even making that request – puts us at risk of him sending out the alert."

Alyssa looked back to Hammond and Ryker. "I think we have to roll the dice on this. Our concern isn't – and shouldn't be – what happens with the media. Our concern isn't and shouldn't be what happens to some movie production. We owe the residents of this state more than that. We owe the victims and their families more than that. I say we track down Hudson Bane for questioning right now."

Alyssa checked her watch. "It's almost nine o'clock. We can either wait until morning or head out there now and hope he's still on set or that someone can point us in his direction. My vote is the sooner the better."

Hammond studied Alyssa for what seemed like an eternity. "You know if we get this wrong, you're not just putting your own reputation at risk; you're putting the entire APD, as well as the FBI at risk. And if you don't think Bane's expensive Hollywood lawyers won't chew you up and spit you out in front of the entire world, you're being foolish."

Alyssa's eyes narrowed. "To hell with my reputation. You know me well enough to know that I'm willing to risk – and take the complete fall for this, on the off chance that we're wrong – if it means bringing justice to the victims. I think we *all* owe it to them."

Hammond let loose another string of colorful curses before he nodded his acceptance. "I figured that's what you'd say. So, what're you still here for? Get going."

Chapter Forty-One

Alyssa hadn't really thought about what they might encounter as far as filming went when they arrived. But she knew she hadn't expected an entire lot full of blazing lights, people, celebrities, extras, film crew, and dozens of people still running around at this hour. It was only when they were stopped at the gate and flashed their credentials to the guard that she began to suspect getting to Hudson Bane might be even more difficult than she had imagined.

She found an empty space in the crowded parking lot and parked the Tahoe. Aside from people darting fleeting but inquisitive glances in their direction as they scurried around the sets like mice trying to navigate a maze, no one paid them a bit of attention. She took a moment to look around, to see if she could spot Hudson Bane anywhere in the throngs of people milling about, but if he was there, she couldn't see him. Not that she'd really expected it to be that easy. It was, after all, a movie set.

A woman balancing two four-cup drink containers rushed past them, and before she even realized her own intent, Alyssa found herself following her. Anyone in that much of a hurry was bound to be headed to someone important, or at least to someone who could point them in the right direction.

Her instincts weren't wrong. Across the lot near a long row of trailers, Hudson Bane sat in a highbacked chair, scrolling through his phone, and looking for all the world like watching the grass grow would be more entertaining. One individual was messing with his hair while another was plastering some kind of thick flesh-colored paste to his face over various scratches and lightly colored bruises. Alyssa thought back to the story she'd heard on the television a few days earlier about the brawl Bane and Remington Everwood had gotten into on set. Were the scratches and bruises a result of that fight – or had they come from his victims fighting for their lives? When she drew closer, neither Bane, nor either of the other men, did more than spare the three newcomers a fleeting glance.

"Hudson Bane?"

The actor's eyes lifted, and after a quick once-over that shouted he was far from impressed, he flicked them away like he might an annoying mosquito. A sneer curled his lips, instantly turning him from Hollywood heartthrob to Hollywood villain. "Extras aren't allowed back here, and they're definitely not allowed to approach me. Leave before I have you booted." A heavy hint of superiority coated Bane's demand as he returned to what he'd been doing before he'd been interrupted.

His attitude hit a nerve, and Alyssa, along with Cord and Ryker, flashed their badges to the two men fixing Bane's hair and makeup. Both men's eyes widened as they threw their hands up and backed away. With her identification still in hand, Alyssa held it over Bane's phone.

She may have succeeded in getting his attention, but his superiority complex remained firmly in place. Alyssa pointed off to the side, and Bane's eyes followed. "Tell me, is that the equipment they use to haul your ego in?"

Bane raked his gaze over Alyssa's body from head to toe and back again in a way that she assumed was meant to insult her. She would've laughed, but she didn't care what the man thought of her, and she most definitely didn't have the time or patience to deal with his overinflated sense of self. She let her voice show it.

"I'm Detective Wyatt with the Albuquerque Police Department. This is my partner, Detective Roberts" – she nodded to Cord – "and Special Agent Newlin with the FBI." She waved her hand toward Ryker. "We need to ask you a few questions. We can go somewhere out of earshot of everyone else, or we can do it here. Your call. But make it fast before I make the decision for you. And trust me when I assure you that I don't give a hot damn about the rumors that are sure to start swirling with so many curious ears listening in."

The veins in Bane's temple throbbed, a clear sign he wasn't used to someone not titled with the label of director or producer telling him what to do. With a sweeping motion of his hands, he shooed everyone away with a barked, "Get out of here." Only after the area cleared did he turn back to the three of them. "My trailer's too small for all of us to fit, so you can talk to me here, I guess. Now, questions about what?"

"About whom," Ryker corrected, working her way backwards through the list of victims. "Macey Travers, Taylor Gray, Jennie Killingbeck, Jaime Asandro, Lauren Grand, Daphne Morrow, Madison Ortega." She paused. "Brooklyn Knox."

While Ryker rattled off the names, Alyssa watched for Hudson Bane's reaction. Instead of recognition, boredom returned to his face. He slouched in his chair and crossed his legs at the ankles. She reminded herself that he was an award-winning actor.

"Are those names supposed to mean something to me?" He flashed the smirky smile that was partly responsible for his skyrocket to fame. "If they're one-night stands, I don't bother to remember their names, and I'm one hundred percent not the baby daddy. I made sure that would never happen." Bane winked at Cord in that, "You're a dude and get it" kind of frat-boy way.

Cord returned the Hollywood star's stare, but not the grin.

Bane squirmed but tried to cover it up by pretending to get more comfortable. He scowled and arched one perfectly groomed eyebrow as if to say, "Well, ask your next question."

Alyssa did. "Where were you on Monday, August twenty-eighth?"

Something flashed in Bane's face. "I don't know where I was. Probably on set. What time Monday?"

Instead of answering, Alyssa pulled her phone from her pocket, brought up the photos Amber had texted, and showed them to the actor.

Confusion replaced his bored expression. He tapped his finger on Alyssa's screen. "The gal who took this selfie one of those people you named?"

The smile Alyssa flashed would never be mistaken for friendly as she, too, tapped her screen. "That windbreaker you're wearing happens to be an exact match to someone the APD and the FBI would like to speak to."

"Okay."

Though Alyssa prided herself on her ability to read people well, she couldn't decide if Bane was playing a game or if he really didn't get it. "Let me be clear here: the person wearing that windbreaker was spotted in the vicinity of a murder victim. You wouldn't know anything about that, would you?"

That got the Hollywood star's attention, and he came flying out of his chair so fast, Alyssa had to step back or get knocked down. Finally catching on, Bane's face paled, and with his attention firmly riveted on Alyssa's screen, he jabbed his finger at the picture. "That exact jacket?"

"Yes, that exact jacket."

Hudson Bane's head whipped back and forth. Both his hands flew up, and he took two steps back. "No. Uh-uh. That's not my jacket. Everwood loaned it to me that day when we were out signing autographs, and the place had its air blasting. I was right under the vent and bitching about it when he tossed me his windbreaker and told me to stop being a little bitch and shut my whining up."

All the air in the area seemed to get sucked out all at once.

"Are you saying that's Remington Everwood's jacket, not yours?" Incredulity rocked Ryker's voice.

The "duh" expression Bane shot in her direction was all the answer Alyssa needed.

"Where's Remington now?" Just as Alyssa put her phone back in her pocket, it vibrated with a message, but whatever it was, it would have to wait.

"He's probably on a flight to Georgia. He's filming another movie right now, and he's been traveling back and forth from here to there. I don't have all the details. All I know is that I'm glad I won't have to deal with him for a while." He touched the bruises and scratches on his face. "Bastard picked a fight with me and did this. Delayed filming my scenes until the swelling went down." Bane puffed his chest out. "Trust me; I gave better than I got. Everwood's nothing but a p—"

A commotion in the background interrupted Bane's rant, and it took a second for Alyssa to decipher that the chatter was about a fire in Taos. Her neck snapped around at Hudson Bane's next words.

"Wonder if the fire's close to Everwood's place up there. Not that I really care," he added.

Ryker's voice stretched tight with tension. "Where in Taos?"

Bane shrugged. "How the hell should I know? I just heard him talking to his agent on the phone about it one day. He was telling the guy to purchase it under an assumed name because he didn't want fans knowing about it."

The hair on the back of Alyssa's neck stood up. She knew in that moment they'd been right about a Hollywood heartthrob committing these murders. They'd just been wrong about which one.

Cord stepped up. "Who's Everwood's agent?"

"Well, it used to be Darren March until a few years ago. But he fired him when his old buddy from some backwoods town showed up. Something Leach is the guy's name, I think. I don't really know him all that well."

Alyssa had one more question. "Where would Everwood be flying out from?"

"He's got a private jet out at Double Eagle II Airport."

Alyssa pulled out a card and handed it to Hudson. "This is a murder investigation. A *serial* murder investigation. I'd advise you to keep your mouth shut, or you could find yourself being arrested for hindering a federal investigation. I'm sure that's not the kind of Hollywood nightmare you'd like to be starring in."

Chapter Forty-Two

Before they reached Alyssa's Tahoe, she was on the phone with Hal, Joe, and Tony. "We need a bead on Leach's whereabouts now. And while you're at it, I need you to track Remington Everwood, too." She raced back onto the interstate, lights flashing, thankful that the Labor Day weekend brought less traffic at this time of night.

"Did you get my text?" Hal asked.

"Yes and no. We were questioning Bane when it came through, and I didn't get a chance to read it yet. What'd it say?"

"I just asked you to call me. I've been flipping through the yearbooks you brought back from Oklahoma, and I kept coming back to one picture that really stood out. A boy by the name of Colton Abbott. I contacted Lindy to ask her about him, but she said she wasn't there during that time and suggested I call the principal. So, I did, and she said she vaguely remembered him. She mentioned how Brooklyn used to let Abbott hang out in her room for lunch whenever his only friend wasn't at school. She couldn't recall the friend's name, and when I asked her if it could've been Leach, she said it was possible, but she couldn't swear to it.

"Anyway, Abbott wasn't the only kid who chose to avoid the lunchroom by hanging in Brooklyn's classroom. He just did it the most often. The principal only remembered him specifically because she remembered that once he started working out, he had a surge in popularity that he kind of ate up. Shortly after that, he moved away. I'm still digging into it, but I'm pretty sure Remington Everwood is the transformed Colton Abbott. I could be wrong here, but there are definite similarities in the facial structure. And just to back up my theory, I can tell you that both Leach and Abbott attended Noble High together, and both moved out of state within a few months of each other."

Hal was still talking when Ryker yanked her phone from her pocket and called her superior at the FBI.

Alyssa punched the gas. Over the road noise and Ryker's conversation, she could hear Hal pecking away on his keyboard.

"By the way, Leach's phone just pinged off towers near I-40 and Atrisco. Looks like he's heading west," Hal said. "Which means he could be heading toward Double Eagle II Airport."

Tony joined the conversation. "Hey, I just got off the phone with Double Eagle. Everwood's plane is still there. I let them know that they needed to be discreet but to do whatever they could to keep that plane from taking off. The gal I spoke with is going to see what she can do. Joe and I are heading out now, so we'll meet you there."

Alyssa breathed a small sigh of relief. "Thanks, Tony. Backup is always appreciated."

After ending the call, Alyssa risked a quick glance at Ryker who had just finished her conversation with her superior.

Ryker's eyes filled with the same excitement racing through Alyssa's veins knowing they were just moments away from closing in on a serial killer. "Let's go get this bastard," she growled.

Chapter Forty-Three

Remington Everwood sat in the soft leather seat of his private plane and stared down at his phone, alternating between pleasure and irritation. Reggie had tried calling him no fewer than once every two to five minutes. His director had tried twice. They wanted him to know there had been an explosion and that his Taos home was burning to the ground.

Disappointed because he'd counted on the fire but not the explosion, he tried to discount his unease. As remote as his place was, it would still take time before they got a fire crew out there. But maybe an explosion was better since it meant Brooklyn would likely die immediately instead of suffocating from smoke inhalation. He shook the image of her body engulfed in flames from his mind, reminding himself that it was time to let her go, to start over fresh.

And he needed her body for the next step in his plan. Framing his old buddy, Reginald Leach.

Leach. Such a fitting name for the person blackmailing him and leaching him of money for the past four years. Ever since Reggie had shown up in Texas, right after Remington had killed Jaime Asandro, he'd been under Leach's control. It had made him feel the same as he had back in the days when he'd been bullied – small and powerless. And that had filled him with rage.

It had been a pure act of obscene luck that the woman he'd killed at Tingley Beach had been the sister of Leach's new love interest. He couldn't have planned that better if he'd tried. Hell, it was better than a Hollywood script. Even when he hadn't realized it, fate had been leading him to this point all along. It wasn't his fault if his one-time only friend was too dumb to find his way off of a flattened box if he was handed the directions.

Remington thought back to when Leach had, quite out of the blue, shown up one day, demanding to speak with him.

Remington offered his on-screen smile to his forgotten friend and brought him in for a quick hug and a clap on the back. "Reggie, long time no talk, man. How've you been?"

Leach's own smile reminded Remington of a slimy con man as he pulled a folder from beneath his arm and tossed it down onto the table before flipping it open and waiting.

Remington glanced down and had to call upon every one of his acting skills to keep his face devoid of emotion. Article after article about Brooklyn's disappearance peeked out. Leach reached down and moved the articles to the side. Photos of Lauren Grand, in addition to articles on Madison Ortega and Daphne Morrow, stared up at him.

Beneath the table, Remington clenched his fists even as he glanced up, adopting a look of confusion.

Reggie pushed the picture of Lauren Grand forward. "I happened to be in Nebraska when I heard you were there filming. I was hoping we'd be able to get together, you know, just two nobodies who'd made it out of that godforsaken town. But you wouldn't return any of my texts or calls. Anyway, I ran into an old buddy of mine while I was there, and he told me his girlfriend had been murdered. Lauren Grand was his girlfriend. He showed me her picture, and I thought to myself, "Now, why does she look so familiar to me?" And then I snapped to it. I gotta say it didn't take much for me to put two and two together. You can go ahead and deny it if you want, but then I'll just go to the police with my concerns, and then you'll be facing a backlash of attention, and your career will be shot. You know it. I know it."

Remington's hands dropped to the knife his grandfather had given him long ago, barely resisting the urge to lunge for Leach, to drive the blade deep into his throat. "What do you want?"

Leach's grin turned feral. "You want me to keep your secret, and I want access to celebrities. You're going to get me that access. And I'm going to need nine grand a month until I get firmly established. I'll give you the account info."

Reeling on the inside, Remington leaned back and sneered. "If you're so sure I'm capable of murder, what makes you think I won't kill you right here and now?"

Leach crowded into Remington's space, bumping his legs up against Remington's. "Go ahead. I left a letter with my attorney. If he doesn't receive a video call from me in twenty-four hours, he's been instructed to open the letter I left him, the one where I've outlined your dirty little secret. How long do you think it'll take for you to fall from that pedestal you've put yourself on? And you will fall. Hard. So, yeah, you might kill me. Or I might survive. Either way, you're finished. My way's better."

Remington hadn't known if he believed him, or if Leach had just watched one too many thrillers. But it hadn't mattered because he couldn't take the chance.

When he'd asked Leach to purchase his Taos property under an assumed name, it really had been to make it harder for fans to find out where he lived. In the whole spirit of "keep your friends close and your enemies closer," he'd even told Leach he could use the place whenever he wasn't around. But after Taylor Gray's death, the idea to frame Leach began to take shape.

Shortly after everything had gone so horribly wrong with Macey Travers, Remington received word from the director of another film he'd signed on for and asked if he could come out to Georgia for a couple of weeks. He'd taken it as another sign.

The house had been easy enough to ignite. All he'd needed to do was turn the gas burners to high on the stove. The moment he'd crossed into the Albuquerque city limits, he'd used his tablet to activate the light switches in the house, starting with the one just outside the door leading to the basement.

Reggie Leach wasn't the only one capable of learning things from the movies. So had Remington. Such as knowing gas was heavy and would sink to the basement before it could all leak out. Within a few hours, enough gas would build up in the basement, and the spark from the light would ignite the fire.

Because of Leach's obsession with becoming an agent to the stars, he'd ended up being in close proximity to every one of the murders except possibly the first two.

He knew Leach would point the finger at him, and if he could've figured out a way to kill him and make it look like an accident, he would've. But he didn't have time, and besides, who would possibly believe a nobody like Leach over a Hollywood heartthrob like him?

He laughed. After Leach's conviction, they'd probably even make a movie about it. Hell, they'd probably ask him to play himself. He'd scoff at first, but he'd agree, and in the end, he'd make a boatload of money off Leach's stupidity. He laughed again when he peered out his window and spotted Reggie heading toward the tarmac.

Let the good times begin.

He instructed his personal flight attendant to let his buddy in. For old time's sake.

Chapter Forty-Four

Before Alyssa made the turn off to Double Eagle II Airport, she cut the lights and instructed Joe and Tony to do the same before they arrived. She wanted to take every precaution to do what she could to avoid alerting Remington Everwood that the police were onto him.

Up ahead, Everwood's plane sat on the tarmac, the lights inside shining brightly. Alyssa pointed to the far corner of the parking lot where a vehicle she recognized as Reggie Leach's sat. "Looks like Hal was right about where Leach was headed." Alyssa parked behind it, boxing it in so he wouldn't be able to leave without ramming her Tahoe.

Though patience had never been her strong suit, and even less so when she was so close to solving one of her cases, she knew she had no choice but to wait for backup. Her entire body vibrated with so much tension that she nearly jumped out of her skin when her phone rang.

"Holy Mary, mother of God," she mumbled as she pulled her phone out of the center console and hit her speaker button. "What's up, Hal?"

"Uh, you're not going to believe this, but that house burning up in Taos—"

Alyssa cut him off. "Belongs to Remington Everwood."

"Well, yeah, but that's not why I'm calling. They just pulled a woman out of the basement. Christ, Lys, she'd been chained to the wall like some kind of wild animal."

Alyssa felt like she'd been sucker-punched. "Brooklyn Knox?"

"Of course, it's just guessing on my part, but yeah, I'm betting that you nailed it with your hunch. For whatever reason, Everwood didn't kill her six years ago, but holy hell, what she must've endured after her attack had to have been just as bad as the attack itself, if not worse."

Ryker's breath rushed out in a loud exhalation of shock. "She's still alive, then?"

Hal's silence didn't bode well. "She's breathing, if that's what you mean. But I've gotta be honest, it doesn't sound promising."

–

A million scattered thoughts jockeyed for position in Alyssa's mind, most of them centered on Brooklyn Knox. She had so many questions, but they'd have to wait because she spotted Joe and Tony coming down the road. "Hal, we've got to go. I'll call you back once we have Everwood in custody."

"Be careful out there."

"You know we will." She ended the call and met Cord's eyes in the rearview mirror before looking over to Ryker. "Let's do this."

The three of them headed over to Joe's squad car so they could work out the details of their approach. Not once did she or Ryker take their focus off the plane's cabin as they discussed the best and safest way to take the men down.

With a plan finally in place, the five of them headed toward the tarmac. Joe and Tony stood off to one side of the steps while Cord moved to the other. Alyssa nodded for Ryker to ascend the steps first, but Ryker stood still, finger to her lips, one hand cupped around her ear.

From the sounds of it, Everwood and Leach were in the middle of a heated conversation. Alyssa pulled her phone out, opened her camera, and though she knew it wouldn't be allowed in any court proceedings, she hit the video recording before handing it to Ryker, who grabbed the phone and crept slowly up another step, then another until she was near the top.

"Your house is burning, and you don't care? Why's that, *Colton*?"

Remington narrowed his eyes at the jab. "It's adobe and wood, man. I can build another. Just like I rebuilt my identity after I left Oklahoma."

"Where's Miss Knox? What'd you do with her?"

Remington's cold laughter flowed out the open cabin door and down to Alyssa. "Always so polite, aren't you. *Miss Knox?* You know we're not teenagers in school anymore, right? You don't have to call her 'Miss.'" The mockery in his voice grated on Alyssa's nerves. "Aren't you more interested in your lover's sister and why I killed her?"

"Because you're a sick sonofabitch?"

"Maybe." Remington's voice lowered. "Or maybe it's *you* who's the sick sonofabitch. I mean, think about it. I didn't know Ms. Gray or her brother. You, on the other hand, did. I imagine there'll be lots of speculation about your jealousy over Jackson's attention being divided between you and his sister. Tsk tsk. Such a shame."

Leach's voice bubbled over with hatred. "My lawyer still has that letter in the safe. And I've added more."

"Yeah, well, it'll be your word against mine then, won't it?"

Alyssa had heard enough, and more importantly, had gotten it on audio. She tapped Ryker on the shoulder and waved for her to go in. Ryker needed no further prodding as she thrust Alyssa's phone back at her and then flew up the last couple of steps into the plane. "FBI and Police. I need both of you to keep your hands up where we can see them."

Alyssa scooted in behind Ryker just in time to watch Remington's Academy Award performance. Sobs wracked his body as he wrapped his arms around his middle. "Thank God, you're here. I thought he was going to kill me."

Alyssa cut him off. "Save it. It's not going to be your word against his. It's going to be your words against yourselves." She held her phone up, still recording.

Leach spoke first. "I'm not saying a word without my lawyer."

Remington wasn't quite ready to give up his game. "He made me do it. He—"

While Alyssa read Leach his rights and placed him in cuffs, Ryker dragged Everwood out of his seat and did the same for him. A smile danced around her lips as she slapped metal bracelets on his wrists and read him his Miranda Rights before donning a pair of gloves and patting him down.

Her hand hit the top of his knife, and she lifted his shirt. "Well, well, what do we have here?" She directed Alyssa's attention to the intricate silver hilt that very much resembled the unique stab wounds on all the victims'

337

bodies, likely the same knife they'd seen on Lois Cutter's security cameras.

"That was a gift from my grandfather," Everwood screamed when Ryker pulled the knife from its sheath and handed it over to Cord to place in an evidence bag.

Alyssa smiled at Everwood's slip. "Good to know it's yours."

As Ryker led the man she'd been hunting for the past five years down the steps of his plane, Alyssa noted the fresh and wicked scratch marks on the back of his hands, up and down his arms, and along his neck. She had a sneaking suspicion that the skin scraped from beneath Macey Travers's fingernails would come back as a match for Remington Everwood. She sincerely hoped so.

With Everwood and Leach secured in the back of Joe's cruiser, Ryker turned to Alyssa. "You know, as great as it feels to finally get some answers, it's all kind of overshadowed by the fact that there are still six dead women. More if Brooklyn or Macey die, too."

Alyssa said nothing because Ryker had just pulled the words right out of her head.

Chapter Forty-Five

News of Remington's arrest hit the news before they'd even made it back to the precinct. Alyssa didn't know who could've leaked the information that quickly, but she suspected it probably had to do with the sophisticated police scanner apps on most reporters' phones. Regardless, the spin doctors were already hard at work trying to figure out how to salvage the movie, as if that were far more important than the six murdered women and the two still fighting for their lives.

After battling their way through the media feeding frenzy, Alyssa excused herself. She closed herself in the closet of an office space she shared with Cord, took out her phone, and placed the most important call she'd make today.

Queenie Knox-Bolton answered on the second ring. "Hello, Detective Wyatt."

Alyssa skipped the pleasantries. "Have you seen the news?"

"No. Why?"

"Two things. First, we've made an arrest. And—"

Queenie's sharp gasp sliced into Alyssa's ear. Half a dozen questions tumbled out one after the other, so Alyssa had to repeat her name several times before the more important news finally sank in.

"Queenie, we found your sister. We found Brooklyn. She's—"

A sound so full of different emotions Alyssa couldn't have picked just one slipped from Queenie's mouth before she screamed for her husband.

When Roy joined his wife on the phone, Alyssa continued. "She's been held prisoner for the past six years."

Queenie's gasp expressed shock mixed with guarded hope. "Are you saying—Oh, my God. Is she *alive*?"

"Yes, but Queenie, I want to be honest. Brooklyn is fighting for her life right now. She suffered from smoke and gas inhalation and burns to her body. And that's not to mention all the trauma she suffered during her years in captivity."

"So, she could still die?"

Alyssa knew she shouldn't offer unrealistic hope, but she couldn't stop herself. "It's possible, yes. But try to remember that your sister survived a vicious attack by a man who turned into a serial killer, six years of being held prisoner, a house explosion, *and* a fire. If there's ever been anyone who can pull through this, it's your sister."

Queenie's voice trembled. "You're right, you're right. Thank you, Detective Wyatt. Thank you so much. Roy's already online buying our plane tickets. Do you mind if I touch base with you after we get to New Mexico?"

"Of course, I wouldn't mind."

Before Alyssa could disconnect, Queenie had one more question. "You said you'd made an arrest. Are you allowed to tell me who?"

Alyssa sucked in a deep breath and let it out, knowing the news of *who* would be just as stunning as learning her sister was still alive. "Remington Everwood."

Absolute silence filled the air before Queenie exploded in disbelief. "As in the *actor*?"

"Yes." Alyssa spent a few more minutes answering what questions she could before finally telling Queenie she needed to go. Her next call was to Sheriff Harold Arnold, who happened to be with his son, Mason.

When she finished telling him what they'd learned, the sheriff said, "I don't know what to say here. I mean, I didn't really know him, but it's hard to believe anyone can have such a complete transformation, isn't it?"

"I don't know. I've seen people I went to school with that I never would've recognized if they hadn't told me who they were. So, I guess it doesn't seem as far-fetched as you'd think."

"Well, I appreciate you calling me personally. I'm going to reach out to Queenie now and see if she minds if Mason and I head over to Albuquerque ourselves. We sure as hell would love to be there for her and Brooklyn both. No matter the outcome. And by God, after all this, she better pull through."

They spoke for a few more minutes, and Alyssa ended the call just as Cord knocked on the door and peeked in. "Leach's attorney is already here, and he's threatening to get everything tossed."

"I'm not surprised," Alyssa said.

"Yeah, well, you might be at this next bit. Everwood is still screaming his innocence and said he 'doesn't need an attorney.' I think we'd better take this opportunity before he realizes he's a damn idiot and changes his mind."

Alyssa flew out of her seat. "Go grab Ryker and meet me in there."

—

Remington Everwood sat on the hard plastic chair in the interrogation room, his body bent forward with his head on the table. When Alyssa, Ryker, and Cord entered the room, his head shot up. Red rimmed his glassy eyes.

Ryker and Alyssa pulled out the two remaining chairs, boxing Everwood into the corner while Cord remained near the door.

Along with the evidence bag holding his knife, Ryker set the same folder she'd brought in for Leach's interview days earlier down on the table and flipped it open. Remington's gaze flitted down and held for a little too long when he saw Brooklyn and Macey's photos.

Ryker didn't give him a chance to speak first. "I can see why you're so in demand in Hollywood right now. Your acting skills are top notch. But not top notch enough. So, why don't you just stop the show and answer some questions for us?"

His lower lip trembling, Remington's eyes darted over to Alyssa. "I swear I didn't do this. Reggie has always been so jealous of me, has always wanted to be me ever since I got famous, but I never thought he'd take things this far."

She arched her brow, her expression clearly showing she wasn't buying a second of his performance. She tapped an image of Taylor Gray's body, specifically the stab wounds in her chest, then tapped the hilt of his knife through the evidence bag. "By your own admission, the knife is yours. So, how do you explain these?"

Stammering over his explanation, Remington's eyes flitted around like a trapped animal's. "I didn't always have it on me. Someone – Leach – could've taken it—"

Alyssa leaned back in her chair and crossed her arms. "You're an actor who likes to share stories with your audience. So, let me share a story with you. There was once a young boy named Colton Abbott. Colton didn't have many friends and was bullied so relentlessly that he used to avoid all those kids who picked on him by taking refuge in one of his teacher's classrooms. That teacher's name was Brooklyn Knox."

Alyssa scooted in closer, watching a muscle begin to tic at the corner of Remington's left eye as he, in turn, tried to scoot back. Alyssa brought her chair in another inch until her knees touched the actor's. "Brooklyn Knox did what she could to protect Colton, and do you know how he repaid her?"

The fake tears evaporated from Remington's eyes.

"He attacked her in her own home. He tried to kill the one woman who treated him with respect and kindness. That's how he repaid her."

Red flooded Remington's face. "I *loved Brooklyn*. That's why I *saved* her." Spittle flew from his mouth and spattered the table, as well as Alyssa's face. She grabbed a tissue and wiped it off.

"You know what I think? I think Remington Everwood is still that little boy who was being bullied and made to feel small and inconsequential, and instead of using your celebrity for good to bring awareness to the issue, you took your anger out on defenseless women. And since you couldn't bring yourself to kill Brooklyn, you killed women who looked like her instead. Which, in effect, means you *did* kill her. Six times, actually." She scoffed. "You're not unique or a star. You just became a worse version of those people who always picked on you."

Hate filled Everwood's eyes before he managed to blink it away.

Alyssa moved back when Ryker leaned across the table and lowered her voice. "I couldn't help but notice how you just now used the past tense: you *loved* Brooklyn Knox. But I have some news for you. Brooklyn didn't die in that fire up at your house in Taos. And Macey Travers survived your attack, too. You know what that means, don't you?"

Remington's face paled.

Alyssa tapped Brooklyn's and Macey's images, a sense of justice settling in her chest at the way Everwood's panic-filled eyes followed her finger. "That means that by the time your case goes to trial, there'll be two women, not one, who can testify to the entire world what you did to them, who will testify that you are not a Hollywood heartthrob but a monster. When all is said and done, Remington Everwood won't be famous; he'll be infamous. People will still know your name, but it won't be for your talents onscreen. You won't be admired and fawned over. You'll be hated for what you've done."

"I want my attorney. I'm not saying another word."

Ryker closed the folder, grabbed the evidence bag with the knife in it, and stood up, as did Alyssa. At the door, she turned around and made a promise. "One more thing before we go. I want to assure you that I, along with Detectives Wyatt and Roberts, will be front and center of your nightmare, reminding the jury and the world every chance we get of the black heart you have hidden inside that chest."

The three of them walked out, closing the door on the curses Remington hurtled at them, the vows that he'd be proven innocent, and how he'd destroy them and their families too.

On the way to the incident room to meet with the rest of the team, Alyssa noted how Ryker walked with a lighter step. In fact, they all did. Because even if Everwood continued to deny everything, even if, God forbid, Brooklyn or Macey died, they'd still have DNA to back up the mountain of evidence stacked up against him. Her guess was that the DNA found beneath Jennie Killingbeck's fingernails, along with the DNA they'd collected from Macey Travers's attack, the DNA found on Taylor Gray's body, and the partial DNA the Slaughterville police had discovered at the Knox crime scene, would match Everwood's.

Chapter Forty-Six

Early Sunday morning, Alyssa and Cord headed back to the hospital to visit Macey Travers again. Yesterday, after debriefing the team, even though it had been late, Alyssa and Cord had driven over to break the news of Everwood's arrest. Macey had broken down and apologized over and over again until Alyssa had squeezed her hand and told her she understood why Macey had been so afraid to tell them, but that she was safe now, that they'd make sure she stayed that way. The doubt in Macey's eyes had stabbed at Alyssa's heart.

Afterwards, they'd stopped in the same intensive care unit Macey had been in just a few days prior, hoping to see Brooklyn, but the doctors were adamant they needed to keep everyone out.

Sometime before dawn, Alyssa had received a text from Queenie that Brooklyn had woken, though she was still heavily sedated.

Alyssa had immediately notified Cord and Ryker and made plans to stop in after they each got a decent night's sleep. However, Ryker's superior had demanded a Zoom call for first thing this morning, so she'd asked Alyssa and Cord to extend her well-wishes to the family.

In the waiting area, Alyssa greeted Queenie and was introduced to her husband, Roy, a big bear of a man who engulfed Alyssa and then Cord in a nearly suffocating hug.

Queenie's hug was just as heartfelt but a little less crushing. "Harold and Mason should get in this afternoon," she explained when she stepped back. "I made sure it was okay with Brooklyn and the doctor, and they said you could have just a couple minutes to speak with her." She wrung her hands together. "I wish I could go back there with you, but the doctors said they can't allow that many people in the intensive care unit." A steady stream of tears ran down her face. "But that's okay because she's going to get better, and then we have the whole rest of our lives."

Before Alyssa understood what Queenie intended, she'd pulled Alyssa into another hug, her anguished but grateful sobbing *thanks* lost in Alyssa's shirt.

A few minutes later, one of Brooklyn's nurses came out and led Alyssa and Cord back to Brooklyn's room. A woman, her tattered red hair faded and knotted, lay on the bed. Alyssa barely stopped herself from reacting to the mutilation done to a woman whose only "crime" was trying to help a bullied kid. In her mind, she pictured each of Everwood's other victims, all brutally murdered or attacked simply because they had the misfortune of resembling Brooklyn Knox.

The damage was far more extensive than anything Alyssa could ever have imagined.

Carefully, she approached the bed, clearing her throat as she did so as not to startle the woman.

Brooklyn's eyes flew open, and even drug-filled and full of tears, the smile in them was unmistakable.

She offered only two strained and muffled words, whispering "thank you" before her eyes closed again, her mind drifting right back to the land of unconsciousness.

After their all-too-short visit with Brooklyn, Alyssa and Cord stopped in to speak with Queenie and Roy one more time and then headed out.

Alyssa dropped Cord off at his house and then headed home to her own family. Isaac, Holly, and Brock were all sitting around the kitchen table when she walked in. In the living room, Nick was yelling at some sports team, and Alyssa smiled at the normalcy of it.

She looked around the room, a little surprised not to see Amber. Before she could decide whether she should ask where she was, Isaac provided an answer. "I broke up with her."

Holly mumbled, "Good riddance" under her breath, and Isaac offered his fist for their sibling fist bump whenever the two of them found themselves in total solidarity.

"Yeah, she, uh, totally freaked when the news broke." Alyssa swore she heard her son's eyes slap the back of his head. "Apparently, since I'm the son of the woman who destroyed her life by arresting Remington Everwood, she expected me to be able to change that outcome, talk 'some sense into you' or some shit, and when I told her that's not how it works, she had a major meltdown. She's already launched a social media campaign to raise money to prove his innocence. Oh, and uh, prove the cops must've planted evidence. What can I say? She's unhinged."

It was Holly's turn to roll her eyes. "God, you're not kidding. That girl had *problems*."

Isaac snorted his agreement. "Uh, yeah. She was way more drama than I could handle. But enough about her and more about me." He grinned the grin that had had girls melting in his presence since he'd turned twelve. "Since you're all here, I might as well tell you I decided to finish my freshman year. But I'm taking Holly and Nick up on their offer to stay with them. No offense to you all, M and D. I just" – he threaded his fingers through his hair – "I'm trying, okay?"

Alyssa walked over to kiss the top of her son's head. "You don't have to explain it to us."

Relief relaxed all the muscles in Isaac's face, and he turned his grin on full force. "So, who's cooking? I'm a growing boy, ya know?"

Brock placed his palms on the table and pushed up. "Glad you brought it up. You, my growing boy, are going to grab Nick, and we men are going to cook dinner for the ladies." He leaned down to stare Isaac in the eyes. "Grandma will be here soon, and you will *not* charm her into feeling sorry for you. When I say we're cooking for the ladies, I mean all of them."

Alyssa and Holly laughed at the way Isaac groaned as they made their way to the living room to break the news to Nick.

Alyssa still had a lot to do to tie up this case, but for today, right this minute, she intended to enjoy this time with her family. Tomorrow would be here soon enough.

A letter from Charly

When *All His Pretty Girls* came out, I wrote a blog titled *Keep on Keeping On*, and wow, have those words ever come in handy lately.

It's been a long couple of years for me, and I wasn't sure I was going to write another Alyssa book. But your emails and amazing messages helped me decide. Because of you, I get to give the make-believe people in my head their own stories and then share those stories with you. Thank you so much for being that voice in my ear.

Thank you, also, for posting your reviews and sharing your love of Alyssa with others.

I really do love hearing from my readers, so if you'd like to get in touch with me, you can email me at charlycox@charlycoxauthor.com or follow me on social media:

IG: @charlycoxauthor
FB: Charly Cox Author (or join my FB group: Charly's Book Chat and More)
TikTok: @charlycoxauthor

For updates on new releases, you can also follow me on Goodreads, Bookbub, and Amazon.

Thanks again, and Happy Reading!
Charly Cox

Acknowledgments

Snap your seatbelts and settle in because I have lots of people to thank.

First and foremost, to my readers: I love seeing your messages and posts, hearing who your favorite characters are, and which scenes had you crying, laughing, cheering, or sitting on the edge of your seats. Thank you for sharing your love of Alyssa and Cord and their families with your own friends, family, and book groups, both online and in-person. And a very special thank you for your patience while I brought these characters to life in this next book! (I hope you enjoyed meeting Ryker!)

Thank you also to Ron (service manager) at First Rate Plumbing, Heating, and Cooling here in Albuquerque for taking a random phone call from a random author, trusting me when I promised my questions were all for research, and then spending a great deal of time talking me through how it would be possible for a person to blow up a house with lights and gas. I hope I got most of it right, but any mistakes are definitely my own.

Kevin: I don't have enough room, know enough languages, or even know where to begin to list all the things I have to thank you for. So, I'll just say I love you, and thanks for always, always, always believing in me, no matter what's going on. You are my very solid rock.

Timothee: Your sense of humor, your advice, the way you see things, and all the ways you encourage me keeps me plugging away. Also, I have to say I stole a few more things from your childhood to put in this book. I can't help it; they're just too much fun.

Melissa: Snort. I've said it before, and I'll say it again… thank you for *all* the things. For not ignoring random text messages full of panic or the equally random phone calls, having more plot hole (and timeline) conversations than two people should probably ever have to have, for not blocking my social media accounts when I send you countless videos I'm positive you must see right now, for making me laugh until it hurts, which granted, doesn't take much, and for just… wait for it… all the things.

Drew: Life's a journey, and damn, I'm glad you're part of mine.

Hallie: Just one word will sum it all up: #HGUS. But I will also add that your unflagging faith in me has picked me up so, so many times. Thank you for seeing the very best in things.

Victoria: For being that voice that whispers NTKA and cheering for me when I succeed. (But also, for being okay if I do. Wink.)

Maureen Downey: For always putting my name, along with Alyssa's, out there, for being an amazing sounding board, and just for being you. Stay strong, my friend.

Darin Miller: For writing one of my favorite mystery series with a character who never fails to make me laugh… and for your constant encouragement behind the scenes.

Keshini: For all your patience, insight, understanding, and just all the millions of other things that help me shape Alyssa's world into one that readers want.

And finally, to the cast of people who are always, always in the wings with their cheers, love, and encouragement... and who tell anyone who will listen to go read these books: Kim, Kerri, Susan, Tam, Ang, Tracy, Annette, Ro, Karen Goeke, Trudy Randour, Mary Ellen, Karen S., and Theresa. As always, your support means more than you could ever know!